P9-CDA-694

The Sheen on the Silk

The Sheen on the Silk

A NOVEL

ANNE PERRY

BALLANTINE BOOKS · NEW YORK

Copyright © 2010 by Anne Perry

Published in the United States by Ballantine Books, an imprint of The Random House Publishing Group, a division of Random House, Inc., New York.

BALLANTINE and colophon are registered trademarks of Random House, Inc.

Library of Congress Cataloging-in-Publication Data
Perry, Anne.
The sheen on the silk : a novel / Anne Perry.—1st ed.
p. cm.
Includes bibliographical references.
ISBN 978-0-345-50065-6 (alk. paper)
1. Young women—Fiction. 2. Disguise—Fiction. 3. Eunuchs—Fiction.
4. Brothers and sisters—Fiction. 5. Thirteenth century—Fiction. 6. Istanbul (Turkey)—
Fiction. I. Title.
PR6066.E693S49 2010
823'.914—dc22   2009052469

Printed in the United States of America on acid-free paper

www.ballantinebooks.com

9 8 7 6 5 4 3 2 1

First Edition

Book design by Caroline Cunningham

Dedicated to Jonathan

Chart of Characters

VENICE

DOGES
{
Lorenzo Tiepolo (1268–1275)
Jacopo Contarini (1275–1280)
Giovanni Dandolo (1280–1289)
}

Giuliano Dandolo
Pietro Contarini

BYZANTIUM

Anna Lascaris (Anastasius Zarides)
Justinian Lascaris (her twin brother)
Bishop Constantine
Zoe Chrysaphes
Helena Comnena (Zoe's daughter)
Emperor Michael Palaeologus
Nicephoras (palace eunuch)
Bessarion Comnenos
Andrea Mocenigo
Avram Shachar

Eirene Vatatzes

Demetrios Vatatzes (her son)

Gregory Vatatzes (her husband)

Arsenios Vatatzes (Gregory's cousin)

Georgios Vatatzes (Arsenios's son)

Cosmas Kantakouzenos

Leo
Simonis } (both servants to Anna)

Sabas
Thomais } (both servants to Zoe)

Charles, Count of Anjou, king of Naples and the Two Sicilies
and younger brother of the king of France

ROME

POPES {
Gregory X (1271–1276)

Innocent V (1276)

Hadrian V (1276)

John XXI (1276–1277)

Nicholas III (1277–1280)

Martin IV (1281–1285)
}

Enrico Palombara

Niccolo Vicenze (both papal legates)

The Sheen on the Silk

Prologue

THE YOUNG MAN STOOD ON THE STEPS, ADJUSTING HIS
eyes to the shadows. The torchlight flickering over the water's surface made the aisles of the great underground cistern look like some half-
drowned cathedral. Only the tops of the columns were visible, holding up
the vaulted ceiling. There was no sound but the whispering of damp air
and the faint echo of dripping somewhere out of sight.

Bessarion was standing on the stone platform a few feet below him,
near the water's edge. He did not look afraid; in fact, his handsome head
with its wavy black hair showed the calm, almost otherworldly repose of
an icon. Was his belief really so all-consuming?

Please God, there was a way to avoid this, even now? The young man
was cold. His heart was pounding in his chest and his hands were stiff. He
had rehearsed all the arguments, but still he was not ready. He never
would be, but there was no more time. Tomorrow it would be too late.

He took another step down. Bessarion turned, fear narrowing his features for an instant, then the ease again as he recognized the intruder.
"What is it?" he said a little sharply.

"I need to speak to you." He walked down the steps until he was on
the level by the water, a couple of yards from Bessarion. Hands clammy,
he was trembling. He would have given everything he possessed to avoid
this.

"What about?" Bessarion said impatiently. "Everything is in place.
What else is there to discuss?"

"We can't do it," he said simply.

"Afraid?" In the wavering light Bessarion's expression was unreadable, but the confidence in his voice was absolute. Did his faith, his certainty of himself, never falter?

"It's not about fear," the young man answered. "Hot blood overcomes that. But it won't make us right if we are wrong."

"But we're not wrong," Bessarion said urgently. "One swift violence to save an age of slow decay into barbarism of the mind and the corruption of our faith. We've been over all that!"

"I'm not talking about moral wrong, I understand sacrificing the one to save the many." He nearly laughed, then choked on his own breath. Could Bessarion understand the impossible irony of that? "I mean wrong in judgment." He hated saying this. "Michael is the right man, you are not. We need his skill to survive, his cunning, his ability to deal, to manipulate, to turn our enemies against each other."

Bessarion was stunned. Even in these changing shadows, it was clear in every line of his face and the angle of his head and shoulders.

"You traitor!" It was a snarl of disbelief. "What about the Church?" Bessarion demanded. "Would you also betray God?"

This was as bad as he had feared. Bessarion saw nothing of his own incompetence to lead. Why had he not seen it sooner himself? His hopes had blinded him, and now he had no choice left.

His voice shook. "We won't save the Church if the city falls, but if we do what we plan to tomorrow, then it will."

"Judas!" Bessarion said bitterly. He swung out wildly but stumbled when he met no resistance.

It was terrible, like killing himself, except that the alternative was unimaginably worse. And there was no time to think. Shuddering, his stomach sick, he did it, lunging at Bessarion as hard as he could. There was a splash as he hit the water, then a cry of surprise. The young man went in after him while Bessarion was still dazed. He found his head and grasped the thick, curling hair with both hands, twisting it and throwing all his weight to submerge him and hold him down under the cold, clear water.

Bessarion struggled, trying to fight upward, with nothing to stand on, against a man leaner and stronger than himself and just as willing to sacrifice everything he had for a belief.

At last the splashing ceased. Silence washed in from the shadows beyond the aisles, and the water became still again.

He crouched on the stones, sick and cold. But he was not yet finished. He forced himself to stand. Aching as if he had been beaten, he climbed back up the steps, his face wet with tears.

One

ANNA ZARIDES STOOD ON THE STONE PIER AND GAZED across the dark waters of the Bosphorus toward the lighthouse of Constantinople. Its fires lit the sky with a great beacon outlined against the paling March stars. It was beautiful, but she was waiting for the dawn to show her the city's rooftops and, one by one, all the marvelous palaces, churches, and towers she knew must be there.

The wind was chill off the waves, whose crests were only barely visible. She heard the sound of them sucking and hissing on the pebbles. Far away on the promontory the first rays of daylight caught a massive dome, a hundred, two hundred feet high. It glowed a dull red, as if with its own inner fire. It had to be the Hagia Sophia, the greatest church in the world, not only the most beautiful, but the heart and soul of the Christian faith.

Anna stared at it as the light strengthened. Other rooftops grew clearer, a jumble of angles, towers, and domes. To the left of the Hagia Sophia she saw four tall, slender columns, like needles against the horizon. She knew what they were, monuments to some of the greatest emperors of the past. The imperial palaces must be there, too, and the Hippodrome, but all she could see were shadows, white gleams of marble here and there, more trees, and the endless roofs of a city larger than Rome or Alexandria, Jerusalem or Athens.

She saw the narrow stretch of the Bosphorus clearly now, already growing busy with ships. With an effort she made out the vast battlements of the shoreline, and something of the harbors below them, crowded with indistinguishable hulls and masts, all riding the safe calm within the break-waters.

The sun was rising, the sky a pale, luminescent arch shot with fire. To the north, the curved inlet of the Golden Horn was molten bronze between its banks—a beautiful spring morning.

The first ferry of the day was making its way toward them. Worried once again how she would appear to strangers, Anna walked over to the edge of the pier and stared down at the still water in the shelter of the stone. She saw her own reflection: steady gray eyes, strong but vulnerable face, high cheekbones, and soft mouth. Her bright hair was jaw length, not dressed and ornamented like a woman's, and with no veil to hide it.

The ferry, a light, wooden boat big enough to carry half a dozen passengers, was less than a hundred yards away now. The oarsman was fighting the stiff breeze and the perverse currents, treacherous here at the narrows where Europe met Asia. She took a deep breath, feeling the bandages tight around her chest and the slight padding at her waist that concealed her woman's shape. In spite of all her practice, it still felt awkward. She shivered, pulling her cloak closer.

"No," Leo said from behind her.

"What's wrong?" She turned to look at him. He was tall, slender-shouldered, and round-faced, with hairless cheeks. His brow was furrowed with anxiety.

"The gesture," the eunuch replied gently. "Don't give in to the cold like a woman."

She jerked away, furious with herself for making such a stupid mistake. She was endangering them all.

"Are you still sure?" Simonis asked, her voice brittle. "It's not too late to . . . to change your mind."

"I'll get it right," Anna said firmly.

"You can't afford mistakes, Anastasius." Leo deliberately used the name Anna had chosen to take. "You would be punished for masquerading as a man—even a eunuch."

"Then I mustn't get caught," she said simply.

She had known it would be difficult. But at least one woman had succeeded in the past. Her name was Marina, and she had entered a monastery as a eunuch. No one had known differently until after her death.

Anna nearly asked Leo if he wished to go back, but it would be insulting, and he did not deserve that. Anyway, she needed to observe and mimic him.

The ferry reached the dock and the oarsman stood up with the peculiar grace of one accustomed to the sea. Young and handsome, he threw a rope around the stanchion, then stepped up onto the boards of the dockside, smiling.

About to smile back, Anna remembered not to only just in time. She let go of her cloak, allowing the wind to chill her, and the boatman passed by her to offer his hand to Simonis, who was older, plumper, and obviously a woman. Anna followed, taking her seat in the ferry. Leo came last, loading their few boxes, which held her precious medicines, herbs, and instruments. The oarsman took his place again and they moved out into the current.

Anna did not look behind. She had left everything that was familiar, and she had no idea when she would see it again. But it was only the task ahead that mattered.

They were far out into the current now. Rising sheer from the waterline like a cliff was the wreckage of the seawalls breached by the Latin crusaders who had looted and burned the city seventy years ago and driven its people into exile. She looked at it now, soaring up as vast as if it had been built by nature rather than man, and wondered how anyone could have dared to attack it, never mind succeeded.

She held on to the gunwale and twisted in her seat to look left and right at the magnitude of the city. It seemed to cover every rock face, inlet, and hillside. The rooftops were so close, they gave the illusion you could walk from one to another.

The oarsman was smiling, amused at her wonder. She felt herself coloring at her naiveté and turned away.

They were now close enough to the city that she could see the broken stones, the thready outlines of weeds, and the darker scars of fire. She was startled how raw it looked, even though eleven years had passed since 1262, when Michael Palaeologus had led the people of Constantinople back home from the provinces where they had been driven.

Now Anna too was here, for the first time in her life, and for all the wrong reasons.

The oarsman strained against the wash that rocked them hard as a trireme went past, bound for the open sea. It was high-sided, three tiers of oars dipping and rising, water running bright from their blades. Beyond it were two other boats almost round, men busy furling their sails, scrambling to lash them fast enough so they could let down anchor in exactly the right place. She wondered if they had come from the Black Sea and what they had brought to sell or trade.

In the shelter of the breakwaters, the sea was calm. Someone somewhere laughed, and the sound carried across the water, above the slap of the waves and the cry of the gulls.

The ferryman guided their way to the quayside and bumped gently against the stones. She paid him four copper folleis, meeting his eyes for no more than a moment, then rose and stepped ashore, leaving him to assist Simonis.

They must hire transport for the boxes, then find an inn to offer them food and shelter until she could look for a house to rent and set up her practice. She would have no help here, no recommendations as she would have had from her father's good name at home in Nicea, the ancient, magnificent capital of Bithynia across the Bosphorus to the southeast. It was only a day's ride away, yet Constantinople was a new world for her. Apart from Leo and Simonis, she was alone. Their loyalty was absolute. Even knowing the truth, they had come with her.

She started along the worn stones of the quayside, making a path between bales of wool, carpets, raw silk, piles of crockery, slabs of marble, exotic woods, and smaller bags that gave off the odors of exotic spices. Heavy in the air were also the less pleasant smells of fish, hides, human sweat, and animal dung.

Twice she turned around to make certain Leo and Simonis were both still with her.

She had grown up knowing that Constantinople was the center of the world, the crossroads of Europe and Asia, and she was proud of it, but now the babel of alien voices in among the Byzantines' native Greek, the teeming, anonymous busyness of it, overwhelmed her.

A bare-chested man with gleaming skin and a sack across his shoulders weighing him down bumped into her and muttered something before staggering on. A tinker laden with pan and kettles laughed loudly and spat on the ground. A turbaned Muslim in a black silk robe walked by without a sound.

Anna stepped off the uneven cobbles and crossed the street, Leo and Simonis close behind. The buildings on the landward side were four or five stories high and the alleys between them narrower than she had expected. The smells of salt and stale wine were heavy and unpleasant, and the noise even here made speaking difficult. She led the way up the hill a little farther from the wharfside.

There were shops to left and right and living quarters above, apparent from the laundry hanging from windows. A hundred yards inland, it was quieter. They passed a bakery, and the smell of fresh bread made her suddenly think of home.

They were still climbing upward, and her arms ached from carrying her medical supplies. Leo must be even more exhausted because he had the heavier boxes, and Simonis carried a bag of clothes.

She stopped and let her case drop for a moment. "We must find somewhere for tonight. At least to leave our belongings. And we need to eat. It is more than five hours since breakfast."

"Six," Simonis observed. "I've never seen so many people in my life."

"Do you want me to carry that?" Leo asked, but his face looked tired and he already had far more weight than either Simonis or Anna.

In answer, Simonis picked up her bag again and started forward.

A hundred yards farther, they found an excellent inn that served food. It had good mattresses stuffed with goose down and was furnished with linen sheets. Each room had a basin large enough for bathing and a latrine with a tile drain. It was eight folleis each, per night, not including meals. That was expensive, but Anna doubted others would be much cheaper.

She dreaded going out in case she made another mistake, another womanish gesture, expression, or even lack of reaction in some way. One error would be enough to make people look harder and perhaps see the differences between her and a real eunuch.

They ate a lunch of fresh gray mullet and wheat bread at a tavern and asked a few discreet questions about cheaper lodgings.

"Oh, inland," a fellow diner told them cheerfully. He was a little gray-haired man in a worn tunic that came no farther than his knees, his legs bound with cloth to keep him warm but leaving him unencumbered for work. "Farther west you go, cheaper they are. You strangers here?"

There was no point in denying it. "From Nicea," Anna told him.

"I'm from Sestos myself." The man gave them a gap-toothed grin. "But everyone comes here, sooner or later."

Anna thanked him, and the following day they hired a donkey to carry their cases and moved to a cheaper inn close to the western edge of the city by the land walls, not far from the Gate of Charisius.

That night, she lay in her bed listening to the unfamiliar sounds of the city around her. This was Constantinople, the heart of Byzantium. She had heard stories of it all her life, from her parents and her grandparents, but now that she was here it was so strange, too big for the imagination to grasp.

But she would accomplish nothing by remaining in her lodgings. Survival demanded that in the morning she go out and begin the search for a house from which she could establish her practice.

In spite of her tiredness, sleep did not come easily, and her dreams were crowded with strange faces and the fear of being lost.

She knew from her father's stories that Constantinople was surrounded by water on three sides, and that the main street, named Mese, was Y shaped. The two arms met at the Amastrianon Forum and continued east toward the sea. All the great buildings she had heard him speak of were along this stretch: the Hagia Sophia, the Forum of Constantine, the Hippodrome, the old imperial palaces, and of course shops with exquisite artifacts, silks, spices, and gems.

They set out in the morning, walking briskly. The air was fresh. Food shops were open, and at practically every corner bakeries were crowded with people, but they had no time to indulge themselves. They were still in the web of narrow streets that threaded the whole city from the calm water of the Golden Horn in the north to the Sea of Marmara in the south. Several times they had to stand aside to let donkey carts pass, piled high with goods for market, mostly fruit and vegetables.

They reached the wide stretch of Mese Street just as a camel swayed past them, high-headed, sour-faced, and a man hurried behind it, bent double under the weight of a bale of cotton. The thoroughfare teemed with people. In among the native Greeks she saw turbaned Muslims, Bulgars with close-cropped heads, dark-skinned Egyptians, blue-eyed Scandinavians, and high-cheeked Mongols. Anna wondered if they felt as strange here as she did, as awed by the size, the vitality, the jumble of vibrant colors in the clothes, on the shop awnings—purples and scarlets, blues and golds, half shades of aquamarine, wine red, and rose pink, wherever she looked.

She had no idea where to start. She needed to make inquiries and learn something about the different residential areas where she might find a house.

"We need a map," Leo said with a frown. "The city is far too big to know where we are without one."

"We need to be in a good residential district," Simonis added, probably thinking about the home they had left in Nicea. But she had willed to come almost as much as Anna herself. Justinian had always been her favorite, even though he and Anna were twins. Simonis had grieved when he left Nicea to come to Constantinople. When Anna had received that last, desperate letter about his exile, Simonis had thought of nothing but rescuing him, at any cost. It was Leo who had had the cooler head and wanted a plan first and who had cared so much for Anna's safety as well.

It took them several more minutes to find a shop selling manuscripts, and they inquired.

"Oh, yes," the shopkeeper said immediately. Short and wiry, with white hair and a quick smile, he opened a drawer behind him and pulled out several scrolls of paper. He unrolled one of them and showed Anna the drawing.

"See? Fourteen districts." He pointed to the loosely triangular shape drawn in black ink.

"This is Mese Street, going this way." He showed them on the map. "There's the Wall of Constantine, and west of that again the Wall of Theodosius. All except district thirteen, across the Golden Horn to the north. That's called Galata. But you don't want to live there. That's for foreigners." He rolled it up and passed it to her. "That will be two solidi."

She was taken aback and more than a little suspicious that he knew she was a stranger and was taking advantage. Still, she passed over the money.

They walked the length of Mese Street, trying not to stare around them like the provincials they were. Row after row of merchants' stalls lined the street. They were shaded by canopies of every color imaginable, tied tightly to wooden posts to anchor them against the wind. Even so they snapped loudly in every gust, as if they were alive and struggling to get free.

In district one there were spice merchants and perfumers. The air was redolent with their wares, and Anna found herself drawing in her breath deeply to savor them. She had neither time nor money to waste, but she could not help gazing at them, lingering a moment to admire their beauty.

No other yellow had the depth of saffron, no brown the multitoned richness of nutmeg. She knew the medical values of all of them, even the rarest, but at home in Nicea she had had to order them specially and pay extra for their freight. Here they were laid out as if they were commonplace.

"There's plenty of money in this district," Simonis observed with a hint of disapproval.

"More important, they'll have their own physician already," Leo replied.

Now they were among the perfumers' shops and there were rather more women than in the other areas, many of them clearly wealthy. As custom required, they wore tunics and dalmaticas from the neck almost to the ground, and their hair was concealed by headdress and veil. One woman walked past them, smiling, and Anna noticed that she had darkened her brows very delicately, and perhaps her lashes. Certainly there was red clay on her lips to make them look so vivid.

Anna heard her laughter as she met a friend, and together they tried one perfume after another. Their embroidered and brocaded silks stirred in the breeze like flower petals. She envied their lightheartedness.

She would have to find more ordinary women, and male patients, too, or she would never learn why Justinian had been a favorite with the emperor's court one day and an exile the next, fortunate to have his life. What had happened? What must Anna do to gain justice for him?

The following day, by mutual agreement, they left the Mese and its immediate surroundings and searched farther into the side streets, in little shops, and in the residential districts north of center, almost under the giant arches of the Aqueduct of Valens, catching occasional glimpses of the light on the water of the Golden Horn beyond.

They were on a narrow street, barely wide enough for two donkeys to pass each other, when they came to a flight of steps up to the left. Thinking the height might give them a better sense of their bearings, they began to climb. The passage turned one way, then the other. Anna nearly stumbled over the rubble on the steps.

Without any warning, the path ended abruptly and they were in a small courtyard. Anna was stunned by what lay around her. All the walls were damaged, some by holes where pieces had fallen out, others by the black stains of fire. The broken mosaic floor was scattered with stones and chips of tile, and the doorways were choked with weeds. The single tower left standing was pitted and dark with the grime of smoke. She heard Simonis stifle a sob, and Leo stood silent, his face pale.

Suddenly the terrible invasion of 1204 was real, as if it had been only a few years ago, not more than half a century. Other things they had seen made sense now, the streets where houses were still derelict, weed-strewn and rotting, the occasional broken wharves she had seen from above, the poverty in what had seemed to her first superficial look to be the richest city in the world. The people had been back for over a decade, but the wounds of conquest and exile were still raw underneath.

Anna turned away, imagined terror gripping her and making her body cold even in the sharp spring sunlight, sheltered here from the wind, where it should have been hot.

By the end of the week, they had found a house in a comfortable residential area on a slope to the north of Mese Street, between the two great walls. From several of the windows Anna could see the light on the Golden Horn, a glimpse of blue between the rooftops that gave her a moment's wild illusion of endlessness, almost as if she could fly.

It was a small house, but in good repair. The tiled floors were beautiful and she particularly liked the courtyard with its simple mosaic and the vines that climbed onto the roof.

Simonis was satisfied with the kitchen, although she made a few disparaging remarks about its size, but Anna could see by the way she poked into every corner and touched the furniture with its marble surfaces, the deep basin and the heavy table, that she liked it. There was a small room for storage of grains and vegetables, racks and drawers for spices, and, like all the rest of the better parts of the city, access to plenty of clean water, even if it was a little salty.

There were enough rooms to have a bedroom each, a dining room, an entrance hall for patients to wait in, and a room for consulting. There was also another room with a heavy door to which Leo could attach a lock and where Anna could keep herbs, ointments, unguents, and tinctures, and of course her surgical blades, needles, and silks. In here she placed the wooden cabinet with its dozens of drawers into which she put the herbs she had, each one labeled, and including one whole leaf or root so one could not be mistaken for another.

But in spite of the discreet notice she put at the front of the house stating her profession, patients would not come to her. She must go out and seek them, let people know of her presence and her skills.

So it was at midday that she stood on the step of a tavern in the hard sunlight and the wind. She pushed open the door and went inside. She walked through the crowd and saw a table with one empty chair. The rest were filled with men eating and talking excitedly. At least one was a eunuch, taller, long-armed, soft-faced, his voice too high, with the strange, altered tone of his gender.

"May I take this seat?" she asked.

It was the eunuch who replied, inviting her in. Perhaps he was pleased to have another of his kind.

A waiter came and offered her food, cut pieces of roast pork wrapped in wheat bread, and she accepted.

"Thank you," she said. "I have just moved in, the house with the blue door, straight up the hill. My name is Anastasius Zarides. I am a physician."

One of the men shrugged and introduced himself. "I'll remember if I am ill," he said good-naturedly. "If you stitch up wounds, you might stay around. There'll be business for you when we've finished arguing."

She was uncertain how to reply, not sure if he was joking or not. She had heard raised voices from the doorway as she came in. "I have needle and silk," she offered.

One of the others laughed. "You'll need more than that if we're invaded. How are you at raising the dead?"

"I've never had the nerve to try," she replied as casually as she could. "Isn't that more of a job for a priest?"

They all laughed, but she heard a hard, bitter sound of fear in it and realized the power of the undercurrents she had barely listened to before, in her own urgency to find a house and begin a practice.

"What kind of a priest?" one of the men said harshly. "Orthodox or Roman, eh? Which side are you on?"

"I'm Orthodox," she said quietly, answering because she felt compelled to say something. Silence would be deceit.

"Then you better pray harder," he told her. "God knows we'll need it. Have some wine, physician."

Anna held out her glass and found her hand was shaking. Quickly she put the glass on the table. "Thank you." When the glass was full she held it up, forcing herself to smile. "Here's to your good health . . . except for perhaps a slight skin rash, or the occasional hives. I'm good at that, for a small sum."

They laughed again and lifted their glasses.

Two

〜

ANNA CALLED UPON HER NEIGHBORS ONE BY ONE, INTRO-
ducing herself and her profession. Several of them already had
physicians they chose to consult, but she had expected that. She told them
that she specialized in complaints of the skin, especially burns, and of the
lungs, then left without pressing the issue.

She also shopped for various household items of as good a quality as she
could afford, buying them from smaller shops within two or three streets
of her house. Here she also introduced herself and told them of her own
skills. For the favor of recommending their wares, they were willing to recommend her to their customers.

In the second week she gained only two consultations, and they were
for ailments so slight as to require only a simple potion to ease itching and
heat. After the busy practice she had inherited from her father in Nicea, it
seemed so small. She had to struggle to keep up her spirits in front of Leo
and Simonis.

The third week was better. She was called to an accident in the street in
which an elderly man had been knocked over and his legs badly scraped.
The boy who came for her described the damage vividly enough that she
knew what lotions and ointments to take with her, and herbs for shock
and pain. Within half an hour the old man felt markedly better, and by
the following day he was speaking her praises. Word spread. In the suc-
ceeding days, the number of patients tripled.

Now she could no longer put it off; she must begin to search for information.

The obvious place to begin was with Bishop Constantine, through whose help Justinian had sent his last letter. He had written of the bishop many times previously, telling her of his loyalty to the Orthodox faith, his courage in the cause of resistance against Rome, and his personal kindness to Justinian, then a stranger in the city. Justinian had also mentioned that Constantine was a eunuch, and that was what made Anna nervous now. She stood in her medicine room amid the familiar odors of nutmeg, musk, cloves, and camphor, and her hands were clenched. Every mannerism, every gesture, must be right. Even the slightest deviation would raise Constantine's suspicion and invite closer scrutiny. More errors would be seen. She might even be perceived to be mocking him.

She found Leo in the kitchen, where Simonis was setting the midday meal on the table: wheat bread, fresh cheese, greens and lettuce dressed with squill vinegar, as prescribed for April. All months had rules for what should be eaten and what should not, and Simonis was well versed in them.

Leo turned as she came in and put down the tools he was using to mend the hinge of the cupboard. She had realized since they moved in just how many skills he had in every practical work.

"It is time I went to see Bishop Constantine," she said quietly. "But before I do, I need one more lesson . . . please."

As a woman, she could have practiced medicine only on female patients and would have been able to learn very little about Justinian's life here, all the myriad small things he had not told her, in spite of their many letters. But as a eunuch, she could go anywhere.

Another consideration, of less importance but still heavy in her mind, was that she did not want the pressure to marry again. She was a widow, and even though she could sometimes think of Eustathius without rage or pain, it would be impossible to take another husband.

"You try too hard to be like a man," Leo said. "There are many kinds of eunuchs, depending on the time of castration, and the degree. Some of us castrated late are nearly men, but with your slender build and soft skin and voice, you are pretending to be one castrated in childhood. You must get it exactly right, or you will draw attention to yourself."

She watched him as he moved about the room. He was tall and slight, a little stooping as the years caught up with him, but surprisingly strong. His thin hands could break wood she could not even bend. He walked with a peculiar grace, neither male nor female. She must copy that gait.

"The way you bend," Leo was saying to her. "Like this . . ." He demonstrated, moving easily. "Not like that." He bent a trifle sideways, like a woman. She immediately saw the difference and cursed her own carelessness.

"And your hands. You don't use them enough when you are speaking. Look . . . like this." He gestured eloquently, his fingers graceful and yet oddly not feminine.

She copied experimentally.

Simonis was watching, her dark, once handsome face creased with anxiety. Was she also afraid? She must see the differences between Anna and Leo, the faults.

"Your food will spoil," she said dryly, her call for them to eat the meal she had prepared so carefully.

Afterward, Anna rose and went to put on her outdoor robe. It was chilly and raining slightly, but it was less than a mile to the bishop's house, just the other side of the Wall of Constantine, near the Church of the Holy Apostles. Walking quickly along the streets, she was aware of the occasional glimpse of light gleaming on the water below.

An elderly servant let her in. He informed her gravely that Bishop Constantine was presently occupied, but he was expecting her and would receive her as soon as he was free. The servant's face was bland, smooth, and beardless. He regarded her completely without interest.

She waited in a great room with a mosaic-tiled floor and ocher-colored walls; two magnificent icons were almost luminous in the somber light. One was of the Virgin Mary, all in blues and golds inside a jeweled frame, the other of Christ Pantocrator, in warm ochers and browns and dark burnt umber.

A slight movement caught her eye and she turned from the icons' quiet, intense beauty and looked through the archway to a brighter room and, beyond it, an inside court. The large, pale-robed figure of the bishop stood in the reflected sun. There was a smile on his face as he extended his hand to the woman who knelt before him, her dark cloak pooling on the floor around her, her hair caught up in an elaborate coil. Her lips touched his fingers, almost covering the gold ring with its jewel. For a moment the scene was like an icon itself, an image of forgiveness stamped on eternity.

The peace of it gripped Anna with a shaft of pain. She ached to kneel and seek absolution also, to feel the weight lift and free her, let her draw the sweet air into her lungs. But that was impossible.

The woman rose and the vision splintered and fell apart. She was Anna's age, and her face was wet with tears of relief.

Constantine made the sign of the cross and said something that was inaudible from this distance. The woman turned and went out by another doorway. Anna moved forward. It was time for the first important lie. If she could pass this test, a thousand more lay ahead.

Constantine welcomed her, smiling.

"Anastasius Zarides, Your Grace," she said deferentially. "Physician, lately come from Nicea."

"Welcome to Constantinople," he replied warmly. His voice was deeper than that of most eunuchs, as if he had been castrated well after puberty. His face was smooth and beardless, his strong jaw becoming a trifle jowly. His light brown eyes were sharp. "How may I be of help to you?" He was courteous, but as yet without interest.

She had the lie well practiced. "A distant kinsman of mine, Justinian Lascaris, wrote to me that you had been of great help to him in a time of difficulty," she began. "Then I did not hear from him again, and there are disturbing rumors of some tragedy, but I do not dare to pursue them, in case I bring him further trouble." She shivered in spite of the warmth in the room. He was looking at her face and the way she stood, her hands loosely at her sides, as a woman would stand, deferentially. She raised her hands in front of her and then did not know what to do with them and let them fall again. How much did the bishop know about Justinian? That his parents were dead? That he was a widower? She must be careful. "His sister is anxious." That, at least, was true.

Constantine's large face was grave, and he nodded slowly. "I am afraid I have not good news for her," he replied. "Justinian is alive, but in exile in the desert beyond Jerusalem."

She contrived to look shocked. "But why? What has he done to warrant such a punishment?"

Constantine compressed his lips. "He was accused of complicity in the murder of Bessarion Comnenos. It was a crime that shocked the city.

Bessarion was not only of noble birth, but regarded by many as something of a saint. Justinian was fortunate not to be executed."

Anna's mouth was dry and she found it hard to draw breath. The Comneni had been emperors for generations, before the Lascaris, and now the Palaeologi.

"That was the difficulty with which you helped him?" she said, as if it were a deduction. "But why would Justinian be accomplice to such a thing?"

Constantine considered for a moment. "Are you aware of the emperor's intention to send envoys to mediate with the pope in little more than a year's time?" he asked, unable to conceal the edge from his voice that betrayed his emotions. They clearly lay harsh and close to the surface, like a woman's feelings, as a eunuch's were said to be.

"I have heard whispers here and there," she answered. "I hoped that it was not true."

"It is true," he rasped, his body stiff, his pale, strong hands half-raised. "The emperor is prepared to capitulate on everything in order to save us from the crusaders, whatever the blasphemy involved."

She was aware that in spite of his passion, Constantine was watching her intently. "The Blessed Virgin will save us, if we trust in her," she replied. "As she has done in the past."

Constantine's fine eyebrows rose. "Are you so new to the city you have not seen the stains of the crusaders' fires seventy years ago?"

Anna swallowed, her mind made up. "If our faith then had been unblemished, I am mistaken," she replied. "I would rather die faithful than live having betrayed my God to Rome."

"You are a man of conviction," Constantine said, a slow, sweet smile lighting his face.

She returned to her first question. "Why would Justinian assist anyone to kill Bessarion Comnenos?"

"He did not, of course," Constantine replied regretfully. "Justinian was a fine man, and as much against the union with Rome as Bessarion was. There were other suggestions, the truth of which I don't know."

"What suggestions?" She remembered her deference just in time and lowered her eyes. "If you can tell me? Who is Justinian suspected of helping, and what happened to him?"

Constantine lifted his hands higher. It was an elegant gesture and yet disturbing in its lack of masculinity. She was sharply aware that he was not a man, but not a woman, either, yet still a passionate and highly intelligent being. He was what she was pretending to be.

"Antoninus Kyriakis." His voice cut across her thoughts. "He was executed. He and Justinian were close friends."

"And you saved Justinian?" Her voice was hoarse, no more than a whisper.

He nodded slowly, allowing his hands to fall. "I did. The sentence was exile in the desert."

She smiled at him, the warmth of her gratitude burning through. "Thank you, Your Grace. You give me great heart for the struggle to keep faith."

He smiled back and made the sign of the cross.

She went out into the street in a turmoil of emotions: fear, gratitude, dread of what she might find in the future, and in them all a powerful awareness of Constantine, strong, generous, firm in a clean and absolute faith.

Of course Justinian had not murdered this Bessarion Comnenos. Although there were marked physical differences between them, in coloring and balance of features, Justinian was her twin brother. Anna knew him as well as she knew herself. He had written to her in the last desperate moments before being taken into exile and told her that Bishop Constantine had helped him, but not why or in what way.

Now her whole purpose was to prove his innocence. She quickened her pace up the incline of the cobbled street.

Three

AFTER ANASTASIUS ZARIDES HAD LEFT, CONSTANTINE remained standing in the ocher-colored room. This physician was interesting and could very possibly prove an ally in the upcoming battle to defend the Orthodox faith from the ambitions of Rome. He was intelligent, subtle, and clearly well educated. With its uncouth ideas and love of violence, Rome could offer nothing to someone like that. If he had a eunuch's patience, suppleness of mind, and instinctive understanding of emotion, then the brashness of the Latins would be as revolting to him as it was to Constantine himself.

But the questions he had asked were troubling. Constantine had assumed that with Antoninus's execution and Justinian's exile, the matter of Bessarion's murder was closed.

He walked back and forth across the colored floor.

Justinian had mentioned no close kinsmen. But then one did not often speak of cousins or those even further removed.

If Constantine were not careful, the questions could become awkward, but it should be easy enough to deal with them. No one else knew Constantine's part, or why he had helped or asked for mercy, and Justinian was safely in Judea, where he could say nothing.

Anastasius Zarides might be useful, if in fact he was a skilled physician. Having come was from Nicea, a city known for its learning, he would have had even better opportunity to mix with Jews and Arabs and perhaps acquire a little of their medical knowledge. Constantine disliked admitting it even to himself, but such people were sometimes more skilled than the physicians who adhered strictly to Christian teaching that all illness was a result of sin.

If Anastasius had greater skills, sooner or later he would gain more patients. When people are ill, they are frightened. When they fear they are dying, sometimes they tell secrets they would otherwise keep.

He spent the rest of the afternoon on Church business, seeing priests and petitioners for one sort of grace or another, guidance or a leniency, an ordinance performed, a permission granted. As soon as the last one was gone, his mind returned to the eunuch from Nicea and the murder of Bessarion. There were precautions to take, in case the young man pursued his questions about Justinian elsewhere.

Constantine had imagined that there was no danger left, but he needed to be certain.

After donning his outdoor cloak over his silk tunic and brocaded and jeweled dalmatica, he went into the street. He walked quickly up the slight incline, raising his eyes to the massive two-tiered Aqueduct of Valens that towered up ahead of him. It had stood there for over six hundred years, bringing millions of gallons of clean water to the people of this region of the city. It pleased him just to look at it. Its great limestone blocks were held in place by the genius of its engineering rather than mortar. It seemed indestructible and timeless, like the Church itself, held upright by truth and the laws of God, bringing the water of life to its faithful members.

He turned left into a quieter street and went on upward, wrapping his cloak more tightly around himself. He was going to see Helena Comnena, Bessarion's widow, just in case Anastasius Zarides should think to do the same. She could be the weak link among those left.

It had stopped raining but the air was damp, and by the time he reached her house he was spattered with mud and his legs ached. He was getting to an age, and a weight, when hills were no longer a pleasure.

He was shown through the large, austere entrance hall and on into an exquisitely tiled anteroom while the servant went to inform his mistress of the bishop's arrival.

From the distance he heard the murmur of voices, then a woman's rich laughter. Not a servant—it sounded too free for that. It had to be Helena herself. Someone else must be here. It would be interesting to know who.

The servant returned, conducted him along a passage to another door, announced him, and then stood back. On the way in, Constantine was passed by a woman servant leaving, carrying a magnificent perfume bottle. It was blue-green glass with gold around the rim, set with pearls—perhaps a gift from the caller who had made Helena laugh?

Helena herself stood in the center of the floor. She was beautiful in an unusual way: quite small and short-waisted. The curves of her bosom and hips were enhanced by the way her tunic was clasped at the shoulder and tied with its girdle. She wore few ornaments in her dark, luxurious hair, and no jewelry, since she was still officially mourning her husband. She had remarkably high cheekbones and a delicate nose and mouth. Under her winged eyebrows, her eyes brimmed with tears.

She came forward to meet him with somber dignity.

"How kind of you to come, Your Grace. It is a strange and lonely time for me."

"I can only imagine how desolate you must be," he replied gently. He knew exactly what she had felt for Bessarion, and far more of the details of what had happened to him than she had any idea. But none of that would ever be acknowledged between them. "If there is any comfort I can offer you, you have but to ask," he continued. "Bessarion was a good man, and loyal to the true faith. It is a double blow that he should be betrayed by those he trusted."

She raised her eyes to his. "I still can hardly believe it," she said huskily. "I keep hoping that something will arise to prove that neither of them was really guilty. I cannot believe it was Justinian. Not on purpose. There is some mistake."

"What could that be?" He asked because he needed to know what she might say to others.

She gave a tiny, delicate shrug. "I have not even thought so far."

It was the answer he wanted.

"Other people may ask," he said quite casually.

Helena lifted her head, her lips parted as she drew in her breath. The fear was there in her eyes only long enough for him to be certain of it, then she masked it. "Perhaps I am fortunate in not knowing anything." There was no lift of question in her voice, and try as he might, he could not read her face.

"Yes," he agreed smoothly. "I will be comforted knowing that you are quite safe from that added distress in your time of mourning."

There was understanding bright in her eyes, and then it was gone again, replaced by the calm, almost blank stare. "You are so kind to have called, Your Grace. Remember me in your prayers."

"Always, my child," he promised, raising his hand piously. "You will never be far from my thoughts."

He felt certain that Helena was not foolish enough to speak too freely to the Nicean eunuch, should Anastasius call and seek further knowledge from her. But as Constantine went out into the brightening sun and the slight wind off the sea, he was equally sure that she knew more than he had supposed and that she would be willing to use it for her own ends.

Who had made Helena laugh so freely and given her the exquisite perfume bottle? Constantine wished he knew.

four

⌒∽⌒

ANNA WENT OUT OF HER WAY TO SPEAK TO NEIGHBORS, prepared to waste time in conversation about the weather, politics, religion, anything they wanted to discuss.

"Can't stand here any longer," one man said finally. It was Paulus, a local shopkeeper. "My feet are so sore I can hardly get them in my shoes."

"Perhaps I can help?" Anna offered.

"Just let me sit down," he said, grimacing.

"I'm a physician. Perhaps I can offer a more permanent solution."

With his face reflecting disbelief, Paulus followed her, walking gingerly along the uneven stones until they covered the fifty yards to her house. Once inside, she examined his swollen feet and ankles. The flesh was red and obviously painful to the touch.

She filled a bowl full of cold water and put an astringent herb in it. Paulus winced as he put in his feet, then she saw his muscles slowly relax and the sense of ease come into his face. It was more the chill than anything else taking the burning out of his skin. What he really needed was to change his diet, but she knew she must be diplomatic about telling him so. She suggested he might care for rice, boiled with seasoning, and should abstain from all fruit, except apples, if he could find some that had been stored and were fit to eat at this time of year.

"And plenty of spring water," she added. "It must be spring, not lake, river, well water, or rain."

"Water?" he said with disbelief.

"Yes. The right water is very good for you. Come back any time you wish to, and I will bathe your feet in herbs again. Would you like some herbs to take with you?"

Paulus accepted them gratefully and paid from the purse he carried with him. She watched him hobble away and knew he would return.

Paulus recommended her to others. She continued to visit the shops within a mile or so of her house, always speaking to the shopkeeper and to other customers as the opportunity arose.

She did not know how far to indulge her own tastes. As a woman, she had loved the feel of silk next to her skin, the soft way it slid through her fingers and pooled on the floor as if it were liquid. Now she held up a length, letting it slither through her hands, watching the colors change as first the warp caught the light, then the weft. Blue turned to peacock and to green; red turned to magenta and purple. Her favorite was a peach burning into flame. In the past, she had worn silks to complement the tawny chestnut of her hair. Perhaps she could still wear them. Vanity was not specifically feminine, nor was the love of beauty.

The next time she had a new patient and earned more than two solidi, she would come back and buy this one.

She stepped out into the brisk wind blowing up from the shore. Walking along the narrow street, she moved aside for a cart to pass. The cool touch of silk had brought back the past with a rush.

She measured her steps carefully on the incline. The street was one of the many still unmended after the return from exile. There were broken walls and windowless houses still dark from the fires. The desolation made her own loneliness overwhelming.

She knew why Justinian had come to Constantinople and had been helpless to stop him. But what passions and entanglements had he become involved in that led him to being blamed for murder? That was what she needed to know. Could it have been love? Unlike her, he had been happy in his marriage.

A small part of Anna had envied him that, but now she had to swallow the hard, choking grief that all but closed her throat. She would give anything she possessed if she could get that happy life back for him. All she had had was medical skill, and it had not been enough to save Justinian's wife, Catalina. The fever had struck, and two weeks later she was dead.

Anna mourned because she had loved Catalina, too, but for Justinian it was as if his wife had taken the light from him with her when she departed. Anna had watched him and ached for his pain, but all the old closeness of heart and mind they shared was insufficient to touch his loss with healing.

She had seen him change, as if he were slowly bleeding to death. He looked for reasons and answers in the intellect. As if he dared not touch the heart, he combed the doctrine of the Church, and God eluded him.

Then two years ago, on the anniversary of Catalina's death, he had announced that he was going to Constantinople. Unable to reach his pain, Anna had stood by and let him leave.

He had written frequently, telling her of everything but himself. Then had come the last terrible letter, scrawled in haste as he was leaving in exile, and after that, only silence.

It was the beginning of June, and she had been in the city two and a half months when Basil first came to her as a patient. He was tall and lean, with an ascetic face, now pinched with anxiety as he stood in her waiting room.

He introduced himself quietly and said that he had come on Paulus's recommendation.

She invited him into the consulting room and inquired after his health, watching him carefully. His body was curiously stiff when he spoke, and she concluded that his pain was more severe than he was admitting.

She invited him to sit and he declined, preferring to remain standing. She concluded that his pain was in the lower stomach and groin, where such a change in position would increase it. After asking his permission, she touched his skin, which was hot and very dry, then tested his pulse. It was regular but not strong.

"I recommend that you abstain from milk and cheese for several weeks, at least," she suggested. "Drink as much spring water as you are able to take. It's all right to flavor it with juice or wine if you prefer." She saw the disappointment in his face. "And I will give you a tincture for the pain. Where do you live?"

His eyes opened in surprise.

"You can come back every day. The dose must be exact. Too little will do no good, and too much will kill you. I have only a small amount in supply, but I will find more."

He smiled. "Can you cure me?"

"It is a stone in your bladder," she told him. "If it passes it will hurt, but then it will be over."

"Thank you for your honesty," he said quietly. "I will take the tincture and come back every day."

She gave him a tiny portion of her precious Theban opium. Sometimes she mixed it with other herbs such as henbane, hellebore, aconite, mandragora, or even lettuce seed, but she did not wish him to fall into unconsciousness, so she kept it pure.

Basil returned regularly, and if she had no other patients, he often remained for a little while and they talked. He was an intelligent man of obvious education, and she found him interesting and likable. But beyond that, Anna hoped to learn something from him.

She broached the subject at the beginning of the second week of his treatment.

"Oh yes, I knew Bessarion Comnenos," he said with a slight shrug. "He cared very much about this proposed union with the Church of Rome. Like everyone else, he hated the thought of the pope taking precedence over the patriarch here in Constantinople. Apart from the insult and our loss of self-governance, it is so impractical. Any appeal for permission, advice, or relief would take six weeks to get to the Vatican, however long it required for the matter to reach the pope's attention, and then another six weeks to get back. By that time it could be too late."

"Of course," she agreed. "And there is the question of money. We can ill afford to send our tithes and offerings to Rome."

He groaned so sharply that for a moment she was afraid his pain was physical.

He smiled with apology. "We are in our own city again, but we balance on the brink of economic ruin. We need to rebuild, but we cannot afford to. Half our trade has gone to the Arabs, and now that Venice has robbed us blind of our holy relics, the pilgrims scarcely bother with us anymore."

They sat in the kitchen. She had made an herbal infusion of mint and camomile, and they were sipping it because it was still hot.

"Added to which," he went on, "there is the major issue of the *filioque* clause, which is the real sticking point. Rome teaches that the Holy Spirit proceeds from both the Father and the Son, making them both equally God. We believe passionately that there is only one God, the Father, and to say otherwise is blasphemy. We cannot condone that!"

"And Bessarion was against it?" she asked, although it was barely a question. Why would anyone think Justinian had killed him? It made no sense. He had always been Orthodox.

"Profoundly," Basil agreed. "Bessarion was a great man. He loved the city and its life. He knew that union with Rome would pollute the true faith and eventually destroy everything we care about."

"What was he going to do about it?" she said tentatively. "If he had lived . . ."

Basil shrugged slightly. "I'm not sure that I know. He spoke well, but he did little enough. It was always 'tomorrow.' And as you know, tomorrow did not come for him."

"I heard he was murdered." She found it difficult to say the words.

Basil looked down at the table and his bony hands holding the cup of mint infusion. "Yes. By Antoninus Kyriakis. He was executed for it."

"And Justinian Lascaris, too?" she prompted. "Was there a trial?"

He looked up. "Of course. Justinian was sent into exile. The emperor himself presided. It appears Justinian helped Antoninus dispose of the body so it might look like an accident. Actually I imagine they thought it would never be found."

She swallowed. "How did he do that? How can a body not be found?"

"At sea. Bessarion's body was discovered tangled in the ropes and nets of Justinian's boat."

"But that could have been without his knowledge!" she protested. "Perhaps Antoninus didn't have a boat, and simply took one!"

"They were close friends," Basil replied quietly. "Antoninus would not have implicated a man he knew so well when there were any number of other boats he could have taken."

It made no sense to Anna. "Was Justinian a man to leave evidence like that, condemning himself?" She knew the answer. She would never have made such a mistake, and neither would he. "Are they even sure Antoninus was guilty? Why would he kill Bessarion?"

Basil shook his head. "I have no idea. Perhaps they quarreled; he fell overboard and panicked. It can be difficult trying to help someone who is thrashing around; they become as much a danger to others as they are to themselves."

Anna had a vision of Justinian losing his temper, striking more forcefully than he had intended. He was strong. Bessarion could have overbalanced. He would flail around in the water and be pulled down, gasping, crying out, drowning. Had Justinian panicked? Not unless he had changed beyond all recognition from the man she had known. He had never been a coward. And if he had intended to kill Bessarion, then he would not have cut the ropes, he would have stayed all night and found the body, then tied weights to it and rowed far out in the Bosphorus and let it sink forever.

She felt a sudden sense of release. It was the first tangible evidence to grasp. She had facts, and even if she could not use them yet, they showed her brother's innocence irrefutably to her. "It sounds like an accident," she pointed out.

"It's possible," Basil conceded. "Perhaps if it had been anyone else, they would have taken it as such."

"Why not for Bessarion?"

Basil made a slight gesture of distaste. "Bessarion's wife, Helena, is very beautiful. Justinian was a handsome man, and while he was religious, he was also imaginative, articulate, and had a dry and sharp sense of humor. He was a widower, and therefore free to follow his inclinations where they led him."

"I see. . . ." Anna was a widow and held a hollow pain of loss inside her, too, but it was different. Eustathius's death had been both a guilt and a release. He had been of good family, wealthy, a soldier of courage and skill. His lack of imagination bored her and eventually made her find him repugnant. And he had been brutal. She still felt nausea rise inside her at the memory. The emptiness within seemed as if it would fill her until it burst through her skin. She was incomplete, maybe as much as the eunuch she pretended to be.

"You think that Justinian cared for Helena?" she asked incredulously. "Is that what people are saying?"

"No." Basil shook his head. "Not really. I should think a quarrel that got out of hand is more likely."

After he had gone, she examined her herb and general medicine store. She needed more opium. Theban was the best, but it was imported from

Egypt and not easily obtained. She might have to settle for second quality. She also needed more black hyoscyamus, mandragora, juice of climbing ivy. She was low in such ordinary herbs as nutmeg, camphor, attar of roses, and a few other of the common remedies.

The following morning, she set out to find a Jewish herbalist whose name she had heard recommended. Like all Jews, he lived across the Golden Horn in district thirteen, Galata. She took as much money as she could afford to spend and set out for the shore. Since having Basil as a patient, she was much better off than previously.

It was hot already, even this early in the day. It was not a long walk, and she enjoyed the sound and bustle as people unloaded donkeys from the day's trade. There was a pleasant smell of baking in the air and the salt breath up from the water.

At the harbor, she waited until there was a taxi going across to Galata that she could share, and fifteen minutes later she was on the northern shore. Here it was even more run-down than the main city. Houses were in need of repair, windows were paned haphazardly with whatever was to hand. The shabbiness of poverty touched every street corner, and she saw people in unembroidered cloaks and tunics, and of course few horses. Jews were not allowed to ride them.

After a few inquiries, she found the small, discreet shop of Avram Shachar, on the Street of the Apothecaries. She knocked on the door. It was opened by a boy of about thirteen, slender and dark, his features Semitic rather than Greek.

"Yes?" he said politely, caution edging his voice. Her fair skin, chestnut hair, and gray eyes would tell him she was unlikely to be of his own people; her robes and beardless face could belong only to a eunuch.

"I am a physician," she replied. "My name is Anastasius Zarides. I came from Nicea, and I need a supplier of herbs of wider origin than usual. Avram Shachar's name was given me."

The boy opened the door wider and called out for his father.

A man appeared from the back of the shop. He was perhaps fifty, his hair streaked with gray, his face dominated by dark, heavy-lidded eyes and a powerful nose. "I am Avram Shachar. How can I help you?"

Anna mentioned the herbs she was short of, adding also ambergris and myrrh.

Shachar's eyes lit with interest. "Unusual needs for a Christian doctor," he observed with humor. He did not say that Christians were not allowed to seek treatment from Jewish physicians, except with the special dispensation that was frequently granted to the rich and the princes of the Church, but his eyes said that he knew it.

She smiled back. She liked his face. And the sharp yet delicate odors of the herbs brought back memories of her father's rooms. Suddenly she was achingly lonely for the past.

"Come in," Shachar invited, mistaking her silence as reluctance.

She followed him as he led the way to the back of the house and into a small room opening onto a garden. Cupboards and chests of carved wood lined three walls, and a worn wooden table stood in the center with brass scales and weights and a mortar and pestle. There were pieces of Egyptian paper and oiled silk in piles, and long-handled spoons of silver, bone, and ceramic set neatly beside glass vials.

"From Nicca?" Shachar repeated curiously. "And you come to practice in Constantinople? Be careful, my friend. The rules are different here."

"I know," she answered. "I use them"—she indicated the cupboards and drawers—"only when necessary to heal. I've learned all my saints' days appropriate to every illness, and every season or day of the week." She looked at him, searching his face for disbelief. She knew too much anatomy and far too much of Arabic and Jewish medicine to believe, as Christian doctors did, that disease was due solely to sin, or that penitence would cure it, but it was not something the wise said aloud.

There was a flicker of understanding in Shachar's eyes, but the dark, subtle amusement did not reach his lips. "I can sell you most of what you need," he said. "What I do not have, perhaps Abd al-Qadir can supply."

"That would be excellent. Do you have Theban opium?"

He pursed his lips. "That is one for Abd al-Qadir. Do you need it urgently?"

"Yes. I have a patient I am treating and I have little left. Do you know a good surgeon if the stone does not pass naturally?"

"I do," he replied. "But give it time. It is not good to use the knife if it can be avoided." He worked as he spoke, weighing, measuring, packing things up for her to take, everything carefully labeled.

When he was finished, she took the parcel and paid him what he asked.

He studied her face for a few moments before making his decision. "Now let us see if Abd al-Qadir can help you with the Theban opium. If not, I have some that is less good, but still perfectly adequate. Come."

Obediently she followed, looking forward to meeting the Arab physician and wondering if perhaps he was the surgeon Shachar would recommend for Basil. How would her very Greek patient accept that? Perhaps it would not be necessary.

Five

ZOE CHRYSAPHES STOOD AT THE WINDOW OF HER FAVORITE room and stared across the rooftops of the city to where the sunlight streamed onto the Golden Horn till the water was like molten metal. Her hands caressed the stones in front of her, still warm in the last glow of the day. Constantinople was spread out below her like a jeweled mosaic. The ancient magnificence of the Aqueduct of Valens was behind her, its arches sweeping in from the north like a Titan from the Roman past, an age when Constantinople was the eastern pillar of an empire that ruled the world. The Acropolis, far to the right, was far more Greek and therefore more comfortable to her, her language, her culture. Although its great days had been before she was born, the elderly woman still felt a pride in the thought of it.

She could see the tops of the trees that hid the ruins of the Bukoleon Palace, where her father had taken her as a child. She tried to bring back those bright memories, but they were too far away and slipped out of her grasp.

The radiance of the setting sun momentarily hid the squalor of the un-mended walls, covering their scars with a veil of gold.

But Zoe never forgot the pain of the enemy invasion, of ignorant and careless feet trampling what had once been beautiful. She looked at the city now and saw it as exquisite and defiled, but still throbbing with a passion to taste every last drop of life and drain it to the lees.

The light was kind to her. She was past seventy, but the skin was smooth over her cheekbones. Her golden eyes were shadowed and hooded under her winged brows. Her mouth had always been too wide, but the curve of it was full. The luster of her hair was less than it had been and closer to brown than chestnut—there was only so much that herbs and dyes could do—but it was still beautiful.

She stared a few moments longer at the glittering skyline of Galata as the torches were lit. The east was fading rapidly, and the harbor was masked in purple. The spires and domes were sharper against the enamel blue of the sky. In thought she communed with the heart of the city, that part of it that was more than palaces or shrines, more even than the Hagia Sophia or the light on the sea. The soul of Constantinople was alive, and that was what she had seen raped by the Latins when she was a small child.

As the sun slid behind the low clouds and the air grew suddenly cold, she turned away at last. She stepped back into the room and its dazzling torchlight. She could smell the tar burning, see the faint shimmer of the flames in the draft. Between two of the finest tapestries in dark reds, purples, and umber, there was a gold crucifix more than a foot's length from top to bottom. She walked over and stood in front of it, staring at the Christ in agony. It was exquisitely wrought: Every fold of His loincloth, the sinews of His limbs, His face hollowed by pain, all were perfect.

Gently she reached up, eased it off its hook, and held it in her hands. She did not need to look at it, knowing as she did every line and shadow of the images on each of the four arms. Her fingers felt them now, going over them softly, like faces of those she loved; except that it was hate that moved Zoe, the envisioning over and over again of revenge: exquisite, slow, and complete.

On the top, above the Christ, was the family emblem of the Vatatzes, who had ruled Byzantium in the past. It was green, with a double-headed eagle in gold, above each head a silver star. They had betrayed Constantinople when the crusaders had come, fleeing the invaded city and taking with them priceless icons, not to save them from the Latins, but to sell for money. They had run like cowards, thieving from the holy sanctuaries as they went, abandoning to fire and the sword what they could not carry.

On the right arm was the emblem of the Doukas family, also rulers until more recently. Their arms were blue, with an imperial crown, a two-headed eagle with a silver sword in each claw; they were traitors as well, plunderers of those already robbed, homeless, and helpless. They would know in time what it was to starve.

On the left arm was the emblem of the Kantakouzenos, an imperial family older still; their arms were red, with the double-headed eagle in gold. They had been greedy, blasphemous, without honor or shame. To the third and fourth generation, they would pay. Constantinople did not forgive the violation of her body or her soul.

On the main trunk, against which hung the figure of Christ, was the emblem of the worst of them all, the Dandolo of Venice. Their coat of arms was just a simple lozenge horizontally halved, white above, red below. It was Doge Enrico Dandolo, over ninety years old and blind as a stone, who had stood in the prow of the leading ship of the Venetian fleet, impatient to invade, despoil, and then burn the Queen of Cities. When no one else had had the courage to be the first ashore, he had leapt down onto the sand, sightless and alone, and charged forward. The Dandolo family would pay for that as long as the scorch marks of ruin scarred the stones of Constantinople.

She heard a sound behind her, a clearing of the throat. It was Thomais, her black serving woman, with her close-cropped head and beautiful, fluid grace. "What is it?" Zoe asked without taking her eyes off the cross.

"Miss Helena has come to see you, my lady," Thomais replied. "Shall I ask her to wait?"

Zoe carefully replaced the cross on the wall and stepped back to regard it. Over the years since her return from exile, she had put it back up there hundreds of times, always perfectly straight.

"Walk slowly," Zoe replied. "Fetch her a glass of wine, then bring her here."

Thomais disappeared to obey. Zoe wanted to keep Helena waiting. Her daughter should not simply walk in at a whim and expect Zoe to be available. Helena was Zoe's only child, and she had molded her carefully, from the cradle; but no matter what she achieved, Helena would never outwit or outwill her mother.

Several minutes later, Helena entered quietly, smoothly. Her eyes were angry. Her respect was in her words, not in the tone of her voice. As was obligatory, she still wore mourning for her murdered husband, and she looked with some resentment at Zoe's amber-colored tunic, its flowing lines accentuated by the height that Zoe had and she did not.

"Good evening, Mother," she said stiffly. "I hope you are well?"

"Very, thank you," Zoe replied with a slight smile of amusement, not warmth. "You look pale, but then mourning is designed to do that. It is appropriate that a new widow should look as if she has been weeping, whether she has or not."

Helena ignored the remark. "Bishop Constantine came to see me."

"Naturally," Zoe responded, sitting down with easy grace. "Considering Bessarion's status, it is his duty. He would be remiss if he didn't, and other people would notice. Did he say something interesting?"

Helena turned away so Zoe did not see her face. "He was probing, as if he wondered how much I knew of Bessarion's death." She looked back at Zoe for a moment with blazing clarity. "And what I might say," she added. "Fool!" It was almost a whisper, but Zoe caught the edge of fear in it.

"Constantine has no choice but to be against union with Rome," she said sharply. "He's a eunuch. With Rome in charge, he would be nothing. Stay loyal to the Orthodox Church, and everything else will be forgiven you."

Helena's eyes widened. "That's cynical."

"It's realistic," Zoe pointed out. "And practical. We are Byzantine. Never forget it." Her voice was savage. "We are the heart and the brain of Christianity, and of light and thought and wisdom—of civilization itself. If we lose our identity, we have given away our purpose in living."

"I know that," Helena replied. "The question is, does he? What does he really want?"

Zoe looked at her with contempt. "Power, of course."

"He's a eunuch!" Helena spat the word. "The days are gone when a eunuch could be everything except emperor. Is he so stupid he doesn't know that yet?"

"In times of enough need, we will turn to anyone we think can save us," Zoe said quietly. "You would be wise not to forget that. Constantine is clever, and he needs to be loved. Don't underestimate him, Helena. He has your weakness for admiration, but he is braver than you are. And you can flatter even a eunuch, if you use your brains as well as your body. In fact, it would be a wise idea if you were to use your brains rather than your body where all men are concerned, for the time being."

Again the color surged up Helena's cheeks. "Said with all the wisdom and rectitude of a woman too old to do anything else," she sneered. She smoothed her hands over her slim waist and flat stomach, lifting her shoulders again, very slightly, to offer an even more voluptuous curve.

The taunt stung Zoe. There were places in her jaw and her neck she hated to see in the glass; the tops of her arms and her thighs no longer had the firmness they used to, even a few years ago.

"Use your beauty while you can," she replied. "You've nothing else. And as short as you are, when your waist thickens, you'll be square, and your breasts will sit on your belly."

Helena snatched up a length of silk tapestry from the chair and swung it as a lash, striking out at Zoe. The end of it caught one of the tall, bronze torch brackets and toppled it over, and burning pitch spilled on the floor. Instantly Zoe's tunic was on fire. She felt the heat of it scorch up her legs.

The pain was intense. She was suffocating in smoke. Her lungs were bursting, yet the shrill sounds deafening her were her own screams. She was hurled back into the far past, the crucible of all she had become. She was engulfed by the flaring red light in the darkness, the noise of walls collapsing, crashing stone on stone, the roar of flames, everywhere terror, confusion, throat and chest seared in the heat.

Helena was there, flinging water at her, shouting something, her voice high-pitched with panic, but Zoe was beyond thought. She was a tiny child clinging to her mother's hand, running, falling, dragged up and on, stumbling over the broken walls, bodies slashed and burned, blood on the pavement. She could smell the stench of human flesh on fire.

She fell again, bruised, aching. She climbed to her feet, and her mother was gone. Then she saw her; one of the crusaders had yanked her mother up off the ground and thrown her against a wall. He slashed at her robe and her tunic with his sword, then leaned against her, jerking violently. Zoe knew now what he had been doing. She could feel it as if it were her own body violated. When he finished, he had cut her mother's throat and let her slide, gushing blood onto the stones.

Zoe's father found them both, too late. Zoe was sitting on the ground as motionless as if she too were dead.

Everything after that was pain and loss. They were always in unfamiliar places, aching with hunger and the terrible emptiness of being dispossessed, and a horror inside her head that Zoe could never lose. And after horror came the hate. Prick her anywhere, and she bled rage.

Helena was close to her, wrapping her in something. The light of flames was gone, but the burning was still there, agonizing. Zoe's legs and thighs were throbbing with pain. She could make out words: Helena's voice, sharp and strained with fear.

"You're safe! You're safe! Thomais has gone for a physician. There's a good one just moved here, good for burns, for skin. You'll be all right."

Zoe wanted to swear at her, curse her for the stupid, vicious thing she had done, wreak a revenge on her that would be so terrible, she would want to die to escape it; but her throat was too tight and she could not speak. The pain robbed her of breath.

Zoe lost all awareness of time. The past was there again, over and over, her mother's face, her mother's bleeding body, the smell of burning. Then at last someone else was there, talking to her, a woman's voice. She was unwrapping the cloths Helena had put around the burns. It hurt appallingly. It felt as if her skin were still on fire. She bit her lips till she tasted blood, to stop herself from screaming. Damn Helena! Damn her, damn her, damn her!

The woman was touching her again, with something cold. The burning eased. She opened her eyes and saw the woman's face. Except it was not a woman, it was a eunuch. He had soft, hairless skin and his features were womanish, but there was a strength in them, and his gestures, the certainty with which he moved his hands, were masculine.

"It hurts, but it's not deep," he told her calmly. "Treat it properly and it'll heal. I'll give you ointment which will take the heat out of it."

It was not the pain now that troubled Zoe but the thought of scarring. She was terrified of disfigurement. She made a gasping sound, but her mouth would not form the words. Her back arched as she struggled.

"Do something!" Helena shouted at the physician. "She's in pain!"

The eunuch did not turn to Helena but looked steadily at Zoe's eyes, as if trying to read the terror in her. His own eyes were a curious gray. He was good-looking, in an effeminate way. Good bones, nice teeth. Pity they hadn't left him whole. Zoe tried to speak again. If she could make some sensible contact with him, she might drive away the panic that was welling up inside her.

"Do something, you fool!" Helena snarled at the eunuch. "Can't you see she's in agony? What are you just kneeling there for? Don't you know anything?"

The eunuch continued to ignore her. He seemed to be studying Zoe's face.

"Get out!" Helena ordered. "We'll get someone else."

"Bring me a goblet of light wine with two spoonfuls of honey in it," the eunuch told her. "Dissolve the honey well."

Helena hesitated.

"Please get it quickly," he urged.

Helena spun on her heel and left.

The eunuch busied himself putting more ointment on the burns, then binding them with cloths, but lightly. He was right; it took the heat away, and gradually the fearful pain subsided.

Helena returned with the wine. The physician took it and eased Zoe up gently until she was sitting and could hold the wine in her own hands. To begin with, her throat felt raw; but each mouthful was easier, and by the time she had drunk half of it, she could speak.

"Thank you," she said a little huskily. "How bad will the scarring be?"

"If you are lucky, keep the wounds clean, and the ointment on them, maybe there will be none at all," he replied.

Burning always scarred. Zoe knew that. She'd seen other people burned. "Liar!" she said between her teeth. Her body was stiff again, resisting his arms around her. "I saw the crusaders sack the city when I was a child," she told him. "I've seen fire burning before. I've smelled the stench of human flesh roasting and seen bodies you wouldn't recognize as having once been human."

There was pity in the eunuch's eyes as he looked at her, but Zoe was not sure whether pity was what she wanted.

"How bad?" Zoe hissed at him again.

"As I told you," he replied calmly. "If you look after the wounds properly, and use the ointment, there will be no scarring. You must take care of them. The burns are not deep; that is why they hurt so much. Deep ones don't, but often they don't heal, either."

"I suppose if you come back in a day or two, you'll want paying twice," Zoe snapped.

The physician smiled, as though it amused him. "Of course. Does that trouble you?"

Zoe leaned back a little. Suddenly she was desperately tired, and the pain had eased so much, she could almost put it from her mind. "Not in the slightest. My servant will attend to you." She closed her eyes. It was dismissal.

Zoe did not remember much of the next few hours, and when she awoke in her own bed, it was the middle of the following day. Helena stood beside her mother, looking down, and the light through the window was clear and harsh on her face. Her daughter's skin was blemishless, but the sun picked out the hardening line of her lips and the faintest slackening of the flesh under her chin. Helena's brow was puckered with anxiety. She smoothed away all sign of it as soon as she realized Zoe was awake.

Zoe looked at her coldly. Let her be afraid. Deliberately Zoe closed her eyes again, shutting her daughter out. The balance of power between them was changed. Helena had caused her both pain and terror, and the terror was worse. Neither of them would forget that.

The burning in her legs was no more than discomfort now. The eunuch was good. If he was right and there was no scarring, she would reward him well. It could also be profitable to cultivate his acquaintance and his gratitude by finding him other patients. Physicians found themselves in places others did not. They saw people at their most vulnerable; they learned their weaknesses, their fears, just as this one had learned Zoe's. He might also learn their strengths. Strength was a good place to attack because no one expected it. People did not realize that their strengths, if nurtured, praised, carried to excess, could also become their undoing.

She was intensely aware that she could have been crippled by the burning, even killed. If she waited any longer to begin her revenge, it could be too late. Something else might happen to her.

Or there was always that other unwelcome possibility—her enemies might die naturally, in their own beds, and she would be robbed of the victory. She had waited so long only that the full flavor might be realized. Before her foes had returned from exile and gained power and wealth in the new empire, there would have been no point. If they had nothing to lose, no riches to hold on to, vengeance would have no sweetness.

She breathed out slowly and smiled. It was time to begin.

Six

ANNA LEFT THE HOUSE OF ZOE CHRYSAPHES WITH A SOAR-
ing sense of achievement. At last she had been able to use her hard-
won skills in the treatment of serious burns, which without the ointment
from Colchis would have left lifelong scars. Her father had brought back
the recipe from his travels in the Black Sea and the home of the legendary
Medea, from whose name and science the very word *medicine* had sprung.
Healing Zoe could bring more patients, if she was fortunate, among them
those who had known Bessarion and therefore Justinian, Antoninus, and
whoever was really responsible for the murder.

As she walked home in the warm night air, she thought of the house she
had just left. Zoe was an extraordinary woman. Even when she was injured, terrified, and in pain, the intensity of feeling in her charged the air
with the kind of tension before a great storm that makes the skin tingle.

What had caused the fire in that gorgeous room with its wrought-iron
torch stands and its rich tapestries? Something deliberate? Was that why
Helena was afraid?

Anna quickened her pace, her mind exploring every possible use she
could make of this opportunity. As a eunuch, she was invisible, like a servant. She could overhear, piece together, make sense of odd threads of information.

She returned to see Zoe every day for the first week. The calls were
brief, simply enough to ensure that the healing was continuing as expected. It was obvious from the texture of her skin and the rich color of

her hair that Zoe herself was skilled in the use of herbs and unguents. Of course, Anna never mentioned it; it would have been tactless. However, on the fourth occasion she found Helena visiting her mother, and she had no such qualms.

Anna was sitting on the edge of Zoe's bed when Helena observed, "That smells disgusting." She wrinkled her nose at the sharp odor of the unguent Anna was using. "At least most of your other oils and creams are pleasant, if a little heavy."

Zoe's eyes narrowed to agate-hard slits. "You should learn their use, and the value of perfume. Beauty begins as a gift, but you are rapidly approaching the age when it begins to become an art."

"Followed by the age when it is a miracle," Helena snapped.

Zoe's golden eyes widened. "Difficult for someone with no soul to conceive of miracles."

"Maybe I will, by the time I need them."

Zoe looked her up and down. "You've left it late," she whispered.

Helena smiled, a slow, secret satisfaction oozing through it. "Not as late as you think. It was my intention that you should think you knew everything—but you didn't. You still don't."

Zoe hid her surprise almost instantly, but Anna saw it.

"If you mean about Bessarion's death," Zoe answered, "then of course I knew it. The poisonings, and the knifing in the street. They had your hand all over them—they failed. Misconceived, and stupid." She sat up a little, pushing Anna aside, her attention fully upon her daughter. "Who did you think would take his place, you fool? Justinian? Demetrios? That's it—Demetrios. I suppose I have Eirene to thank for that." It was a conclusion, not a question. She sank back against the pillows, the pain showing in her face again. And Helena walked out.

Anna tried to keep her concentration on the slowly healing skin, but the thoughts raced in her mind. There had been other attempts on Bessarion's life. By whom? Apparently Zoe thought by Helena. Why? Who was Demetrios? Who was Eirene? Now she had something concrete to seek.

She finished the bandages, willing herself to keep her fingers steady.

It was not difficult to make the initial inquiries. Eirene was a woman of great note, ugly, clever, of ancient imperial family both by birth as a

Doukas and by marriage as a Vatatzes. Gossip had it that she was responsible for the steady increase of her husband's fortune, even though he had not yet returned from exile, for most of which he had been in Alexandria.

She had one son—Demetrios. There the information stopped, and as yet Anna dared not press it any further. The connections she was looking for now were more sinister, perhaps dangerous.

By August, Zoe's burns were almost entirely healed and her patronage was bringing other patients to Anna. Some of these were wealthy merchants, dealers in furs and spices, silver, gems, and silks. They were happy to pay two or three solidi for the best herbs and even more for personal attention on demand.

Anna told Simonis to buy lamb or kid, even though they were recommended only for the first half of the month. They had been frugal ever since they had arrived in March. Now it was time for a celebration. She should serve it hot, with honey-vinegar and perhaps some fresh gourd.

"You know what vegetables to eat in August," Anna added. "And yellow plums."

"I'll get some rose wine." Simonis had the last word.

Anna went back to the local silk shop and picked up the length she had admired before. She let the soft, cool fabric slide through her fingers, almost like liquid, and watched as the light fell on it, turning it slowly. The sheen was first amber, then apricot, then fire, changing as it moved like a living thing. People said that of eunuchs, that the essence of them was elusive, never the same twice. It was meant as condemnation—that they were unreliable.

She saw it only that they were different as they were viewed, because they needed to be to survive; and that they were human, full of hungers, fears, and dreams like everyone else, and had the same ability to be hurt.

She bought a length of the silk sufficient to make a dalmatica for herself and accepted the shop owner's offer to have it cut and stitched and delivered to her home. She thanked him and left, smiling even in the heat of the road outside and the dust of too many rainless days.

Then she went south toward Mese Street and looked at the shops there. She bought new linen tunics for both Leo and Simonis and a new outdoor cloak for each of them, requesting that they be delivered.

She had attended the nearest church every Sunday except when a patient required her urgent presence, but now she felt like taking a water taxi the considerable distance to the great cathedral of the Hagia Sophia. It stood out on the promontory, at the farthest end of Mese Street, between the Acropolis and the Hippodrome.

It was a calm evening, the air still close and warm, even on the water. As the sun sank lower in the west, color spilled across the Golden Horn, making it look like a sheet of silk. It was its brilliant reflection at sunrise that had given it its name.

The water taxi put ashore at dusk, and she climbed the steep streets up from the harbor as the lamps and torches were lit.

She approached the Hagia Sophia, now black against the fading sky, with a sense of awe and excitement. For a thousand years it had stood on this spot, the largest church in Christendom. It had been completely destroyed by fire in 532. The great dome had collapsed in 558, brought down by an earthquake, and been replaced almost immediately by the dome that now soared huge and dark against the sky.

Of course she had seen it many times from the outside. The building itself was over 250 feet in either direction. The stucco was of a reddish color, and in the rising or setting sun it glowed with such warmth that mariners approaching the city could see it from afar.

She went in through the bronze doors and then stopped in amazement. The vast interior was bathed in light from countless candles. It was like being in the heart of a jewel. The porphyry marble columns were deep red. Her father had told her they were originally from the Egyptian temple in Heliopolis, ancient, beautiful, and priceless. The polychrome marble in the walls was cool green and white, from Greece or Italy. The white of it was inlaid with ivory and pearls, and there were gold icons from the ancient temples of Ephesus. It far surpassed every description she had heard.

The impression of light was everywhere, as if the whole structure floated in the air, needing no physical support. The arches were inlaid with mosaics of staggering beauty, somber blues, grays, and browns against backgrounds of countless tiny squares of gold: pictures of saints and angels, Mary with the child Christ, prophets and martyrs from all the ages. Her eyes were dragged away from them only by the beginning of the Mass and the voices rising in unison and then in harmony.

Moved by the sacred solemnity of it, uplifted by a surge of her own faith and an ache to belong, she went toward the steps to the upper level. Head bent, she was carried forward by the others around her. This was the familiar ritual and the creed that had nourished her all her life. She had walked up to the women's section of her own church in Nicea as a little girl with her mother, while Justinian and her father went with the men to the main body of the hall.

She reached the top and stood with the others staring down into the heart of the church as, in profound reverence, the priests performed the blessing and the taking of the sacrament of Christ's body and blood, given to redeem mankind. The ritual was Byzantine to the heart, solemn and subtle, ancient as the trust between man and God.

The sermon was about the faith of Gideon leading the armies of the children of Israel against a force that seemed overwhelming. Again and again God commanded Gideon to reduce his meager army until it seemed absurd even to attempt a battle. The priest pointed out that this was so that when they won, as they would do, they would know that it was God who had made it possible. They would be victorious, but also both humble and grateful. They would know upon whom to rely in all future paths. First obey, and nothing is impossible, no matter what appearances suggest.

Was he speaking of the threat to the Church posed by the union with Rome? Or an invasion by crusading forces again, if the union was refused and the Latins returned, violent and bloody as before?

After the last notes of the singing faded away, she turned to leave, and then the horror dawned on her. Unthinking, she had followed the other women up to the women's section. She had utterly forgotten she was supposed to be a eunuch. What on earth could she do? How could she escape now? The sweat broke out on her body, drenching her and leaving her cold. Everyone knew that the balconies of the upper floor were for women. She was agonized with shame.

The women were streaming past her, eyes downcast, heads veiled, unlike hers. None of them looked back up to where she stood clinging to the banister, swaying a little as dizziness overwhelmed her. She must find an excuse, but what? Nothing could account for coming up here.

An old woman stopped beside her, her skin pale, her face withered. Dear heaven, was she going to demand an explanation? She looked ashen. Was she going to faint and draw the attention of the entire crowd?

The old woman swayed and gave a hacking cough; a spot of blood stained her lips.

The answer came like a shaft of light. Anna put her arm around the woman and eased her down to sit on the steps. "I'm a physician," she said gently. "I'll help you. I'll see you home."

A younger woman turned and saw them. She quickly came back up a step.

"I'm a physician," Anna said quickly. "I saw her looking ill and I came up to help her. I'll take her home." She assisted the old woman to her feet, arm around her again, supporting most of her weight. "Come," she encouraged. "Direct me where to go."

The younger woman smiled and made way for them, nodding approval.

Nevertheless, afterward, Anna arrived home trembling with relief. Simonis looked at her anxiously, knowing there was something wrong, but Anna was too ashamed of her stupidity to tell her what it was.

"Have you found anything further?" Simonis asked, holding out a goblet of wine and placing a dish of bread and chives in front of Anna.

"No," Anna said quietly. "Not yet."

Simonis said nothing, but her look was eloquent. They were not here risking their lives a hundred miles from home so Anna could gain a new medical practice. In Simonis's opinion, there was nothing wrong with the one Anna had had in Nicea. Their only reason for leaving it, and the places and friends they had known all their lives, was to rescue Justinian.

"My tunics are very good," Simonis said quietly. "Thank you. You must be getting new patients. Rich ones."

Anna could see the disapproval in her stiff shoulders and the way she pretended to be concentrating on grinding the mustard seeds to make the sauce for the flatfish she would cook tomorrow.

"Rich is incidental," she told her. "They knew Justinian and the other people around Bessarion. I am learning about his friends, and perhaps Bessarion's enemies."

Simonis looked up quickly, her eyes bright. She smiled briefly; it was as far as she dared go, in case her belief invited bad luck, and the prize slipped away. "Good." She nodded. "I see."

"You don't like the city much, do you?" Anna said softly. "I know you miss the people you knew at home. So do I."

"It's necessary," Simonis replied. "We've got to find the truth of what happened, and get Justinian back. You just keep trying. I'll make new friends. Now go to bed. It's late."

Seven

᎒᎒

IN EARLY OCTOBER, ZOE SENT A MESSENGER TO ANNA, RE-
questing that she attend her immediately. Zoe drew her like a flame
that was dangerous, unpredictable, at times destructive, but above all a
blazing light, and Anna was in urgent need of more information.

When she arrived Zoe received her at once, which was in itself a compliment. Today she was dressed in a wine red tunic with a lighter red dalmatica over it, clasped at the shoulder with an enormous gold-and-amber
jewel. More gold and amber hung on her ears and around her neck and
was echoed at the embroidered hems of her garments. With her topaz eyes
and deep bronze hair, Zoe was breathtaking.

"Ah! Anastasius," she said eagerly, walking toward Anna, smiling. "How
is your business? I hear good reports of you from my friends." It was a
courteous question and asked with enthusiasm. It was also a reminder that
most of Anna's best patients—the ones with money who paid on time and
recommended her further—had come because of Zoe.

"Good, and getting better all the time," Anna answered. "I thank you
for your recommendations."

"I am happy they have been useful." Zoe waved one elegant hand,
sharp-nailed and decorated with rings, indicating the table with a jug of
wine, several goblets, and a green glass bowl of almonds.

"Thank you," Anna said, as if accepting, but she made no move toward
it. She was too tense with expectation as to what Zoe wanted. She looked

in good health, even if some of it was achieved with her own salves and potions and a great deal of willpower.

"How can I be of service?" Anna asked. She had learned not to compliment women as if she were a whole man or to commiserate as if she were another woman.

Zoe smiled, amused. "Quick to the point, Anastasius. Have I drawn you away from another patient?" She was probing, seeing how Anastasius would walk the razor's edge between flattery and truth, keeping his own dignity, maintaining the respect for his skill, yet also being available to do whatever Zoe wished. He could not yet afford to refuse, and they both knew it. Zoe was not a patient in this instance, yet it would be absurdly arrogant for Anastasius ever to imagine they were social acquaintances. He was a eunuch from the provinces who earned his own living; Zoe was of an aristocratic family and not just a native of the city, but almost an embodiment of its soul.

Anna measured her words, smiling a little. "Is this not business?"

Zoe's golden eyes flashed with laughter. "Of course. It is a friend, a young woman named Euphrosane Dalassena. She has a disease of the skin, and it is somewhat embarrassing to her. You seem to be skilled in such things. I have told her you will come."

Anna swallowed the sting of arrogance at being so taken for granted. Even so, Zoe saw the flicker and knew what it meant. It pleased her.

"If you tell me where I may find her, I shall call," Anna answered.

Zoe nodded slowly, satisfied, and named the house and the street. "Urgently, if you please. Study her carefully, consider her mind as well as her body. It is of concern to me how she progresses. Do you understand?"

"I shall be happy to tell you that she is doing well, or not so well," she replied.

"I don't care about her skin!" Zoe snapped. "You can take care of that, I have no doubt. She is recently widowed. I am interested in her state of mind, the strength of her character."

Anna hesitated on the brink of further restrictions on what she felt free to say, then decided it would be pointless. It would anger Zoe for no reason. She would decide how much to tell her later.

"I'll go straight away," she said graciously.

Zoe smiled. "Thank you."

.   .   .

Euphrosane Dalassena was in her late twenties, but at first she seemed younger. Her features were excellent and she should have been lovely, but there was a certain insipidity about her, and Anna wondered if it were due to illness. She lay on a couch, her light brown hair unadorned, her skin a little waxy. Anna had been shown in by a serving woman, who remained in the unimaginatively ornamented room, standing by the doorway.

Anna introduced herself and asked all the usual questions about symptoms. Then she examined the painful rash that spread across Euphrosane's back and lower abdomen. She seemed to have a slight temperature and was clearly both embarrassed and distressed by her condition. Her eyes never left Anna's face, always waiting for the verdict, trying to interpret every expression.

Finally she could bear it no longer. "I go to confession every other day, and I know of no sin of which I have not repented," she exclaimed. "I've fasted and prayed, but nothing comes to my mind. Please help me!"

"God does not punish you for what you can't help," Anna said quickly, then immediately wondered at her daring. That was her own conviction, but was it the doctrine of the Church? She felt the blood burn up her face.

Euphrosane's logic was perfect. "Then I must be able to help it," she said plaintively. "What haven't I done? I have prayed to Saint George, who is the patron saint of skin diseases, but he is patron saint of a lot of things. So I have also prayed to Saint Anthony the Abbot, just in case I should be more specific. I attend Mass every day, I go to confession, I give alms to the poor and offerings to the Church. Where have I fallen so far short that this has happened to me? I don't understand." She lay back on the couch.

Anna drew in her breath to say that it was nothing to do with sin of any kind, omission or commission, but realized that that might be viewed as heresy.

Euphrosane was still watching her, the sweat dampening her skin and making her hair lank. Anna must answer or lose Euphrosane's faith in her.

"Could it be that your sin lies in not trusting God's love enough?" she said, shocked at her own words. "I will give you medicine to take, and ointment to have your maid put on the blisters. Each time you do so, pray, and believe that God loves you, personally."

"How could He?" Euphrosane said wretchedly. "My husband died young, before he had achieved half the things he could have, and I did not even bear a child! Now I am afflicted with an illness so ugly no other man will want me. How could God love me? I am doing something terribly wrong, and I don't even know what it is."

"Yes, you are," Anna said vehemently. "How dare you dismiss yourself as useless or ugly? God does not need you to get everything right, because nobody is going to do that, but He does expect you to try, and to trust Him."

Euphrosane stared at her in wonder. "I understand," she said, the confusion gone. "I shall repent, immediately."

"And use the medicine as well," Anna warned. "He gave us herbs and oils, and intelligence to understand their purpose. Don't throw His gift back at Him. That would be ingratitude, which is also a very serious sin indeed." And it would make the whole exercise pointless, but she could not tell her that.

"I will! I will!" Euphrosane promised.

A week later, Euphrosane was completely healed, which made Anna wonder if perhaps much of her fever had been due to fear of an imagined guilt.

She went to report to Zoe, as asked, and this time she had to wait nearly half an hour before being admitted. She knew the moment she saw Zoe's face that she was already aware of Euphrosane's recovery. Quite probably she also knew how much Anna had been paid, but she could not afford to let her irritation show. She thanked Zoe again for the referral.

"What did you think of her?" Zoe asked casually. Today she wore dark blue and gold. With her warm hair and eyes, the effect was superb. There were times when Anna longed, with almost physical pain, to dress as a woman again herself and to ornament her hair. Then she could face Zoe on an even footing. She forced herself to remember Justinian somewhere in the sterility of the Judean desert, possibly even wearing sackcloth, and the reason she was here posing as a eunuch. Did he imagine she had forgotten him?

Zoe was waiting, her expression impatient. "Is your opinion of Euphrosane so bad you cannot answer me honestly? You owe me that, Anastasius."

"Gullible," Anna replied. "A sweet young woman, painfully honest, but easily persuaded. Obedient. Too fearful not to be."

Zoe's golden eyes opened wide. "So you bite," she said with amusement. "Be careful. You cannot afford to nip the wrong person."

The sweat broke out on Anna's skin, but she did not look away. She knew never to let Zoe sense weakness. "You asked for the truth. Should I tell you less?"

"Never," Zoe replied, her eyes bright as faceted gems. "Or if you lie, then do it so well that I never find out."

Anna smiled. "I doubt I could do that."

"Interesting that you are wise enough to say so," Zoe replied softly, almost a purr. "There is something I would like you to do for me. If a merchant named Cosmas Kantakouzenos should ask your opinion of Euphrosane's character, as he might, would you be as candid with him? Tell him she is honest, guileless, and obedient."

"Of course," Anna replied. "I would be grateful if you would tell me more about Bessarion Comnenos." It was a bold question, and she had not had time to think of any explanation for her interest. But Zoe had not given any reason why she wished Euphrosane recommended to Cosmas.

Zoe walked over to the window and stared out at the complex pattern of rooftops. "I suppose you mean his death," she said dryly. "Bessarion's life was uninteresting. He married my daughter, but he was a bore. Pious and chilly."

"And he was killed for that?" Anna said with disbelief.

Zoe turned around slowly, her eyes sweeping up and down Anna from her woman's face in the guise of a eunuch, naked of a masculine beard and unsoftened by the lushness of feminine curls and ornaments. Zoe's eyes traveled down her body, bound at the chest, padded out from shoulder to hip to hide the natural curve.

Anna knew what she looked like. She had worked hard on her appearance. Yet at times like these, in the presence of a woman who was beautiful, even now, she hated it. Her hair no longer than to her shoulders actually became her face. It was less stiff than the highly dressed styles women wore, but still she missed the combs and ornaments she had once had. More than that she missed the color for her brows, the powder to even out the tones of the skin, the artificial color to make her lips less pale.

A servant's footsteps passed audibly across the floor in the next room.

Deliberately, Anna forced herself to remember Zoe's terror when she had been burned, the nakedness of the pain in her. It reduced her to a human being in need.

Zoe saw some change in her but did not comprehend it. She gave the slightest shrug of one shoulder. "It was not an isolated incident," she remarked. "A year before his death he was attacked in the street. We never learned if it was an attempt at robbery, or one of his own bodyguards, perhaps, seizing a chance to stab him in the scuffle but making a mess of it. He was cut only once, but it was quite deep."

"Why would one of his own bodyguards do that?" Anna asked.

"I have no idea," Zoe answered, then saw instantly from Anna's face that that was an error. Zoe would always know, and she would never admit ignorance. Now to cover the disadvantage Zoe would attack. "It was before you came," she said. "Why does it concern you?"

"I need to know friends and enemies," Anna answered her. "Bessarion's death still seems to be of interest to many people."

"Of course," Zoe said tartly. "He was of one of the old imperial families, and led the cause against union with Rome. Many people placed their hopes in him."

"And now in whom?" Anna asked—too quickly.

There was a flash of humor in Zoe's eyes. "And you imagine this was a bid for sainthood. Or that Bessarion is some kind of martyr?"

Anna blushed, angry with herself for opening the way for such a remark. "I want to know the allegiances, for my own safety."

"Very wise," Zoe said softly with a flicker of appreciation, an inner light of laughter. "And if you succeed, you will be cleverer than anyone else in Byzantium."

Eight

∽

WHEN ANASTASIUS WAS GONE, ZOE REMAINED ALONE IN the room, standing at the window. She never tired of the view. Up that shining strip of water had sailed Jason and his Argonauts in search of the Golden Fleece. He had found Medea and betrayed her. Her revenge had been terrible. Zoe could well understand. She was nearly ready to exact her own revenge on the Kantakouzenos. Cosmas was Zoe's age. It was his father, Andreas, who had told the crusaders where the vial was with the blood of Christ in it, in order to save himself. Dead now, he was beyond Zoe's reach, let God burn him in hell. But Cosmas was alive and well and now here again in Constantinople, prospering. He had much to lose. She watched him as she would watch a fruit ripening, read to be plucked.

Her eyes moved to the golden bowl on the table. It was full of apricots, like liquid amber touched with the red of the sun. She picked one up and bit into it, crushing its flesh between her teeth and letting the juice run over her lips onto her chin.

Euphrosane's grandfather Georgios Doukas had helped steal icons from the Hagia Sophia, the Mother Church of Byzantium. He had even helped them take the Holy Shroud of Christ itself. Its loss to the Orthodox faith could never be forgiven. Now the coarse, irreverent fingers of the Latins would hold it. Zoe's whole body shuddered at the thought, as if she herself had been touched intimately by something foul.

It was a stroke of good fortune that Euphrosane had fallen ill with a disease of the skin that her own physician could not heal. It had enabled Zoe to send the eunuch physician to her, and he in turn would get Cosmas to trust her.

She took another apricot; this one was less ripe than the first, a little like Anastasius. He had surprised her with his sharpness in judging Euphrosane. Not that he was wrong, of course; she simply had expected him to be more mealy-mouthed in expressing it. But liking him could not be allowed to get in the way of Zoe's plans for revenge. If Anastasius was useful, that was all that mattered.

And he had one weakness she should not forget—he forgave. Some of the patients she had recommended had treated him badly, but he did not seem to bear a grudge. He had had opportunity to take advantage of them in return, and he had not taken it. Zoe did not think it was cowardice; there would have been no danger to himself—indeed, no price to pay of any sort. That was stupid. With no fear there would be no respect. She would have known better. She would have to protect Anastasius, as long as he was useful. All scores must be evened.

She turned back and faced the room and the great gold crucifix on the wall. She would help the physician in his quest for information about Bessarion, but she knew it had nothing to do with understanding alliances in Constantinople. Then why was he asking about it?

Naturally she could not tell him even a whisper of the truth. Could she say that Helena had been bored witless by Bessarion and that he had probably never been interested in her—not as a man should be interested in a woman?

She relaxed and threw back her head, smiling in a rare moment of self-mockery. She had tried to seduce Bessarion herself once, just to see if there was any fire in his loins, or his soul. There wasn't. He was willing, eventually, but it wasn't worth the trouble.

No wonder Helena's eyes were wandering! Far cleverer to seduce Antoninus and then use him to dispose of Bessarion and so get rid of both of them—if that was what had happened. That was worthy of a daughter of Zoe's. She had been slow to learn, but apparently she had succeeded well enough in the end. Pity Helena had compromised Justinian, too. He was a real man, too much for Helena. If she had caused that, Zoe would not forgive her for it.

She walked slowly across the room to the doorway, swinging her arm out a fraction to make the silk of her robe flutter and shine in the light. The sheen changed color from russet to gold and back again, deceiving the eye, firing the imagination.

A week later, the emperor sent for her. There was a man worth lying with. The memory was still a good one, even all these years after. Not the best; Gregory Vatatzes would always be that. But Zoe forced him out of her mind. There was pain in every thought of him, as well as pleasure.

Michael wanted something, or he would not have sent for her. She dressed carefully, gorgeous in a bronze and black silk tunic that clung to her. A high necklace would conceal the aging of her skin under her jaw. Her hands were soft. She knew exactly what ingredients to use in unguents to keep them pale and the knuckles from swelling. She wore topaz, set in gold. None of it was to seduce him; their relationship was beyond that now. He wanted her skill, her cunning, not her flesh.

Since the return of the empire from exile in Nicea and scattered cities to the north along the coast of the Black Sea, Michael had made his residence in the Blachernae Palace, on the other side of the city from the old Imperial Palace. The Blachernae overlooked the Golden Horn, as did her own house, and it was not more than a mile and a half away. She could walk it easily, accompanied by Sabas, her most loyal servant.

She did not hurry, it was unseemly. She had time to notice the weeds where paving stones were missing, the broken windows in a church, never replaced.

Even the Blachernae Palace itself was scarred, some of the magnificent arches of its upper windows shattered, threatening to topple over and smash on the steps below.

The Imperial Varangian Guard did not question her. They knew better than to ask who she was. No doubt they had been told to expect her. She swept past them with just a slight inclination of her head.

She remembered the old days, before the Latins came, when she was a tiny child and her father had taken her to the old Imperial Palace, high up on the headland overlooking the city and the sea. Alexios V had been emperor of Byzantium, which to her was the world. That was just before the terrible days of the invasion.

She waited in a huge room with high windows that let the light fill the space and magnify the perfect proportions. The walls were inlaid with pink marble and the floor with porphyry. The torch brackets were high, slender, and decorated in gold. Her surroundings pleased her profoundly, and she was happy to gaze at them until she was sent for.

She was conducted by a tall eunuch with a soft face, tired eyes, and an irritating manner of waving his hands. He led her through the halls and galleries into the emperor's private rooms. There were some conversations that should not be overheard by anyone. Even the ever-present Varangian Guard would stand at a distance, out of earshot. Many of them were yellow-haired, blue-eyed, from God-knew-what remote lands.

This private room was totally restored, the walls repainted with exquisite murals of pastoral scenes at harvesttime. The tall, bronze candle stands were ornate and gleaming, the few statues left undamaged.

She made the usual obeisance. She was twenty-five years older than Michael, and a woman, but he was emperor and Equal of the Apostles. He did not rise to greet her but remained seated, his knees a little apart, covered by the woven, brocaded silk of his dalmatica and the scarlet of the tunic underneath. He was a handsome man with his heavy black hair and beard, fine eyes, and slightly ruddy complexion. He had good hands. Zoe remembered the touch of them with pleasure, even now. They were surprisingly sensitive for a man who had been a brilliant soldier in his prime and still knew more of military strategy than most generals. In battle he had led his army rather than followed it. He was busy now reorganizing the army and the navy and overseeing the repair of the city walls. He was above all a practical man. What he wanted of Zoe would also be practical.

"Come forward, Zoe," he commanded. "We are alone. There is no need for pretense." His voice was soft and deep, as a man's should be.

She stepped closer to him, but slowly. She would never presume and so give him the chance to rebuff her. Let him do the asking, the requesting.

"There is a matter in which you may be of assistance," he said, watching her intently, his eyes searching her face. She was never sure how far he could read her. He was Byzantine to the core; nothing of the imagination passed him by. He was subtle, devious, and brave, but at the moment he had a heavy burden to carry and a broken and obstinate people to lead. They were blind to the realities of the new threat, because they dared not look at it clearly.

Since Bessarion's death, Zoe was beginning to see the political situation differently. There was a betrayal still being planned somewhere, and when Zoe found it out, she would punish whoever was responsible, even if it was Helena.

She wished she could have spoken to Justinian before he went into exile, but Constantine had accomplished his rescue so smoothly, and so quickly, that that had not been possible.

Now she needed to know what Michael wanted of her. "Whatever I can do," she murmured respectfully.

"There are certain people whose services you use . . ." He measured his words with care. "I would prefer not to be seen to use them, but they have skills I need. I wish for information. Later it may be more than that."

"Sicily?" She breathed out the word; it was really more of an acknowledgment than a question.

He nodded assent.

She waited. A new bargain must be made, and that was good. She would deal with anyone if it was for Byzantium's sake, but she would not do it cheaply. The Sicilian she employed was a weasel of a man, a double spy, but she had caught his one mistake and kept the proof of it where all his cunning would never find it. He was dangerous, and she must handle him with care, as one did a serpent. She knew why Michael could not afford to have any connection with him, even through his own spies. Nothing escaped the eunuchs closest to him, or the house servants and palace guards, the priests forever coming and going. He needed someone like Zoe, who was just as clever as he was but who could afford to be ruthless in ways he dared not. There were too many pretenders to the throne, would-be usurpers, plots and counterplots. Michael was only too bitterly aware of it, always watching over his shoulder.

He leaned forward, less than a yard from her now. "I need this man of yours," he said quietly. "Not to strike yet, but in a while. And I need someone else in Rome also, a second voice."

"I can find someone," she promised. "What do you wish to know?"

He smiled. He had no intention of telling her. "Someone close to the pope," he said. "And to the king of the Two Sicilies."

"Someone with courage?" Hope flared inside her that after all, he meant to fight. Perhaps Michael would even assassinate the pope? After all, the pope was the enemy of Byzantium, and this was war.

He read her instantly. "Not that kind of courage, Zoe. Those days are past. Popes can be replaced easily enough." There was anger in his eyes and something that might have been fear. "The king of the Two Sicilies is the real danger, and the pope is the only one who can hold him back. If we are to survive, we must compromise."

"You cannot compromise the faith," she retorted.

Temper burned the skin under his heavy beard. She saw the flush across his cheekbones. He leaned even closer to her. "We need skill, Zoe, not bravado. We must use one against the other, in the way we always have. But I will not lose Constantinople again, to pay for anything on earth. I'll bow the knee to Rome, or let them think I do, but the crusaders will not break one stone of my city, nor tax the smallest coin of tribute from my people." His black eyes bored into hers. "Sicily may starve, and may even turn to bite the hand that robs it, and if it does, so much the better for us. Until then, I will trade in words and symbols with the pope, or the devil, or King Charles of Anjou and the Two Sicilies, if I have to. Are you with me or against me?"

"I am with you," she said softly, aware now of a subtle and disturbing irony. "I will defend Byzantium against anyone, within or without. Are you with me?"

He looked straight back at her, unblinking. "Oh yes, Zoe Chrysaphes. You may trust me to choose what I see, and what I don't."

"I have my spies by the neck. I shall see they do as you wish," she promised, smiling also and stepping back. Her mind was busy already. Sicily rising against their king? There was a thought.

Nine

∽

OE DID AS MICHAEL HAD REQUESTED, THEN SHE TURNED her mind to revenge. She had not forgotten the bitter lesson of her own brush with death. There was no time to wait.

The eunuch Anastasius was exactly the tool she needed. He had intelligence and the kind of honesty to his profession that made people trust him. She was quite aware that he did not trust her, and there was also this hunger in him to know about Bessarion's death. One day Zoe would take time to find out exactly why that was.

In the meantime, there was a delicate balance of irony in using him to trick and ruin Cosmas Kantakouzenos, whose family's greed had robbed Byzantium of some of its greatest art.

Zoe was dressed in a tunic the color of dark wine in shadow and an even darker dalmatica, burgundy warp shot with a black weft, which caught the warmth of reds in the firelight as she passed through the glow of the torches.

She crossed herself and stepped out into the night, Sabas following behind her, for safety in the shadows of twilight and for their return in the dark.

She stood for a moment in the street, reciting the Ave Maria to herself, hands folded. Then she started to walk again.

She drew a deep breath into her lungs. This was her vengeance at last. By tomorrow, the first of those whose emblems were on the back of her crucifix would be dead.

She left Sabas outside as the servant showed her in to Cosmas's house. Even the entrance hall was magnificent, especially the marble bust of a Roman senator on a plinth, his elderly face lined with the emotion and experience of a lifetime. Blue Venetian glasses stood on a table, the light making them look like jewels. An Egyptian alabaster dog with huge ears took pride of place on a carved wooden table.

When she was shown into his room, Cosmas was sitting in a wide chair, staring at an inlaid table on which stood a jug of Sicilian wine, which was now more than half-empty. Beside it was a dish of dates and honeyed fruits. He was a short man with a curved nose and heavy-lidded eyes, red-rimmed in shadowed sockets.

"I don't owe you anything," he said sourly. "So I assume you have come to see what you can plunder."

She wanted to do more than gloat; she needed a quarrel, one that could be escalated into violence.

"You are a wretched judge of character," she replied, still standing. He did not rise. "I have not come to make financial profit out of you. I will buy icons to give to the church so all may worship them there and be blessed. I will pay you a fair price."

His shoulders straightened and his head lifted a little.

"But I will see them first," she added with a slight smile.

"Of course. Wine?"

"With pleasure." She had no intention of drinking anything in his house, but she wanted the glass. A pity to break it—it was exquisite.

He rose stiffly, knees creaking, and fetched another glass from a cupboard. He poured it half-full for her and set it within her reach. "Let us talk money. The icons are on the wall in there." He indicated an archway leading to a dimly lit room beyond.

She accepted the invitation and walked through. Then she stopped, her heart pounding. There were still half a dozen icons left, images of St. Peter and St. Paul, of Christ. One icon of the Virgin was in gold leaf and green-and-azure enamel, and blue so dark as to be almost black. She was somber-faced, with a tenderness that held the viewer in amazement.

Others had jewels encrusted on the clothes of the figures or were inlaid with ivory. There was such beauty in them that momentarily she forgot why she was here or why the hatred scorched inside her.

There was a sound behind her, and she froze. Very slowly she turned. He was there in the doorway, fat and soft, full of good living and the savor of profit.

"I would rather destroy them than be robbed," he said between his teeth. "I know you, Zoe Chrysaphes. You do nothing without a reason. Why are you really here?"

"The icons are beautiful," she said, as if that were a reply.

"Worth a great deal of money." His merchant's heart was in his face.

"Then let us haggle," she said, unable to keep the contempt out of her voice as she brushed past him, accidentally touching the protrusion of his belly as he stood in the middle of the archway. "Let us argue how many byzants the face of Mary is worth."

"It is an icon," he said with a sneer. "The creation of man's hands, made of wood and paint."

"And of gold leaf, Cosmas; never forget the gold leaf or the gems," she responded.

He frowned at her. "Do you want to buy one of them or not?" he snapped.

"How many pieces of silver, Cosmas, for the Mother of God? Forty seems an appropriate number." She took a small purse of silver solidi out of her robe and placed the coins on the table.

Temper flared up his face. "It is an icon, you stupid woman! An artist's work, no more. It is not Christ I sell!"

"Blasphemy!" she shrieked at him, her fury only in part pretense. She lunged for one of the glasses, her hand sweeping high, making clear her intention to smash it and use it as a weapon.

He darted forward first and seized it, dashing off the lovely golden rim of it and leaving jagged ends bristling from the stem. He held it out like a dagger, his eyes wide, flickering with fear, his lips parted.

She hesitated. She had borne pain before, and she hated it. Body's ecstasy and agony were equally deep for her, right on the cliff edge of the unbearable. But this was revenge—what she had lived for over the long, arid years. She pushed forward again, using the end of her cloak to dull some of the cutting edge when he struck her.

He jerked upward at her with the ragged stem, impelled by fear.

She felt the glass cut, and she twisted away and grasped it with the other hand, screaming out, intending the servants to hear her. Afterward, she would need their testimony. He must be the aggressor, only one glass broken, she merely defending herself.

He was caught by surprise. He had expected her to fall backward, bleeding. Instead she pressed on up to him, turning the stem against him with her weight and her other hand over his. The broken edge caught him, a thin, slashing cut.

Then she drew back, allowing surprise into her face as servants came rushing into the room.

"It's nothing!" Cosmas said angrily, shouting at them but still looking at her. His face was red, his eyes blazing.

Zoe turned toward the two men and the woman, forcing herself to sound apologetic. This was what they must remember. "I dropped a glass and it broke," she said with a charming smile, rueful, just a little ashamed. "We reached for it at the same moment and . . . and bumped into each other. I am afraid we both grasped for the glass, and have cut ourselves on its shards. Perhaps you would bring water, and bandages."

They hesitated.

"Do it!" Cosmas yelled at them, clutching the wound where the blood was already staining his robe.

"I have a tincture to ease pain," Zoe said helpfully, reaching inside her tunic for the fold of oiled silk with the antidote in it.

"No," he refused instantly. "I will use my own." There was a slight sneer in his voice, as if he had seen her trick and sidestepped it.

"As you please." She emptied the powder into her mouth and took a sip of the wine from his glass, still whole on the table.

"What's that?" he demanded.

"A powder against the pain," she replied, holding up her bleeding arm. "Do you want some?"

"No!" There was derision in his eyes.

The servants returned and carefully washed the wounds of both of them.

"I have a salve. . . ." Zoe reached with her other hand for the porcelain jar of ointment with its painted chrysanthemums. She put a little on her wound. It was mildly soothing, but she relaxed her body, as if it had brought great ease. She held out the open jar to Cosmas; her face was composed, as close to indifferent as she could make it.

"Master?" one of the servants offered.

"Oh, do it," Cosmos told him impatiently. Now that the servants were returned, being seen to be afraid demeaned him.

The servant obeyed, using it liberally.

Both wounds were bound, and the servants fetched more wine, more glasses, and a blue porcelain dish of sweet honey cakes.

Within fifteen minutes, Cosmos began to sweat profusely and have some difficulty in getting his breath. The glass slipped from his hand and spilled wine onto the floor, rolling away with a hollow sound. He put his hand to his throat as though to loosen a tight garment, but there was nothing there. He began to shake uncontrollably.

Zoe stood up. "Apoplexy," she said, looking down at him. Then she turned and walked unhurriedly to the door and called the servants. "He is taking a fit. You had better send for a physician," she told them.

When she had seen them leave, their faces white with panic, she went back to where Cosmas was collapsed, half-fallen to the floor. He should live for another hour, at least, but the poison was working rapidly.

Cosmos gasped and seemed to recover a little. Although she found it revolting to touch his fat body, she bent and helped him ease his position to one where he was better able to breathe. She might have to explain it afterward if she had not.

"You did this to me!" he gasped, curling his lips in a snarl. "You are going to steal my icons. Thief!"

She bent even closer to him, the fear draining out of her and vanishing. "Your father stole them from mine," she hissed in his ear. "I want them back in the churches so pilgrims will come here and make Byzantium rich and safe again. You, your family, and your blood are the thieves. And yes, I did this to you! Know it and taste it, Cosmas. Believe it!"

"Murderer!" he spat back at her, but it was no more than a sigh.

She went into the room with the icons. After lifting the one of the Virgin off the wall, she wrapped it in the folds of her cloak.

She smiled and walked on to the door where the servants were waiting to let her out.

Revenge was perfect, richer than laughter, sweeter than honey, more lasting than the scent of jasmine in the air.

Ten

෴

ON THE LAST DAY OF APRIL IN THE FOLLOWING YEAR, 1274, Enrico Palombara was standing in the central courtyard of his villa a mile beyond the Vatican walls. The sunlight had the limpid clarity one sees only in spring. The arid heat of summer was still far away. The walls were ocher-colored, and the new leaves of the vines made a lacework of green against them. The sound of falling water was a constant music.

He could hear the chattering of birds in the eaves as they worked. He loved their ceaseless industry, as if they could not imagine failure. They did not pray, as men did, so the answering silence would not frighten them.

He turned and went inside. It was time for him to walk to the Vatican and present himself to the pope. He had been sent for, and he must make certain he was there well in time. He did not know the reason Gregory X wished to speak to him, but he profoundly hoped that it would be the chance of office again—and not merely as secretary or assistant to some cardinal or other.

He increased his pace along the street, his long bishop's robes swirling. He nodded to people he knew, exchanging a greeting here and there, but his mind was on the meeting ahead. Perhaps he would be sent as a papal legate to one of the great courts of Europe, such as Aragon, Castile, Portugal, or, above all, the Holy Roman Empire. Any such position would offer vast opportunities out of which could be carved a superb career, possibly even elevation to the papal throne itself one day. Urban IV had been a papal legate before his election.

Five minutes later, Palombara walked across the square, up the wide, shallow steps of the Vatican Palace, and into the shade under the huge arches. He reported his presence and was conducted to the pope's private apartments, still fifteen minutes before the appointed time.

As he expected, he was kept waiting. He did not feel free to pace back and forth over the smooth marble floor as he would have liked.

Then suddenly he was summoned, and the next moment he was in the pope's chamber, a formal room still, but brighter and more comfortable. Sunlight streamed in through the window, making it seem airy. He had no time to look at the murals, but they were in softer colors, muted pinks and golds.

He knelt to kiss the ring of Tebaldo Visconti, now Gregory X. "Your Holiness," he murmured.

"How are you, Enrico?" Gregory asked. "Let us walk in the inner court-yard for a while. There is much to discuss."

Palombara rose to his feet, noticeably taller and leaner than the rather rotund figure of the pope. He looked down into the pope's face with its large, dark eyes and magnificent nose, long, heavy, and straight. "As Your Holiness pleases," he said obediently.

Gregory had been pope for two and a half years already. This was the first time he had spoken with Palombara alone. He led the way out through the wide doors into the inner courtyard, where they were ob-served but not overheard.

"We have much work to do, Enrico," Gregory said quietly. "We live in a dangerous age, but one of great opportunity. We have enemies all around us. We cannot afford dissension within." He glanced at Palombara sharply.

Palombara murmured a reply to show his attention.

"The Germans have chosen a new king, Rudolph of Hapsburg, whom I shall crown Holy Roman Emperor in due time. He has renounced all claims to our territories, and to Sicily," Gregory continued.

Now Palombara understood. Gregory was clearing all threats one by one toward some further great plan.

They crossed into a brief open space, and Palombara shaded his eyes against the sunlight so he could read Gregory's expression.

"The power of Islam is increasing," Gregory continued, his voice growing sharper. "They hold much of the Holy Land, all Arabia south and east, Egypt and North Africa, and up into the south of Spain. Their trade is expanding, their science and their arts thrive, their mathematics, their medicine, lead the way in thought. Their ships sail the eastern Mediterranean, and there is nothing to stop them."

Palombara felt a chill in the air in spite of the brilliance of the sun.

Gregory stopped. "If they move north toward Nicea, and they well could, then there is nothing to stop them taking Constantinople, and the whole of the old Byzantine Empire piece by piece after that. Then they will be at the very gates of Europe. Disunited, we will not stand."

"We must not permit it to happen," Palombara said simply, although the answer was anything but simple. The two-hundred-year-old schism between Rome and Byzantium was deep and had resisted all previous attempts at reconciliation. They were now not only doctrinally apart on many issues, most intractably the issue of the Holy Spirit proceeding from the Father and the Son or the Father only. They were also culturally different in a hundred patterns, beliefs, and observances. These distinctions had become a matter of human pride and identity.

"The emperor Michael Palaeologus has consented to send delegates to the council I have called in Lyons this June," Gregory continued. "I wish you to come also, Enrico. Listen carefully to everything that you hear. I need to know my friends, and my enemies."

Palombara felt a surge of excitement. Healing the schism would be the greatest single achievement for Christianity within the last two centuries. Rome would control all the land and command the obedience of every soul from the Atlantic to the Black Sea.

"How can I serve this cause?" Palombara surprised himself with how honestly he meant it.

"You have a fine mind, Enrico," Gregory said smoothly, the harsh lines of his face softening. "You have great skills, a nice balance between caution and strength. You understand necessity."

"Thank you, Holy Father."

"Do not thank me, it is not flattery," Gregory said a trifle tartly. "I am merely reminding you of the qualities you possess which will be needed. I wish you to go to Byzantium, as legate of the Holy See, with special duties to end this quarrel which divides the Christian Church."

A smile curved Gregory's wide lips. "I perceive you have grasped the vision. I knew you would. I know you better than you imagine, Enrico. I have great faith in your skill. As always, of course, you will be accompanied by another legate. I have chosen Bishop Vicenze. His abilities will be the right complement for yours." There was a flicker of amusement in his eyes, almost too slight to be seen, yet for an instant it was unmistakable.

"Yes, Holy Father." Palombara knew Niccolo Vicenze and disliked him profoundly. He was single-minded, unimaginative, and dedicated to the point of obsession. He was also completely without humor. Even his pleasure was ritualistic, as if he must follow a precise order or lose his control over it. "We will balance each other, Holy Father," he said aloud. It was his first lie of the encounter. If he were pope, he too would have sent Niccolo Vicenze as far away as possible.

Gregory permitted himself a wide, generous smile. "Oh, I know that, Enrico, I know that. I will look forward to seeing you in Lyons. I think perhaps you will enjoy it."

Palombara inclined his head. "Yes, Holy Father."

In June, Palombara was in the central French city of Lyons. It was hot, dry, and dusty underfoot. He had watched and listened all week as the pope had commanded, and he had heard a score of opinions, most with little presentiment of the danger from the east and south that Gregory perceived so sharply.

The promised delegates from the emperor of Byzantium were not here yet. No one knew why.

Now he walked up a flight of shallow steps to the thoroughfare above. Ahead of him was a cardinal in purple, his robes vivid in the June sun. Lyons was a beautiful city, dignified and imaginative, built upon two rivers. This month, the men and women in the streets and byways were used to the sight of princes of the Church and they took no more notice than a polite bow or curtsy, and moved on about the business of their lives.

Palombara turned, hearing a disturbance in the street ahead, movement, men stepping aside. There was a flowing of color, purples and reds and whites, and flashes of gold, like wind in a field of poppies. King James l of Aragon came out of one of the great palace entrances, surrounded by courtiers. Everyone made way for him.

He was totally unlike the bold and arrogant Charles of Anjou, king of the Two Sicilies, which in effect meant all Italy from Naples southward. Charles was as unsaintly as possible, yet it could be he who would lead the crusade that the pope so badly wanted. It was an interesting contrast in the holy and practical, one that Palombara was contemplating with some indecision.

That evening, he attended the Mass in the Cathedral of Saint Jean. Work on the building had begun nearly a century ago and was still far from finished. Even so it looked magnificent, severe and elegantly Romanesque.

The sweet perfume of incense filled his head, and it all swelled in a complex rhythm, carrying him along toward that exquisite moment when the sacrament of bread and wine would become the body and blood of Christ, and in some mystical way they would be united, cleansed of sin and renewed in spirit.

Was there such a thing as communication with God? Did these men around him experience it? Or was it just the music and the incense, the hunger to believe, creating the longed-for illusion?

Or was it the lies and the doubts Palombara allowed to poison his soul that rendered his ears deaf to the voices of angels? Memory returned with a jolt of sensual pleasure and emotional guilt. As a young priest, he had counseled a woman whose husband was distant and humorless, not unlike Vicenze. Palombara had been gentle with her and made her laugh. She had fallen in love with him. He saw it happening and enjoyed it. She was warm and lovely. He had lain with her. Even as he stood here in this cathedral, while some cardinal offered up the Mass, the incense in his nose and throat was gone for a moment and he could smell the fragrance of her hair, feel the warmth of her flesh, and see her smile.

She became with child, Palombara's child, and they had agreed to let her husband believe it was his. Was that wrong? Wise or not, it was a coward's lie.

Palombara had confessed to his bishop, chosen his penance, and received absolution. Better for the Church, and so the welfare of the people, if it was never known. But was penance enough? There was no peace inside him, no sense of having been forgiven.

Standing here with the music, the color and light, the rapt faces of men whose minds could be as far from God as his own, he had a sense of not having tasted the fullness of life, and the beginning of a terrible fear came to him that maybe there was no more than this. Maybe real hell was the fact that there was no heaven?

The embassy of Michael Palaeologus finally arrived in Lyons on June 24. They had been delayed by bad weather at sea and were too late for much of the discussion. They presented a letter from the emperor, signed by fifty archbishops and five hundred bishops or synods. Their good faith could not be denied. It seemed victory for Rome had come easily.

On June 29, Gregory celebrated the Mass in the Cathedral of St. Jean again. The Epistle, Gospel, and Creed were sung both in Latin and in Greek.

On July 6, the emperor's letter was read aloud and the Byzantine ambassadors promised fidelity to the Latin Church and abjured all the propositions it denied.

Gregory held the world in his hands. It was all accomplished; unworthy bishops had been deposed, certain mendicant orders suppressed, and the orders of St. Francis and St. Dominic warmly approved. The cardinals would no longer be able to dither and delay the election of a new pope. Rudolph of Hapsburg was recognized as the future monarch of the Holy Roman Empire.

In spite of the death of Thomas Aquinas on his way to Lyons, and of St. Bonaventure in Lyons itself, Gregory's cup of triumph ran over.

Palombara felt as if there was nothing left for him to do.

Still, Gregory wished both Palombara and Vicenze to return briefly to Rome and then prepare to sail to Constantinople. If they met with the same weather the Byzantine envoys had, this could take as long as six weeks. They would not arrive until October. But they had something priceless to deliver: an embassy of hope for the unity of the Christian world.

It was August and miserably hot in Rome when Palombara, returning from Lyons, walked across the familiar square toward the great arches in front of the Vatican Palace, the enormous building stretching left and right to either side, windows glinting in the sun. As always, people came and went; the wide steps were dotted with the colors of pale robes, purple hats and capes, touches of scarlet.

This was to be Palombara's last audience before departing again. He already knew their purpose was to make sure that the emperor Michael Palaeologus kept all the great promises he had written to the pope, that there was indeed substance behind the words. It might become necessary to warn Michael of the cost to his own people should they fail. The balance of power was delicate. Another crusade led by Charles of Anjou might not be far away. Men and ships would sail for Constantinople by the thousand, armed for war. The city's survival depended upon them coming in peace, as brothers in Christ, not as invading conquerors of an alien faith, as they had been at the beginning of the century, killing and burning, destroying the last bastion against Islam.

Palombara looked forward to the challenge of it, and the adventure. It would stretch his intelligence, test his judgment, and, if he was successful, considerably advance his career. And he also looked forward to being immersed in a new culture. The great buildings were still left, the Hagia Sophia, at least, and the libraries, the markets with all the spices, silks, and artifacts of the East. He would enjoy a different lifestyle, more of the Arab and the Jewish thought, and of course more of the Greek than was easy to find here in Rome.

But he would miss what he was leaving behind. Rome was the city of the Caesars, the heart of the greatest empire the world had ever seen. Even St. Paul had been proud to claim its citizenship.

But Palombara was also an intruder here, a Tuscan, not a Roman, and he missed the beauty of his own land. He loved the long view of rolling hills, so many of them forested. He missed the light on them at dawn, the color of sunset and shadow, the silence of the olive groves.

He smiled as he walked toward the wide steps. He was halfway up when he realized that one of the men standing waiting was Niccolo Vicenze, his pale, zealous eyes studying Palombara.

He looked at Vicenze's dour face with its pale brows and felt a chill of warning.

Vicenze smiled with his lips, his eyes unchanging as he moved into Palombara's path. "I have our instructions from the Holy Father," he said with no inflection in his voice except a slight lift. It almost hid his satisfaction. "But no doubt you would like the Holy Father's blessing upon you also, before we leave."

In one sentence he had made Palombara redundant: an escort, there simply because one was customary.

"How considerate of you," Palombara replied, as if Vicenze had been a servant who had obliged him beyond his duty.

Vicenze looked momentarily confused. Their natures were so utterly disparate that they could have used the same words to convey opposite meanings.

"It will be a great achievement to bring Byzantium back into the true Church," Vicenze added.

"Let us hope we can accomplish it," Palombara observed dryly, then saw the gleam in Vicenze's pale eyes and wished he had not been so candid. There were seldom meanings behind meaning with Vicenze, only the obsession for control and conformity. It was a strangely inhuman trait of character. Was it holiness, the dedication of a saintly man, or the madness of one who had not too much love of God so much as too little of mankind? Since he last saw him, he had forgotten how much he disliked Vicenze.

"We will be equal to the task. We will not cease until we are," Vicenze said slowly, giving each word weight. Perhaps he had a sense of humor after all.

Palombara stood in the sun and watched Vicenze walk down the steps and into the square with a slight swagger, papers in his hand. Then he turned and went up past the guard and into the coolness of the shadowed hall.

Eleven

By September, Anna had discovered more information about both Antoninus and Justinian himself, but what she had found all seemed superficial, and she could see in it no meaning or connection with the murder of Bessarion. There seemed nothing the three men all had in common except a dislike for the proposed union with Rome.

From all accounts, Bessarion had been not only serious-minded, but extremely sober of nature and spoke often and with great passion about the doctrine and history of the Orthodox Church. While respected, even admired, he allowed no intimacy. She felt an unwilling flicker of sympathy for Helena.

Like Bessarion, Justinian was a member of an imperial family, but much further from the center of it. Unlike Bessarion, he had no inherited wealth. His importing business was necessary for his survival, and he appeared to have succeeded with it, although with his exile all his property had been forfeited. The merchants of the city and ships' captains in the harbors all still knew his name. They were shocked that he had stooped to murder Bessarion. They had not only trusted Justinian, they had liked him.

It was hard for Anna to listen and control her sense of loss. The bitter loneliness inside her was so vast, it threatened to tear through her skin.

Antoninus had been a soldier. It was far more difficult for her to learn more of him. The few soldiers she treated spoke well of him, but he had been their senior in rank, and all they knew was repute and hearsay. He was strict and he was unquestionably brave. He enjoyed wine and a good joke—not the sort of man Bessarion would have liked.

But Justinian would. It made no sense, no pattern.

She sought the only person she trusted—Bishop Constantine. He had helped Justinian, even at risk to his own safety.

He welcomed her into a smaller room in his house than the warm, ocher one with the marvelous icons. This had cooler earth tones and looked down at a courtyard. The murals were pastoral, with muted colors. The floor was green-tiled, and there was a table set for dining and two chairs beside it. At his insistence, she sat in one of them to leave sufficient space for him to walk gently back and forth, deep in thought.

"You ask about Bessarion," he said, absentmindedly smoothing his fingers over the embroidered silk of his dalmatica. "He was a good man, but perhaps lacking the fire to stir men's souls. He weighed, he measured, he judged. How can a man be at once so passionate of mind and so indecisive?"

"Was he a coward?" she asked quietly.

A look of sadness came across Constantine's face. It was several moments before he spoke again. "I presumed he was simply cautious." He crossed himself. "God forgive them all. They wished for so much, and all to save the true Church from the dominion of Rome, and the pollution of the faith that will bring."

She echoed his sign of the cross. She wanted more than anything else to lay the burden of her own guilt at God's feet and seek His absolution. She remembered her dead husband, Eustathius, with a coldness that still struck: the quarrel, the isolation, the blood, and then the never-ending grief. She would never carry another child. She was fortunate to have healed without crippling. She ached to tell Constantine, to spread all her guilt before him and be cleansed, whatever penance was necessary. But the confession of her imposture would rob her of any chance to help Justinian. There was no punishment fixed for such an offense, it would fall under other laws, but it would be harsh. No one liked to be made a fool of.

Her thoughts were interrupted by a knock on the door. A young priest came in, white-faced and struggling to control his emotion.

"What is it?" Constantine said. "Are you ill? Anastasius is a physician." He gestured briefly to include Anna.

The priest waved a thin hand. "I am well enough. No physician can heal what ails us all. The envoys are back from Lyons. It was a complete capitulation! They gave up everything! Appeals to the pope, money, the *filioque* clause." Tears glistened in his eyes.

Constantine stared at the priest, his face white with horror. Then slowly the blood suffused his skin. "Cowards!" he snarled between his teeth. "What did they bring back with them—thirty pieces of silver?"

"Safety from the crusading armies when they pass this way on their path to Jerusalem," the priest said wretchedly, his voice quavering.

Anna knew this was a higher reward than perhaps this young priest understood. With a chill passing through her, she remembered Zoe Chrysaphes and the terror that so clearly still haunted her when she felt the flame sear her skin, seventy years afterward.

Constantine was watching her. "They have no faith!" he snapped, his lips drawn back in contempt. "Do you know what happened when we were besieged by barbarians, but kept our faith with the Holy Virgin, and carried her image in our hearts and before our eyes? Do you?"

"Yes." Anna's father had told her the story many times, his eyes wistful, half smiling.

Constantine was waiting, standing with his arms spread out, his pale robes splendid in the light. He looked enormous, intimidating.

"The barbarian armies stood before the city," Anna recounted obediently. "We were vastly outnumbered. Their leader rode forward on his horse, a huge, heavy man, savage as an animal. The emperor went out to meet him, carrying the icon of the Virgin Mary before him. The barbarian leader was struck dead on the spot, and his army fled. Not one of our men was injured and not a stone of the city broken." Such perfect faith still gave her a strange bubble of excitement inside, as if a warmth had broken open within her. She did not know if the year or the details were exact, but she believed the spirit of it.

"You knew it," Constantine said triumphantly. "And also when we were besieged by the Avars in 626, we carried the icon of the Blessed Virgin along the halls, and the siege was raised." He turned to the priest, his face glowing. "Then why is it that the envoys of our emperor, who styles himself 'Equal of the Apostles,' do not? How can he even bargain with the devil, let alone yield to him? It's not the barbarians who will defeat us this time, it's our own doubt."

His hands clenched. "We are not conquered by the hordes of Charles of Anjou, or even the liars and hucksters of Rome, but betrayed by our own princes who have lost their faith in Christ and the Holy Virgin." He swung around to Anna. "You understand, don't you?"

She saw a desperate loneliness in his eyes. "Michael does not speak for the people," he said in little more than a whisper. "If we believe enough, we'll be strong; we may persuade them to trust in God."

Emotion thickened his voice. "Help me, Anastasius. Be strong. Help me keep the faith we have nurtured and guarded for a thousand years."

The passions churned inside her, conflicting faith and guilt, love of the beautiful and loathing of the darkness within herself, the memories of hate.

Constantine was quick, sensitive, as if he could taste Anna's turmoil, even without understanding it. "Be strong," he urged, his voice now gentle. "You have a great work in your hands. God will help you, if only you believe."

She was startled. "How? I have no calling."

"Of course you have," he answered. "You are a healer. You are the left hand of the priest, the mender of the body, the comforter of pain, the silencer of fears. Speak truth to those to whom you minister. The word of God can heal all ills, protect from the darkness without—but even more, from that within."

"I will," she whispered. "We can turn the tide. We will look to God, not to Rome."

Constantine smiled. He lifted his large white hand in the sign of the cross.

Behind him, the thin young priest echoed it.

"We'd know what to do about it if Justinian were here," Simonis said grimly as Anna later stood in the warm, herb-scented kitchen, telling her the news. "It's a disgrace, a blasphemy." Simonis took a deep breath and turned away from the table to face Anna. "What else have you learned about this Bessarion? We've been here almost a year and a half, and his real murderer is still free. Someone must know!" As soon as the words were out of her mouth, her face pinched with guilt. She resumed her work slicing onions and mixing them with aromatic leaves.

"If I'm clumsy, I could make it worse," Anna tried to explain. "As you said, whoever really killed Bessarion is still here."

Simonis froze, her body stiffening. "Are you in danger?"

"I don't think so," Anna replied. "But you are right. I should look more closely at money. Bessarion was very wealthy, but I can't find even a whisper that he came by it at anyone else's cost. He doesn't seem to have cared very much. He was all about faith."

"And power," Simonis added. "Perhaps you should look at that?"

"I will, although I can't see that it has anything to do with Justinian or Antoninus."

Twelve

PALOMBARA AND VICENZE WERE HELD UP BY BAD WEATHER as the year waned and did not reach Constantinople until November. But their first formal duty would be to witness the signing by the emperor and the bishops of the Orthodox Church of the agreement reached at the Council of Lyons. This was to take place on January 16 of the following year, 1275. After that, they would continue as papal legates to Byzantium. It was the job of each to report to His Holiness upon the other, which made the whole exercise a juggling act of lies, evasions, and power.

As envoys of the pope, it was expected that they would live well. Neither humility nor abstinence was expected of them, and their choice of house immediately made even more obvious the differences in their characters.

"This is magnificent," Vicenze said approvingly of a great house not far from the Blachernae Palace, which would be made available to them at a reasonable price. "No one calling here will mistake our mission or whom we represent." He stood in the middle of the tessellated floor and surveyed the exquisitely painted walls, the arched ceiling with its perfect proportions, and the ornate pillars.

Palombara looked at it with distaste. "It's expensive," he agreed. "But it's vulgar. I think it's new."

"Would you prefer some nice Aretino castle, perhaps? Familiar and comfortable?" Vicenze said sarcastically. "All little stones and sharp angles?"

"I would like something a little less brash," Palombara replied, trying to keep the coldness out of his voice. Vicenze was from Florence, which had been engaged in a bitter artistic and political rivalry with Arezzo for years. He knew that was what lay behind the remark.

Vicenze regarded him sourly. "This will impress people. And it is convenient. We can walk to most of the places we shall need to go. It is near the palace the emperor lives in now."

Palombara turned around slowly, his eyes stopping at the heavily crowned pillars. "They will think we are barbarians. It's money without taste."

Vicenze's long, bony face was bleak with incomprehension and a growing impatience. He considered preoccupation with the arts to be effete, a digression from the work of God. "It doesn't matter whether they like us or not, only whether they believe what we say."

Palombara settled to the conflict with a sense of satisfaction. The man was obedient without imagination, and dogged as an animal following a scent. In fact, there was something faintly canine in the way he sniffed. Vicenze sought nothing but a sterile, obedient power for himself.

"It is ugly," Palombara insisted with harshness in his voice. "The other house, to the north, has grace of proportion, and quite sufficient room for us. And we can see the Golden Horn from the windows."

"To what purpose?" Vicenze asked, his face completely innocent.

"We are here to learn, not to teach," Palombara said, as if explaining to someone slow of wit. "We wish people to feel comfortable when we speak with them, and let down their guard. We need to know them."

"Know your enemy," Vicenze said with a slight smile, as if the answer had satisfied him. He conceded to Palombara's choice of a more modest house.

"Our brothers in Christ!" Palombara retorted. "Temporarily alienated," he added dryly, the humor there only to please himself.

Palombara set out to explore the city, which in spite of the winter weather, brisk winds off the water, and occasional rain, he found fascinating. It was not particularly cold, and he was perfectly comfortable to walk. A Roman bishop's dress was not remarkable here in streets where so many nations and faiths passed one another every day. After a long day of studious walking, he was exhausted and his feet were blistered, but he understood the broad layout of the city.

The following day he was stiff, to Vicenze's sarcastic pleasure. But the day after, ignoring blisters, he wandered in his own neighborhood. The weather was fine, with bright sun and little wind. The streets were narrow, old, and bustling, not unlike the Roman ones he was accustomed to.

He bought lunch from a peddler and ate it while watching two old men playing chess. The board was set out on a table barely large enough to hold it. The carved wooden pieces were worn from use and darkened with the natural oils of the hands that had held them.

One old man had a lean face, a white beard, and black eyes almost hidden in the wrinkles of his skin. The other was bearded also, but nearly bald. They played with total dedication, oblivious to the world around them. Other people passed by, children shouted across the street, donkey carts rumbled over the stones. A peddler asked them if they wished for anything and was not heard.

Palombara watched their faces and saw the intense pleasure in them, an almost fierce joy at the intricacy of the mental battle. He waited for a full hour until it was finished. The thin man won and ordered the best wine in the house and fresh bread, goat cheese, and dried fruit so they could both celebrate, which they did with as great a delight as they had in playing.

He returned earlier the next day and watched the game from the beginning. This time the other man won, but there was just the same celebration at the end.

Suddenly he was overwhelmed by the arrogance of coming here to tell old men like these what they should believe. He stood up and walked away into the wind and sun, too disturbed in mind to think clearly; yet the ideas raced in his head.

One day in early January, having forced himself to work with Vicenze on the coming signing of the agreement, Palombara escaped to a public restaurant.

He sat deliberately close to another table where two middle-aged men were involved in a fierce debate on the Byzantines' favorite subject—religion. One of the men observed Palombara listening and immediately drew him in, asking his opinion.

"Yes," the other added eagerly. "What do you think?"

Palombara considered for several seconds before plunging in with a quote from Saint Thomas Aquinas, the brilliant theologian who had died on his way to the Council of Lyons.

"Ah!" the first man said quickly. "Doctor Angelicus! Very good. Do you agree that his choosing to stop his own greatest work, the *Summa Theologica*, was right?"

Palombara was taken aback. He hesitated.

"Good!" the man said with a brilliant smile. "You don't know. That is the beginning of wisdom. Didn't he say that all he had written was as straw compared with what he had seen in a vision?"

"Albertus Magnus, who knew him well, said that his works would fill the world," his friend argued. He swung around to Palombara. "He was Italian, may God rest his soul. Did you know him?"

Palombara remembered meeting him once: a large man, corpulent, dark-skinned, and immensely courteous. One could not help but like him. "Yes," he answered, and described the occasion and what had been said.

The second man seized on it as if he had found a treasure, and both attacked the ideas with intense enjoyment. Then they immediately moved on to discuss Francis of Assisi and his refusal to be ordained. Was that good or bad, arrogance or humility?

Palombara was delighted. The free-flowing urgency of it was like the wind off an ocean, erratic, undisciplined, dangerous, but sweeping in from an endless horizon. It was not until he was joined unexpectedly by Vicenze that suddenly he realized how far he had strayed from the accepted doctrine.

Having overheard some of the conversation, Vicenze interrupted in a tone barely civil, saying that he had urgent news and Palombara was to come immediately. Since it was merely an acquaintance fallen into by chance, Palombara had no excuse to finish the discussion. He pardoned himself reluctantly and walked out into the street with Vicenze, angry and frustrated, startled by his sense of loss.

"What is this news?" he asked coldly. He resented not only the interruption, but the high-handed manner in which Vicenze had made it, and now his tight-lipped expression of disapproval.

"We have been summoned to present ourselves to the emperor," Vicenze replied. "I have been arranging this, while you have been philosophizing with atheists. Try to remember: You serve the pope!"

"I would like to think I serve God," Palombara said quietly.

"I would like to think you do, too," Vicenze retaliated. "But I doubt it."

Palombara changed the subject. "Why does the emperor wish to see us?"

"If I knew what he wanted, I would have told you," Vicenze snapped.

Palombara didn't think so, but it was not worth an argument.

Their audience with Emperor Michael Palaeologus was held in the Blachernae Palace. To Palombara, who had learned a little of its history, the glories of the past seemed to haunt the air like bright ghosts lost in the grayer present.

All the walls he passed had once been without blemish, inlaid with porphyry and alabaster, hung with icons. Every niche had had its statue or its bronze. Some of the greatest works of art in the world had stood here, marbles of Phidias and Praxiteles from the classical age before Christ.

He had seen the smoke stains of the crusader invasion in the city and was ashamed of it. Here he saw the scars of poverty also: the tapestries unmended, the mosaics with broken pieces, columns and pilasters chipped. For all their pretense in serving God, what barbarians of the heart the crusaders were. There were many kinds of unbelief.

They were conducted into the presence of the emperor in a magnificent hall with huge windows overlooking the Golden Horn. The view of the city far below was a vast panorama of roofs and towers, spires, masts of ships in the harbor, and clustered houses on the far shore.

The hall itself was marble-floored with porphyry columns that held up a ceiling ornately decorated with mosaic arches that flickered here and there with gold.

But all that was only a fleeting impression. As Palombara walked toward the emperor, he was startled by the inner vitality of the man. He was dark, with thick hair and a full beard. His clothes were silk, heavily embroidered and jeweled, as one would expect. He wore not only the customary tunic and dalmatica, but also a sort of collar that ended with something like a priest's breastplate at the front. This was crusted with gems and ringed around the edges with pearls and gold thread. He wore it as if he were accustomed to it and it were of no importance. Palombara remembered with a jolt that Michael was considered to be Equal of the Apostles. He was a brilliant soldier who had led his people through battle and exile and back to their own city. He had regained his empire by his own hand. They would be foolish to underestimate him.

The emperor gave Palombara and Vicenze all the appropriate formal greetings and invited them to be seated. The protocol for the signing of the agreement had already been arranged, there did not seem to be anything further to discuss, but if there were, it would be done with less senior officials.

"The princes and prelates of the Orthodox Church are aware of the choices facing us, and the necessities driving us," Michael said quietly, glancing from one to the other. "However, the cost to us is high, and not all are willing to pay."

"We are here to be of any assistance we may, Majesty." Vicenze felt compelled to fill the silence.

"I know." A faint smile played on Michael's lips. "And you, Bishop Palombara?" he asked softly. "Do you also offer your assistance to our cause? Or does Bishop Vicenze speak for both of you?"

Palombara felt the blood burn up his face. He must not give Michael leverage so quickly.

The emperor's black eyes reflected his laughter. He nodded. "Good. Then we wish for the same result, but for different reasons, and perhaps in different ways—I for the safety of my people, and perhaps for the survival of my city; you for your ambition. You do not want to return to Rome empty-handed. You will get no cardinal's hat. Not for failure."

Palombara winced. Michael was rather too much of a realist, but life had given him little chance to be anything else. The emperor chose union under Rome as the only chance for survival, not for any meeting of beliefs. He was letting them know that, in case they cherished any notions that they could reach him with a religious conversion. He was Orthodox to the bone, but he meant to survive.

"I understand, Majesty," Palombara answered. "We are faced with hard choices. We pick the best of them."

Vicenze bowed so slightly, it was barely discernible. "We will do what is right, Majesty. We understand that haste would be unfortunate."

Michael looked at him dubiously. "Very unfortunate," he agreed.

Vicenze drew in his breath sharply.

Palombara froze, dreading the clumsiness of what Vicenze might say and yet a tiny part of him wishing for his downfall.

Michael waited.

"There would be little to recommend failure, in any way," Palombara said quietly. As a matter of pride, he wanted Michael to see him quite separately from Vicenze.

"Indeed." Michael nodded. Then he looked beyond them and signaled for someone to come forward. He was obeyed by a person of curious stature, walking with an oddly graceful gate. His face was large and beardless, and when he spoke, with the emperor's permission, his voice was as soft as a woman's and yet not feminine.

Michael introduced him as Bishop Constantine.

They acknowledged each other formally and with some discomfort.

Constantine turned to Michael. "Majesty," he said emphatically, "the patriarch, Cyril Choniates, should also be consulted. His approval would be of great service toward persuading the people to accept unity with Rome. Perhaps you have not been advised of the depth of feeling there is?" He phrased it as a question, but the emotion in his voice made it into a warning.

Palombara found him an uncomfortable presence because of his indeterminate masculinity, but the strange person also seemed to be laboring to hide some passion he was afraid to show. Yet it was so powerful that it broke through in the ridiculous gestures of his pale, heavy hands and now and then in a loss of control in his voice.

Michael's face darkened. "Cyril Choniates is no longer in office."

Constantine was not deflected. "The monks are likely to be the most difficult section of the Church to convince that we should forfeit our ancient ways and submit to Rome, Majesty," he stated. "Cyril could help with that."

Michael stared at him, the expression in his face changing from certainty to doubt. "You puzzle me, Constantine," he said at last. "First you are against union, now you are addressing me how best to smooth the path for it. You seem to change like water in the wind."

Suddenly Palombara had an acutely awkward awareness, as if someone had taken a blindfold from his eyes. How could he have been so slow to see? Bishop Constantine was one of the eunuchs of the court of Byzantium. Palombara found himself looking away and was aware of a heat in his cheeks and a disturbing consciousness of his own wholeness. He had associated passion and strength with masculinity, and effeminacy with change, weakness, lack of decision or courage. It seemed Michael felt the same.

"The sea is made of water, Majesty," Constantine said softly, staring at Michael without lowering his glance. "Christ walked upon the lake of Gennesareth, but we would be wise to treat it with greater caution and respect. Or else lacking faith, as Peter did, we may drown without a divine hand reaching to save us."

The silence prickled in the great room.

Michael drew in his breath slowly, then let it out again. He studied the bishop's face for a long time. Constantine did not waver.

Vicenze drew in his breath to speak, and Palombara poked him sharply, with his elbow. He heard Vicenze gasp.

"I have no confidence that Cyril Choniates will see the necessity of union," Michael said at last. "He is an idealist, and I am guardian of the practical."

"Practicality is the art of what will work, Majesty," Constantine replied. "I know you are too good a son of the Church to suggest that faith in God does not work."

Palombara barely hid a smile, but no one was looking at him.

"If I decide to seek Cyril's help," Michael said carefully, his eyes unwavering, "I know you will be the man to send to him, Constantine. Until then I look to you to persuade your flock to keep faith both in God and in your emperor."

Constantine bowed, but there was little obeisance in it.

A few moments later, Palombara and Vicenze were permitted to leave.

"That eunuch could prove a nuisance," Vicenze said in Italian as the Varangian Guard accompanied them on their way out into the air where there was a breathtaking view of the city beneath them. He gave a little shiver, and his lip curled with distaste. "If we cannot convert people like that"—he carefully avoided using the term *man*—"then we will have to think of a way of subverting their power."

"At the height of their power eunuchs ran the whole court and much of the government," Palombara informed Vicenze with perverse satisfaction. "They were bishops, generals in the army, ministers of government and law, mathematicians, philosophers, and physicians."

"Well, Rome will put an end to that!" Vicenze said with savage satisfaction. "We are not come a day too late." And he marched forward, leaving Palombara to catch up with him.

Thirteen

∽

PALOMBARA BUSIED HIMSELF LEARNING MORE ABOUT HOW the emperor might strengthen his position in the eyes of his people. If they truly regarded him as "Equal of the Apostles," then they might believe he guided them righteously in their religious choice, as he had in their military and governmental ones.

He went to the great cathedral of the Hagia Sophia, but it was not to worship, and certainly not to partake in the Orthodox Mass. He wished to experience the differences between the Greek and the Roman.

The service was more emotionally moving than he had expected. There was a passionate solemnity to it in this ancient cathedral with its mosaics, its icons, and its pillars, the gold-surfaced niches surrounding the marvelous, somber-eyed figures of saints, the Madonna, and Christ Himself. In the dim light they glowed with an almost animate presence, and in spite of himself he found his intellectual appreciation overtaken by awe for the genius and the beauty of it. The vast dome seemed almost to float above its high circle of windows, as if there were no support for it of brick or stone. He had heard the legend that the building of it was beyond human ability, and that the dome itself had been miraculously suspended from heaven by a golden chain, held by angels until the pillars could be secured. The tale had amused him at the time, but here in this glory it did not seem impossible.

He was on the outer steps when he saw, a little apart from the crowd, a woman of more than average height. She had an extraordinary face. She was at least sixty, possibly more, but she stood with a perfect, even arrogant posture. She had high cheekbones, a mouth too wide, too sensuous, and heavy-lidded, golden eyes. She was looking at him, singling him out. He felt both flattered and uncomfortable as she approached him.

"You are the papal legate from Rome." Her voice was strong, and seen closer up her face was full of a vitality that demanded his attention and his interest.

"I am," he agreed. "Enrico Palombara."

She gave a slight shrug; it was almost a voluptuous gesture. "Zoe Chrysaphes," she answered. "Have you come to see the home of the Holy Wisdom, before you attempt to destroy it? Does its beauty touch your soul, or only your eyes?"

Nothing in her invited pity. She was an aspect of Byzantium he had not seen before—perhaps the ancient spirit that had survived the barbarians when Rome had fallen: passionate, dangerous, and intensely Greek. The energy in her fascinated him, as a flame draws a night insect.

"What is perceived only by the eyes does not necessarily have meaning," he replied.

She smiled, instantly aware of the subtle flattery implied and amused by it. This could be the beginning of a long duel, if she really cared about the Orthodox faith and keeping it from Roman contamination.

She arched her fine brows. "How could I know? We have nothing meaningless." The laughter in her was almost expressed.

He waited.

"Have you no fear that perhaps you are wrong to demand our submission?" she asked at length. "Does it not waken you in the night, when you are alone, and the darkness around you is full of thoughts, good and evil? Then do you not wonder if it is the devil who speaks to you and not God?"

He was startled. It was not what he had expected her to say.

She was staring at him, searching his eyes. Then she laughed, a full-throated, rich sound of pulsing life. "Ah, I see! You don't hear anyone's voice at all—do you—only silence. Eternal silence. That is Rome's secret—there is no one there except yourselves!"

He looked at the intelligence and the victory in her face. She had seen the emptiness inside him.

He stood still facing her while the departing people swirled around them. He could sense her pain, like the touch of fire. He could even empathize with her, but in the end the union was going to happen, with or without Zoe Chrysaphes's agreement. All this unique glory of the eye, the ear, and, above all, the mind could be destroyed by the ignorant, if the crusader armies stormed through here yet again.

Knowing her might give him an advantage it would be wise not to let Vicenze know about.

In the weeks that followed, Palombara pursued his interest in Zoe Chrysaphes discreetly, listening for her name rather than raising it himself, collecting many facts about her once powerful family. Her only child, Helena, who had married into the ancient imperial house of Comnenos, had been recently widowed by murder.

It was rumored that Zoe had been mistress to many men, possibly Michael Palaeologus himself. Palombara was inclined to believe it. Even now there was a sensuality about her, a savagery and a life force that made other women seem tame.

For a moment, he regretted that he was a papal legate, abroad where he dared not slip the traces. Vicenze was always watching; and anyway, Zoe would not entertain lovers simply for the pleasure of it. Physical passion with her would have been a good battle, one worth the fighting, win or lose. It would always have been of the mind as well, even if rarely of the heart.

It was up to him to bring about the next encounter, which he did by hunting along Mese Street for an unusual gift for her. He wanted something individual that would earn her curiosity. Then he could visit her, ostensibly to seek her advice. He knew enough about her now to make that credible.

He was shown into her magnificent room, which overlooked the city and the Bosphorus beyond. It was like stepping back into the old city, before the sack: its glory fading only a little, its pride still secure. There were tapestries on the walls, rich and dark. Their colors were subdued by the centuries but not worn dim, only muted in places where the light had softened their tones. The floor was marble, smoothed by the passage of generations of feet. The ceiling in places was inlaid with gold. On one wall hung a gold cross nearly two feet long, the figure on it so exquisitely crafted that it seemed about to twist in a last agony.

Zoe wore a tunic of amber color under a darker, more vibrant dalmatica, and it was fastened with a gold pin set with garnets. She looked amused, as if she had known he would come, but perhaps not so soon.

There was another person present, about Zoe's height but dressed in a plain tunic and dark blue dalmatica. He stood nearer the corner of the room, occupied with packing away powders into little boxes. Palombara could smell the rich aroma of them: some sort of crushed herbs.

Zoe ignored the other person, so Palombara did also.

"I found a small gift I hope will interest you," he said, holding out what he had brought, wrapped in red silk. It fitted neatly into the palm of his lean, outstretched hand.

She looked at it, her golden eyes curious, as yet unimpressed. "Why?" she asked.

"Because from you I can learn more of the soul of Byzantium than from anyone else," he replied with total honesty. "And I wish to have that knowledge, rather than my fellow legate, Vicenze." He allowed himself to smile.

A flash of amusement lighting her expression, she then opened the silk and took out a piece of amber the size of a small bird's egg. Inside it a spider was caught perfectly, immortalized in the moment before victory, the fly a hairbreadth beyond its reach. She did not hide her fascination with it, or her pleasure. "Anastasius!" she said, turning to the person with the herbs. "Come see what the papal legate from Rome has brought me!"

Palombara saw that it was another eunuch, smaller in stature and younger than Bishop Constantine, but with the same smooth, hairless face and—when he spoke—the same unbroken voice.

"Disturbing," he remarked, looking at it closely. "Very clever."

"You think so?" Zoe asked him.

Anastasius smiled. "A graphic picture of the instant, and of eternity," he replied. "You think the prize is in your grasp, and it eludes you forever. That moment is frozen, and a thousand years later you are still poised, and empty-handed." He looked across at Palombara, who was struck by the intelligence and the courage in his eyes. They were cool and gray, utterly unlike Zoe's, although the rest of his coloring was almost the same. And he too had high cheekbones and a sensuous mouth. It disturbed Palombara that Anastasius had seen so much in the amber, more than he had himself.

Zoe was watching. "Is that what you mean to say to me, Enrico Palombara?" she asked. She refused to call him "Your Grace," because he was a bishop of Rome, not of Byzantium.

"I wished it to give you pleasure, and interest," he answered, speaking to her, not the eunuch. "It will say whatever you read into it."

"Speaking of mortality," Zoe went on, "if you should fall ill while you are in Constantinople, I can recommend Anastasius. He is an excellent physician. And he will cure your illness without preaching to you of your sins. A trifle Jewish, but very effective. I know my sins already, and find it tedious being told of them again, don't you? Especially when I am not feeling well."

"That depends upon whether they are being envied or despised," Palombara said lightly.

He saw a flicker of laughter in the eunuch's face, but it was gone again almost before he was certain of it.

Zoe saw it also. "Explain yourself," she ordered Anastasius.

Anastasius shrugged. It was a gesture oddly feminine, yet he seemed not to have the volatile emotionalism of Constantine. "I think that contempt is the cloak that envy wears," he replied to Zoe, smiling as he said it.

"What should we feel for sin?" Palombara asked quickly, before Zoe could speak. "Anger?"

Anastasius looked at him steadily, with an oddly unnerving stare. "Not unless one is afraid of it," he said. "Do you suppose God is afraid of sin?"

Palombara's reply was instant. "That would be ridiculous. But we are not God. At least we in Rome do not think we are," he added.

Anastasius's smile broadened. "We in Byzantium do not think you are either," he agreed.

Palombara laughed in spite of himself, but it was out of embarrassment as well as humor. He did not know what to make of Anastasius. One moment he seemed lucid, intellectual like a man, and the next joltingly feminine. Palombara found himself wrong-footed too often. He thought of one of the silks he had seen in the markets: Hold it up one way and the light picked up the blue; then turn it, and it was green. The character of eunuchs was like the sheen on the silk—fluid, unpredictable. A third gender, male and female, yet neither.

Zoe turned the amber over in her hand. "This is worthy of a favor," she said to Palombara, her eyes bright. "What is it you want?" She flashed a glance at the eunuch. Palombara saw irritation in it and perhaps a momentary contempt. But then a woman of passion and sensuality like Zoe would never forget that Anastasius was not a whole man. What did it feel like to be denied that most basic of appetites? To be hungry is to be alive. Palombara wondered if there was anything Anastasius wanted with that intensity burning in his eyes.

He told her what he had come for. "Knowledge, of course."

Zoe blinked. "Knowledge of whom?"

He glanced at Anastasius.

Zoe smiled, looking Anastasius up and down, as if measuring whether he was worthy of dismissing or, like a servant, too unimportant to matter.

Anastasius took the decision himself. "The herbs are on the table," he told Zoe. "If they please you, I will bring more. If not, then I shall suggest something else." He turned to Palombara. "Your Grace. I hope your stay in Constantinople will be interesting." He bowed to Zoe and walked away, picking up his bag of herbs as he left. He moved stiffly, as if he had to be careful to keep his balance or maybe his dignity. Palombara wondered if perhaps he had pain of some acutely private nature, a wound never entirely healed. How could a man endure such a thing—such an indignity, a mutilation—without a bitterness of soul? He was sufficiently effeminate; perhaps they had removed not only his testicles, but everything? What an incomprehensible mixture of beauty, wisdom, and barbarity eunuchs were. Rome should fear them more than it did.

He turned back to Zoe, prepared to listen to all she would say of her city and regard it all with interest and skepticism.

Fourteen

ONSTANTINE STOOD IN HIS FAVORITE ROOM OF THE
house, his hand caressing the smooth marble of the statue. Its head
was buried in thought, its naked limbs perfect. He passed his hand over it
again, moving his fingers as if he could knead it and feel muscle and nerve
in the stone shoulders.

His own body was so tightly knotted that he ached.

Michael had reenacted the signing, affirming it for all Constantinople
to see, and to satisfy Rome, and Constantine had been helpless to prevent
it. It would be a mark of subservience, a signal to the world, and above all
to God, that the people of Byzantium had forsaken their faith. Those who
had trusted the leadership of the Church would be destroyed by the very
men sworn to save their souls. How infinitely shortsighted! Selling today
to purchase tomorrow's safety. What about their salvation in eternity? Was
that not more important than any earthly thing?

But he had known what to do, and he had done it.

As he thought of it the sweat broke out on his body, even here in this
cool room. The Byzantime people had a right to fight for life!

And that he had done. He had lit the fire in their hearts and it had exploded into a riot in the streets, scores and then hundreds pouring into the
squares and marketplaces, crying out against the union with Rome and
everything alien and forced.

Of course Constantine had contrived to look as if he were doing all in
his power to stop them, to sympathize and yet try to stem the violence, to

plead for order and respect while leading them on. What difference was there between a gesture of blessing and one of encouragement? It lay in the angle of the hand, the inflection of a voice carefully raised not quite loudly enough to be heard above the din.

It had been marvelous, superb. They had come in their thousands, filling the streets until they choked the byways. He could still hear their voices as he stood here in his quiet room. There the blood had pounded in his veins, his heart racing, sweat of heat and danger running off his skin as the noise carried him along.

"Constantine! Constantine! In the name of God and the Holy Virgin, Constantine for the faith!"

He had smiled at them, stepping back a pace or two as if to decline in modesty, but they had shouted the louder.

"Constantine! Lead us to victory, for the Holy Virgin's sake!"

He had lifted his hands in blessing, and gradually they had calmed, the shouting ceased. They stood in the square and in the streets beyond, silent, waiting for him to tell them what to do.

"Have faith! God's power is greater than that of any man!" he had told them. "We know what is truth and what is false, what is of Christ and what of the devil. Go home. Fast and pray. Be loyal to the Church, and God will be loyal to you."

God would save them from Rome only if their faith were perfect, and it was Constantine's mission to do everything heavenly possible to see that it was.

A few days later, Michael retaliated. The vacant throne of the patriarch of Byzantium was given not to the eunuch Constantine, but to a whole man, John Beccus.

The servant who brought Constantine the news was white-faced, as if he carried word of death. He stood in front of Constantine, eyes lowered, his breath loud in the room.

Constantine wanted to scream at the man, but that would expose his pain like his own nakedness, incomplete, marred by circumstance outside his mastery. He had been doubly castrated, robbed of the office that was rightfully his by virtue, faith, and the will to fight. John Beccus was for the union with Rome, a coward and a traitor to his Church.

"Go!" Constantine's voice was rasping from a throat raw with pain.

The servant stared at him and then fled.

When his footsteps had ceased to sound on the stones, Constantine let out a howl of fury and humiliation. Hatred was like fire in his soul. He could have torn John Beccus apart if he had laid hands on him at this moment. A whole man, an insult to Constantine's existence. As if organs made the soul! A man was his passions of the heart, his dreams, the things he longed for, the fears he had overcome, the wholeness of his sacrifice, not of his body.

Was a man better because he could put his seed into a woman? Beasts of the field could do that. Was a man holier because he had that power and abstained from using it?

Constantine could take a knife and slice Beccus's testicles: see the blood flow, as it had from his own body as a boy; see the agony, the terror of bleeding to death! Then watch him clutch at what was left of his manhood with a horror at his loss that would never leave him as long as he existed. They would be equal then. See who could lead the Church and save it from Rome!

But it was only a dream, like other images in the night. He could not do it. His power was in the love and the belief of the people. They must never see his hatred. It was weakness. It was sin.

Could the Holy Virgin read his heart? His face burned scarlet with shame. Slowly he knelt, tears wet on his face.

Beccus was wrong! He was a liar, a time server, a seeker after favor and office and his own power. How could a good man pretend to approve that?

Constantine asked himself whether he was a good man. He could make himself be, and he must.

He rose to his feet to begin: now, today. There was no time to waste. He would show John Beccus, he would show them all. The people loved him, his faith, his mercy, his humility and courage, his will to fight.

In the uncounted days that followed, he worked until exhaustion overcame him, taking no thought or care for his own needs. He answered every call he could, walking miles from one house to another to hear confessions of the dying and give them absolution. Families wept with gratitude for such peace of heart. He left with aching legs and blistered feet, but soaring spirits in the certainty that he was loved, and for his sake an ever increasing number of people would remain loyal to the true Church.

He celebrated the Mass so often, he felt sometimes as if he were doing it in his sleep, the words reciting themselves. But the eager faces were all the reward he wanted, the humble, grateful hearts. When he lay down, exhausted, it was often on the floor of wherever he was when night came, and he thought nothing of it. He rose at daybreak and ate what the wretched could spare him.

It was very late one night when he was listening to the confession of a bull-chested man, something of a local leader and a bully, that he began to feel ill.

"I beat him," the man said quietly, his eyes meeting Constantine's uncertainly, clouded with fear. "I broke some of his bones."

"Did he . . . ," Constantine began, and then found he could not draw his breath. His heart was beating so loudly, he thought the man kneeling before him must hear it also. He was dizzy. He tried to speak again, but he could hear nothing but a roaring in his ears, and the moment after he was plunging into oblivion, for all he knew death itself.

He awoke in his own house, his head pounding, his stomach sick and cramped with pain. His servant Manuel stood beside the bed.

"Let me send for a physician," he begged. "We have prayed, but it is not enough."

"No," Constantine said quickly, but even his voice was weak. His stomach knotted again, and he was afraid he was going to be sick.

He tried to get up to relieve himself urgently, but the pain doubled him over. He called for Manuel to help him. Twenty minutes later, drenched in sweat and so weak that he could not stand without help, he collapsed on the bed and allowed Manuel to pull the covers over him. Now suddenly he was cold, but at least he could lie still.

Manual asked again for permission to send for a physician, and again Constantine refused. Sleep would cure him.

Constantine lay still, his belly quiet. But the fear gripped his heart like an iron clamp, twisting inside him. He dared not lie down in the dark when the light spiraled away from him, his skin slick with sweat again and yet his limbs ice cold.

"Manuel!" His voice was shrill, almost hysterical.

Manuel appeared, candle in his hand, his face tight with fear.

"Get Anastasius for me," Constantine conceded at last. "Tell him it is urgent." The pain shot through his belly again. "But first assist me." He must relieve himself again, quickly. He must have help. He also thought he was about to be sick. Anastasius was another eunuch and would not pity his mutilation or be repelled by it. He had had a whole physician once and seen the prurient revulsion in the man's eyes. Never again; he'd rather die.

Anastasius would have only understanding. He too was lost, uncertain, carrying a burden somewhere inside him that was too heavy. Constantine had seen it in his face in unguarded moments. One day he would learn what it was.

Yes, send for Anastasius. Quickly.

Fifteen

ANNA COULD SEE FROM THE SERVANT'S MANNER AND THE high pitch of his voice that he was seriously alarmed. But quite apart from that, she knew that Constantine, a proud and private man, would not have sent for her were the matter not grave.

"How does the illness show itself?" she asked. "Where is the pain?"

"I don't know. Please come."

"I want to know what to bring with me," Anna explained. "It would be far better than having to return for it."

"Oh." Now the man understood. "In his abdomen. He does not eat or drink, relieves himself often, and yet the pain does not go." He shifted his weight from one foot to the other impatiently.

As quickly as she could, she packed in a small case all the herbs she thought mostly likely to help. She also took a few Eastern herbs from Shachar and from al-Qadir, whose names she would not tell Constantine.

She informed Simonis where she was going, then followed the man out into the street and down the hill as rapidly as she could walk.

She was ushered straight into the bedchamber where Constantine was lying, his night tunic tangled and soaked with sweat and his skin a pasty gray.

"I'm sorry you feel so ill," she said quietly. "When did it begin?" She was startled to see the fear in his sunken eyes, naked and out of control.

"Last night," he answered. "I was listening to confession and suddenly the room went black."

She touched his brow with her hand. It was cool and clammy. She could smell the sharp, stale odor of sweat and sour body waste. She found his pulse. It was strong, but racing.

"Do you have pain now?" she asked.

"Not now."

She judged that to be only a half-truth. "When did you last eat?"

He looked puzzled.

"If you don't remember, it was too long ago." She studied his arm where it lay across his chest. She must never let him know she had seen the terror in him. He would not forgive her that. She must examine him intimately also—at least his belly, to see if it was swollen or perhaps if his bowel was obstructed. He might never forgive her that, either, if his castration was untidy—a bad mutilation. She had heard that they varied a great deal. Some eunuchs had had all organs removed and needed to insert a tube to pass water.

She hesitated. She was taking a terrible risk; it was an intrusion from which there was no return. Yet her medical duty to him forbade that she withhold any treatment she believed could help. She had no choice.

Gently she took the skin of his arm between her thumb and finger. It was slack, loose on the underlying flesh. "Bring me water," she told the servant still waiting at the door. "And get the juice of pomegranates, preferably not quite ripe, if you have them. Bring it to me in a jug. One jugful will do to start with." She handed the servant the honey and spikenard and told him the proportions to add. Constantine's body was drained of fluids.

"Have you vomited?" she asked him.

He winced. "Yes. Only once."

She knew from the feel of his skin and his sunken eyes that he had lost far too much fluid from his body.

"Perhaps it was unintentional," she told him, "but you have starved yourself, and drunk too little."

"I was working with the poor," he answered weakly. His eyes avoided hers, but she did not think it was because he was lying. She suspected that he loathed the intrusion of anyone seeing him like this.

"What is wrong with me?" he asked. "Is it a sin unto death?"

She was stunned. The fear was deep and raw in him, indecently exposed. How could she answer him with honesty that was true both to medicine and to faith?

"It is not only guilt which afflicts," she said gently. "Anger can also, and sometimes grief. You have spent too much of your strength in ministering to others and have neglected yourself. And yes, perhaps that is a sin. God gave you your body to use in His service, not to ill-treat it. That is an ungrateful thing to do. Maybe you need to repent of that."

He stared at her, grasping at what she had said, turning it over and weighing it. Gradually some of the fear eased away, as if miraculously she had not said what he dreaded. His hand gripping the sheet loosed a little.

She smiled. "Take better thought for yourself in future. You cannot serve either God or man in this state."

He breathed in deeply and let out a sigh.

"You must drink," she told him. "I have brought herbs which will cleanse and strengthen you. You must eat, but with care. Bread that has been well kneaded, hens' eggs lightly boiled, not goose or duck eggs. You may eat lightly boiled meat of partridge or francolin, or young kid, not older animals. A little stewed apple with honey would be good, but avoid nuts. Then when you are ready, in two or three days, take a little fish; gray mullet is good. Mostly you must drink water with juice mixed in. Have your servant wash you and bring you clean linen. Have him help you so you do not fall. You are weak. I shall give him a list of what other food to buy."

She saw in his face that he wished to ask more. Afraid it would be questions she could not answer without causing him confusion or distress, she gave him no time, bidding him good-bye and promising to return soon.

Early the following morning, she went to check his progress. He looked gaunt in the full daylight, his cheeks sunken, his skin colorless, papery; oddly like a very large old woman. His pale hands on the bedcover seemed enormous, his arms fleshy. She was moved with a wave of intense pity for him but was careful that he should not see it in her eyes.

"The people are praying for you," she told him. "Philippos, Maria, and Angelos stopped me when they heard I had called on you. They are very concerned."

He smiled, the light returning to his eyes. "Really?"

Did he fear she was saying it to please him? "Yes, some even fast and keep vigil. They love you, and I think also they are very afraid of facing the future without you."

"Tell them I need their support, Anastasius. Thank them for me."

"I will," she promised, embarrassed by his need for so much reassurance. When he was better, would he remember this and hate her for having seen too much?

The following day, Manuel once again opened the door to Anna. His eyes went immediately to the basket she was carrying: strengthening foods prepared by Simonis for the ailing bishop.

"Food for the bishop," she explained. "How is he?"

"Much better," Manuel replied. "The pain is less, but he is still very weak indeed."

"It will take time, but he will recover." She passed him the soup with instructions to heat it and left the bread on the table. She went through to Constantine's bedroom, knocking on the door and waiting for his answer before she went in.

While he was sitting up in bed, he still looked hollow-eyed and pale. A whole man would have been stubble-chinned by now, but Constantine's face looked curiously soft.

"How are you?" she asked.

"Improved," he replied, but she could see he was tired.

She felt his brow, then his pulse, then gently pinched the skin on his forearm again. He was still clammy and his flesh slack, but his pulse was steadier. She made a few more inquiries about his pain, by which time Manuel arrived with the soup and bread. She sat beside Constantine, steadying his hand as he ate, gently helping him, steeling herself to ask the questions.

"Please eat," she encouraged. "We need you to be strong. I do not wish to be governed by Rome. It will destroy a great deal of what I believe to be true, and of infinite value. It is a tragedy that Bessarion Comnenos was murdered." She hesitated. "Do you think that could have been prompted by Rome?"

His eyes widened and his hand stopped with the spoon in the air. The thought had not occurred to him. She could see him searching for the answer he wanted to give.

"I had not considered it," he admitted finally. "Perhaps I should have."

"Would it not have served their interest?" she pressed. "Bessarion was passionately against union. He was of imperial blood. Might he have led a resurgence of faith among the people that would have made union impossible?"

He was still staring at her, the last of the soup temporarily forgotten. "Have you heard anyone say so?" he asked, his voice low and with a sudden, sharp note of fear in it.

"If I were of the Roman faith, perhaps hoping to assist the union myself, either for religious reasons or ambition, I would not want a leader such as Bessarion alive and well," she said urgently.

A curious look passed over Constantine's face, a mixture of surprise and wariness.

She plunged on. "Might Justinian Lascaris have been in the pay of Rome, do you suppose?"

"Never," he said instantly. Then he stopped, as if he had committed himself too quickly. "At least, he is the last man I would have thought it of."

She could not let this opportunity slip by. "What other reason do you think Justinian could have had for killing Bessarion? Did he hate him? Was there a rivalry between them? Or money?"

"No," he said quickly, pushing aside the tray that held his food. "There was no rivalry or hate, at least on Justinian's part. And no money. Justinian was a wealthy man, and prospering more each year. Every reason I know of says he would wish Bessarion alive. He was profoundly against the union and supported Bessarion in his work against it. At times I thought he did the more work of the two."

"Against the union?"

"Of course." Constantine shook his head. "I cannot believe Justinian would work for Rome. He was an honorable man, of more courage and decisiveness than Bessarion, I think. That is why I spoke for him to the emperor in plea that the sentence be commuted to exile. It was certainly his boat that was used to dispose of the body, but it might have been without his knowledge. Antoninus confessed, but he did not implicate Justinian."

"What do you think was the truth?" She could not leave it now. She touched on the subject ugliest in her mind. "Could it not have been personal? To do with Helena?"

"I do not believe Justinian had any feelings for Helena, most certainly not of that kind."

"She is beautiful," Anna pointed out.

Constantine looked slightly surprised. "I suppose so. There is no modesty in her, no humility."

"True," Anna conceded, "but those are not always qualities that men look for."

Constantine shifted a little in the bed, as if he were uncomfortable. "Justinian told me that Helena had once made it very clear that she wished him to lie with her, and he had refused. He told me that he still loved his wife, who had died not long before, and he could not yet think of another woman, least of all Helena." Constantine smoothed his hands over the rumpled sheet. "He showed me a painting of his wife, very small, only a couple of inches square, so that he could carry it with him. She looked very beautiful to me, a gentle face, intelligent. Her name was Catalina. The way Justinian said it made me believe everything he said."

Anna took the tray from the side of the bed and rose to put them on a table at the far side of the room. It gave her a chance to compose herself. His words, the story of Justinian and Catalina's portrait, brought their presence so sharply to her mind that the loss was almost like a physical pain.

She put down the tray and turned back to Constantine. "Then he would have wanted Bessarion alive, wouldn't he?" she asked. "Both to lead the struggle against the union and to excuse him from having to justify his refusal of Helena?"

"That is another reason I pleaded for his exile," Constantine said sadly.

"Then who did help kill Bessarion? Could we not prove it, and have Justinian freed?" She saw the surprise in his face. "Would it not be our holy duty?" she amended quickly. "Added to which, of course, he could return and continue in the struggle against Rome."

"I don't know who helped kill Bessarion," he said, spreading his hands in a gesture of helplessness. "If I did, don't you think I would already have told the emperor?"

His tone had changed. She was convinced he was lying, but it was impossible to challenge him. She should retreat now, before she antagonized him or aroused his suspicion as to why she should care so much.

"I suppose it was some other friend of Antoninus," she said as lightly as she could. "Why did he kill him, anyway?"

"I don't know that, either." Constantine sighed.

Again she was certain he was lying.

"I'm glad you liked the soup," she said with a slight smile.

"Thank you." He smiled back. "Now I think I will go to sleep for a while."

Sixteen

GIULIANO DANDOLO STOOD ON THE STEPS OF THE LAND-
ing stage and watched the water of the canal rippling in the torchlight. He smiled in spite of the faint sense of unrest he felt. One moment
the wavelets were crested with glittering ribbons of light, the next they
were shadowed and as dense as if he could walk out over them and they
would bear his weight. Everything was shifting, beautiful and uncertain,
like Venice itself.

His thoughts were disturbed by the sharper slap of water on the steps,
and as he moved forward he saw the outline of a small, swiftly moving
barge. There were armed men standing on the sides, and it slid smoothly
to the mooring post and stopped. The torches blazed up and the slender,
heavily robed figure of Doge Lorenzo Tiepolo rose and in an easy movement stepped ashore. He was in his later years. His sons had all risen to
eminence, and many suggested it was purely by their father's favor. But
then people always said such things.

Tiepolo walked forward across the marble as the torchlight wavered in
the rising breeze. He was smiling, his small, heavy-lidded eyes bright and
his hair silver like a halo.

"Good evening, Giuliano," he said warmly. "Did I keep you waiting?"
It was a rhetorical question. He was ruler of Venice; everyone waited for
him. He had known Giuliano since he had been brought here as a small
child nearly thirty years ago, as he had known and loved Giuliano's father
also.

Still, one did not take liberties. "A spring evening on the canal can hardly be thought of as waiting, Excellency," Giuliano replied, falling into step with the doge, but just behind him.

"Always the courtier," Tiepolo murmured as they crossed the piazza in front of the ornate Ducal Palace. "Perhaps it is a good thing. We have sufficient enemies." He led the way inside through the great doors, the guard before and behind him silent and watchful.

"The day we have no enemies it will mean we have nothing for any man to envy," Giuliano replied a trifle dryly. They took off their outdoor cloaks and walked along the high-ceilinged hall with its painted walls, their feet loud on the inlaid floor.

Tiepolo's smile widened. "And no teeth to bite with," he added. He turned right into a high anteroom and then into his own chambers with their frescoed walls and heavy chandeliers. The sandalwood table held dishes of dried dates and apricots and a selection of nuts. The torches glimmered, throwing warm light over the tessellated floor.

"Sit!" He waved his arm in the general direction of the carved chairs around the huge fireplace, where a fire burned to warm the still chilly March air. The great portrait of his father, Doge Jacopo Tiepolo, hung above it. "Wine?" he offered. "The red is from Fiesole, very good." Without waiting for an answer, he took two of the glass tumblers and filled them, then passed one to Giuliano.

Giuliano accepted it, thanking him. Tiepolo had been his friend and patron since his own father's death, but he knew he had not been summoned simply for the pleasure of conversation. That happened quite often, but it was late at night for casual talk of art or food, boat races, beautiful women, or, far more entertainingly, scandalous ones—and, of course, of the sea. Tonight the doge was serious; his narrow face with its long nose had a pensive expression, and he moved uneasily, as if paying more heed to the thoughts occupying his mind than to his actions.

Giuliano waited.

Tiepolo looked at the light through the wine in his glass but did not yet drink. "Charles of Anjou still cherishes his dreams of uniting the five ancient patriarchies of Rome, Antioch, Jerusalem, Alexandria, and Byzantium again." His look was bleak. "All under his own sovereignty, of course. Then he would be Count of Anjou, senator of Rome, king of Naples and Sicily and Albania, king of Jerusalem, lord of the patriarchates, and of course uncle to the king of France. Such power in any one man would make me uneasy, but in him it is a danger not only to Venice, but to the whole world.

"His success would threaten our interests right along the east coast of the Adriatic. Michael Palaeologus has signed the agreement of unity with Rome, but my information tells me he will have considerably more difficulty in taking his people with him than the pope may imagine. And we all know that the Holy Father is a passionate crusader." He smiled bleakly. "He is reputed to have sworn the skill of his right hand that he will never forget Jerusalem. We would be wise to remember that."

Giuliano waited.

"Which means he will aid Charles, at least in that," Tiepolo added.

"Then he would have Rome on his side, and Jerusalem and Antioch in his hands." Giuliano spoke at last. "Would Charles attack Byzantium, even though the emperor has signed the agreement of union and submitted to the pope? Surely he would then be attacking an equally Christian city, and the Holy Father could not countenance that."

Tiepolo lifted one shoulder very slightly. "That might depend whether the people of Byzantium, especially the city of Constantinople, will honor the union."

Giuliano thought about it, aware of the doge's eyes probing, watching every flicker and shadow of his expression. If Charles of Anjou took all five of the old patriarchies, including Constantinople astride the Bosphorus, he would hold the gateway to the Black Sea and everything beyond it: Trebizond, Samarkand, and the old Silk Road to the East. If he also gained control of Alexandria and thus the Nile, and so Egypt, he would be the most powerful man in Europe. The trade of the world would pass through his hands. Popes came and went, and the election of them would be his decision.

"We have a dilemma," Tiepolo continued. "There are many elements to Charles's possible success. Our building ships for his crusade is only one of them. And if we do not, then Genoa will. We have to consider the profit and loss of our naval yards, and of course our bankers and merchants, and those who supply the knights, foot soldiers, and pilgrims. We want them to pass through Venice, as they have always done. It is a very considerable revenue."

Giuliano sipped his wine and reached across to take half a dozen almonds.

"There are other factors far less certain," Tiepolo continued. "Michael Palaeologus is a clever man. He could not have retaken Constantinople were he not. He will have the same information we have, or more." He said the last with a rueful amusement in his eyes. At last he also took a handful of nuts.

"He will know what Charles of Anjou plans, and he will know what Rome intends to do to assist him," he went on. "He will take all measures he can to prevent their success." His eyes were steady on Giuliano's dark, handsome face, watching his reaction.

"Yes, Excellency," Giuliano answered. "But Michael has a small navy, and his army is already fully occupied elsewhere." He said it with little pity. He did not want to think of Constantinople. His father was Venetian to the bone, a junior son of the great Dandolo family, but his mother had been Byzantine, and he never willingly brought her back to his mind. What sane man looks for pain?

"So he will use guile," Tiepolo concluded. "In his place, wouldn't you? Michael has just regained his capital city, one of the great jewels of the world. He will fight to the death before he gives it up again."

Giuliano could remember his mother only as a sort of warmth, a sweet smell and the touch of soft skin, and then afterward an emptiness that nothing since had ever filled. He had been about three when she had gone, as bereaved as if she had died. Only she hadn't; she had simply left him and his father, choosing to stay in Byzantium rather than be with them.

If Constantinople were sacked again, burned and looted by Latin crusaders, robbed of its treasures, its palaces left charred and in ruins, it would be a kind of justice. But the thought gave him no pleasure; the savage satisfaction was more pain than joy. Charles of Anjou's success would alter the fate of Europe and of both the Catholic Church and the Orthodox. It might also quell the rising power of Islam and redeem the Holy Land.

Tiepolo leaned forward a little. "I don't know what Michael Palaeologus will do, but I know what I would do in his place. Men can lead nations only so far. Charles of Anjou is a Frenchman, king of Naples by chance and ambition, not birth. The same is true of Sicily. If rumor is correct, they have no love for him."

Giuliano had heard the same whispers. "Michael will use it?" he asked.

"Wouldn't you?" Tiepolo said softly.

"Yes."

"Go to Naples and see what manner of fleet Charles plans. How many ships, what size. When he plans to sail. Talk bargains and prices with him. We will need even more good hardwood than usual if we are to build his fleet. But also see what the people think." Tiepolo lowered his voice. "What do they say when they are hungry, afraid, when they have drunk too much and tongues are unguarded? Look for troublemakers. See what strength they have, and what weaknesses. Then go to Sicily and do the same. Look for the poverty, the discontent, the love and hate beneath the surface."

Giuliano should have realized what Tiepolo wanted of him. He was the ideal man for the job, a skilled sailor who could command his own ship, the son of a merchant father who knew the trade of the whole Mediterranean, and above all a man who had inherited the blood and the name of one of the greatest of all Venetian families, even if not their wealth. It was his great-grandfather Doge Enrico Dandolo who had led the crusade that had taken Constantinople in 1204, and when Venice was cheated of its just payment for the ships and supplies, he had brought the greatest of its treasures home in recompense.

Tiepolo was smiling openly now, the wineglass glinting in his hand. "And from Sicily go to Constantinople," he went on. "See if they are repairing their defenses, but more than that, stay in the Venetian Quarter down by the Golden Horn. See how strong it is, how prosperous. If Charles attacks in Venetian ships, judge what they will do. Where are their loyalties, their interests? They are Venetian, and by now part Byzantine. How deep are their roots? I need to know, Giuliano. I give you no more than four months. I cannot afford longer."

"Of course," Giuliano agreed.

"Good." Tiepolo nodded. "I will see that you have all you need: money, a good ship, cargo to give you excuse and reason, and men who will obey you, and to whom you can trust your trade while you are ashore. You will leave the day after tomorrow. Now drink your wine. It's excellent." He lifted his own glass higher as if to demonstrate and put it to his lips.

In the evening of the following day, Giuliano met his closest friend, Pietro Contarini, and they dined together. Giuliano savored the tastes of wine and food as if he might be hungry for months to come. They laughed over old jokes and sang songs they had known for years. They had grown up together, learned the same lessons, discovered the pleasures of wine and women and the misfortunes as well.

They had fallen in love for the first time in the same month, each confiding to the other the doubts and the pains, the triumphs, and then the agony of rejection. When they had discovered that it was the same girl, they had fought like wild dogs until first blood was drawn, Giuliano's. Then instantly friendship was more important, and they had ended laughing at themselves. No woman had come between them since.

Pietro had married several years ago and had a son of whom he was immensely proud, and then two daughters. However, domestic responsibility had not dulled his eye for a pretty woman or robbed him of his joy in adventure.

Now they sat in the tavern facing the long sweep of the Grand Canal amid the laughter and clink of glasses, the smells of wine and salt water, food and leather, and smoke from cooling fires.

"Here's to adventure. . . ." Pietro raised his glass of rather good red wine to which Giuliano had treated them both, in honor of the occasion.

They touched glasses and drank.

"Here's to Venice, and everything Venetian," Giuliano added. "May her glory never grow dim." He emptied his glass. "What time is it, do you think?"

"No idea. Why?"

"Going to say good-bye to Lucrezia," Giuliano replied. "Won't see her for a while."

"Will you miss her?" Pietro asked curiously.

"Not much," Giuliano said. Pietro had been nagging him to marry for some time. Even the thought of it made him feel trapped. Lucrezia was fun, warm, and generous, at least physically—but she was also cloying at times. The thought of committing himself to her was like locking a door that trapped him inside.

He put his empty glass on the table and stood up. He would enjoy being with Lucrezia. He had bought a gold filigree necklace to take her as a gift. He had chosen it with care, and he knew she would love it. He would miss her, her quiet laughter, the softness of her touch. But it still would not be hard to leave in the morning.

.   .   .

Giuliano found Naples a frightening and disturbingly beautiful place, full of unexpected impressions. The city had a vitality that excited him, as if the people tasted both the joy and the tragedy of life with a wholehearted intensity greater than that of others.

It had been founded by the Greeks, hence its name—Neapolis, New City—and the narrow streets followed a pattern like a grid, which the Greeks had formed. Many of them were well over a thousand years old, steep and shadowed by high houses. Giuliano listened to the laughter and the quarrels, the haggling over olives and fruit and fish, the splashing of fountains and the rattle of wheels. He smelled cooking and clogged drains, the perfume of bright trailing vines and flowers, and human and animal waste. He watched women scrubbing laundry by the fountains, gossiping with one another, laughing, scolding their children. Their loyalty was to life, not to any king, Italian or French.

The sun was bright and hotter than he was accustomed to. He was familiar with light on water, but the burning blue of the Bay of Naples, stretching to the horizon, had a brilliance to it that dazzled his eyes, yet he was drawn again and again to stand and stare at it.

But always intruding into his mind was the ominous presence of Mount Vesuvius looming behind the city to the south, now and then sending a breath of smoke up gently into the glittering peace of the sky. Looking at it, Giuliano could see so easily how it could drive people mad with the hunger for life, the craving that would make you seize everything, gorging on every taste, in case tomorrow was too late.

He was in a deeply contemplative mood when finally he approached the palace and was invited into the presence of the Frenchman who ruled as king. Giuliano knew of his considerable military successes, particularly in the war with Genoa, barely over, and his victories in the East that had made him king of Albania as well as of the Two Sicilies. He expected a warrior, a man a little drunk with the triumph of his own violence. And he thought all Franks were unsophisticated compared with any Latin, never mind a Venetian who had so much of the delicate subtlety of Byzantium as well as his native love of beauty.

Giuliano found a large, barrel-chested man in his late forties, olive-skinned, dark-eyed, his powerful face dominated by an enormous nose. His dress was quite modest; nothing marked him out from those around him except the restless energy of his manner and the confidence that burned through even in the moments when he stood in repose.

When he was commanded to speak, Giuliano introduced himself as a sailor familiar with most of the ports of the eastern Mediterranean and currently an emissary of the doge of Venice.

Charles welcomed him and invited him to sit at the table, which was richly set with food and drink. It seemed like an order, so Giuliano obeyed. But instead of eating, Charles paced back and forth in vigorous strides, firing questions at him.

"Dandolo, you said?"

"Yes, sire."

"A great name! A great name indeed. And you know the East? Cyprus? Rhodes? Crete? Acre? Do you know Acre?"

Giuliano briefly described these places to him.

Charles surely knew them already. Presumably he was comparing one account with another. Only occasionally did he pick up a leg of roast fowl and a piece of bread or fruit and bite into it, and he took little wine. Now and again he gave orders, and there seemed to be scribes taking them down in notes all over the place, as if he required three copies of everything. Giuliano was impressed that he seemed able to think of so many things at once.

His grasp of politics in Europe was encyclopedic, and he knew much of North Africa and the Holy Land and beyond, as far as the Mongol Empire. Giuliano found himself dazzled and had to struggle to keep up, quickly coming to the decision that to admit his limitations would be not only more courteous, but wiser in the presence of one who would take only moments to realize the relative ignorance of somebody who was younger and less experienced.

Should he ask about ships for a coming crusade? It was what Tiepolo had sent him for.

"It would need a great fleet," Giuliano observed.

Charles laughed, a rich sound of amusement. "Always the Venetian. Of course it will. Much money and many pilgrims. Are you going to offer me a bargain?"

Giuliano leaned back a little and smiled. "We could bargain. Much timber would be needed, far more than usual. All our shipyards would be engaged, possibly day and night."

"In a holy cause," Charles pointed out.

"Conquest or profit?" Giuliano asked.

Charles roared with laughter and slapped him on the shoulder, a blow that jarred his teeth. "I could like you, Dandolo," he said heartily. "We'll talk numbers, and money, in a little while. Have another glass of wine."

Three hours later Giuliano left with his mind whirling, walking back through the halls hardly less ornate than the Doge's Palace in Venice, although the courtiers were less sophisticated, even coarse in their habits by comparison.

Some said Charles was stern but fair, others that he taxed his subjects into penury, almost to starvation, and that he had neither love for nor interest in the people of Italy.

Yet for ambition's sake, he chose to have his court so often here in Naples, passionately, intensely, almost madly alive and placed like a jewel on the side of a sleeping dragon whose smoke even now scarred the horizon. Charles too was a force of nature that might destroy those who took him too lightly.

Guiliano must learn a great deal more, study, listen, watch, and take intense care as to exactly what he reported back to the doge. He went down the steps into the blinding sunlight, and the heat from the stones embraced him.

When Charles moved his court from Naples south to Messina on the island of Sicily, Giuliano followed after him a week later. As in Naples, he watched and listened. The talk was of the reconquest of Outremer, as the old kingdom of Christian Palestine was known.

"Just the beginning," one sailor said cheerfully, drinking down half a pint of wine and water with gusto. "More than time we took the war back to the Muslims. They're all over the place, and spreading."

"Time we got our own back," another said savagely. He was a big man with a red beard. "Fifteen years ago they killed a hundred and fifty Teutonic knights at Durbe. Then all the people in Osel apostatized and slaughtered every Christian in their territory."

"At least they stopped the Mongols going into Egypt," Giuliano volunteered, interested to see their answer to that. "Better the Muslims fight them than we have to."

"Let the Mongols soften them up for us," the first man rejoined. "Then we'll finish them. I'm not choosy who's on my side." He guffawed with laughter.

"Clearly," a small man with a pointed beard put in.

The red-haired man slammed his tankard on the tabletop. "And what the hell is that supposed to mean?" he challenged, his face flushing with anger.

"It is supposed to mean that if you had ever seen an army of Mongol horsemen, you'd be damn glad to have the Muslims between you and them," the other rejoined.

"And the Byzantines?" Giuliano asked, hoping to provoke an informative reply.

The small man shrugged. "Between us and Islam?"

"Why not?" Giuliano urged. "Isn't it better they fight Islam than we have to?"

The man with the red beard shifted in his seat. "King Charles will take them when we pass that way, just like before. Plenty of treasure there for the picking."

"We can't do that," Giuliano told him. "They've agreed to union with Rome, which makes them fellow believers in the one faith with us. Taking them by force would be a sin unpardonable by the pope."

Redbeard grinned. "The king'll take care of that, never you worry. He's writing to Rome even now, asking the pope to excommunicate the emperor, which will take all protection from him. Then we can do as we like."

Giuliano sat stunned, the room melting into a blur of sound, senseless around him.

Two days later, Giuliano set out for Constantinople. The voyage east was calm and swifter than he had expected, lasting only eighteen days. Like most other ships, theirs hugged the shore all the way, often unloading cargo and taking on more. It was to be a profitable journey in money as well as information.

However, as they sailed up the Sea of Marmara in the early May morning, the mares-tail clouds high and fragile, the wind painting brushstrokes on the sea, he admitted to himself that no matter how long it took, or however he steeled himself, he would never be ready to see the homeland of the mother who had given him birth and yet loved him so little that she had been willing to abandon him.

He had looked at women with their children passing him in the street. They might be tired, worried, heartbroken for a hundred reasons, but they never took their eyes from their children. Every step was watched. A hand was ever ready to support or to chastise, but it was always there.

They might scold the child, slap it in temper, but let anyone else threaten it and they would learn what anger really was.

At midday he stood on the deck of the ship, heart pounding as they slid across the smooth, shining water of the Bosphorus and the great city grew closer and more detailed. His sailor's eye was drawn to the lighthouse. It was magnificent, visible to approaching mariners at night from miles away.

The harbor was crowded, scores of fishing boats and ferries and cargo carriers scudding about the huge hulls of the triremes hailing from the Atlantic to the Black Sea. And across that narrow channel of water, Europe met Asia. This was the crossroads of the world.

"Captain?"

There was no more time for self-indulgence. He must turn his attention to making harbor, seeing the ship safely anchored and the cargo unloaded before turning over command to his first officer. They had already agreed that the ship would return for him at the beginning of July.

It was the following day before he stepped ashore with his chest packed—a few clothes and books, sufficient to last him for nearly two months. The doge had given him a generous allowance.

It was an alien feeling to stand on the cobbles of the street. Half Byzantine, he should have embraced this as a homecoming, yet all he felt was rejection. He came as a spy.

He turned and looked back at the harbor teeming with ships. He might know the men on some of them, even have sailed with them, faced the same storms and hardships, the same excitement. The light on the water had the same strange, luminous quality that it had in Venice, the sky, the familiar softness.

He spent three nights in lodgings and the intervening days walking around the city, gaining a feel for its nature, its customs, its geography, even the food, the jokes, and the taste of the air.

He sat in a restaurant having an excellent meal of savory goat meat with garlic and vegetables, then a glass of wine that he thought not nearly as good as Venetian. He watched the people in the street, overhearing snatches of conversation, much of which he did not understand. He studied faces and listened to the tones of voice. The Greek he spoke, and of course the Genoese he heard disturbingly often. He understood snatches from the Arabs and Persians whose dress was so easy to distinguish. The Albanians, Bulgars, and high-cheeked Mongols were alien, and he was reminded with a tingle of discomfort just how far east he was and how close to the lands of the Great Khan or the Muslims the red-bearded man had spoken of in Messina.

He would find a Venetian family down by the shore of the Golden Horn. He wondered idly where his mother had lived. She had been born during the exile, perhaps in Nicea or farther north? Then he was furious with himself for allowing in the pain that always came with thoughts of her. He couldn't stop himself.

He closed his eyes hard against the sunlight and the busyness of the street, but nothing shut out the inner vision of his father, gray-haired, his face lined with sorrow, the locket open in his hand showing the tiny painting of a young woman with dark eyes and laughing face. How could she laugh and leave them? Giuliano had never once heard him speak ill of her. He had died still loving her.

He lurched to his feet. The wine would choke him now. He left it and strode out into the street. This was an alien city, full of people he would never be foolish enough to trust. Know your enemy, learn from them, understand them, but never, ever be seduced by their art, their skill, or their beauty; just judge whose side they would be on when it mattered.

The Venetian Quarter was just a few streets, and they made no great show of their origins. No one had forgotten whose fleet had brought the invaders who had burned the city and stolen the holy relics.

He found a family with the old, proud name of Mocenigo and immediately liked the man, Andrea. He had an ascetic face, bordering on plain until he smiled; then he was almost beautiful. And it was not until he moved that Giuliano noticed he had a slight limp. His wife, Teresa, was shy but offered to make Giuliano welcome, and his five children seemed happily unaware that he was a stranger. They asked him numerous questions as to where he was from and why he was here, until their parents told them that interest was friendly, but to be inquisitive was rude. They apologized and stood in a row, eyes downcast.

"You have not been the least bit rude," Giuliano said quickly in Italian.

"One day, when we have time, I will tell you about some of the other places I have been to, and what they were like. And if you will, you can tell me about Constantinople. This is the first time I have been here."

That settled the issue immediately; this was the house in which he would lodge. He accepted with pleasure.

"I am Venetian," Mocenigo explained with a smile. "But I have chosen to make my life here because my wife is Byzantine, and I find a certain freedom of the mind in the Orthodox faith." His tone was half-apologetic because he assumed Giuliano would be of the Roman Church, but his eyes were unflinching. He would not choose an argument, but if one arose, he would be ready to defend his belief.

Giuliano held out his hand. "Then perhaps I shall learn something deeper of Byzantium than the merchants will tell me."

Mocenigo clasped it, and the bargain was made. The financial agreement was far outweighed in importance by the promise of the future.

It was natural that they should ask Giuliano his business, and he was prepared with an answer.

"My family have been merchants for a long time," he said easily. That, at least, was true, if he intended the term to include all those descended from the great doge Enrico Dandolo. "I've come to see more directly what is bought and sold here, and what more we could do to increase our trade. There must be needs unmet, new opportunities." He wanted the freedom to ask as many questions as possible without raising suspicion. "The new union with the Church of Rome should make many things simpler."

Mocenigo shrugged and pulled his face into an expression of doubt. "The paper is signed, but that's a long way from a reality yet."

Giuliano managed to look slightly surprised. "You think the agreement may not be kept? Surely Byzantium wants peace? Constantinople in particular cannot afford war again, and if they are not of one faith with Rome, war is what it will be, in fact, even if they don't call it that."

"Probably." Mocenigo's voice was soft and sad. "Most sane people don't want war, but wars still happen. The only way you change people's religion is by convincing them of something better, not by threatening to destroy them if they refuse."

Giuliano stared at him. "Is that how they see it?"

"Don't you?" Mocenigo countered.

Giuliano realized that Mocenigo identified with Constantinople, not with Rome. "Do you think other Venetians here feel the same?" he asked. Then instantly he wondered if it was too soon to have been so blunt.

Mocenigo shook his head. "I can't answer for others. None of us knows yet what obedience to Rome will mean, apart from months of delay before we get answers to appeals, and money paid out of the country in tithes, instead of it staying here, where we desperately need it. Will our churches still be cared for, mended, filled with beauty? Will our priests still be paid well, and left their consciences and their dignity?"

"Well, there cannot be a crusade before '78 or '79 at the soonest," Giuliano reasoned aloud. "By then we may have reached a more sensible understanding, earned a little latitude, perhaps."

Mocenigo smiled—a sudden radiance in his face. "I love a man with hope," he said, shaking his head. "But find out all you can about trade, by all means. There's profit to be made, even in a short time. See what others think. Many believe the Holy Virgin will protect us."

Giuliano thanked him and let the subject fall for the time being. But the easy way in which Mocenigo, a Venetian, had said "us" when referring to Constantinople remained in his mind. It suggested a sense of belonging that he could neither dismiss nor forget.

In the following days, he explored the shops along Mese Street and the spice market with its rich, aromatic perfumes and bright colors. He talked to the Venetians in the quarter, listened to the jokes and the arguments. At home in Venice most quarrels were about trade; here they were about religion, faith versus pragmatism, conciliation versus loyalty. Sometimes he joined in, more with questions than opinions.

It was not until his third week that he went farther up the hills and into the old back streets, where he found the dark stains of fire on the stones and every now and then rubble and weeds where there had been people's homes at the turn of the century; and for the first time in his life, he was ashamed of being Venetian.

One house in particular caught his attention as he stood in a brief shower of rain, the water running down his face and plastering his hair to his head. He stared at the faded paint of a mural showing a woman with a child in her arms. His mother would not have been born when the city was broken and burned, but she might have looked like that, young and slender, in a Byzantine tunic, with a child close to her, proud, gentle, smiling out at the world.

Seventeen

∾

"FROM THE EMPEROR," SIMONIS SAID, HER EYES WIDE AS she stood in the doorway of the herb room. "They want you to go with them, immediately. He is ill."

"I expect someone is ill," Anna replied, following after Simonis toward the outer room. "A servant, perhaps."

Simonis snorted with impatience and pushed open the door for Anna to go in.

Simonis was right: It was Michael himself who wished to consult Anna. Almost lost for words, she gathered up her case of herbs and ointments and accompanied the servants out along the street and up toward the Blachernae Palace.

Inside, she was met by a court official and together they were escorted by two of the Varangian Guard, the emperor's personal troops. They led her through the magnificent, crumbling aisles and galleries to his private apartments. He was apparently suffering from some complaint of the skin that was causing him severe discomfort.

It must have been Zoe who had spoken of her in such a way that the emperor would call her. What would she want in return? Without any doubt at all, it would be a large favor and probably dangerous. Yet it would never have been possible for Anna not to accept. One did not refuse the emperor.

She would have liked to. Failing to cure him might be the end of her ca-reer, at least among the wealthy and influential. Zoe would certainly not favor her again. She would be fortunate if that were all the revenge she took for such an embarrassment to her own reputation. And not every ailment was curable, even with the Jewish and Arabic medicine Anna used, let alone Christian.

Even though the great days of the court eunuchs were past, and the emperor no longer spoke to or listened to the world solely through them, there were still many here. She would have to deceive them with her imposture.

She had tried so hard to mimic Leo that she was losing her own identity, pretending to dislike apricots when she loved them, to like sweet pastries full of honey when they made her gag. She had had to spit out a hazelnut because it revolted her, after she had seen him take one and copied without thinking. She was using his phrases, adopting his voice, and she despised herself for it. She did it because it was safe. Nothing of her old, female self must be left to betray her.

How great a fool was she making of herself now, hurrying along the vast gallery behind a somber-robed official and the huge Varangian Guardsmen, hoping to practice the medicine her father had taught her—on the emperor, no less—because she thought she could rescue Justinian? Her father would have understood, and even approved her aims, but would he question her sanity in trying to put it into practice? What would he think of her if he knew the truth of what she owed Justinian? He had died before she had found the courage to confess to him.

The official had stopped, and there was another man in front of Anna. He was tall and broad-shouldered, but with the smooth face of a eunuch, the long arms and slightly odd grace of movement. She could not judge his age, except that he was certainly older than her. The skin of a eunuch was like that of a woman, softer, more prone to fine lines, and a eunuch's hair seldom receded as a whole man's often did. When he spoke, his voice was low-pitched and his diction beautiful.

"I am Nicephoras," he introduced himself. "I will conduct you to the emperor. Is there anything you need that we may bring to you? Water? Incense? Sweet oils?"

She met his eyes for an instant, then looked down. She must not forget that this eunuch was one of the most senior courtiers in Byzantium. "Water would be helpful, and whatever sweet oils the emperor most favors," she replied.

Nicephoras gave the order to a servant waiting in a farther doorway almost out of sight. Then he dismissed the official who had brought Anna, and the guards, and he himself led the way forward.

Outside the emperor's room, he stopped. Anna felt as if he must see through her disguise and was about to tell her so. She wondered for a hideous moment if they might actually search her before allowing her into Michael's presence. Then she had an appalling thought as to where his skin rash might be, and after she looked at it she would never be forgiven for the intimacy. It even came to her in a wild instant to confess now, before it was beyond recall. The sweat broke out on her skin, and the blood beat so loudly in her ears that it almost deafened her.

Nicephoras was speaking, and she had not heard him.

He realized it.

"He is in some pain," he repeated patiently. "Do not ask him anything unless it is necessary for you to know it, and address him formally at all times. Do not stare. Thank him if you wish, but do not embarrass him. Are you ready?"

She would never be ready, but it was too late to run away. She must have courage. Whatever lay ahead, it would not be as terrible as turning back. "Yes . . . I am." Her voice came out as a squeak. This was ridiculous. Suddenly she wanted to giggle. It welled up inside her like hysteria, and she had to pretend to sneeze to hide it. Nicephoras must think she was a simpleton.

Nicephoras led the way into the bedchamber. It was huge, and unlike the official room, this was barely refurnished even after more than eleven years. Michael lay on the bed with a loose tunic on the upper part of his body and linen bedding over his thighs up to the waist. He looked flushed, his face and neck mottled red. His mane of black hair, threaded with gray, was damp and bedraggled.

"Majesty, the physician, Anastasius Zarides," Nicephoras said distinctly, but keeping his voice lowered. He gestured for Anna to approach the emperor. She obeyed as confidently as she could. The more afraid you were, the more important it was to carry yourself with courage. Her father had told her that over and over.

"Majesty, may I be of service?" she asked.

Michael looked her up and down curiously. "The Jews don't have eunuchs, yet Zoe Chrysaphes said you know Jewish medicine."

The room swam in her vision, heat burning up her cheeks. "Majesty, I am Byzantine, from Nicea, but I have learned as much as I could of all forms of medicine." She almost added, "from my father," and realized just in time that that might be a fatal error. She bit her tongue, hoping the pain would remind her of her lapse.

"Born in Nicea?" he asked.

"No, Majesty, Thessalonica."

His eyes widened fractionally. "So was I. If I wanted a priest, I'd send for one. I have hundreds at my beck and call, all of them more than will-ing to tell me my sins." He smiled bleakly and winced. "And give me due penance, I'm sure." He pulled his tunic apart at the neck, showing the red, blistered weals across his chest. "What is wrong with me?"

She saw the anxiety in his eyes and the sweat beading his brow.

She studied the rash, memorizing the pattern of it, the frequency of the blisters, and the degree to which they were raised. "Please cover yourself again, in case you get chilled," she requested. "May I touch your brow to gauge your fever?"

"Do it," he responded.

She did so and was unhappy with how hot he seemed. "Does the rash burn?"

"Don't they all?" he said tersely.

"No, Majesty. Sometimes they only itch, sometimes they ache, others are very painful, like lots of little stings. Does your head ache? Have you any difficulty in breathing? Does your throat hurt?" She wanted to ask him also if his belly hurt, if he had vomited or suffered diarrhea or consti-pation, but how could she ask an emperor such things? Perhaps she could ask Nicephoras later.

He answered all her questions, mostly in the affirmative. She asked for permission to withdraw and spoke privately with Nicephoras.

"What is it?" he asked her with deep concern. "Is he poisoned?"

She realized with a jolt of horror how realistic was that suspicion. She had never considered what it must be like to live forever in the shadow of envy and hate such that you never know which of your servants, or even your fam-ily, might wish you dead passionately enough to connive at bringing it about.

"I don't know yet," she said aloud to Nicephoras. "Wash gently wher-ever the rash has come. Make sure the water is clean. I will prepare medi-cines, and unguents to relieve the pain."

She took a bold step. Timidity would cause even greater fear. "Then I will learn what it is, and prepare an antidote," she said. A hideous thought flashed through her mind that it could be Zoe herself who might have poisoned him. She was highly skilled in beauty preparations; her own superbly preserved appearance was testimony to that. Possibly she knew poison just as well.

"Nicephoras!" she called as he moved away.

He turned, waiting for her to speak, his dark eyes anxious.

"Use new oils, ones that you have purchased yourself," she warned. "Nothing that is a gift from anyone at all. Purify the water. Give him nothing to eat that you have not prepared, and has not already been tasted."

"I will," he promised, and then added wryly, "and for my own safety, I will have a companion watch my every move, and we will both touch and taste everything." His features were powerful, though they had no beauty, except for his mouth. But when he smiled, even ruefully as now, it lit his entire face.

Anna realized with a shiver one small shadow of what she had stepped into.

When she returned to the palace the following day, she saw Nicephoras first. He looked anxious, and he made no pretense at conversation.

"He is no worse," he said immediately they were alone. "But he still finds eating painful, and the rash has not subsided. Is it poison?"

"There is accidental poison, as well as intentional," she prevaricated. "Some foods spoil, or are poisonous if unripe, or if they are touched by things unclean. One may cut an apricot with a knife, one side of which has been smeared with poison, the other not. Eat one half—"

"I see," he interrupted. "I must be more careful." He caught her flash of understanding. "For my own sake," he added with an ironic curl of his lip.

"Do you fear anyone in particular?" she asked.

"There are factions all over the city," he replied. "Mostly those who feel passionately against the union with Rome; or who are exploiting those who do. You've seen the riots yourself."

She felt the sweat prickle her skin, acutely conscious of Constantine's part in the unrest and now her knowledge of it. "Yes."

"And of course there are always those who have their own ambitions to the throne," he added, his voice lower. "Our history is full of usurpation and overthrow. And there are those who harbor desires of revenge for what they see as past wrongs."

"Past wrongs?" She swallowed hard. This was getting painfully close to Justinian, and if she was honest, to herself. "You mean personal enmity?" she said softly.

"There are those who feel that John Lascaris should have remained emperor, regardless of his youth, inexperience, and profoundly contemplative nature." His face creased with pain for that old, terrible mutilation. "There was a man in the city until recently—Justinian Lascaris," he said quietly. "Presumably a kinsman. He came to the palace several times. The emperor spoke with him out of our hearing, and I don't know what about. But he was involved in the murder of Bessarion Comnenos, and he is now exiled in Palestine."

"Could he have returned and done this?" Her voice shook, and she did not know what to do to control her hands. She pushed them half under her robes, twisting the cloth.

"No." The idea brought a flicker of bleak humor to his eyes. "He is locked in a monastery in Sinai. He will never leave it."

"Why did he collude in killing Bessarion Comnenos?" She had to ask, in spite of the danger to herself and her fear of the answer.

"I don't know," he admitted. "Bessarion was one of many who hated the union with Rome, and he was gathering a considerable following."

"And was this Justinian Lascaris for union with Rome, then?" Surely that could not be?

"No." Nicephoras smiled with a surprising softness. "He was profoundly against it. Justinian's arguments were less theological, but more telling than Bessarion's."

"Then it couldn't have been a religious disagreement," she said, grasping at straws of hope.

"No. The enmity, if it was such, seems to have been born of his friendship with Antoninus, who appears to have been the one actually to have killed Bessarion."

"Why would he? Was he not a soldier, a very practical man?" She felt she must explain herself. "I have treated men, soldiers, who knew him."

He looked at her directly. "There was a suggestion that Antoninus and Bessarion's wife were lovers."

"Helena Comnena? She's very beautiful. . . ."

"Do you think so?" He seemed interested, even puzzled. "I find her empty, like a painting whose colors are flat. There is no passion in her, and little ability to know the pain of high dreams one cannot grasp."

"Did Antoninus see that in her? Why else would he kill Bessarion?"

"I don't know," Nicephoras admitted. "I keep coming back to the union with Rome and his passion against it, his attempt to stir up the people to resist. Which leads me nowhere, because both Justinian and Antoninus were against it also."

She sensed a complexity of emotions in him and wondered what Nicephoras's own feelings were about the union.

"Does Bessarion still have followers alive?" She dragged his attention back to the present issue. "Not just admirers, but people who would continue his cause?"

"Justinian and Antoninus are gone," he replied with an edge of sadness. "I think the others have drifted back to their own concerns, other loyalties. Bessarion was a dreamer, like Bishop Constantine, imagining Byzantium can be saved by faith rather than diplomacy. We have never relied on great armies or navies. We have always pitted our enemies against each other, and stood apart from their battles ourselves. But that takes skill, willingness to compromise, and above all the nerve to hold on and wait."

"A rare kind of courage," she conceded, while thinking of Constantine's passionate belief in the Virgin's power to protect them, if they kept the Orthodox faith. Constantine's way of defending the city was surely what God wanted; the emperor's was the intellectual way of man trusting to himself and the arm of flesh—or, more accurately, of cunning.

She wondered what Justinian had really believed rather than what it was politic to say.

A servant had come to call them, and she followed Nicephoras into the emperor's presence.

Michael was still a little feverish, but the rash was definitely improved and no longer spreading. This time, she had brought leaves to make an infusion—a different sort that would reduce fever and pain—and also more ointment of frankincense, mastic, and elder bark, mixed with oil and white of egg.

Two days after that when she came again, the emperor was up and dressed. He had sent for her to thank her for her skill and to pay her handsomely. She did not allow him to see the intensity of her relief.

"Was I poisoned, Anastasius Zarides?" Michael asked, his black eyes searching her face.

She had expected the question. "No, Majesty."

His arched eyebrows rose even higher. "Then I have sinned, but you did not tell me?"

She had expected that also. "I am not a priest, Majesty."

He considered a moment. "Nicephoras says you have intelligence, and that you are honest. Is he wrong, then?"

"I hope not." She made her voice as pious as she could and avoided his eyes.

"Do I sin in seeking union with Rome, and you have not the courage or the faith to tell me?" he persisted.

This question she had not foreseen. There was laughter in his eyes, and impatience. She had only seconds to think. "I believe in medicine, Majesty. I do not know enough about faith. It did not save us in 1204, but I don't know why not."

"Perhaps we had not enough?" he suggested, looking her up and down slowly, as if he might read her answer in the way she stood or the hands knotted together in front of her. "Is lack of faith a sin, or is it an afflic-tion?"

"To know whether to have faith or not, one has to understand what it is that God has promised," she replied, searching her mind frantically. "To have faith that God will give you something merely because you want it is foolish."

"Will He not protect His true Church, because He wants it?" he re-sponded. "Or does it depend upon us observing every detail, and then standing against Rome?"

He was playing with her. Nothing she said would change his mind, but it might decide her fate. Perhaps he would know if she was lying about her beliefs to please him, and then he would not believe her medical opinions as honest, either.

"I think our blind trust dissolved in blood and ashes seventy years ago," she said. "Maybe God expects us to find a way to use both our intelligence and our faith this time. We will never all be just, or all be wise. The strong must defend the weak."

He appeared satisfied and changed the subject.

"So how did you cure me, Anastasius Zarides? I wish to know."

"With herbs to reduce the fever and the pain, Majesty, ointment to heal the rash, and care to make sure you were not infected by spoiled food, or cloth or oils that were not clean. Your other servants would take care you were not deliberately poisoned. You have tasters. I advised them to be careful of all knives, spoons, and dishes for themselves also."

"And prayer?"

"Most profoundly, Majesty, but I did not need to tell them that."

"For my health, and your survival, no doubt." This time there was quite open laughter in his face.

On the way home, she still wondered if he had been poisoned and if Zoe had had anything to do with it. To be subject to Rome might feel like rape to her. Had she convinced herself that this time blind, passionate faith would save them?

Suddenly Anna was aware of the depth of her own doubt, and perhaps the weight of sin that might have caused it. Were the differences between one church and another of any importance to God, or were they only matters of philosophy, rituals of men adapted to suit one culture or another?

She wished she could have asked Justinian what he believed now, what it was he had learned in Constantinople that he had been willing to fight for to prevent union with Rome and survival against the next crusade.

The loneliness of mind without him was all but crippling.

Eighteen

❦

ANNA HAD BEEN IN THE CITY OVER TWO YEARS. SHE NOW knew exactly what Justinian had been charged with and what the evidence seemed to have been. His trial had been secret and had been held before the emperor himself. Michael was the last resort to justice in all cases, so it was not unusual, particularly since both the victim and one of the accused were of once imperial families.

She had also learned far more about Antoninus, but nothing of it suggested a man prone to violence. On the contrary, he sounded most likable. He was brave and fair as a soldier and reputedly even liked music. People said he and Justinian were good companions, and it was easy to believe it.

Bessarion, on the other hand, was admirable but seemed a solitary man. While gifted with crowds, he was not at ease with his equals and perhaps a bit obsessive in his views.

The more she knew of it, the less sense it made. What possible bond could link Bessarion the religious leader to Antoninus the soldier and good comrade; Justinian the merchant and believer; Zoe the wounded and passionate lover of Byzantium; Helena, her shallow daughter; the lightweight Esaias Glabas, whose name turned up every so often; Eirene Vatatzes, clever but reputedly ugly; and Constantine, the powerful, vulnerable eunuch bishop?

It had to be more than religion. That was shared to a greater or lesser degree by the entire nation.

There was no one she dared speak to about it apart from Leo and Simonis.

Simonis had been there since both Anna and Justinian had studied medicine under their father's tutelage. She had no children of her own, and when their mother had been ill, as she was increasingly often, it was Simonis who had looked after them.

Then had come Anna's first practice with real patients, always carefully supervised, every movement watched, every calculation checked, encouraged, or corrected.

That was when it had happened. In her eagerness, Anna had misread a label and prescribed too strong a dosage of opiates for pain. She had left immediately afterward on an errand that took several hours. Her father had been called to a serious accident, and it was Justinian who had discovered the mistake.

He had had sufficient knowledge to realize what had happened and also to understand the treatment. He had prepared it, then raced to the home of the patient, where he had found him already feeling dizzy and lethargic. Justinian had forced the patient to take a strong emetic and then, after he had vomited, a laxative to get rid of the rest of the opiate. He took on himself the blame for the error. To save both his father's practice and Anna's future, Justinian had placated the irate and wretched patient by promising to give up all medical studies himself, and the man had accepted and agreed to remain silent as long as Justinian kept his word.

He had kept it. He had turned instead to trade, at which he had proved both gifted and successful. But it was not medicine!

Her brother had never once chided Anna for her error or its cost to him, nor had he spoken of it in front of their father. Justinian had said his decision to leave study and turn to business was simply a personal choice. To his mind, Anna was the better physician. Their mother was bitterly disappointed, but their father had said nothing.

Shame still burned inside Anna like acid. She had begged Justinian to tell the truth and allow her to carry her own guilt, but he had warned her that the patient was sworn to silence only on the conditions now agreed. If she now went to him, it would ruin her career without restoring his, and it might also bring their father down. A second story now would seem devious at best, at worst doubly incompetent. She'd known that was true, and for her father's sake she had said nothing. She never knew how much he had known or guessed of the truth.

Her mistake had cost Justinian his life in medicine. He had earned the right to ask almost anything of her, yet beyond her marriage to Eustathius—which he had believed at the time to be for her happiness and security—he had sought nothing. Anything she could do now to clear his name and effect his release was little enough, and she had no shadow of hesitation.

Nineteen

❧

ANNA WAS AWARE OF THE DANGERS OF ASKING ABOUT RE-
ligious contention in a climate already riven with differences and a
sense of impending danger. Yet the answer as to who had killed Bessarion
was not going to fall into her hands without her actively seeking it.

What did Constantine know? That seemed the best place to begin.

He was in his room by the courtyard with the summer sun bright on
the water and the stones beyond the arches, and the shadows cool inside.
He looked almost fully recovered from his illness.

"What can I do for you, Anastasius?" he asked.

"I have been thinking how you wear yourself out in helping the poor
and those in trouble of heart or conscience . . ." she began.

He smiled, his shoulders easing as if he had expected something more
critical from her.

"My medical practice is sufficiently established to provide for the needs
of my household," she continued. "I would like to offer some of my time
to caring for those who cannot pay . . . with your guidance as to who is
the most in need." She hesitated only a moment. "Perhaps you would like
me with you, so I could act both wisely and without delay?"

His eyes widened and his face filled with pleasure. "That is a truly noble
desire, and I accept. We will begin straightaway—tomorrow. I was dis-
couraged, uncertain what next to do for the best, but God has answered
my prayers in you, Anastasius."

Surprised and pleased by the vehemence of his response, she found herself smiling. "What ailments will we be most likely to find, so I can bring the best herbs?"

"Hunger and fear," he replied ruefully. "But we will also find diseases of the lungs and of the stomach, and no doubt of the skin, from poverty, insect infestations, and dirt. Bring what you can."

"I'll be here," she promised.

She went with Constantine at least two days in every week. They traveled the poorer areas down by the docksides, the back streets, narrow and cramped. There were so many sick, especially during the summer heat when there was little rain to clear the gutters and flies swarmed everywhere. It was a difficult course to steer between the spiritual ailments and the bodily ones. It was even more so with Constantine so close and the certainty that all she said to a patient could be repeated back to him.

Often a patient would say to her, "I've repented, why aren't I getting better?"

"You are," she would reply. "But you must also take the medicine. It will help." Then she tried to bring back to her memory all the appropriate saints to pray to for the specific illness and realized in doing so that she did not believe it at all. But they did, and that was what mattered. "Pray to St. Anthony the Abbot," she would add. "And put on the ointment." Or whatever was right for the problem.

Gradually she let slip from her mind the part Constantine had played in the riots. He loved the people, and he was tireless in ministering to them. He had a purity of thought and a strength of faith that eased away the fear that crippled so many.

Always he comforted them. "God will never abandon you, but you must have faith. Be loyal to the Church. Do the best you can, always."

She too felt the need for someone who knew more than she did and whose certainty healed her own gnawing doubts. How could she deny it to anyone else?

At the end of one particularly long day, tired and hungry, she was glad to accept the invitation to return to his home and eat with him.

The meal was simple, bread and oil, fish, and a little wine, but with the poverty she had seen in the last weeks, abundance would have been close to obscene.

She sat opposite Constantine at the table in the quiet summer evening. It was late and the torches were all that lit the night, throwing warm, yellow radiance onto the walls, catching the flash of a gold icon. The fish was finished and the plates removed, only bread, oil, and wine were left, along with an elegant ceramic bowl of figs.

She looked across at him. The lines in his smooth face were deep with tiredness, his shoulders slumped under the weight of other people's pain.

He became aware of her glance and looked up, smiling. "Something troubles you, Anastasius?" he asked.

She ached to tell him and be rid of the burden of guilt that sometimes weighed so heavily that she was not sure she could ever stand upright beneath it. And of course she could say nothing.

He was watching her now, his eyes searching.

"Yes, I am troubled," she said at last, crumbling bread absentmindedly in her fingers. "But then I imagine many people are. I was called to treat the emperor a short time ago . . ."

He looked up, startled, and then a darkness came into his face, but he did not interrupt her.

"I could not help becoming more aware of some of his views," she continued. "Of course, I didn't discuss such things with him. I think he is committed to union with Rome, whatever the cost, because he believes there will be another invasion if we remain separate." She gazed at Constantine steadily. "You know better than he does the poverty we have. How much worse will it be if there is another crusade, and it comes through here again?"

His heavy hand on the table clenched until it formed a fist, knuckles white. "Look about you!" he said urgently. "What is beautiful, precious, and honest in our lives? What keeps us from the sins of greed and cruelty, of the violence that despoils what is good? Tell me, Anastasius, what is it?"

"Our knowledge of God," she said immediately. "Our need for the light we have seen, and can never wholly forget. We have to believe that it exists and that if life is lived well, in the end we can become part of it."

His body eased, and he let out his breath slowly. "Exactly." A smile ironed the weariness from his face. "Faith. I tried to tell the emperor that,

only two days ago. I said to him that the people of Byzantium will not accept any pollution of who we are, and what we have believed since the first
days of Christianity. Accepting Rome tells God that we will sacrifice our
beliefs when it is expedient to us."

He saw the understanding in her face, and perhaps something of the
peace that he had brought her. "The emperor agreed with me, of course,"
he went on. "He said that Charles of Anjou is planning another crusade
even now, and that we have no defense. We will be slaughtered, our city
burned, and those of our people who survive will be exiled, perhaps this
time forever."

She stared into his face, his eyes. "God can save us, if it is His will," she
said softly.

"God has always saved His people. But only when we are faithful." He
leaned across the table toward her. "We cannot put our trust in the arm of
flesh, deny our loyalties, and then when we are losing, turn back to God
and expect Him to rescue us."

"What should we do?" she asked quickly. She must not let him deviate
too far in the conversation. "Bessarion Comnenos was passionately against
the union, and for the sanctity of the Church as we know it. I have heard
so many people praise him and say what a great man he was. What did he
plan?" She tried to make it sound almost casual.

Constantine stiffened. Suddenly the room was so silent, she could hear
a servant's feet on the tiles in the outer corridor. At last he sighed. He
looked down at the dishes on the table when he spoke.

"I fear Bessarion was something of a dreamer. His plans may not have
been as practical as people thought."

Anna was startled. Was she at last close to the truth? She kept her expression deliberately innocent. "What did they think?"

"He spoke a great deal about the Holy Virgin protecting us," Constantine began.

"Oh yes," she said quickly. "I heard that he told the story many times
of the emperor riding out of the city when they were besieged by barbarians long ago. He carried an icon of the Virgin with him, and when the
barbarian leader saw it he fell dead on the spot, and all the besiegers fled."

Constantine smiled.

"Do you think the emperor Michael would do that again?" she asked.
"Do you think it would stop the Venetians, or the Latins from invading us

from the sea? They may be barbarians of the soul," she added wryly, "but they are sophisticated in the mind."

"No," Constantine said reluctantly.

"I cannot imagine Michael Palaeologus doing that," she admitted. "And Bessarion was neither emperor nor patriarch."

Was Bessarion looking to be patriarch? He was not even ordained! Or was he? Was that his secret? She could not let the chance slip away. "If Bessarion was no more than a dreamer, why would anyone bother to kill him?"

This time his answer was instant. "I don't know."

She had half expected that, but looking at his smooth face, the anxiety easing away from it now, she did not entirely believe him. There was something he felt unable to tell her, possibly something Justinian had told him in the bonds of the confessional. She tried another approach.

"They tried to kill him several times—before they succeeded," she said gravely. "Someone must have felt he was a very serious threat to them, or to some principle they valued above even safety, or morality."

Constantine did not disagree, but neither did he interrupt her.

She leaned a little farther across the table. "No one could care for the Church more than you do. Nor, I believe, could anyone serve it so whole-heartedly and with such honor that all the people of Constantinople must be aware of it. Your courage has never deserted you."

"Thank you," he said modestly, but his intense pleasure was almost like a physical warmth radiating from him.

She lowered her voice. "I fear for you. If someone would murder Bessarion, who was so much less effective than you are, might they not attempt to kill you also?"

His head jerked up, eyes wide. "Do you think so? Who would murder a bishop for preaching the word of God?"

She looked down at the table, then up at him again quickly. "If the emperor thought Bessarion was going to make union with Rome more difficult, and so endanger the city, might not he himself have had Bessarion killed?"

Twice Constantine started to speak and then stopped again.

Had he really not thought of it? Or was it that he knew it was not true, because he knew what was? "That is what I was afraid of." She nodded as if it were confirmed. "Please be very careful. You are our best leader, our only honest hope. What will we do if you are killed? There would be despair, and it might end in the sort of violence that would be not only the ruin of the city, and any chance of unity within ourselves, but think of what it would do to the souls of those involved, who would be so stained by sin. They would die without absolution, because who would there be to offer it to them?"

He was still staring at her, appalled at what she had said.

"I must continue," he said. His body was shaking, his face suffused with color. "The emperor and all who advise him, the new patriarch, have forgotten the culture we have inherited, the ancient learning that disciplines the mind and the soul. They would sacrifice all of it for physical survival under the dominion of Rome with its superstitions, its gaudy saints, and its easy answers. Their creed is violence and opportunism, the selling of indulgences for more and more money. They are the barbarians of the heart." He looked at her as if at this moment it were almost a physical need within him that she understand.

It made her uncomfortable, embarrassed by the intimacy of it. She could think of nothing to say that was even remotely adequate.

His voice was thin with pain when he spoke again. "Anastasius, tell me, what use is it to survive if we are no longer ourselves, but something dirtier and infinitely smaller? What is our generation worth if we betray all that our forebears loved and died for?"

"Nothing," she said simply. "But be careful. Someone murdered Bessarion for leading the cause against Rome, and made it look as if Justinian were to blame. And you say he felt equally strongly." She leaned forward again. "If that was not the reason, then what was?"

He drew in a deep breath and let it out in a sigh. "You are right, there is no other."

"Then please take care," she said again. "We have powerful enemies."

"We need powerful people on our side." He nodded slowly, as if it were she who had pointed it out. "The rich and the noble of the old families, the people others will listen to, before it's too late."

Anna felt her stomach tighten and her hands grow slick with the sweat of fear.

"Zoe Chrysaphes could be such a person," he said thoughtfully. "She has much influence. She is close to the Comneni, as well as to the emperor. She would do things for Byzantium that many others would not."

He nodded his head slightly, the shadow of a smile on his lips. "If I make her see that an act has the Virgin's blessing, then she will do it. And there is also Theodosia Skleros and all her family. They have great wealth, and they are all devout, she most of all. I have but to preach, and she will obey." His eyes were bright and he leaned closer toward her. "You are right, Anastasius, there is great hope, if we have the courage and the faith to seize it. Thank you. You give me heart."

Anna felt the first stab of doubt, fine as a needle. Could holiness use such shadowed means and remain pure? The torches burned in their stands, and there was no wind, no sound outside, but suddenly she was colder.

Anna was still troubled with doubts and aware of the tensions in the city. She had warned Constantine of the personal dangers to him because she needed to raise the subject of Bessarion's murder, but some of her fear for him was real. And she also knew that by asking questions, she drew attention to herself. There was no question of stopping her inquiry, but she took more care about walking alone, even though to everyone else she appeared to be a eunuch, and there was nothing lacking of propriety in going wherever she chose. But when called out late, after dark, which happened only rarely at this time of year with the short summer nights, she took Leo with her.

With all she had used in her own practice, and the extra needed for assisting the poor, she was running short of herbs. It was time she replenished her supply.

She walked down the hill to the dockside in the warm light, the sun still well above the hills to the west, the breeze blowing and smelling a little salt. She had to wait only twenty minutes, listening to the shouts and laughter of fishermen, before a water taxi came, and she shared it with a couple of other passengers going across the Golden Horn to Galata.

She relaxed in the taxi; the slight rocking of the boat and the steady slap of the water were soothing, and the other passengers seemed to feel the same. They smiled but did not disturb the evening with unnecessary conversation.

Avram Shachar welcomed her as always, taking her into the back room with its shelves and cupboards full of supplies.

She made her purchases and then was happy to accept his invitation to stay and dine with his family. They ate well, then the two of them sat in the small garden late into the evening, discussing some of the physicians of the past, especially Maimonides, the great Jewish physician and philosopher who had died in Egypt the same year the crusaders had stormed Constantinople.

"He is something of a hero to me," Shachar said. "He also wrote a guide to the entire Mishnah, in Arabic. He was born in Spain, you know."

"Not Arabia?" she asked.

"No, no. His name was really Moses ben Maimon, but he had to flee when the Muslim overlord, Almohades, gave people no choice except to convert to Islam or be put to death."

Anna shivered. "They're to the south and to the west of us. And they seem to be getting more powerful all the time."

Shachar made a gesture of dismissal. "There is enough evil and pain to fight today, don't look for tomorrow's. Now tell me about your medicine."

It was with pleasure and some surprise that she realized he was interested in her growing practice. She found herself answering his questions about her treatment of Michael, although she was discreet enough to say only that she was afraid for him because of the anger among the people regarding the union with Rome.

"That is something of an honor for you to attend him," he said gravely, but he looked more anxious than happy.

"It was Zoe Chrysaphes's recommendation that earned it," she assured him.

"Ah . . . Zoe Chrysaphes." He leaned forward. "Tell her nothing you do not have to. While I know her only by repute, I cannot afford to be ignorant of where the power lies. I am a Jew in a Christian city. You would do well to be careful also, my friend. Do not assume that everything is as it seems."

Why did he warn her? Surely she had been discreet enough with her inquiries. "I'm Byzantine, and Orthodox Christian," she said aloud.

"And a eunuch?" he added softly, a question in his eyes. "Who uses Jewish herbs and practices medicine on both men and women, and who asks a lot of questions." He touched her arm where her robe covered it, very lightly, barely enough for her to feel, and not on her skin, just as he would if she were a woman. Then he withdrew it and sat back.

She felt the horror surge through her and bring the sweat out on her body. Somewhere she had made mistakes, perhaps many. Who else knew she was a woman?

Seeing her fear and understanding it, he shook his head fractionally, still smiling. "No one," he said gently. "But you cannot hide everything, especially from an herbalist." His nostrils flared slightly. "I have a keener sense of smell than most men. I had sisters, and I have a wife."

She knew with a rage of embarrassment what he was referring to. It was her time of the month; in spite of her injuries it still came, and with it, of course, the warm, intimate odor of blood. She thought she had masked it.

"I will give you herbs which will keep you safe from others' suspicion, and perhaps ease the pain a little," he offered.

She could only nod. In spite of his kindness, she felt humiliated and deeply afraid.

Twenty

∽

WHEN ANNA NEXT VISITED CONSTANTINE, HIS SERVANT conducted her into the room with the icons, apparently unaware that Constantine himself was in the next room, deep in conversation with someone.

Anna walked to the farther end, hoping to be out of earshot, because whatever it concerned, confession or simply the arrangement of some ceremony, it was being said in the belief that it was private.

But as Constantine and the man walked slowly from the courtyard closer to the archway into the room, she could actually see the other man, whom she knew because she had once treated his mother. His name was Manuel Synopoulos; almost thirty, he was a rather brisk, confident young man of unusually plain appearance, but the family possessed great wealth, and he could at times be charming.

Now he pulled out of his dalmatica a soft leather pouch fat with coins and passed it to Constantine.

"For the feeding of the poor," he said quietly.

Constantine's reply was gentle, but there was a high, sharp note of excitement underneath it.

"Thank you. You are a good man and will be a noble addition to the Church, a great warrior in the cause of Christ."

"A captain," Synopoulos said, and as he turned he smiled.

Anna wouldn't admit to herself what had happened. It could not be that Constantine had just sold an office in the Church in return for money, even though he gave it all to the poor and more besides, just as Synopoulos had directed.

Manuel Synopoulos was no more a worthy priest, a man of God, than any young man who studied nothing, bought his way out of his mistakes, and took his pleasures where he wished and as his right.

His family would be grateful, and as long as the Greek Church stayed independent of Rome, a high office would bring in even more wealth. But far above money was the pride and the respect.

When Constantine did come to her, he looked elated, his face a little flushed.

"I have just received a new donation to the poor. We are gathering strength, Anastasius. Men are repenting of their sins, confessing and putting the past away. They will not join Rome but will fight beside us for the truth."

She forced an answering smile. "Good."

He heard the effort in her voice. "Is something wrong?"

"No," she lied, then knew he would not believe her. "It is simply that there is so far to go."

"We are gaining allies all the time. Now the Synopoulos are with us, and the Skleros have always been."

She wanted to ask at what cost, but she was not yet ready to challenge him. "I came about another matter, a patient I am concerned for. . . ." And she addressed the cause of her visit.

He listened patiently, but it was clear to Anna that his mind was still in the exhilaration of his achievement.

Anna found Zoe in her bedroom, lying on the great bed. Its tightly laced sheep-fleece mattress was covered with further goose-down ones and then clean, embroidered linen. It was so soft, Zoe had sunk into the depths in great comfort; still, she was tired and bad-tempered. Her lungs were congested, and she complained that it kept her from sleeping. She blamed Helena for having brought the affliction into the house.

"Then she is ill, too," Anna said. "I am sorry. Shall I take some herbs to her, also? Or does she prefer a . . . a more traditional physician?" It was a delicate way of asking if she would accept medicine rather than a priest's treatment by prayer and confession.

Zoe laughed harshly. "Don't mince words around me, Anastasius!" she snapped, sitting up a little farther against the pillows. "Helena is a coward. She will confess to anything trivial, and take the herbs if she likes them well enough, which I think you already know perfectly well. Isn't that what you do for most people—comfort their guilty consciences with the doctrine they expect, and then give them the medicine that actually treats the illness?"

It gave Anna a chill to realize Zoe saw through her so easily. She struggled for an answer. "Some people are more honest, others less," she equivocated.

"Well, Helena is less," Zoe said coldly. "Anyway, why do you care about her? I called you, she didn't. Is it because she's Bessarion's widow? You've been unusually curious about him from the beginning."

Lies would never work with Zoe. "Yes, I have," Anna said boldly. "From what I have heard, he was fervently against the union with Rome, and he was murdered for it. I care very strongly that we do not lose ourselves and all that we believe to what is in effect a conquest by deception. This seems to be surrender. I would rather be conquered still fighting."

Zoe propped herself up on her elbows. "Well, well. Such spirit! You would have been disappointed in Bessarion, I promise you." Her voice was laced with disgust. "He had less manhood than you have, God help you!"

"Then why bother to murder him?" Anna asked. "Or was it to replace him with someone better?"

Zoe stopped, remaining motionless on one elbow, even though it must have been uncomfortable. "Such as whom?" she asked.

Anna took the plunge. "Antoninus?" she said. "Or Justinian Lascaris? Some people are saying he was man enough for it. Did he not have the courage?" She was trying to sound casual, although her body was stiff and her hands rigid. She had said it to begin with merely as a spur to make Zoe deny it and perhaps give away more. Now the idea danced wildly in her mind as a possibility.

"You think I know?" That was a demand, and the edge of Zoe's voice was razor-sharp.

Anna held her gaze. "I would be very surprised if you didn't."

Zoe leaned back against her pillows, her rich, bright hair fanning out. "Of course I do. Bessarion was a fool. He trusted all sorts of people, and look where it got him! Esaias Glabas is charming, but a player of games, a manipulator. Only a fool needs to be loved, although it is pleasant, of course, and useful—but it is not necessary. Antoninus was loyal, a good right hand. Yes, Justinian was the only one with the brains, and the steel in his bones, to do it. Pity Bessarion was such a damn fool to drop his amulet in the cisterns. God knows what he was doing there anyway! I wish I did."

"In the cisterns?" Anna repeated, playing for time. "I thought Bessarion was supposed to have died at sea? Did someone steal the amulet?"

Zoe shrugged. "Who knows? It wasn't found until several days later, so perhaps the thief put it there."

"An amulet?" Anna asked. "What was it like?"

"Oh, it was Bessarion's," Zoe assured her. "Very Orthodox, but unimaginative. Rather a graceless thing, really. Justinian had one far better, and he wore it all the time. Still had it when they took him away."

"Really?" Anna could not control the wavering in her voice. "What was his like?"

Zoe stared at her. "St. Peter walking on the waves, and Christ holding out his hands to him," she answered, and for a moment there was emotion in her voice as well, a mixture of pain and wonder.

Anna knew it. It was the one Catalina had given him. It was a joke between them, gentle and very deep: a reference to the ultimate faith, the weakness it mastered, the love it extended. So Justinian still wore it. She must not cry in front of Zoe, but tears choked her throat.

"Justinian was dining with friends half a mile away," Zoe explained. "I presume that is why they suspected him of complicity. That, and the fact that it was the nets from his boat that Bessarion was found caught in and drowned."

"Bessarion's amulet could have got into the cisterns at any time," Anna argued. "When was it stolen?"

Zoe settled a little more against her pillows. "The night he was killed," she replied. "He wore it that day. Not only Helena said so, but his servants as well. She might lie, but they have not the sense to do so consistently, not all of them."

"Justinian! I thought . . ." Anna stopped, not knowing what to say. She was betraying herself. None of it was what she had wanted to hear. "What . . . what was this Justinian like?" She did not wish to know, but she could no longer avoid asking. She remembered him as he had been, how they had shared so much, in thought and passion almost mirror images.

"Justinian?" Zoe rolled the name over on her tongue. "Sometimes he made me laugh. He could be abrupt and single-minded, but he wasn't weak." Her wide mouth tightened. "I hate weakness! Never trust a weak person, Anastasius, man or woman—or eunuch. Never trust someone who needs to be approved of. When things get hard, they'll go with the winner, whatever they stand for. And don't trust someone who needs to be praised. They'll buy approval, regardless of the price." She lifted one long, slender finger. "Above all, don't trust someone who has no belief bigger than the comfort of not being alone. He'll sell his soul for what looks like love, whatever it really is." In the torchlight her face was hard and full of pain, as if she had stared at the first great disillusion.

"So whom do I trust?" Anna asked, forcing the same harsh humor into her own voice.

Zoe looked at her, taking in every line of her face, her eyes, her mouth, her hairless cheeks and soft throat. "Trust your enemies, if you know who they are. At least they'll be predictable. And don't look at me like that! I'm not your enemy—or your friend. And you will never predict me, because I'll do whatever I need to, of God or of the devil, to get what I want."

Anna believed her, but she did not say so.

Zoe saw it in her face and laughed.

Twenty-one

A NNA PUT AWAY THE HERBS INTO HER CASE, SAID A FEW
last words of advice to the patient, then excused herself.

"Thank you," Nicephoras said sincerely as she came out into the hall-
way. He had obviously been waiting for her. "Will Meletios recover?" The
concern was apparent in the slight strain in his voice. He was sending for
her more and more often lately.

"Oh yes," she said confidently, praying she was right. "His fever's broken. Just get him to drink, and then start him eating again soon, perhaps
tomorrow."

Nicephoras was clearly relieved. She had found him to be both com-
passionate and highly intelligent. She had become increasingly aware of a
loneliness in him to share the excitement of his knowledge. He not only
collected works of art, especially from antiquity, but even more he loved
the treasures of the mind and hungered to share them.

They walked together from the anteroom to one of the great galleries.
He guided her a little to the left. "Have you met John Beccus, the new patriarch?"

"No." She was interested and knew that it showed in her voice. This
was the calling that Constantine had wanted, even though he was obliged
to hide it.

"He is with the emperor now. If you wait a short while, I shall introduce you," Nicephoras offered.

"Thank you," she accepted quickly. They fell into conversation about art, moving into history and the events that had inspired certain styles, and from that into philosophy and religion. She found his views more liberal than she had expected, teasing her mind with new and broader ideas.

"I have just been reading some works by an Englishman named Roger Bacon," he said with intense enthusiasm. "I have never discovered a mind like his. He writes of mathematics, optics, alchemy, and the manufacture of a fine black powder which can explode"—he jerked his hands apart to demonstrate—"with great force, when it is ignited. The thought is exciting and terrifying. It could be used for immense good, and perhaps even greater evil." He looked at Anna's face to judge her appreciation of what he had said, the sheer intellectual excitement of it.

"He is an Englishman?" Anna repeated. "Did he discover this stuff, or invent it?"

"I don't know. Why?" Then he understood. "He is a Franciscan, not a crusader," he said quickly. "He has many practical ideas, such as how lenses could be ground and then assembled into a machine so that the tiniest objects could appear enormous, and you could see them quite clearly." His voice lifted again with the love of pure knowledge. "And other lenses so that objects miles distant could seem to be only yards away. Consider what that could do for the traveler, especially at sea. He is either one of the greatest geniuses in the world, or he lives in an ecstasy of madness."

She looked down, hating what she was thinking. "Perhaps he is a genius, and can see all these things, but is he wise? The two are not the same."

"I have no idea," Nicephoras answered gently. "What is it you are afraid of? Would it be bad to see things in the distance more clearly? He writes of being able to fix some of these lenses in a contraption so you could wear them on your nose, and those who cannot now see would be able to read." His voice rose with his excitement. "And he studies also the size, position, and paths of celestial bodies. He has worked out great theories on the movement of water, and how it could be used in machines to lift and carry things, and to create an engine that transforms steam into power which could drive ships across the sea, regardless of the wind or the oar! Imagine it."

"Can we make these things that explode?" she asked softly. "Machines that create steam to drive ships across the sea, without the wind in the sails, or men at the oars?" She could not rid herself of the fear of such things, the power it would give the nation that possessed them.

"I expect so." He frowned slightly, as if at the first touch of a chill. "Then we need not be prisoners of the wind."

She looked up at him. "The kings and princes of England come on crusade, don't they?" It was a statement. Everyone knew of Richard, known as the Lionheart, and of course more recently Prince Edward.

"You think they will use these things in war?" Nicephoras was pale now, his excitement bled away, leaving horror like an open wound.

"Would you trust them not to?"

"Bacon is a scientist, an inventor, a discoverer of the miracles of God in the universe." He shook his head. "He is not a man of war. His religion is one of wonder, the conquest of ignorance, not of lands."

"And perhaps he thinks all other men are the same," she said dryly, an edge of sarcasm in her tone. "I don't, do you?"

He was about to respond again when the door opened and John Beccus emerged from the emperor's presence. He was imposing, a gaunt and hatchet-faced man. He wore his magnificent robes with elegance, the silk tunic under a heavy, sweeping dalmatica. But far more than his mere physical presence, there was a power of emotion in him that commanded attention.

After acknowledging Anna, he looked at Nicephoras. "There will be a great deal to do," he said almost by way of an order. "We must have no more disturbances like that last miserable affair. Constantine seems incapable of controlling his adherents. Personally, I have doubts about his own loyalties." He frowned. "We must either persuade him, or silence him. The union must be carried through. You understand that? Independence is no longer a luxury we can afford. We must pay a certain price in order to avoid having to pay everything. Is that not obvious enough? The survival of both church and state are tied to the issue."

He chopped his large-knuckled hand savagely in the air, his rings gleaming. "If Charles of Anjou invades—and make no mistake, if we are separate from Rome he will—then it will be the end of Byzantium. Our people will be decimated, exiled to who knows where? And without our churches, our city, our culture, how will the faith survive?"

"I know that, Your Grace," Nicephoras answered gravely, his face pale. "Either we yield something now, or everything later. I have spoken to Bishop Constantine, but he believes that faith is our best shield, and I cannot shake him from that."

A shadow crossed Beccus's high face, and a flash of arrogance. "Fortunately, the emperor sees the stakes even more clearly than I do," he replied. "And he will save every jot he can, whether some of our more naive religious orders can see that or not." He made an almost cursory sign of the cross and swept away in a swirl of jewel-encrusted robes, the light flickering on him as if it were fire.

Walking away from the palace and back down the hill toward her own house, the wind in her face, Anna thought hard about the passions and the issues she had heard, both from Nicephoras and from the new patriarch.

There was ruthlessness in John Beccus she had not expected, yet she realized that without it he would be useless. Maybe she had been too emotional and simplistic in her judgment? Constantine might need to be just as devious to succeed, just as willing to use all the weapons he could reach.

And what of this Englishman who could see for miles, drive ships without wind or oar, and, perhaps worst of all, create a powder that exploded? Whose hands might that fall into? Charles of Anjou? If Nicephoras knew of it, who else did?

Now murder did not seem so unlikely, to get rid of both Bessarion and Justinian by murdering one and contriving that the other should be blamed for it. Antoninus might be incidental, not an intended victim at all. She shivered as she realized how much more likely it was that whoever had done this, one person or several, had actually intended Justinian to be the one executed.

When she knew just a little more, she must find a way to ask Nicephoras about the trial of Justinian and Antoninus. As one of the most intimate advisers of the emperor, he had to know. There was no office of prosecutor. The emperor himself was regarded as "living law," and his word was final, as to both verdict and punishment. Michael had chosen to execute one man and yet only exile the other.

The punishment of Justinian and Antoninus not only would get rid of them from the scene, but would also frighten and confuse any other conspirators against union, leaving only Constantine and the leaderless masses who were against every disturbance and change.

Who was the real killer? A betrayer among them, an infiltrator or intruder? Even an agent provocateur on Michael's behalf? It would be understandable. The emperor was embattled on all sides, surrounded by ambition, bigotry, religious fanaticism. Yet he alone was responsible to make the final decisions for his people's survival, not only in the world, but perhaps in heaven also.

Twenty-two

ANNA CONTINUED TO WATCH AND LISTEN, BUT THE AN-
swer was always the same: She needed to know more about the
people surrounding Bessarion in the last years of his life. Perhaps the
women he had known might reveal more to her; she would certainly understand them better. Naturally she did not say this to Zoe when she visited her to offer her some new and interesting herbs, but she did ask her
help in widening her practice.

Her reward came a week later, when Zoe asked her to call again. This
time she was shown into a different room from the one in which she was
usually received. This was more formal and beautiful in a traditional way.
There was nothing here that seemed to reveal Zoe's character, as if in this
part of the house she received people whom she wished to keep at arm's
length.

Helena was there, exquisitely dressed in dark wine red set with jewels.
Her hair was ornamented and gleamed like black silk. Clearly she was no
longer in mourning. She watched Anna with an interest devoid of kindness.

There was another, older woman present of commanding demeanor, as
different from Zoe as possible. She was barely of average height and
uniquely ugly. Her expensively embroidered blue green dalmatica could not
disguise her wide, bony, almost masculine shoulders or her lack of bosom.
Her broad nose was too strong for her face. Her light eyes were brilliant with
intelligence, and her mouth was delicate but without sensuality.

Zoe introduced her as Eirene Vatatzes, and only then, when she smiled, did she momentarily possess an illusion of loveliness. Then it was gone.

With her was a tall young man. His long, dark face was not quite handsome but held a promise of considerable power to come, perhaps in ten years' time when he was in his late forties. He was a startling contrast to Eirene, and Anna was surprised when he was introduced as her son, Demetrios.

They spoke politely of trivial matters until finally Zoe mentioned that she had been badly burned in an accident. She told how Anna had healed her, holding out her arm to display the unblemished skin for Eirene's appreciation. She also looked at Helena with a flash of amusement that was very easy for Anna to read.

From then on, the conversation was less comfortable. Helena was sharp, walking across the room with an exaggeratedly graceful movement as if to display her youth in front of the two older women. She did not even glance at Demetrios, but she might as well have stared at him. It was for his attention; she clearly did not care in the least what Anna thought of her. She passed by her as if she barely existed.

Suddenly, Anna found the muted blues of her own tunic and the necessity of her eunuch mannerisms more than usually imprisoning. She felt as if she stood on the edge of the room like a cipher, while the exchanges, spoken and unspoken, passed in front of her. Did all eunuchs feel like this? Did a woman as unlovely as Eirene Vatatzes feel a little of the same thing?

She saw Zoe looking at her with bright, clever eyes. Too much understanding.

The conversation turned to religion, as sooner or later every conversation in Byzantium did. Helena had no particular faith, which was clear from her manner as much as her words. She was beautiful, physically very immediate, but there was no soul in her. Anna could see that, but was it invisible to a man?

She listened to them, averting her eyes slightly so as not to be noticed.

"Very tedious," Zoe said with a shrug. "But it all comes to money, in the end." She was looking at Eirene.

Helena looked from her mother to Eirene and back again. "With Bessarion, it was the faith, pure and simple," she contradicted.

Eirene's face flickered with impatience, but she kept it in check. "To organize a faith and keep it alive you need a Church, and to keep a Church you need money, my dear." The words were gentle, even affectionate, but there was a condescension in them of the highly intelligent to the intellectually shallow. "And to defend a city we need both faith and armaments. Since the Venetians stole our relics we have far fewer pilgrims, even since our return in 1262. And most of the silk trade has gone to Arabia, Egypt, and Venice. Trade may be tedious to you, and perhaps to many of those who buy the artifacts, the games, and the fabrics. Perhaps you find blood messy, it smells ugly, it soils the linen, it attracts flies—but try living without it."

Helena wrinkled her nose in slight revulsion at the simile, but she did not dare argue.

Amusement flashed in Zoe's eyes. "Eirene understands finances better than most men do," she observed, not entirely with kindness. "In fact, I have sometimes wondered if Theodorus Doukas really runs the Treasury, or if it is you, most discreetly, of course."

Eirene smiled, a faint flush in her sallow cheeks. Anna had the sudden thought that there was much truth in Zoe's remark, and the fact that she perceived it was not entirely displeasing to Eirene.

Conspicuously, Helena said nothing.

Anna became aware that Zoe was watching her, half smiling.

"Do we bore you with our talk of doctrine and politics?" Zoe asked her. "Perhaps we should ask Demetrios for some tales of his Varangian Guard? Colorful men, from all sorts of barbarous places. Lands where the sun shines at midnight in the summer, and it is dark all winter long."

"One or two of them," Demetrios agreed. "Others are from Kiev, or Bulgaria, or the principalities of the Danube, or the Rhine."

Zoe shrugged. "You see?"

Anna felt herself blushing. She had not been listening. "I was thinking," she lied. "Realizing how much I still have to learn of politics."

"Well, if you've learned that, I suppose you have achieved something," Helena said waspishly.

Zoe did not hide her laughter, but there was a crackle of ice in her voice when she turned to Helena. "Your tongue is sharper than your mind, my dear," she said softly. "Anastasius knows how to dissemble, and mask his intelligence with humility. You would do well to learn the same trick. It is not always wise to appear clever." She blinked. "Even if you were."

Eirene smiled, then instantly looked away, and the moment after,

Anna found her bright, clear eyes fixed steadily on her, curious and interested.

Helena was talking again, looking at Demetrios.

Antoninus might have loved her because he alone could find the tenderness in her. Anna had no idea what they might have shared. Helena might suffer alone now, not daring to let anyone else see, least of all her mother or this other clever, ugly woman who carried such hurt in her face.

Anna looked across to where Helena was standing with Demetrios. She was smiling, and he appeared self-conscious.

"He is beginning to look like his father," Zoe observed, glancing sideways at Eirene, then back at Demetrios. "Have you heard from Gregory lately?" she continued.

"Yes," Eirene said tersely.

Anna saw that she stiffened, her body becoming more angular just in the way she stood.

Zoe seemed amused. "Is he still in Alexandria? I see no reason for him to remain there now. Or does he believe we are going to be decimated by the Latins again? I never knew him to care a jot about the intricacies of religion."

"Really?" Eirene said with raised eyebrows, her brilliant eyes ice cold. "But then perhaps you did not know him nearly as well as you imagined."

The color was brighter in Zoe's cheeks. "Perhaps not," she agreed. "We had some wonderful conversations, but I cannot recall that they were ever about religion." She smiled.

"Hardly the circumstances conducive to matters of the spirit," Eirene agreed. She turned to look at Demetrios again. "Yes, he does look like his father," she said. "A pity you did not have a son . . . by any of your . . . lovers."

Zoe's face tightened as if she had been slapped. "I would not advise allowing Demetrios to admire Helena too much," she said softly, in little more than a whisper. "It could be . . . unfortunate."

Eirene lost the last trace of blood from beneath her skin. She stared at Zoe, then turned with a freezing look to Anna. "It is agreeable to make your acquaintance, Anastasius, but I shall not be availing myself of your services. I do not put potions on my face in a desperate attempt to cling to youth, and fortunately my health is excellent, as is my conscience. Should it not be, I have my own physician to consult. A Christian one. I have heard that you use Jewish remedies on occasion. I prefer not to. I am sure you will understand, especially in these strange and disloyal times." Without waiting for Anna to reply, Eirene nodded briefly to Zoe and took her leave, Demetrios following after her.

Helena looked at her mother, appeared to consider picking a quarrel over the issue, and decided better of it. "So much for your further clientele," she said to Anna. "I don't know what you were hoping for, but Mother seems to have made it impossible." She smiled brightly. "You will have to seek your business elsewhere."

Anna excused herself also and left. There had been no possible retaliation she could afford to make, dearly as she would have liked to.

She spent a long evening turning over and over in her mind what bound these people together who seemed to have so little in common. Anna could not believe it was faith, but it could perhaps be hatred of Rome.

The following morning was Sunday, and she walked alone to the Hagia Sophia to attend the Mass. She wanted to be where neither Simonis nor Leo could see her or question her mood. Perhaps the glory of the building and the power of the familiar words would comfort her, remind her of the certainties that mattered.

On the steps almost in the shadow of the dome, she nearly bumped into Zoe. It was impossible to avoid her without being both rude and slightly absurd.

"Ah, Anastasius," Zoe said blandly. "How are you? I apologize for Eirene's odd manners. She is a woman of peculiar moods. Perhaps you could treat her for it? She would benefit greatly." She fell into step beside Anna as they moved toward the Tarsus doors. "As would all those around her," she added.

Once they entered the building, it was as if Anna had ceased to exist. Zoe was as wrapped in the intensity of her thoughts as she was in the dark folds of her robe. Zoe stepped to one side, at the tomb of Doge Enrico Dandolo. A look of scalding hate filled her face; her eyes narrowed, and her lips curled into a snarl. Her body clenched, and she spat violently onto the cursed name. Then, chin high, she moved away.

Without looking to left or right, she went straight to one of the outer colonnades of arches and found an icon of the Virgin. She stood before it with her head bowed.

Anna was a little to the left of her and saw her face, eyes closed, mouth soft, and lips slightly parted, as though she breathed in the essence of a holy place. Anna believed she prayed quite genuinely, several times repeating the same words over and over.

Anna looked at the Madonna holding her child, the calm joy radiating from her face more than from the gold of the mosaic creator's art. There was something purely human in it, a power of the spirit to which she had been a witness.

Anna felt it like an ache within herself for something forever lost, a grief for what could not be. And she felt guilt because she herself had given it away, not in generosity or sacrifice, but in fury and in a revulsion so savage that she had allowed it to possess her. Was there forgiveness for that? She left, tears spilling hot on her face, all but choking her.

As she passed the tomb of Enrico Dandolo on the way out, she saw a man there, a cloth in his hand, carefully wiping away the spittle where Zoe, and others, had vented their hatred. He stopped and looked up at her, his dark eyes finding hers, recognizing the pain but puzzled.

Another woman walked past and, disregarding him, spat on the tomb.

He turned back to it and began patiently cleaning it again.

Anna stood and watched. His hands were beautiful, strong and slender, working as if nothing had happened.

She regarded his face, knowing he was unaware of her, set on his task. There was power in the line of his bones, vulnerability in his mouth. She would like to think he could laugh, quickly, easily if the wit was good, but there was nothing of ease in him now, only an intense loneliness.

Anna felt it also, an ache inside her almost beyond bearing, because outwardly she was neither man nor woman, only a solitary person loved perhaps only by God—but not yet forgiven by Him.

Twenty-three

GIULIANO DANDOLO WALKED OUT INTO THE LIGHT, AL-
most unaware of the heat of the sun on the stones or the glare. This
was only the second time he had been inside the Hagia Sophia. Around
the base of the vast central dome was a ring of high windows, and the light
poured in, making the whole interior like the heart of some great jewel
burning with its own fire.

He was used to the veneration of the Virgin Mary, but this was a different kind of femininity; holy wisdom as a woman was a strange concept
to him. Surely wisdom was unwavering light, anything but feminine?

Then he had seen the tomb of Enrico Dandolo, soiled with spittle, and
stood in front of it confused by loyalty and shame, both tearing at him in
the same moment. Since coming here, he had learned far more about the
looting of the city on the last crusade. It was the doge Enrico Dandolo
who had been personally responsible for taking the four great bronze
horses that now adorned St. Mark's Cathedral in Venice. He also had
taken first choice among the holiest of the relics stolen, including the vial
of Christ's blood, one of the nails from the Cross, the gold-encased cross
that Constantine the Great had carried into battle with him, and much
more besides. Yet Enrico had been his great-grandfather. He was part of
Giuliano's history, good or bad.

As he had stood by the tomb, another person had walked past and spat
on the plaque inlaid on the floor. This time Giuliano had come deter-

mined to clean it, even if only for a few moments, until the next violation.

The person who had watched him today had awoken a different feeling in him. He had seen eunuchs before, but they still made him uncomfortable. He had recognized without question what he was. It was nothing of the man's gender that disturbed him; it was the pain in his eyes and in the lines of his mouth. For a moment Giuliano, a complete stranger, had looked inside him at a raw and terrible wound.

Why did Giuliano clean the plaque over the tomb? He had never known his great-grandfather; there were no memories, no personal stories. It was only because the name on it was Dandolo. It was someone to whom he could belong, a tie to the past that had nothing to do with the Byzantine mother who had not wanted him.

He left the church and walked rapidly, as if following a known path, yet he had no distinct idea except to climb upward to where he could look out over the sea. Always he went toward light on the water and the limitless horizon, as if in looking at it, he might free his mind.

What had he expected to find when he came here to Constantinople at last? A city alien to him, too Eastern, too decadent, so he could hate it and return to Venice having exorcised it from his heart. That was it. So he could think of his mother with indifference and recognize nothing of her in himself.

He came to a small place, a side turning off the path, just large enough for two or three people to stand and stare at the shifting patterns of current and wind as the tide swept through the narrows between Europe and Asia. It looked like the brushstrokes of an artist, except that it moved. It was a living thing, as though it had a pulse. The air was a breath on his skin, warm and clean, a little salt.

The city below him was like Venice and yet so unlike. The architecture was lighter in Venice, yet there were echoes in it of this. There was the same teeming vitality and trade, always trade, the eye for a bargain, the weighing of value, buying and selling. And there was the same knowledge of the sea in all its moods: subtle, dangerous, beautiful, boundless with chance and possibility.

Yet the similarities were superficial. He did not belong here. No one really knew him except in brief friendship, such as Andrea Mocenigo, who had allowed him to become so much a part of his family. But that was kindness. They would have done the same for anyone. Being a stranger in Constantinople gave Giuliano a freedom to grow, to change if he wished to, to embrace new ideas, no matter how wild or foolish.

Belonging was safety, but it was also constriction. Not belonging was boundless, as if his feet knew no weight and his horizons were endless. But he had no roots, either, and at unexpected moments there was a loneliness that was almost unbearable.

He could not clear from his mind the passion and grief on the face of the eunuch who had watched him in the Hagia Sophia. There was a tenderness in it that haunted him.

He must finish collecting and assessing his information for the doge and return home.

When finally his first officer returned, Giuliano was ready to leave. He had all the information he needed. At least he thought so, although even as he said good-bye to Mocenigo and his family and carried his chest out to the waiting cart, a doubt stirred in him that again he was escaping. Did the feeling of completion come from his finishing his task here for the doge? Or was it that he had satisfied his own thirst for knowledge—and rejected Byzantium?

He put it from his mind. He was returning home.

The voyage was swift, and by mid-August he stood on the deck gazing at the skyline of the city that seemed to float on the face of the lagoon. Byzantium was a bright memory like the colors of a mosaic in someone else's ceiling: touched with gold, but too far away to see clearly. Only an impression remained on his mind in a multitude of facets, tiny and beautiful—and beyond his reach.

It was 1275. In Rome, Pope Gregory X arranged a one-year-long truce between Emperor Michael Palaeologus of Byzantium and Charles of Anjou, king of the Two Sicilies. Anna never learned how much the papal legate in Constantinople had had to do with that.

Twenty-four

∾

GIULIANO DOCKED IN THE OUTER HARBOR, INTENDING to make his way to his own home just off the Grand Canal. First he would wash and change his clothes, rest a little, then eat a good meal in one of the cafés—something different from shipboard fare. After that he would report to the doge. He would probably have to wait some time for an audience.

However, he had barely stepped beyond the dock when he overheard hushed voices speculating as to who the next doge would be.

"Is the doge ill?" he demanded, pulling at the man's shoulder to gain his attention.

The man turned, regarding his travel-stained seaman's britches with pity. "Just landed?" he asked. "Yes, friend, it is feared he will not last long. If you have news for him, you'd better give it now."

Giuliano thanked him and, with a hollow sense of loss gnawing at him, made his way as quickly as he could to the Doge's Palace. Received by somber servants, he was told in a quiet voice to wait until he was called.

He paced back and forth from sunlight to shadow under the long windows, his feet whispering on the marble, the sound of muted voices beyond the door. Finally he was called in and told by a grim-faced, elderly man in black doublet and stockings that he must be brief.

The doge's bedroom had the stale, sharp smell of illness and the watchful gloom of those who have urgent tasks to perform but want to seem as if they have all the time in the world.

Tiepolo lay propped against pillows, his cheeks sunken, his eyes hollow.

"Giuliano!" he said hoarsely. "Come! Tell me about Charles of Anjou, and the Sicilians. Will they rise, do you think? How is Byzantium? What of the Venetians there? Whose side will they be on if there is another invasion? Tell me the truth, good or bad."

Giuliano smiled at him and put his hand over the old man's frail fingers where they rested on the sheet. "I wasn't going to lie," he said so quietly that he hoped the others in the room would not hear him. This last conversation between them should have the dignity of not being overheard, so it could include all that either of them wished to say.

"Well?" Tiepolo asked.

As briefly as he could, Giuliano told him his opinion of Charles of Anjou and the differences he could see between his rule in Naples and that in Sicily and the corresponding reactions of the subject peoples.

"Good." Tiepolo smiled faintly. "So you think Sicily could be made to rise against him, if the circumstances were right?"

"Certainly they hate him, but that will be a long way from rebellion."

"Possibly." Tiepolo's voice was weak. "Now tell me about Constantinople."

"I loved it and hated it," Giuliano answered, remembering the soaring thoughts, the turmoil of ideas, the drowning pain of rejection.

"Of course," Tiepolo said with a faint smile. "What did you love, Giuliano?"

"The freedom of ideas," he replied. "The sense of being at the crossroads of East and West. The adventure of the mind."

Tiepolo nodded. "And you loved the parts that were like Venice, and hated them because of your mother." His eyes were gentle in spite of his own pain.

Giuliano picked up the thread of his mission. "None of them want war," he said urgently. "Not the Byzantines and not the Venetians there—or the Genoese or the Jews or the Muslims. They'll never hold off a crusader army, but I fear that most will fight to protect their own, and die with it."

Tiepolo sighed. "Never trust the pope, Giuliano, not this pope or any other. They have no love for Venice, not as you and I do. There are turbulent times ahead. Charles of Anjou wants to be king of Jerusalem, and he will bathe the Holy Land in blood to do it." His blue-veined hand tightened on the sheet. "Venice must keep its freedom, never forget that. Never give it up, to anyone, emperor or pope. We stand alone." His voice sank a little lower, and Giuliano had to lean forward to hear him. "Promise me that."

There was no choice. The hand on the sheet was cold when he placed his own over it. The pull of Byzantium was strong, the world was full of danger, enticement, and promise, but this man had nurtured him after his own father had died. A man who forsook his debts was worth nothing. Venice was the cradle of his heart. "Of course I promise," Giuliano answered.

Tiepolo smiled for an instant, then the light faded from his eyes and he did not blink again.

Giuliano felt a prickling in his throat and a tightness inside him so he could barely breathe. It was like his father's death repeated, the beginning of a new loneliness that would go on forever. He slipped his hand off the old man's and stood up slowly, turning to face the shadowed room.

The physician looked at him and understood. Giuliano found his throat too tight to speak, and he refused to embarrass himself. He nodded his thanks and walked past them, outside into the cool, marble-floored anteroom and then into the hall.

Tiepolo's funeral was a magnificent occasion, too profound for the clatter of words to intrude on. The day was misty and suffocatingly hot, with a fine summer rain drifting like streamers of silk as the black-ribboned barge moved slowly and almost soundlessly along the Grand Canal, seeming already a ghost ship.

The way was lined with people, either on balconies above the water or in small boats tucked in well to the sides to allow the procession and the mourners to pass on their way from the Doge's Palace through the city, then back again as far as the Rialto Bridge, then through the smaller canals more directly to the Cathedral of Saint Mark, almost where they began.

Giuliano came in the first boat behind it, not in the prow—he was not family—but toward the stern. He stood watching the high facades of the buildings and the pale, rain-dappled light on the water, blurring the images. He was intensely alone, in spite of Pietro only a few yards away. In the death of a leader was the passing of an age, and they were both indissolubly bound in something unique and as deep as blood or bone.

They moved through silver bars of weak sunlight that struck the canal's face into luminescence and made the barge ahead momentarily stark, oars shining. Then the shadows closed over again, and colors faded. There was no sound but the swirl and dip of water.

A week later, he sat over wine again with Pietro. They had spent the day out in the lagoon talking, remembering, watching the sunset colors touch the facades of the palaces opposite, making them seem to float on the face of the water, insubstantial as a dream. Now they were sitting, wet-footed, a little cold, in one of their favorite taverns off a small canal five hundred yards from the Church of San Zamipolo.

Giuliano stared moodily into his glass. He liked red wine, and this one was good. He was quite aware that he was drinking too much. The heat clung like damp cloth, and his thirst was never quenched.

"I imagine they are choosing the inquisori to go through all his acts and pass judgment," he said angrily.

"They always do," Pietro responded, taking more wine himself. "They'll have to find something to complain about. Or people will say they aren't doing their jobs. You can't win."

"What could he do wrong, for God's sake?" Giuliano demanded angrily. "They kept him under surveillance all the time! He couldn't open dispatches from foreign powers without them peering over his shoulder and reading behind him."

Pietro laughed. "It's human nature. Venetians will always be pulling someone apart. Be glad he wasn't a pope." He grinned suddenly. "They dug one of them up and hanged the poor sod. Ambrosius the Second, I think. Twice! Buried him, then a flood in the river uncovered the grave and washed him away, or something of the sort. All after a proper trial, of course. Didn't matter the accused was a corpse, God rest his soul."

Pietro put his empty glass on the table. "Do you want to go down to the canal near the arsenal tomorrow night? I know a great café where the wine is excellent and the women are young, rounded in all the right places, and smooth-skinned."

"You make them sound like something to eat," Giuliano said, but the idea appealed to him. Easy pleasure, music, a little anonymous kindness with no obligation, no one to hurt or be hurt by. And Pietro was good company, kind and funny, and he never complained. "Yes," he agreed. "Why not?"

The process for electing a new doge was vastly complicated. It had been instituted by Tiepolo himself, in the year of his accession. It was intended to reduce the power of the great families who had led the city from the reign of the first doge five hundred years before. Giuliano wondered if Tiepolo had had the Dandolo in mind specifically.

In the end, when all the due process had been filled to the letter, a new doge was duly elected. He was Jacopo Contarini, an octogenarian cousin of Pietro's.

A week later, he sent for Giuliano.

He was uncomfortable going to the Doge's Palace and finding someone else in Tiepolo's place. The halls and corridors were just the same, the marble columns, the pattern of sunlight streaming through the windows onto the floor. Even the servants had not changed except for a few of the most personal. It was probably right that the sense of continuity be so powerful, but it made him painfully aware that Venice was so much larger than the individual men who were its life.

"Come in, Dandolo," Contarini said formally, still unused to his office, although he may well have coveted it most of his life.

"My lord," Giuliano replied, bowing and waiting until he was told to relax. This was not Tiepolo. To this new doge he meant nothing.

"You have recently returned from Constantinople," Contarini said with interest. "Tell me what you learned. I know Doge Tiepolo sent you, God rest him. What is your judgment of the emperor Michael, and of the king of the Two Sicilies?"

"The emperor Michael is a clever and subtle man," Giuliano answered. "A strong soldier, but without the navy he needs to defend from a sea attack. The city is recovering slowly. They are still poor, and it will be a long time before trade brings in the kind of wealth they need to rebuild the sea defenses sufficiently to withstand another assault."

"And the king of the Two Sicilies?" Contarini pressed.

Giuliano remembered Charles of Anjou with sharp clarity and told the doge how as king he lacked the loyalty of his people.

Contarini nodded. "Indeed. And did Doge Tiepolo tell you his reasons for seeking this information?"

"A crusade by Charles would require a vast fleet, and either we or the Genoese will build it. If the crusade should succeed, the spoils will be enormous. Not as rich as in 1204, because there are not so many treasures left, but still well worth the taking. We should make a contract now, and secure the wood we will need. It will be far beyond our usual purchase."

Contarini smiled. "Tell me, did Tiepolo assume that a contract made with Charles of Anjou would be kept?"

"It would be to his advantage to do so. Charles would not wish to make an enemy of Venice until after he has conquered Byzantium, Jerusalem, and possibly Antioch. And we have long memories for an injury," Giuliano answered.

The smile reached Contarini's eyes. "Very good. And your time in Constantinople?"

"To consider the mood and the loyalties of the Venetians and Genoese there, Excellency. There are many of them, mostly in the harbor areas."

Contarini nodded. "And would they be with us or against us?"

"Those who are now married to Byzantines might find their loyalties torn. And there are surprisingly many."

"To be expected." Contarini nodded. "In time I will send you to look again, to keep me informed. First I would like you to go to France and secure wood for us. You will need to make careful bargains. We do not wish to be committed, and then learn that the crusade is delayed, or worse, canceled. The situation is lightly balanced." His smile lost its warmth. "I need you to be very precise, Dandolo. Do you understand me?"

"Yes, Excellency." He did understand, but oddly the sense of excitement had died away. It was a good task, necessary. It could not be given to a man whose skill or whose loyalty was not absolute. Yet it was also impersonal. There was none of the fire he had shared with Tiepolo.

Giuliano took his leave and went out into the sun in the piazza. The light off the water was as clean and bright as always, but it was cold.

Twenty-five

PALOMBARA AND VICENZE ARRIVED BACK IN ROME IN January 1276. They had been at sea for nineteen days and were both glad to make landfall at last, even though they knew that it was a race to report to the pope, which of course they would do separately, neither knowing what the other would say.

Two days later, when the messenger finally came to conduct Palombara to the pope's presence, they walked together along the street and across the windy square, robes swirling. Palombara tried to think of anything he could ask the man that would tell him if Vicenze had already been or not, but every question sounded ridiculously transparent. He ended by walking the entire distance in silence.

His Holiness Gregory X looked tired, even in the quiet sunlight of his room and the magnificence of his robes. He had an irritating cough, which he tried to mask. After the usual ritual of greeting he went straight to the subject, as if short of time. Or perhaps he had already seen Vicenze, and this was merely a courtesy to Palombara and of no more meaning than that.

"You have done well, Enrico," he said gravely. "We did not expect that such a great undertaking as the unity of all Christendom could be achieved without difficulty, and some loss of life among the most obdurate."

Palombara knew instantly that Vicenze had already been here and reported a greater success than in fact they had had.

He had a sudden acute sense that the man opposite him was weighed down beyond his ability to bear. There were heavy shadows in his face. Was that repetitive cough more than a cold come with the beginning of winter?

"There are too many people whose reputation, and all the honor or power they have, lies in their allegiance to the Orthodox Church," Palombara replied. "One cannot claim divine guidance and then change one's mind." He wished to smile at the irony of it, but he saw no glimpse of humor in Gregory's eyes, only indecision and a coming darkness. It frightened him, because it was one more piece of evidence that even the pope did not have that bright certainty of God that surely came with true sanctity. Palombara saw only a tired man searching for the best of many resolutions, none of them complete.

"The resistance is mostly among the monks," Palombara continued. "And high clergy whose offices will no longer exist once the center of power has moved here to Rome. And there are the eunuchs. There is no place for them in the Roman Church. They have much to lose, and as they see it, nothing to gain."

Gregory frowned. "Can they cause us trouble? Palace servants? Churchmen without . . ." He shrugged slightly and coughed again. "Without temptation of the flesh, and therefore without the possibility of true holiness. Is it not better for all that their species die out?"

Intellectually, Palombara agreed with him. The mutilation repelled him, and if he thought about it in detail, it frightened him. Yet when he had said the word *eunuch,* he had been thinking of Nicephoras, the wisest and most cultured man he had encountered at Michael's court. And of Anastasius, who was even more effeminate; there was nothing manly about him at all. Anastasius's intelligence, and even more the fire of his emotions, had caught Palombara in a way he could not dismiss. In spite of his loss of manhood, the healer had a passion for life that Palombara had never felt. He both pitied and envied him, and the contradiction of it was disturbing.

"It is an offense, a denial, Holy Father," he agreed. "And yet they have merit, even if their abstinence is enforced. I doubt it is of their own choosing in most cases, so there can be no blame. . . ."

Gregory's expression hardened in the pale winter sun slanting in through the windows. "If a child is not baptized, it is not the child's choosing, Enrico, yet it is still lost to Paradise. Be careful when you make such sweeping statements. You tread on delicate ground where doctrine is concerned. We do not question the judgments of God."

Palombara felt a chill. It was not the warning or the chastisement, it was far deeper than that. It was the denial of passion, of certainty, of knowing everything was perfectly and brilliantly true, beautiful to the mind and the soul, as the things of God should be. Did he know an unbaptized child was lost to Paradise? He knew that was taught, but was it by God? Or was it by man, in order to enlarge the flock and therefore the power of the Church, ultimately their own dominion?

How did Gregory, and the Church, conceive of God? Were they creating Him in their own image, essentially shallow, seeking more and more praise, obedience, purchased by fear of damnation? Was man seeking anything beyond himself, not curtailed by the boundaries of his own imagination?

Who dared beyond that, crashing alone into the bright, silent world of . . . what? Infinite light? Or just a white void?

Palombara knew now, in this beautiful winter-pale room in the Vatican, that in his soul he believed that Gregory had no more idea than he had, simply no desire or compulsion to ask.

"I apologize, Holy Father," he said contritely, sorry for having disheartened an old man whose life hung upon his certainties. "I spoke hastily, because I gained respect for the wisdom of some of the eunuchs at the emperor's court, and I would exclude no one from the saving grace of truth. I fear we have much work yet to do in Byzantium before we win any loyalty deeper than the fear of our physical violence toward them if they fail."

"Fear can be the beginning of wisdom," Gregory pointed out. He looked up suddenly and met Palombara's eyes. He saw the skepticism in them, and possibly something of the darkness inside.

Palombara nodded in acquiescence.

"But I have other plans to discuss," Gregory said with sudden vigor. "The momentum is building for a new crusade, without the bloodshed of the past. I have decided to write to the emperor Michael inviting him to meet us in Brindisi next year. I will be able to speak to him, make better judgments of his strength, and his sincerity, and perhaps allay some of his fears." He waited for Palombara's reaction.

"Admirable, Holy Father," he said with as much enthusiasm as he could put into his voice. "It will stiffen his resolve, and perhaps you will be able to suggest to him ways in which he can deal with his bishops of the old faith, and still retain their loyalty. He will be grateful to you, as will the Byzantine people. More important than that, of course, it is the right thing to do."

Gregory smiled, quite clearly pleased with the response. "I am glad you see it so clearly, Enrico. I fear not everyone will."

Palombara wondered instantly if Vicenze had argued. That would have been daring of him, or, more likely, simply highly insensitive. Had he seen Gregory's failing health and already changed his allegiance? Perhaps Vicenze had information Palombara did not; otherwise it would be out of character. He never took risks.

"Others will understand in time, Holy Father," Palombara said, despising the hypocrisy in himself.

"Yes indeed." Gregory pursed his lips. "But we have much to do to prepare." He leaned forward a little. "We need all Italy with us, Enrico. There is much money to raise, and of course men, horses, armor, machines of war. And food, and ships. I have legates in all the capitals of Europe, and Venice will come because there is so much profit in it for them, as there always has been. Naples and the south will have no choice, because Charles of Anjou will see to it. It is the cities of Tuscany, Umbria, and the Regno that concern me."

In spite of his desire to be impervious to the fires of ambition, Palombara felt a flutter of excitement inside himself. "Yes, Holy Father. . . ."

"Begin with Florence," Gregory said. "It is rich. There is a stirring of life and thought there that will reward us well, if we nurture it. They are loyal to us. Then I want you to seek out what support we have in Arezzo. That will be harder, I know. Their loyalties are to the Holy Roman Emperor. But you have proved your mettle in Byzantium." He smiled bleakly. "I know what you have told me of Michael Palaeologus, Enrico, and I am not as blind as your tact imagines. I know what you have not told me, by virtue of your silences. Go, and report back to me by the middle of January."

"Yes, Holy Father," Palombara said with an enthusiasm he could not conceal. "Yes, I will."

.   .   .

On the last night before leaving Florence, Palombara dined with his old friend Alighiero de Belincione and Lapa, the woman he had lived with since the death of his wife. They had two small children, Francesco and Gaetana, and Alighiero's son Dante, from his previous marriage.

As always, they made Palombara feel welcome, gave him excellent food, and afterward sat around the fire and brought him up-to-date on all the latest news and gossip.

They were fascinated by Palombara's experiences in Constantinople. Lapa wished to hear all about the court of Michael, particularly the fashions and the food. Alighiero was more interested in the spices and silks in the market and the artifacts to be purchased from the fabled cities farther east along the old Silk Road.

They were discussing the life of those who traveled it when a boy came into the room, tentatively at first, knowing he was interrupting. He was about ten years old, slender, almost thin; the bones of his shoulders were visible even through his winter jerkin. But it was his face that held Palombara's attention. He was pale and his features were already losing the softness of the child, and his eyes burned with a passion that seemed almost to consume him.

Lapa looked at him with anxiety. "Dante, you missed supper. Let me get you something now." She half rose to her feet.

Alighiero put out his hand to restrain her. "He'll eat when he's hungry. Don't worry so much."

She brushed him away. "He needs to eat every day. Dante, let me present you to Bishop Palombara, from Rome, then I'll make you something."

Alighiero sat back again, probably in deference to Palombara, rather than have a disagreement in front of him, which would have been embarrassing.

"Welcome to Florence, Your Grace," the boy said politely.

Palombara looked into his eyes and saw in them an emotion so powerful that it seemed to light him from within, and Palombara had a sudden conviction that he himself scarcely impinged upon the boy's world. He wanted to make some mark on this extraordinary child.

"Thank you, Dante," he replied. "I have already been given the hospitality of friends, and there is no greater gift of welcome than that."

Now Dante looked at him, then he smiled. For an instant Palombara was real to him, it was there in his eyes.

"Come," Lapa said, standing. "I will make you something to eat. I have a little of your favorite caramel." She led the way out of the room, and with a brief glance at Palombara, the boy followed her obediently.

"I apologize for him," Alighiero said with a smile to cover his embarrassment. "Ten years old and he believes he has seen heaven in a girl's face. Portinari's daughter, Bice, Beatrice. He barely saw her. It was last year, and he still can't get over it." His eyes were puzzled. "He lives in another world. I don't know what to do with him." He shrugged slightly. "I suppose it will pass. But at the moment poor Lapa's worrying about him." He picked up the jug of wine. "Have some more?"

Palombara accepted, and they spent the rest of the evening in agreeable conversation. For once, Palombara was able to indulge in friendship and forget about the moral ambiguities of the crusade.

When he left to ride to Arezzo the following morning, he could not rid his mind of the solemn, passionate face of the boy who was convinced he had seen the face of the girl he would love all his life. The fire had consumed the boy, had lit him from within. Ahead of him were both heaven and hell, but never the corrosion of doubt or the yawning wasteland of indifference. Yes, Palombara envied the boy, and whether he dared to grasp at it or not, he needed to know that heaven existed.

Palombara rode through the winter rain, feeling it on his face, smelling the wet earth, the tangle of fallen leaves rotted beneath the trees. It was a clean, living odor. The day would be short and dark, night crowding in from the east, closing the colors across the sky into hot reds on the horizon. Tomorrow he would be back in Rome.

Palombara sought out old friends in Arezzo and put to them the same questions he had to others in Florence. By January 10 in the new year of 1276, he was back in Rome, to report to Gregory.

He was crossing the square toward the broad steps up to the Vatican Palace, aware of a certain hush in the gray winter air, like a presage of rain. It was late afternoon, and it looked as if darkness were going to come early.

He saw a cardinal he was acquainted with walking toward him with a heavy tread, his face pinched.

"Good evening, Your Eminence," Palombara said courteously.

The cardinal stopped, shaking his head from side to side. "Too soon," he said sadly. "Too soon. We don't need change at the moment."

Palombara was seized with a presentiment of loss. "The Holy Father?"

"Just today," the cardinal replied, looking Palombara up and down, seeing the marks of travel on his clothes. "You're too late."

Palombara should not have been surprised. Gregory had looked exhausted both in body and in spirit when he had last seen him. Palombara was touched with a grief greater than his disappointment at his own loss of office or the confusion of the future, everything plunged into uncertainty again. There was an emptiness where he had had a friend, a mentor, someone whose judgments he understood.

"Thank you," he said quietly. "I did not know." He crossed himself. "May he rest in peace."

It rained all day, and he stayed at home, supposedly writing a report on his work in Tuscany to give to the new pope, should he want it. Actually he paced the floor, deep in thought, turning over all the decisions he would have to make. There was everything to win . . . or lose.

He had been in high office several years now and earned both friends and enemies. Most important, perhaps, he had earned favors, and chief among his many enemies was Niccolo Vicenze.

Over the next few weeks, if he was to retain any power, he would need more than skill, he would need luck. He should have been better prepared for Gregory's death. The signs of it had been there in the hollows around his eyes, the constant cough, the pain and weariness in him.

Palombara stopped at the window and stared out at the rain. The new crusade had been a passion with Gregory, but what about his successor?

He was surprised how much Constantinople dominated his thoughts. Would the new pope care about the Eastern Church, try to bridge the differences between them and treat them with respect as fellow Christians? Would he begin a real healing of the schism?

During the following days, tension mounted, speculation was rampant, but for the most part concealed by the decencies of mourning and of Gregory's burial in Arezzo. Above all, of course, was expediency. No one wished to wear his ambition naked. People said one thing and meant another.

Palombara listened and considered which faction he should be seen to back. This was much on his mind when a Neapolitan priest named Masari fell into step with him, crossing the square toward the Vatican Palace in the feeble light of the January sun only a week after Gregory's death.

"A dangerous time," Masari observed conversationally, avoiding the puddles with his exquisite boots.

Palombara smiled. "You fear the cardinals will choose other than by the will of God?" he said with only the barest suggestion of humor in his voice. He knew Masari, but not well enough to trust him.

"I fear that without a little help they may be fallible, like all men," Masari replied, an answering gleam in his eyes. "It is a fine thing to be pope, and great power is destructive of all manner of qualities, regrettably, sometimes most of all of wisdom."

"But far from ending with it," Palombara said dryly. "Give me the benefit of your knowledge, brother. What, in your opinion, would wisdom dictate?"

Masari appeared to consider. "Intelligence rather than passion," he replied at length as they continued up a flight of steps. It was starting to rain harder. "A gift for diplomacy rather than a tangle of family connections," he went on. "It is most awkward to owe one's relations for the favor of their support. Debts have a way of requiring payment at most inconvenient times."

Palombara was amused and interested in spite of himself. He felt the quickening of his pulse. "But how is one to gain any level of support without obligation, probably of several kinds? Cardinals do not cast their ballots without a reason." He did not say "unless they are bought," but Masari knew the sense behind his words.

"Regrettably not." Masari bent forward, shielding his dark face from a spout of water off a high roof guttering. "But there are many sorts of reasons. One of the best might be the belief that the new pope, whoever he is, would succeed in unifying the whole Christian faith, while not yielding any holy doctrine to the false teaching of the Greek Church. That would surely be most displeasing to God."

"I do not know the mind of God," Palombara said acerbically.

"Of course," Masari agreed. "Only the Holy Father himself knows that beyond doubt. We must pray, and hope, and seek after wisdom."

Palombara had a fleeting memory of standing in the Hagia Sophia and the beginning of his understanding of how much subtler a thing the wisdom of Byzantium was than that of Rome. For a start, it incorporated the feminine element: gentler, more elusive, harder to define. Perhaps it was also more open to variance and alteration, more nurturing to the infinite spirit of humanity.

"I hope we don't have to wait until we find it," he said aloud. "Or we might not elect a new pope in our lifetime."

"You jest, Your Grace," Masari said softly, his black eyes steady on Palombara's face for a moment, then moving swiftly away again. "But I think perhaps you understand wisdom more than most men."

Again the stab of surprise jolted Palombara, and the racing of his heart. Masari was testing him, even courting him?

"I value it more than wealth or favors," he answered with total solemnity. "But I think it does not come cheaply."

"Little that is good comes cheaply, Your Grace," Masari agreed. "We look toward a pope who is uniquely fitted to be leader of the Christian world."

"We?" Palombara kept walking, but now unmindful of the wind, the puddles gathering in the stones, or the passersby.

"Such men as His Majesty of the Two Sicilies and lord of Anjou," Masari answered. "But of more import to this issue, of course, he is also senator of Rome."

Palombara knew precisely what he meant—someone with a powerful influence over who would become pope. The implication and the offer were both plain. Temptation roared through his mind like a great wind, scattering everything else. Already? A serious chance to become pope! He was young for it, not yet fifty, but there had been far younger. In 955, John XII had been eighteen, ordained, made bishop, and crowned pope all in a day, so it was said. His reign had been short and disastrous.

Masari was waiting, watching not only for the words, but for all the unspoken patterns and betrayals in his face.

Palombara said what he believed was probably true, but also what he knew Charles would want to hear. "I doubt Christendom will be wholly united by anything except conquest of the old Orthodox patriarchies," he said, hearing his own voice as if it were someone else's. "I have recently returned from Constantinople, and the resistance there, and in the surrounding countryside especially, is still strong. A man who has given his career to one faith does not easily sacrifice his identity. If he loses that, what else has he?"

"His life?" Masari suggested, but there was no seriousness in his voice, only satisfaction and a passing regret, as for the inevitable.

"That is the stuff martyrs are made of," Palombara retorted a trifle sharply. The triple crown was closer to his grasp than it had ever been, perhaps than he had ever seriously believed possible. But what would he have to pay for such a favor from Charles of Anjou and whoever else was in his debt?

If he hesitated now, Charles would never back him. A man fit to be pope did not need time to weigh his courage. Did he have that clarity of mind so that he would understand the voice of God telling him how to lead the world, or what was true and what was false? Did he have the fire of soul that could bear it? Did such a thing even exist?

He thought again of the strange, effeminate eunuch Anastasius and his plea for gentleness and the humility to learn, to crush the appetite for exclusivity, and to tolerate the different.

"You hesitate," Masari observed. The withdrawal was already in his voice.

Palombara was angry with himself for his equivocation, his cowardice. A year ago, he would have accepted and considered the cost, even the morality, afterward.

"No," Palombara denied it. "I have not the stomach to rule a Rome that starts another war with Byzantium. We will lose more than we gain."

"Is that what God tells you?" Masari asked with a smile.

"It is what my common sense tells me," Palombara answered him. "God speaks only to the pope."

Masari shrugged and with a little salute turned and walked away.

The decision came remarkably quickly. It was eleven days later, January 21, a dark, windy day, when Palombara's servant came running across the courtyard, his feet splashing in the puddles. He barely knocked on the carved wooden door before entering the study, his face flushed with exertion.

"They have chosen Pierre de Tarentaise, Cardinal Bishop of Ostia," he said breathlessly. "He has taken the name of Innocent the Fifth, Your Grace."

Palombara was stunned. His immediate thought was that Charles of Anjou had supported him all along, and Palombara had been ridiculous to imagine that Masari had been offering him anything except a chance to declare his loyalties. He was a pawn, no more.

"Thank you, Filippo," Palombara said absently. "I am obliged you came so hastily."

Filippo withdrew.

Palombara sat at his desk, his body frozen, his mind whirling. Pierre de Tarentaise. Palombara knew him, at least to speak to. They had both been at the Council of Lyons; Tarentaise had actually read the sermon.

Then another thought came to him: Apparently he was taking the name of Innocent V. It was Innocent III who had been pope when Enrico Dandolo had set off on the crusade whose soldiers had sacked and burned Constantinople in 1204. Choosing the name of Innocent was a statement of intent, as such choices always were. Palombara must think carefully indeed where his own path lay.

He entered the familiar high-windowed rooms, his heart pounding with anticipation, already hardening himself against failure, as though bracing himself would make the pain less.

It was only now that he realized how keenly he wanted to return to Constantinople. He longed for the complexity of the East and to be part of the struggle he had seen begin there. He wanted to persuade at least some of those clerics to bend and save what was good of their belief so it was not lost to the wider faith. He wanted to explore their different concept of wisdom; it intrigued him, promising a more rounded explanation of thought, less didactic and in the end more tolerant.

He was finally ushered into the Holy Father's presence and entered with all the appropriate humility. Innocent was already over fifty, a fair, mild-faced man, nearly bald, and now dressed in the magnificent regalia of his new office.

Palombara knelt and kissed his ring, making the usual formal protestations of his loyalty. Then on Innocent's invitation, he rose to his feet again.

"I am familiar with your opinions on Byzantium and the Greek Church in general," Innocent began. "Your work has been excellent."

"Thank you, Holy Father," Palombara said humbly.

"His Holiness Pope Gregory informed me that he had sent you to Tuscany to see what support you could raise for the crusade," Innocent continued. "It will take time, of course, possibly five or six years. Success cannot be hurried."

Palombara agreed, wondering what Innocent really meant. He looked at his calm face, completely unreadable. He could see nothing changed in him except his clothes and the confidence in his manner, a kind of benign glow; but every now and again he glanced around the room, as if to make certain he was really here.

"There are matters of reform within our own numbers," Innocent said, "that we cannot pursue for the time being." That was a flat contradiction of Gregory's view, and he had felt strongly about it, certain that it was God's will. Had he been wrong? Or was Innocent not listening to the whisper of the spirit now?

The void was there again at Palombara's feet, the fear that there was no revelation at all, simply human ambition and chaos, fed by the desperate need for meaning.

"I have been giving both thought and prayer to the situation in Byzantium," Innocent continued. "It seems to me that you have a feeling for the people. . . ."

"I have come to know them far better than at first," Palombara answered what he took to be a question. He felt the need to justify himself and not allow the implication of disloyalty, however slight, to go uncorrected. "I do not think they will be easily persuaded from their beliefs, especially those who have placed themselves in a position from which there is no retreat."

Innocent pursed his lips. "It is a pity we ever allowed it to become such. We should have begun negotiations long ago. But whenever it is done, as you say, it will not be without loss. No war for the cause of the Mother Church was ever fought without casualties." He shook his head fractionally. "Give me your report on your findings in Tuscany, then I wish you to go to other cities here in Italy and encourage their support." He smiled. "Perhaps in time to Naples, even to Palermo. We shall see."

Palombara felt a sudden coldness seize him. Did Innocent know that Masari had approached him and that he had been tempted, even if only for a moment? There would be an exquisite irony in sending Palombara to the court of Charles of Anjou to raise support for a new crusade.

"Yes, Holy Father," he said, keeping his voice level with an effort. "I shall give you the report on Tuscany tomorrow, then leave for whatever city you judge best."

·"Thank you, Enrico," Innocent said mildly. "Perhaps you could begin with Urbino. And then perhaps Ferrara?"

Palombara accepted and looked into Innocent's face with a new awareness of his power and a certain foreboding. Would it be possible to mount a crusade that would not ravage Constantinople again?

Was his new mission a beginning of undoing all that his last had sought to achieve? Any certainty of faith eluded him.

Twenty-six

◦◦◦

B UT PALOMBARA'S CALLING WAS SHORT-LIVED. INNOCENT died in the middle of the year, after just five months in office. After a short conclave, Ottobono Fieschi had been chosen, and taken the title of Adrian V. Then, incredibly, after only five weeks this pope too was dead. He had not even had time to be consecrated! It was lunacy. How could it be attributed to God? Or was it God's way of telling them that they had chosen the wrong man? It was descending into farce. Didn't anyone hear the voice of divine prompting?

Or was it as Palombara had always feared in the darkness of his own soul, that there was no divine voice? If God had indeed made the world, then He had long since lost interest in its self-destructive indulgences, its frail dreams, and its incessant, pointless quarreling. Man was simply too busy looking after himself either to have noticed or to have understood.

It was hot outside, the smoldering heat of midsummer in Rome. And now the cardinals from all corners of Europe would have to come back to begin again. Some of them might not even be home yet from the last conclave. What absurdity.

Palombara walked slowly around the house he had once loved so much. He looked at the beautiful paintings he had collected over the years and saw the skill of the brushstrokes, the mastery of balance and line, but the fire in the artist's soul failed to warm him.

He would go to Charles of Anjou himself, not wasting time and words with someone like Masari. He would see if his interest was still alive in the possibility of backing Palombara for the throne. He would decide before he got there exactly what he would offer the king of Naples and what he would not.

Thirteen days later, he was in Charles's presence in his huge villa on the outskirts of Rome. He was a man of immense physical power, barrel-chested, pulsing with energy like the fires of a forge. He seemed unable to stand still, moving from one place to another in the room, from one pile of papers of his compulsive triplicate of orders to a scribe making notes, then on to another. On a table were his own pen and ink, where he corrected what he considered mistakes. His broad brow was sheened with sweat and his heavy face high-colored.

"Well?" he inquired. "What have you come to see me for, Your Grace?" There was amusement in his face and a penetrating intelligence. Palombara was sharply aware that he could not manipulate this man, and only a fool would try.

"As a senator of Rome, you will have a powerful vote to cast on the papal conclave, sire," he replied.

"One vote," Charles observed dryly.

"I think more than that, my lord," Palombara answered him. "Many men care what your judgment might be."

"For their ambition." It was not a question but an answer.

"Of course. But also for the future of Christendom," Palombara pointed out. "More hangs in the balance now than perhaps at any time since the days of Saint Peter." He smiled, not hesitating. "And possibly hanging over it all, can we unite Byzantium with us in any sense that has value, not a source of constant strife?"

"Byzantium . . ." Charles repeated the word, rolling it on his tongue. "Indeed."

The silence prickled in the room.

"You've been legate to Constantinople," Charles observed, continuing again to walk around the room, his leather-clad feet slapping on the marble floor. He passed from shadow into the sunlight falling from the high windows and back into shadow again. "You told the Holy Father the Byzantines would not yield to Rome." He swung around in time to catch the surprise in Palombara's face before he could mask it. "Is that tide of resistance strong enough to last, shall we say, another three years or so?"

Palombara understood immediately. "That might depend upon the terms on which Rome insisted, sire."

Charles breathed out softly. "As I assumed. And if you were pope, what sorts of conditions would you feel could not be abandoned, even to secure such a prize as the submission of the Orthodox Church and the uniting of Christendom?"

Palombara knew exactly what he meant. "We are speaking of political unity," he said carefully, but his tone was light, as if it were well understood between them. "Unity of intent was never a possibility. Obedience, perhaps, but not belief."

Charles waited, smiling slowly.

"I see no virtue in facilitating such a union if it means giving away any of the tenets of faith that have kept the loyalties we have elsewhere," Palombara answered. It was a nicely sanctimonious speech, but he knew Charles would understand it. Charles needed a pope who would delay any act of unity by making demands to which he knew Byzantium would not yield. Who better to judge that precisely than Palombara, who had argued the case with Michael?

"Your understanding matches my own." Charles relaxed and moved away, walking easily, the tension drained out of him. "I can see how it might very well be God's will to have a pope with such perception of the true nature of people, rather than some ideal which does not conform to reality. I shall use such influence as I have to that end. Thank you for sparing me your time, and your knowledge, Your Grace." His smile broadened. "We shall be able to be of service to each other—and to the Holy Mother Church, of course."

Palombara excused himself and walked out through the shadow of the arches and into the blistering sun. Even the cypresses, like motionless flames in the still air, looked tired. There was no wind to stir them at all.

It was absurd to suppose that popes kept dying because they were not enacting the will of God, yet Palombara could not rid his mind of the thought. It kept dancing at the edge of his grasp all the time, a single reason that made sense of all of it.

He let his imagination roam, tasting ideas, soaking them in as a cat basks in the sun.

The conclave was divided into two great factions, the pro–Charles of Anjou Frenchmen and the anti-Charles Italians. They cast the first ballot, and Palombara was deliriously on the crest of the wave, only two votes short of being elected. His outstretched fingers all but touched the crown.

On September 13, the final vote was cast.

Palombara waited. He had hardly slept for days, lying awake, his mind in a turmoil of hope and self-mockery. He had even stood before the glass and imagined himself in the robes of office, looked at his strong, slender hand and seen the papal ring on it.

Now he waited, like everyone else, too tense to remain seated, too tired to pace more than a few moments. He lost count of time. He was hungry, and even more he was thirsty, but he could not bring himself to leave.

Then at last it was over. A fat cardinal in billowing robes, the sweat streaming down his face, announced that Christendom had a pope again.

Palombara's heart nearly deafened him. The seventy-one-year-old Portuguese philosopher, theologian, and doctor of medicine, Peter Juliani Rebolo, was elected, as John XXI. Palombara was furious with himself for not having expected it. How could he have been such a fool? He stood in the beautiful hall with a fixed smile on his face as if there were no leaden weight of disappointment crushing inside him, as if he did not hurt intolerably. He smiled at men he hated, connivers and time servers he had courted only hours before. Was this Portuguese philosopher and ex-doctor really God's choice for the throne of Saint Peter?

The people around him were cheering, voices too loud, filled with false joy, some, like his own, strident with disappointment and fear for their own positions. Everyone knew who had leaned which way openly, for or against. No one knew what deals had been done, bargains made, prices offered or taken in secret.

Within days, he was sent for by yet another new Holy Father, and once again he walked across the square and up the shallow steps through the great arches. Inside, he walked the familiar ornate passageways to the papal apartments.

He knelt and kissed the pope's ring and repeated his faith and loyalty, his mind racing as to why he had been sent for. What miserable task would he be given to remove him from Rome to where his ambition could be nicely cooled? Where could he do no harm? Probably somewhere in northern Europe, where he would freeze all summer as well as all winter.

John was smiling when Palombara looked up. "My predecessor, God rest his soul in peace, wasted your talents in chasing support for the crusade here in Italy," he said smoothly. "As did the good Innocent."

Palombara waited for the blow.

John sighed. "You have both skill and experience regarding the schism between ourselves and the Greek Orthodox Church. I have studied your letters on the subject. You would best serve God and the cause of Christendom if you were to return to Constantinople, as legate to Byzantium, with a special responsibility to continue in the work of healing the differences between us and our brethren."

Palombara drew in his breath slowly and let it out in silence. The sunlight in the room was so bright, it hurt his eyes.

"It is of the greatest importance," John said gravely, his words chosen with care and only slightly accented with his native Portuguese. "You must work with all prayer and diligence to this end." He smiled. "We need Byzantium not only to give lip service to its union with Rome, we need it to be real. We need to see the obedience and be able to prove it to the world. The days when we can afford leniency are past. Do you understand, Enrico?"

Palombara studied the new pope's face. Was John XXI, under his bland exterior, far subtler than anyone had guessed, and willing to use whatever tool was to hand, turning its blade to suit his own purposes? Was this new office given in order to have Palombara safely out of Rome and in Constantinople, which he knew and loved as much as he loved anything? To whom did he owe this debt? Someone would seek to collect whatever favor he had given, but who?

"Yes, Holy Father," he accepted. "I will do all I can to serve God, and the Church."

John nodded again, still smiling.

Twenty-seven

༄

IN THE YEAR AFTER THE DEATH OF GREGORY X, ANNA HAD
little chance to pursue any further information about Justinian or his
disillusionment with Bessarion, or even the courage or strength of the
Church. There was little rain in the spring, and the summer's heat came
early.

Disease started in the poorer quarters where there was insufficient
water. Rapidly the outbreak spread, and the situation spiraled out of control. The stench of sickness filled the air, clogging mouth and nose.

"What can you do?" Constantine said desperately as he stood in his
beautiful arcade, gazing at Anna. His pained eyes were hollow with exhaustion, red-rimmed, his face pasty gray. "I have done all I know, but it
is so little. They need your help."

There was no possible answer but to make arrangements for someone
else to see her regular patients and for Leo to turn away new ones until this
fever and flux were past. If afterward she had to begin again and build up
a new practice, it was the price that must be paid. She could not walk away
from Constantine, and deeper and more lasting than that, she could not
leave the sick without help.

When she told Leo he shook his head, but he did not argue. It was Simonis who did.

"And what about your brother?" she said, her face tight, eyes angry.
"While you're tending to the poor night and day, running yourself into the

ground, risking your own health, who's going to work to save him? He waits in the desert, wherever he is, for another summer?"

"If we could ask him, wouldn't he say that I should help the sick?" Anna asked.

"Of course he would!" Simonis snapped, her voice sharp with frustration. "That doesn't mean it's what you should do."

Anna worked night and day. She slept only in snatches here and there as exhaustion overtook her. She ate bread and drank a little sour wine, cleaner than water. She had no time to think of anything but how to get more herbs, more ointments, more food. There was no money. Without the generosity of Shachar and al-Qadir, all real help would have ceased.

Constantine worked also. She saw him only as he called on her because he knew of someone in need so desperate that he was willing to interrupt whatever she was doing or even to waken her when she slept.

Sometimes they ate together or merely spent the last hours of a dreadful day in wordless comfort, each knowing that the other had had experiences equally harsh and also ending in death.

Then as the year waned, at last the infection ebbed. The dead were buried, and the business of ordinary life slowly took over again.

Twenty-eight

A S WAS INEVITABLE, POPE JOHN XXI ALSO BECAME BIT-
terly aware of the reality in Byzantium with regard to the faith. He
was not inclined to be as lenient as his predecessors. He sent letters to
Constantinople demanding a public and unqualified acceptance of the *filioque* clause about the nature of God, of Christ, and of the Holy Spirit, the
Roman doctrine of purgatory, the seven sacraments as held by Rome, and
papal primacy over all other princes of the Church, with the right of appeal to the Holy See and submission of all churches to Rome.

All Michael's appeals for the Greek Church to retain its ancient rites, as
before the Schism, were refused.

Palombara was present at the great ceremony in April 1277 when this
new document was signed by Emperor Michael, his son, Andronicus, and
the new bishops whom he had created because the established bishops
would not yield their faith or their old allegiances. Of course, in that sense
it was a farce. Michael knew it, and so did the new bishops. Their calling
existed only on the condition of their abject and public surrender.

Palombara also knew it, and he watched the splendor of the ritual with
no sense of victory. He stood in the magnificent hall and wondered how
many of these men in their silks and gems felt any passion at all, and if
they did, what it was. Was such a prize of any worth? Indeed, was it a service to God or to any kind of morality?

What was the difference between the whisper of the Holy Spirit, the
hysteria born of the need for God to exist, and the terror and isolation of

seeking Him alone? Was the darkness too big to look at? Or had they seen some light in it that he had not?

He turned slightly sideways to watch Vicenze, a couple of feet away. He stood upright, his eyes bright, his face totally unmoving. He reminded Palombara of nothing so much as a soldier at a victory parade.

How was Michael going to control his people after this? Was he realist enough to have some plan? Or was he shortsighted and utterly lost as well? All shorn lambs, struggling alone through the same gale, not seeing one another.

If only the monk Cyril Choniates would sign, then his followers would. It would be a giant step toward pacifying the opposition. Perhaps it could be brought about? But Palombara must do it, not Vicenze; at all costs, not Vicenze.

He smiled at himself and at his own weakness for victory.

But the main document was already signed. What he needed was an addendum. At first he saw it as a setback that Cyril Choniates was apparently quite seriously ill. Then he thought of Anastasius, the eunuch physician.

A few inquiries elicited the information that he was willing to treat anyone who needed his skills, Christian, Arab, or Jew. He would not rant on about sin or foolish talk of penitence, but would treat the illness, whether provoked by the mind or not.

The next thing for Palombara to do was have Anastasius recommended to whoever was caring for Cyril in his captivity. Who was powerful enough to do that and could be persuaded to?

The answer to that question was undoubtedly Zoe Chrysaphes.

Two days later, he called upon her, bringing with him as a gift this time a small but very beautiful Neapolitan cameo, carved with amazing delicacy. He had chosen it himself and was reluctant to give it away, although that was why he had bought it in the first place.

He saw in her eyes that it pleased her. She turned it over in her fingers, feeling the surface, smiling, then looked up at him.

"Exquisite, Your Grace," she said softly. "But I am past the days when men give me such gifts for my favors, and you are a priest anyway. If that was what you wanted, you would have to be much subtler. I think far more to the issue is the fact that I am Byzantine and you are Roman. What is it you are looking for?"

He was amused by her directness and forbore from telling her that he was not Roman but Aretino, to him an important difference, but not to her.

"You are right, of course," he conceded, looking her up and down slowly, with candid appreciation. "As for your favors, I would rather earn them than buy them. What is purchased is of little worth, and has no taste to linger in the mind."

He was delighted to see the color in her cheeks and realized that he had momentarily disconcerted her. He met her eyes boldly. "What I want is for you to recommend a good physician for the deposed and now exiled subpatriarch Cyril Choniates, who is presently quite seriously ill in the monastery at Bithynia. I have Anastasius Zarides in mind. I believe your influence would be sufficient to have the abbot send for him."

"It would," she agreed, her golden eyes quickening with interest. "And why do you care in the slightest what happens to Cyril Choniates?"

"I wish the union with Rome to proceed with as little bloodshed as possible," he answered. "For Rome's sake—as you wish it for Byzantium's. I have an addendum to the treaty of union which I believe Cyril will sign, even though he has refused the main agreement. If he did, then the many monks loyal to him would do so as well. It will be a break in the resistance, perhaps sufficient to bring peace."

She thought for several minutes, turning away from him to stare at the window and the magnificent view across the rooftops toward the water.

"I assume that this addendum will never be added to the agreement," she said at last. "At least the main body of it will not. Perhaps a sentence or two, with Cyril's name, and those of as many of his followers as you may obtain?"

"Precisely," he agreed. "But it will bring peace. We do not want any more martyrs to a cause which cannot succeed."

She measured her words very carefully. "There are two of you, are there not? Legates from the pope in Rome?"

"Yes. . . ."

"Is your companion aware that you have come to me with this?"

She might already have the answer, and to affirm it would be an unnecessary lie. "No. We are not allies. Why do you ask?" He kept the irritation out of his voice.

Her smile widened, vivid with amusement. "Cyril will not sign anything for you."

He felt a chill and a sudden awareness that she was playing, manipulating him far more than he was her. "Have you some other suggestion?" he asked.

She turned to face him, looking up at last, her gaze steady. "What you need is Cyril's silence, and word that he agreed, which he cannot contest."

"Why would he not contest it, if as you say he will not agree?"

"He is ill. He is also old. Perhaps he will die?" She raised her superbly arched brows.

Was she really suggesting what he thought? Why would she? She was Byzantine to the core and against anything and everything Roman.

"I shall recommend Anastasius," she went on. "He is known to be a clever physician, and still resolutely Orthodox. In fact, he is a good friend and something of a disciple of Bishop Constantine, the most Orthodox of all the bishops. I myself will provide him with a medicine to help poor Cyril."

He let out his breath slowly. "I see."

"Possibly you do," she agreed skeptically. "Are you sure you would not prefer that Bishop Vicenze should take this document to Cyril after all? I shall suggest it to him, if you wish."

"Perhaps that would be a good idea," Palombara said slowly, the blood roaring in his ears. "I would owe you much."

"Yes." Her smile widened. "You would. But peace is in both our interests, even in that of Cyril Choniates, if he were but well enough to see it. We must do for him what he cannot do for himself."

Twenty-nine

ANNA ENTERED ZOE'S ROOM EXPECTING TO FIND HER ill and was surprised when Zoe walked toward her with all the grace and vitality of a woman on the verge of a huge endeavor.

"I am obliged you came so quickly," she said to Anna, regarding her with a slight smile. "Cyril Choniates is very ill indeed. He is a man I used to know, before his banishment, and for whom I had the greatest admiration."

She regarded Anna with a sudden solemnity. "He needs a far better physician than his current exile affords him." She frowned. "One who will disregard his sins, which I doubt are many, and anyway, sin is largely a matter of opinion. One man's virtue may be another man's vice." She looked grave. "Anastasius, you can treat him with herbs and tinctures, medicines which will actually help his illness, or at the very least, if he is ill unto death, ease his distress. He deserves that. Do you take deserving into account?"

"No," Anna replied with a faint gleam of humor herself. "You know that. As you say, it is often only a point of view anyway. I despise hypocrisy, which would place me against half of the most pious people I know."

Zoe laughed. "Your frankness could prove your undoing, Anastasius. I advise you to watch your tongue. Hypocrites have absolutely no sense of humor at all, or they would see their own absurdity. Will you go and do what you can for Cyril Choniates?"

"Will I be allowed to?"

"I shall see to it," Zoe replied. "He is at a monastery in Bithynia. And the papal legate Bishop Niccolo Vicenze will accompany you there. He has business with Cyril, which means he will organize and pay for the travel and the lodging. That seems a good arrangement. The weather is pleasant. The journey on horseback will take you a few days, but it will not be over-arduous. You know Bithynia better than he can. You will leave tomorrow morning. There is no time to waste."

She moved slowly back across the room toward the table and smooth, comfortable chairs. "I have an herbal mixture I would like you to take for Cyril. He used to enjoy it when I knew him in the past. It is a simple restorative, but it will give him pleasure, and perhaps it will give him also an increase in strength. I will take a little myself. Perhaps you would like some also?"

Anna hesitated.

"As you please," Zoe said lightly, reaching for the door of a carved wooden cabinet and opening it. Inside were many drawers, each only a few inches square. She pulled one open and took out a silk pouch full of fragments of leaves, crushed so finely as to be almost a powder. "One takes it in a little wine," she said, suiting the action to the words. She poured two goblets of red wine and sprinkled a little powder into each. It dissolved almost immediately.

Her eyes met Anna's as she picked up one of them and put it to her lips. "To Cyril Choniates," she said softly, and drank.

Anna picked up the other and sipped. There was no alteration to the flavor; even the scent of the herb had vanished.

Zoe emptied her goblet and offered a honey cake, taking one herself and biting into it with pleasure.

Anna drained her goblet as well.

"Honey cake?" Zoe offered. "I recommend it. It will take the aftertaste away."

Anna accepted and ate.

Zoe gave her the rest in the silk pouch.

"Thank you." Anna took it. "I will offer it to him."

Anna made the short journey across the Bosphorus to the Nicean shore, where she found Bishop Niccolo Vicenze waiting for her somewhat impatiently. He was pacing back and forth on the quayside, his pale hair gleaming in the cool, early light, his face set in harsh lines of displeasure. He was dressed for traveling, as she was, in shorter robes and soft leather boots covering his lower legs. Even so, he managed to look severely clerical, as if his office were part of himself.

Their greeting was brief, no more than an acknowledgment, then they mounted the waiting horses and began the long journey inland through country she already knew.

The sun rose in a clear sky and the day was warm with only the slightest breeze. But it was a long time since Anna had ridden a horse for more than a couple of miles, and she quickly grew both sore and tired, although Bishop Vicenze was the last person to whom she would have displayed any weakness.

She had ridden in this land before, years earlier, with Justinian. If she closed her eyes and felt the sun on her face, the strength of the animal beneath her, she could imagine it was he riding ahead of her.

But it was Vicenze who was there now along the track between the bracken, the wild blackberries, and the gorse, and he shared nothing. He never even looked back to see if she was keeping up.

It was familiar territory to her, at least to begin with. After that they followed Vicenze's guidance from a map, which appeared to be perfect. It was fortunate, but somehow it gave her little pleasure. She had fully expected he would be infallible in such technical skills. Nevertheless, she thanked him, because she did not wish to be at fault in courtesy. It would be a sign of weakness, and although he was a priest, she sensed no mercy in him.

They arrived at the massive, fortresslike monastery after dark, on the third day, having found wayside lodging each night.

They were made welcome. Zoe's messenger had arrived and left before them, and Anna at least was eagerly awaited. As soon as she had been given the barest food and water, and had washed her hands and face from the dust of the journey, she was taken to see Cyril.

With gratitude and anxiety, a young monk took her along the silent corridors to Cyril's cool stone cell. It was a simple room, no more than five paces by five, the walls bare except for a large crucifix. He lay on a narrow cot, pale-faced and exhausted from the pain in his chest and entire abdominal area. That was not unusual with a long-term fever. The normal functions do not occur, and pain is natural.

She greeted him gently, introducing herself and expressing sorrow for his illness. He was not an old man as she considered age, certainly not over seventy, but his body was wasted from years of self-denial and now also from illness. His hair was thin and white and his face sunken; his skin felt like old paper to her touch.

She asked him the usual questions and heard the answers she had expected. She had brought herbs that were pleasant tasting but purgative. To begin with, what she wanted most was to give him some ease, a better chance to sleep for a length of time, and to restore the balance of fluid in his body.

"Drink as much as you can of this I have brewed for you," she told him. "It will ease your pain considerably. I shall make a jug full every few hours, and bring it to you. By tomorrow this time, you will be less distressed." She hoped that was true, but belief was a large part of recovery, Christian or not.

"It would be more comfortable if you were to be attended by someone you know well," she said to him. "But I shall be as close by as your brethren will permit, and will come at a moment's notice if you call."

"Should I fast?" he inquired anxiously. "With Brother Thomas's help I will pray. I have already confessed my sins and received absolution."

"Prayer is always good," she agreed. "But be brief. Do not weary God with what He already knows. And no, do not fast," she added. "Your spirit is strong enough. In order to continue in service to God and man, you need to regain the strength of your body. Take a little wine, mixed with water, and honey if you wish."

"I abstain from wine." He shook his head fractionally.

"It's not important." She smiled at him. "Now I shall make the herbal infusion for you, and come back with it."

"Thank you, Brother Anastasius," he said weakly. "God be with you."

She sat up most of the night with him. He was feverish and restless, and she began to fear she would not be able to save him. By morning he was very weak, and she found it difficult to persuade him to drink the stronger herbs she had prepared. He was in much distress, and she became concerned that he had an internal obstruction rather than merely the natural effects of fever and ill diet. She increased the strength of the purgative, feeling she had little to lose. This time she added sandalwood for the liver, aloeswood to treat blockage in the liver and urinary system, and again more calamint.

By nightfall he was in even greater distress, but he had passed a large amount of water and seemed less pinched and his eyes less sunken.

Sometime in the middle of the night, the monk who was with him reported to her that Cyril had passed a quantity of waste and seemed relieved in his pain. He was now asleep.

She did not disturb him in the morning but looked at him closely and felt his brow. He was no more than warm, and he stirred vaguely at her touch without wakening. She allowed herself to hope he might recover.

Later in the day, Vicenze insisted on obtaining his audience. As far as the monks were concerned, it was he who had brought the physician under whose care Cyril had begun to recover, even though he was still desperately weak. In gratitude, the abbot could not refuse. Anna was kept from the room.

When finally she was allowed in again, Cyril was exhausted and he looked as if his fever were returning. The young monk who had attended him all through his illness looked anxiously at Anna but did not speak.

"I will not," Cyril said hoarsely. "Even if it costs me my life. I will not sign a paper which swears away my faith and leads my people into apostasy." He gulped, his eyes fixed on Anna's face, frightened and stubborn. "If I do, I will lose my soul. You understand that, don't you, Anastasius?"

"I am not always sure what is right," she began slowly, choosing her words and watching his eyes. "But of course, like everyone else, I have thought very hard about loyalty to our faith, and also the terrible danger of the Latin crusaders storming the city again. They will kill and burn everything in their path. We have a duty to the lives of the people who trust us to care for them, and for those they love, their children, their wives, and their mothers. I have heard stories of the sack in 1204, of a child who watched her mother raped and murdered in front of her . . ."

He winced and the tears filled his eyes, rolling down his tired cheeks.

"But to deny our faith is a destruction even worse," she went on, hating herself for distressing him. "If you have the light of the Holy Spirit of God to tell you what is right, then you can never deny it, whatever the cost. Denial is not merely death, it is hell."

He nodded slowly. "You are wise, Anastasius. Wiser, I think, than some of my own brethren. Certainly wiser than that cold-hearted priest from Rome." He smiled weakly, a flash of light in his eyes. "The only wisdom is to trust God." He made the sign of the cross, conspicuously in the Orthodox way, then lay back on his pillows and drifted into sleep, a slight smile still on his face.

The next time she went to him, he was awake and feverish, his fingers trembling so it was difficult to hold the cup with the herbal infusion in it. She had to put her own hands around his to help him. This was the time to offer Zoe's restorative. Normally she would not give any herbs but those she had brought and mixed herself, but she had already tried everything else she had.

She told him she was going to mix something more, sent for him by Zoe Chrysaphes, and left him with the young monk while she did so. When she returned he looked tired, and she offered him the new drink.

"It may be bitter," she warned. "I drank some myself, as did Zoe, but we took it with wine, and I know you do not wish for that."

He shook his head. "No wine." He reached for the cup, and she gave it to him. He drank and pulled his mouth into a grimace. "It's most unpleasant," he said ruefully. "For once I wish I—" He stopped abruptly, his face pale, his eyes wide. He gasped and clutched at his throat, struggling for breath.

"It's poison!" the young monk cried out in terror. "You've poisoned him!" He scrambled to his feet and ran to the door. "Help! Help! Cyril is poisoned! Come quickly!"

There were footsteps clattering along the corridor, loud with panic. The young monk was still shouting. In front of her Cyril was gasping, his eyes wild, his skin drained of even the last vestige of color and turning blue as he choked.

But she herself had drunk exactly the same! She had seen Zoe take it out of the same silk purse, and she had given Cyril no more than a pinch. She had not tasted bitterness, but then she had taken it with wine and immediately after had cakes with honey.

Was that it? Wine? Did Zoe know Cyril did not drink it?

She leapt up and ran to the door. "Wine!" she shouted almost into the face of the monk only feet away from her. "Get me wine and honey now! This second, for his life!"

"You poisoned him!" the monk accused, his face contorted with loathing.

"Not I!" She said the first thing that would make any sense. "The Roman! Don't stand there like a fool, fetch wine and honey, or do you want him dead?"

That accusation moved him. He swiveled on his heel and ran back down the corridor, his sandals slapping on the stone.

She waited in an agony of fear, dashing back into the room to hold Cyril up in her arms, trying to ease his breathing. His throat had closed up and his chest heaved with the effort to fill his lungs. It seemed to be endless, one long, dreadful breath after another, rasping in pain.

At last the monk returned, followed by another. They had wine and honey. She snatched it from them and mixed the two together, not caring a bit how they tasted, and held it to Cyril's lips.

"Drink!" she commanded. "I don't care how hard it is, drink! Your life depends on it." She tried to pry his jaws apart and force it into his mouth. He was barely breathing at all now, his eyes rolled back into his head. "Hold him!" she ordered the nearest monk. "Do it!"

He obeyed, shivering with terror.

With two hands she was more able to force his lips apart and his head back. A little of the liquid went into his mouth, and he swallowed it convulsively. He gagged, then gulped again, and it went down. She gave him more, and more. Infinitely slowly his throat eased, his breathing became less labored, and at last when he focused his eyes the panic had died out of them.

"Enough," he said hoarsely. "A moment and I will take it all, I promise."

She laid him back gently and sank to her knees on the hard floor, the prayer of gratitude more audible than she had intended. It was not just for Cyril's life, but perhaps for her own.

"Explain," the abbot demanded when she stood before him in his beautiful, sparse office later that evening. He was gaunt, his face lined with anxiety and the long battle against grief. He deserved the truth, absolute and not diminished or twisted by emotion. But he also did not deserve her burden of suspicion that could not be proved. She had had time to weigh what she should tell him.

"Zoe Chrysaphes gave me an herb to offer to Cyril," she answered. "She told me it was a restorative. She emptied some of it into her own wine goblet, and then into mine, and we both drank it with no ill effects. She gave me the pouch of herbs and I took it. It was from that that I mixed an infusion for Cyril."

The abbot frowned. "That does not seem possible."

"Not until I remembered that Zoe and I drank the herbs mixed with wine, and Cyril took his with water," she explained. "Also we ate honey cakes. She said it prevented an aftertaste. Those were the only differences I knew, so I immediately sent for wine and honey, and forced Cyril to take them. He began to recover. I assume it was the wine, and that Zoe Chrysaphes had never taken it with water, and did not know of its hideously different effect." That of course was a lie, but neither of them could prove it, nor could they afford the truth.

"I see," he said slowly. "And what of the Roman? What part has he in this?"

"None that I know," she said. Again it was a lie. If he had not wished to persuade Cyril to sign the addendum, and Zoe had not feared that he might succeed, then Cyril would simply have died quietly here in this monastery, and public opinion regarding the union would have been unaffected. Zoe would choose that before his surrender. Anna's visit had offered her the chance to make certain of Cyril's refusal, or, if at the worst he had signed, then Anna and Vicenze would be blamed for his murder and the document accounted worthless.

But the abbot did not need to know that.

"We are grateful for your quick thought in saving him," he said gravely. "Perhaps you will tell Zoe Chrysaphes that?"

"I will convey whatever message you wish," she replied.

"Thank you," the abbot said gravely. "One of the brothers told me you are from Nicea. Is that correct?"

"Yes. I grew up a little distance from here."

He smiled, a slight, sad gesture, but it reached his eyes with a startling tenderness. "One of our brethren does not ever leave here. There was a man who visited him, but he has not been lately. I think it would be a great kindness if you would spend an hour with Brother John." He barely made it a question.

Anna did not hesitate. "Of course. It would be my pleasure."

"Thank you," the abbot said again. "I shall take you." And without hesitation he led her out of the room, along a narrow, slightly echoing passage and through a huge carved door studded with brass, then up a steep and winding stairway. He stopped on a small landing at the top, high over the rest of the vast building. He knocked at the only door, and at the word of command, he opened it and went in ahead of Anna, holding it for her to follow.

"Brother John," he said quietly, "Brother Cyril has been ill and a physician has come from Constantinople to help him. He has done well, and will shortly leave, but he is from Nicea, and I thought you might like to speak with him for a while first. His name is Anastasius. He reminds me somewhat of the man who used to come to see you three or four years ago."

Anna looked at the young man who rose slowly from the hard wooden chair and thought how odd it was for the abbot to describe her when she was only a step behind him. Then she saw the man's face, thin and worn with pain and yet startlingly gentle. He was no more than in his twenties, but the thing that made her heart beat wildly so the blood thundered in her head and her mouth went dry was that he had no eyes. The ugly sockets were sunken, giving his face a hollow, mutilated look. With a shock like fire, she knew who he was—this was John Lascaris, whose eyes had been put out by Michael Palaeologus so he could not succeed to the throne. No wonder she reminded the abbot of the man who had come to see him—it could only be Justinian.

She choked on her own breath as it caught in her throat. "Brother John . . . ," she began. How desperately she wanted to tell him that she too was a Lascaris, Zarides was merely her married name, but of course that was impossible.

He nodded slowly, an instant of surprise in his expression because the abbot had not told him she was a eunuch, and her voice betrayed her. "Come in," he invited. "Please sit down. I believe there is another chair."

"Yes, thank you," she accepted. This man was not only the rightful emperor, he was now held by many to be a saint, a man of holiness so close to God as to be capable of calling upon Him for miracles. But it was Justinian's time with him that filled her mind.

"The Father Abbot told me that you had a friend who came to visit you some years ago, a man from Nicea . . . ," she began.

John's face lit with pleasure. "Ah, yes. What a fire there was in him to learn. He was truly seeking God."

"He sounds like a fine person," she said carefully. "Would that more of us were seeking, rather than assuming we already know."

He smiled, a sudden, radiant warmth in his sightless face. "You sound like him," he said simply. "But perhaps a little wiser. You already begin to know how vast is our capacity yet to learn, and what we do not know is without end."

"Is that heaven?" she asked impulsively. "Is it heaven to learn endlessly, and to love?" she explained herself. "Is that what he was looking for?"

"You care about him," he said gently. It was not entirely a question, more a realization. "A friend? A kinsman? He did not have a brother, he said so, but a sister. He said she was a physician, a very gifted one."

She was glad he could not see her sudden tears.

Justinian had spoken of her, even here with John Lascaris. She swallowed the tightness in her throat. "A kinsman," she replied, needing to tell him as much truth as she could and claim the tie that was so close inside her. "But distant."

"He was a Lascaris," he said softly, rolling the name in his mouth as if the sound of it were sweet. "He doesn't come anymore. I fear he was involved in something dangerous. He spoke of Michael Palaeologus, and a union with Rome, and how he wanted to save the city without either the bloodshed of war or the corruption of betrayal, but it would be almost infinitely difficult." John Lascaris frowned, the lines puckering his forehead and deepening the other lines of pain in his face. "Something happened to him, didn't it?"

There was no possibility of lying. "Yes, but I don't know what it truly was. I am trying to find out. Bessarion Comnenos was murdered, and Justinian was implicated in helping the man who did it. He is in exile in Judea."

John let out his breath in a sigh. It carried sorrow and infinite weariness. "I'm sorry. If he could have anything to do with that, then he did not find what he was seeking. I sensed that the last time he was here. He was different. It was in his voice. A disillusion."

"Disillusion?" she asked, leaning closer to him. "With the Church . . . or something else?"

"My dear friend," John said, shaking his head a fraction from side to side. "Justinian was looking for answers to questions of purpose and loneliness. He wanted reasons that made sense to our incomplete grasp. He would have been a better emperor himself than Bessarion Comnenos, and I think he knew that. But the throne would not have made him a better man. I'm not sure if he understood that also."

Emperor! Justinian? He must have misunderstood. "But he loved the Church," she insisted. "He would have fought for it!"

"Oh yes," he agreed. "He hungered to belong to it, to preserve its place, its rituals, its beauty, and above all its identity."

A new idea flared up in her mind. "Enough to die for it?"

"I cannot answer that," John replied. "No man knows what he will die for until the moment comes. Do you know what you would die for, Anastasius?"

She was taken aback. She had no answer.

He smiled. "What do you want of God? And what do you believe He wants of you? I asked Justinian that, and he did not answer me. I think he did not yet know what he believed."

"You said he loved the Church," she said softly. "Why the Orthodox, and not the Roman? They have beauty, too, and faith, and ritual. What did he believe in that he was willing to pay so much to keep it?"

"We love a familiar path," John said simply. "None of us like to be told what to think, what to do, by a stranger imposing his will from another land in another tongue."

"Is that all?"

"It is a great deal," he said with a small, weary smile. "There are not many certainties in life, not much that does not change, wither, deceive, or disappoint at some time or other. The sanctities of the Church are the only things I know of. Are not these things worth living or dying for?"

"Yes," she said immediately. "Did he find that . . . at least that hope?"

"I don't know," he answered, his voice sad and very lonely. "But I miss him." He looked tired, the strength gone from his voice, the sunken eye sockets more deeply shadowed.

"I am doing what I can to prove he was wrongly accused," she said impulsively. "If I succeed, they will have to pardon him and he will return."

"A cousin of a cousin?" He smiled at her.

"And a friend," she added. "I don't wish to tire you." She rose, frightened now in case she was tempted into betraying herself irreparably.

He lifted his hand in the old blessing. "May God light your path in the darkness, and comfort your aloneness in the cold of the night, Anna Lascaris."

The heat washed up her in a wave like fire, yet it was sweet, in spite of all the fear there should have been. He knew her; hc had used her own name. For a long, terrible, wonderful moment, she was herself.

She leaned forward and touched his hand softly, a totally feminine gesture. Then she turned and walked to the door. The instant she was beyond it, she would resume her role.

When she had made the long journey back to Constantinople, saying nothing but the few civil words necessary to Vicenze, she called upon Zoe.

Anna stood in the same room as always, with its great golden cross on the wall and its magnificent view, and faced Zoe with a smile, tasting the moment.

"Were you able to save the good Cyril?" Zoe asked, her topaz eyes hard and too bright to hide her eagerness or the strange, powerful emotions warring inside her.

"Yes indeed," she replied levelly. "He may live for many years yet."

There was a flicker in Zoe's eyes. "And the legate Vicenze—did he succeed in his purpose?"

Anna raised her eyebrows. "His purpose?"

"He did not go merely to accompany you!" Zoe said, keeping the temper out of her voice with difficulty.

"Oh, he had an audience with Cyril," Anna replied quite casually. "Of course I was not present. Poor Cyril was taken ill after that, and all my attention was bent on treating him."

Zoe's anger burned behind her glittering gaze. For the first time, she had been balked by Anna. Suddenly they met as equals.

Anna smiled. "That was when I gave Cyril the herbs that you so thoughtfully provided."

Zoe took a deep breath and let it out slowly. In that moment something changed in her, a knowledge of having been confounded. "And they helped?" she asked, knowing the answer already.

"Not at first," Anna told her. "In fact, the effect was most unpleasant. I quite feared for his life. Then I remembered that when you and I had taken them, we did so with wine. It made all the difference." She smiled, meeting Zoe's eyes unflinchingly. "I am grateful to you for your foresight. I explained to the abbot exactly what had happened. I would not wish such a holy man to imagine you had attempted to poison poor Cyril. That would be fearful."

Zoe's expression froze like white marble, so tightly controlled that neither fury nor relief showed. Then something quite remarkable was there, just for a second, but long enough that Anna was perfectly certain of what it was—admiration.

"How kind of you," Zoe said in a low voice. "I shall not forget it."

Thirty

V ICENZE RETURNED TO THE HOUSE IN A VICIOUS TEMPER. "How was your journey to Bithynia?" Palombara asked.

"Pointless," Vicenze snapped. "I went only because it was my holy duty to try." He looked at Palombara malevolently, faintly suspicious as to how much he might know or guess. "One of us must do something to win over these obdurate people, or give them room to condemn themselves utterly."

"So that whatever we do, we are justified." Palombara was surprised at how bitter he sounded.

"Exactly," Vicenze agreed. "It was a last attempt."

"Last?"

Vicenze's eyebrows rose and there was a gleam of satisfaction in his cold eyes. "Next week we return to Rome. Had you forgotten?"

"Of course not," Palombara told him. Actually, he had thought it was a little longer than that. He had been considering with some anxiety exactly what he would report to the pope, in what terms he would explain the nature of their failure to gain any more support for the agreement. He had come to the point where he believed that Michael could carry his people sufficiently for the appearance of union with Rome and that the fact of a degree of independence could be disguised. People would always believe differently from one place to another, one social class, one degree of wealth or education or emotional need to another. But he did not think the pope would be well pleased with that. It was an eminently practical answer, but it was not a political victory.

Thirty-one

❧

IT WAS ONLY DAYS AFTER THAT WHEN ANNA ATTENDED AN
accident in the street. An old man had tripped and bruised himself
badly. She was bending over his leg, examining it, when there was a disturbance in the crowd that had gathered, and a young priest, ashen-faced,
elbowed his way through, pushing people aside roughly, calling out her
name.

"Is it an emergency?" she asked without looking up. "This man has had
a bad shock and needs—"

"Yes, you may already be too late." The priest reached for her arm and
pulled her to her feet. "He is bleeding to death. They have torn his tongue
out."

She turned to the crowd and gestured to the old man. "Take him home.
Give him hot drinks and keep him wrapped up. I have to go."

She picked up her bag and allowed the priest to half drag her around the
corner and up an alley to a small house where the door was open. She could
hear gagging and wails of fear and distress even before she was inside.

The scene that met her was appalling. A monk knelt sprawled on the
floor, blood streaming from his mouth, pooling scarlet on the tiles in front
of him, covering his hands and forearms and the front of his robe. He
gasped, gagged again, and more blood gushed out of him. His face was
gray with pain and terror, his eyes staring. Around him three other monks
stood helplessly, not knowing what to do. The man was bleeding to death
in front of them.

Anna put down her bag and seized a piece of cloth from one of them, glanced at it quickly to make certain it was clean, then went to the man on the floor. Someone said his name was Nicodemus.

"I can help you," she said firmly, praying that please God she could. "I'm going to stop the bleeding, and you won't choke. You'll have to breathe through your nose. It may be difficult, but you can do it. Keep still and let me press this. It's going to hurt, but it's necessary." And before he could pull away, she put her arm around him. One of the monks suddenly grasped what she was going to do and moved forward to help. Together they held the terrified man while Anna forced his mouth open wider and placed the cloth as hard as she could on the bloody remnant of his tongue.

It must have been agony, but after the first convulsive jerk and shudder he kept as still as he could.

In a perfectly level voice she ordered the other monks, and the priest who had come for her, to fetch more clean cloths, to open her case and take out certain herbs and spirits in small vials, also her surgical needles and silk. She directed two of them to fetch water and clean up the blood from the tiles.

All the time she kept the pressure on the stump of tongue, trying desperately to prevent the man from bleeding to death, choking on blood, or suffocating because he could not draw air into his lungs.

She changed one blood-soaked cloth for another, still holding the man with her left arm. She could hear the rhythmic murmur of prayer and wished she could join in.

Finally, more than half an hour after she had begun, she pulled the cloth away slowly and judged that if she was quick, she would be able to stitch the flesh and seal off the vessels enough to remove the cloth permanently.

It was a difficult task in the wavering candlelight, and she was acutely conscious of the pain she must be causing; unlike most other patients, he could not even be given any herbs to drink to deaden the sensation. His mouth and throat were a mass of swollen scarlet flesh, terribly mutilated, but all she had time to consider was saving his life from hemorrhaging away. She worked as quickly as she could, stitching, pulling, tying, cutting, stanching again, always with too much blood and with pain almost palpable in the air.

Finally, she finished and swabbed away the remaining blood. She gently washed his face, meeting his eyes, remembering that although he would never speak again, he could hear everything. She picked up herbs to show to all of them, saying when to use them and how and in what proportions.

"And you must keep his lips and his mouth moist," she went on. "But don't touch the wound yet, especially not with water. If he will take it, give him a little honeyed wine to drink, but carefully. Don't let him choke."

"Food?" someone asked. "What can he eat?"

"Gruel," she replied. "Warm, not too hot. And soups. He will learn to chew and to swallow properly, but give him time." She hoped that was true. She had no prior experience with such a mutilation.

"Thank you," the priest who had called her said sincerely. "Your name will always be in our prayers."

She waited with them all night, watching, listening to them trying to reassure one another and find courage for what they knew lay ahead, perhaps for all of them. Nicodemus was the first, but he would not be the last.

"Who did this?" she asked, dreading the answer.

The monks glanced at one another, then at her. "We do not know who they were," one of them replied. "They had the emperor's authority, but they were led by a foreigner, a Roman priest with light-colored hair and eyes like a winter sea." He breathed in and out slowly, and his voice dropped even lower. "He had a list."

Anna felt the coldness scour through her as if strength drained away. She was wrong to have doubted Constantine, too squeamish, too cowardly of spirit to acknowledge the truth because she wanted to keep her hands clean. She was ashamed of her stupidity.

Faith called for high prices—faith in God, the light, and the hope. Crucifixion was brutal. She was sick at the thought of it, the reality of the gasping for breath, the agony through belly and loins and every sinew, the sheer terror. Why did the images soften it, as if Christ had not been flesh like everyone else, as if His searing horror had been different? The answer was obvious—to escape knowing it, because it made our own betrayal of Him easier.

Then a curious peace filled her. Se had been wrong in her judgment of Constantine, wrong, ignorant, and shallow. She was crushed with penitence. They would all have to fight, to pick up and use weapons that would hurt them as well as the enemy. But the conflict inside her had ceased, and instead there was the wide, sweet balm of assurance.

She was called again to help other monks who had been tortured, but none afflicted her with the same panic as the first one had. She did not save everyone. Sometimes all she could do was ease the agony, stay with them to be there in the last moments. It was never enough.

She hated to be thanked, to accept their gratitude even when she failed. She did not feel brave. She wanted to run away, but the nightmares she would suffer forever, if she left a dying man, would have been worse than any waking horror.

At home she tossed and turned in the night and often woke gasping, her face wet with tears, her lungs aching.

She crept out of bed and knelt in prayer: "Father, help me, teach me. Why do You let this happen? They are good men, peaceable men, trying with all their hearts and bodies, all their time every day, to serve You. Why can't You help them? Or don't You care?"

Nothing answered her but the silence, void as the night. If there were real stars, not just dreams and illusion, they were infinitely out of reach.

Once she only just escaped the emperor's men when they broke into the house, and she ran, half dragged out of the back door by others who were just as passionately against the union. They were willing to forfeit their homes and possessions to rescue the monks who still preached against it and were made martyrs for their faith.

She ran with them through the wind and rain, their feet splashing in the rivulets of water streaming along the gutters, bumping into blind walls and tripping over steps in the darkness. She was pulled along, someone else carrying her bag and her instruments. She had little idea who they were, only gratitude for their courage.

When eventually they burst into a quiet room with an old woman alone beside the fire, she saw in the torchlight that there were three of them, two men and a young woman with long, wet hair.

"You must be more careful," the woman said, gasping as she struggled to allow the breath into her lungs. "You have answered too many of these calls. They know you now."

"Why me? Who knows me?" she asked, fighting against the truth.

"Bishop Constantine," he answered. "People know you are his physician, and you have helped him with the poor."

No more was said of it. Of course it was Constantine who was behind the rescues, the medicines, the whole resistance of the mass of ordinary people. It had been he who had fought to have Justinian exiled instead of put to death for his involvement in Bessarion's murder. They were all battling for the same cause, the survival of the faith, the life, the existence of Byzantium, and the freedom to worship as they knew to be right.

She went to Constantine in the quietness of his own house, in the gallery where his favorite icon hung.

"Thank you," she said simply, standing hungry and bruised, still exhausted in body from the night's loss and flight, the whole bitter failure of it. "Thank you for all you do, for having the courage to lead us, holding the light high for us to see. I don't really know how much I care passionately for one faith over another, one creed in the nature of God and the Holy Spirit, but I know absolutely that I care for the love of humanity that Christ taught us. I know with all my heart that it is worth everything we can pay for it. It is worth living and dying for. Without it, in the end the darkness takes everything."

There was a moment's prickling silence. She realized what she had said. "If hell were not so deep that it could break your soul, then heaven could not be so high. Would we want God to lower heaven?"

She drew in her breath as he lifted his head from prayer and looked at her.

"Could he ever do that, and still be God?" she asked, although she could have answered it herself.

He said nothing, but he made the sign of the cross in the air.

It did not matter; she did not need his reply.

Thirty-two

∾

HELENA HAD A MILD BUT EMBARRASSING AILMENT THAT she preferred Anna to treat rather than the physician she usually called.

It was the middle of the afternoon, and Simonis woke Anna from a briefly snatched rest. She was exhausted from treating the mutilated and dying, and her first instinct when Simonis told her Helena had sent for her was to refuse. How could she ever keep patience with a little irritation to the skin when men were being tortured to death?

"Bessarion's widow," Simonis said sharply, looking at Anna's face. "I know you're tired." Her voice softened, but there was still urgency in it and an edge of fear. "You haven't slept properly for weeks. But you can't afford to refuse Helena Comnena. She knew Justinian." She said his name gently. "And his friends." She did not add any more, but it hung in the air between them.

Helena received Anna in a newly painted, lush room next to her bedchamber. The murals had been redesigned, far closer to the erotic than Bessarion would have allowed. Anna hid her smile.

Helena was dressed in a loose tunic. She had an ugly rash on her arms. At first, she was frightened and polite. Then, as the herbs and advice began to take effect, she was no longer so concerned and her natural arrogance reasserted itself.

"It still hurts," Helena said sharply, pulling her arm away.

"It will hurt for a little while longer," Anna told her. "You must keep the ointment on it, and take the herbs at least twice a day."

"They're disgusting!" Helena responded, curling her lip. "Haven't you got anything that doesn't taste as if you're trying to poison me?"

"If I were trying to poison you, I would make it sweet," Anna replied with a slight smile.

Helena paled. Anna saw it and her interest sharpened. Why had Helena mentioned poison so easily? She looked away and allowed the silk of Helena's robes to fall back into a more modest position.

"Do you really have any idea what you're doing?" Helena snapped.

Anna decided on the risk. "If you are worried, I know other physicians who might suit you. And I am sure Zoe would know even more."

Helena's eyes were bright and hard, her cheeks flushed. She swallowed as if there were something rank in her throat. "I'm sorry. I spoke in haste. Your skill is quite sufficient. I am unused to pain."

Anna kept her eyes lowered in case Helena saw in them the contempt she felt. "You are right to be apprehensive. Such things, if not treated quickly, can become serious."

Helena drew in her breath with a little hiss. "Really? How quickly?"

"As you have done." Anna had exaggerated the danger. "I have another herb here which will help, but if you wish, I will stay with you, so that if it should have any ill effects in other ways, I can give you the antidote." That was an invention, but it would take time even to broach the subjects she wished to explore.

Helena gulped. "What sort of effects? Will it make me ill?"

"Faint," Anna replied, thinking of something not too distressing. "Perhaps a little hot. But it will pass quickly, if I give you the herb which counteracts it. You mustn't take it if it isn't needed. I'll stay with you."

"And charge extra, no doubt!" Helena snapped.

"For the herb, not for the time."

Helena considered for several seconds, then accepted. Anna mixed a number of herbs for her and had them steeped in hot water. It would be relaxing, good for the digestion. She soothed her conscience by telling herself she had kept her oath: If she was doing no good, at least she was doing no harm.

Helena saw Anna's eyes on the murals. "Do you like them?" she asked.

Anna drew in her breath. "I've seen nothing like them before."

"Nor in the flesh, I suppose," Helena observed with a sneer.

Anna longed to say that she had tended patients in a brothel once and seen something of the sort, but she could not afford to. "No," she said, clenching her teeth.

Helena laughed.

The servant returned with the steeped herbs in a glass.

Helena sipped it. "It's sour," she remarked. She looked at Anna over the top of the glass.

Anna could not afford to delay any longer. "You should look after yourself," she said, trying to invest her expression with concern. "You have suffered a good deal." She realized with a jolt that for all she knew, that could be true.

Helena struggled to mask her surprise, not entirely successfully. "My husband was murdered. Of course it is not easy."

As Anna stood looking at her, she knew it was perfectly possible Helena had actually assisted in his murder, but she hid her disgust behind a pretense of anxiety. "Surely it was worse than that? Was he not killed by men you had supposed to be his friends, and yours?"

"Yes," Helena said slowly. "I had thought so."

"I'm sorry," Anna murmured. "I cannot imagine what it must have been like for you."

"Of course you can't," Helena agreed, a shadow across her face that might have been contempt or only a movement of the light. "Justinian was in love with me, you know?"

Anna gulped. "Really? I had heard it was Antoninus, but perhaps I misunderstood. It was only gossip."

Helena did not move. "No," she denied. "Antoninus admired me, perhaps, but that is hardly love, is it?"

"I don't know," Anna lied.

Helena smiled. "It isn't. It is a hunger. Or don't you know what I mean?" She turned and looked at Anna appraisingly. "It was a euphemism for lust, Anastasius."

Anna lowered her eyes to prevent Helena from reading them.

"Do I embarrass you?" Helena asked with obvious pleasure.

Anna ached to fight back, to blaze at her that no, she didn't, she revolted her with greed, manipulation, and lies. But she could not afford to.

"I do embarrass you," Helena concluded happily. "But you didn't know Antoninus. He was handsome, in a fashion," she continued. "But he had not the depth of character of Justinian. He was extraordinary. . . ." She let it hang in the air, the suggestion infinite.

"Were they friends?" Anna asked.

"Oh yes, in many things," Helena replied. "But Antoninus liked parties, drinking, games, horses, that sort of thing. He was a good friend of Andronicus, the emperor's son—although perhaps not as much as Esaias. Justinian was an excellent rider, too, but he had more intelligence. He read all sorts of things. He liked architecture, mosaics, philosophy, things that were beautiful." Regret touched her face, only momentarily, but it was deep.

Anna was touched by it also, with pity, and with a closeness so in that instant she cared for Helena as if they had been one in grief, and perhaps they were.

Then the mood shattered, before she was ready for it.

"You're right," Helena said huskily. "I have suffered far more than most people realize. You must take care of me. Don't look so crushed. You're a good physician."

Anna forced her attention back to the present. "I didn't know that Justinian loved you," she said, hearing her own voice artificial in her ears. She remembered Constantine saying how Justinian had been revolted by Helena's advances and rebuffed her. Surely that was the truth? "You must miss him," Anna added.

"I do," Helena said with a tight, gleaming smile, unreadable except as a mask for something else. Anna was a servant and a eunuch; why should Helena show her anything she did not have to?

"And your husband, too," Anna added judiciously.

Helena shrugged. "He was a bore. He was always talking about religion and politics. Away with the damn bishop half the time."

"Constantine?" Anna said in surprise.

"Of course Constantine," Helena snapped. She looked at the glass in her hand. "This is disgusting, but it doesn't make me feel ill. You don't need to stay," she dismissed her. "Come again in three days. I'll pay you then."

When Anna returned, she had been with Helena only ten minutes when another visitor was announced, Eulogia Mouzakios. Helena had little choice but either to invite her in as soon as she was dressed again or to allow Eulogia to know that she had a physician present—or, more dangerous than that, some other caller she did not wish her to meet.

"If you dare tell her what you came to treat me for, I shall see you never work again," she snarled. "Do you understand me?"

"Say you have sprained your ankle," Anna advised. "She will smell the unguent in the air. I will not contradict you."

Helena straightened her tunic. She did not bother to answer.

Eulogia came in a few moments later, bearing a gift of honeyed fruit. She was an elegant woman, fair-haired and a little thin, several inches taller than Helena. There was a jolting familiarity about her that froze Anna in sudden confusion. She searched her mind for the name and found nothing.

"My physician," Helena said, waving an arm at Anna after she had greeted her guest. "Anastasius." She gave a slight smile, infinitely condescending. She was saying the name so Eulogia would recognize Anna instantly as a eunuch, a womanish creature with a man's name and no gender at all.

Eulogia stared at Anna for a moment, then looked away, entering conversation with Helena as if Anna had been a servant.

In that instant, Anna recognized her. Eulogia was Catalina's sister. They had met several times in Nicea years ago, when Catalina was alive. No wonder Eulogia had been disturbed by memory at first.

The sweat broke out on Anna's skin, and her breath was shaky, her hands trembling. She must watch every gesture. Nothing must remind Eulogia of Justinian's sister.

She had not finished prescribing for Helena, who would be angry if she left. She was imprisoned here by obligation and circumstance.

Helena sensed her discomfort and smiled. She turned to Eulogia. "Have some wine, and figs. These are very good, very quickly dried to produce excellent humors. It's kind of you to call."

She ordered the servant to bring refreshments, including a glass for Anna. It seemed to amuse her.

Anna considered refusing. Eulogia was watching her, the puzzled look in her face again. Anna dared not let Helena believe she was afraid of staying. "Thank you," she accepted, smiling back. "I'll have time to prepare your . . . herbs."

"Ointment!" Helena snapped, then blushed, aware she might have made a mistake. "I have a sprain," she said to Eulogia.

Eulogia nodded and offered her sympathy. They moved to sit together, leaving Anna to look in her bag for the appropriate items.

"How is Demetrios?" Eulogia inquired.

"Well, I imagine," Helena said casually. The wine, figs, and nuts came. She poured, leaving aside a glass for Anna but not offering it.

"I imagine Justinian will not be returning," Eulogia remarked, looking obliquely at Helena.

Helena allowed herself to look sad. "No. They believe he was deeply implicated in Bessarion's death. Of course he wasn't!" She smiled. "Whoever it was tried before, you know, when Justinian was in Bithynia, miles from here."

Anna's hand froze over the herbs. Fortunately her back was to the room, and neither Helena nor Eulogia could see her face.

"Tried to kill him?" Eulogia said in amazement. "How?"

"Poison," Helena said simply. "I've no idea who it was." She took a bite out of a dried fig and chewed it slowly. "And Bessarion was attacked in the street a few months after that, also. It looked like an attempted robbery, but afterward Bessarion himself thought it was one of his own men. But Demetrios found them for him, from friends of his—the Varangian Guard, so it seems unlikely."

Eulogia was curious. "Demetrios Vatatzes has friends in the Varangian Guard? How interesting. Unusual, for a man of an old imperial family. But then his mother, Eirene, is unusual."

Helena shrugged it off. "That's what I thought he said. Perhaps I was wrong."

Eulogia was concerned. "That's dreadful. Why would anyone wish to harm Bessarion? He was the noblest of men."

Helena hid her impatience. "It was always religion with him, so it was probably something to do with that. Of course, he and Justinian quarreled terribly about it, twice that I know of, and then Justinian went to Eirene. Heaven knows why! After that, of course, Bessarion really was killed by Antoninus. Funny thing is that I never knew that Antoninus cared about religion all that much. He was a soldier, for heaven's sake!"

Anna turned around, the herbs in her hand and a small jar of ointment. She held them out.

"Why, thank you, Anastasius," Helena said charmingly, meeting Anna's eyes. "I'll pay you if you come tomorrow, when I'm not busy."

Anna returned as commanded to collect the money.

When she arrived, Helena received her after only fifteen minutes' wait and made her almost welcome. They were in the newly decorated room with its exotic murals. She was dressed in a soft deep plum color that became her excellently. She had a minimum of jewelry, but with her warm skin and rich hair, she did not need it. The silk of her dalmatica billowed around her as she came across the room. It was one of the rare moments when Helena was as beautiful as her mother.

"Thank you for coming," she said warmly. "My ankle is so much better, I shall recommend you to everyone I know." She smiled, but she made no reference to the money.

"Thank you," Anna replied, taken by surprise.

"Odd that Eulogia should call just as you were here," Helena went on. "She was related to Justinian Lascaris, you know?"

Anna felt herself tense. "Was she?"

"He was married, some time ago." Helena's tone dismissed it as if it were not relevant anymore. "She died. She was Eulogia's sister." She was watching Anna's face as she spoke.

Anna stood motionless, awkward. Her hands seemed clumsy and in the way, as if she had no idea what to do with them. She swallowed. "Really?" She tried to sound uninterested. She was trembling.

Helena picked up a small jeweled box from the table. It was exquisite, silver set with chalcedony and surrounded by pearls. Anna could not help looking at it.

"You like it?" Helena held it out for Anna to see.

"It's very beautiful," Anna replied sincerely.

Helena smiled. "Justinian gave it to me. Unwise, I suppose, but as I told you, he loved me." She said it with satisfaction, but still looking at Anna under her eyelashes. "Bessarion gave me very little that I can recall. If he had chosen anything, it would have been books, or icons; dark ones, of course, heavy and very serious." She looked back at Anna. "Justinian was fun, you know? Or don't you know that? He had an elusive quality about

him, as if you could never really know all of him. He would always surprise you. I like that."

Anna's sense of discomfort grew. Why was Helena telling her all this?
Surely it was lies, as Constantine had said? Helena was beautiful and profoundly sensuous, but Justinian must have seen what was ugly inside her,
if not immediately, then soon after. Helena turned the box in her hand, its
pearls catching the light. Why had Justinian spent so much on her? Or
was that a lie, too?

Helena was watching her. There was an intensity in her gaze that was almost mesmeric. The light was shining on the box, on the plum silk of her
dalmatica, on the gloss of her hair. "Do you like beautiful things, Anastasius?" she asked.

There was only one possible answer to that. "Yes."

Helena's winged eyebrows rose, her eyes wide and dark. "Just 'yes'? How
unimaginative of you. What kinds of beautiful things?" she insisted. "Jewelry, ornaments, glass, paintings, tapestries, statuary? Or do you like
music, and good food? Or something you can touch, like silk or fur? What
gives you pleasure, Anastasius?" She put the box on the table and walked
three steps closer to Anna. "Do eunuchs have pleasure?" she said softly.

Was this what had happened to Justinian? Anna felt the sweat run
down her body and the blood hot in her face. Helena was trying to
awaken her sexually for entertainment, power, simply to see if she could.

The air in the room prickled as if a storm were about to break. Anna
would have given anything on earth to escape. It was excruciating.

Helena's eyes swept down Anna's body. "Do you have anything left,
Anastasius?" she asked, her voice soft not with pity, but with a sharp and
curiously coarse interest. Her small hand reached out to touch Anna's
groin where her male organs would have been, had she had them. They
met nothing.

Anna panicked, and hysteria welled up as if she were going to choke.
Helena's eyes were bright, laughing, at once both inviting and contemptu-
ous.

No man, however mutilated, would refuse to speak at all. And whatever
Anna said, it must be what a man would say, not the revulsion that was
beating inside her now like a huge bird trapped and breaking itself to force
a way out.

Helena was still waiting. She would never either forget or forgive a rebuff. She was so close, Anna could feel the warmth of her and see the pulse beating in her throat.

"Pleasure must be mutual, my lady," Anna said, her voice catching in her throat. "I think it would take a remarkable man to please you."

Helena stood absolutely still, her features slack with surprise and disappointment. Anastasius had been polite to her, flattering, yet she knew she had been robbed of something. She made a sharp little sound of annoyance and stepped back. Now it was she who did not know how to answer without giving herself away.

"Your money is on the table by the door," she said between her teeth. "You bore me. Take it and go."

Anna swiveled and went out, forcing herself not to run.

Thirty-three

ANNA ARRIVED HOME AFTER HER ENCOUNTER WITH HE-lena with her mind racing and her body still trembling as if she had been physically assaulted. She strode past Simonis with barely a word and went to her own room. She took off her clothes and bandages and stood naked, then washed herself over and over again, as though she could cleanse herself with harsh, astringent lotion, smelling the bite of it with pleasure. It stung, even hurt, but the pain pleased her.

She dressed again in her plain golden brown tunic and dalmatica and left the house without eating or drinking. She was fortunate that Constantine was at home.

He rose from his seat, his broad face filled with anxiety the moment after she entered. "What is it?" he demanded. "What's happened? Is it another monk tortured? Dead?"

It was preposterous! Her obsession with her own, so desperately trivial hurt, when people were dying terribly. She started to laugh, hearing it run out of control and end in sobbing. "No," she gasped, fumbling her way forward to sit in her accustomed chair. "No, it's nothing at all, nothing that matters." She put her elbows on the table and dropped her head into her hands. "I saw Helena. I've been treating her—nothing serious, just painful. She . . ."

"What?" he demanded, sitting opposite her. His voice was gentle, but there was an edge of alarm in it.

She looked up at him, steadying herself. "Really nothing," she repeated.

"You told me that she made an advance to Justinian, which he found acutely embarrassing." She did not add her own experience, but he understood it. She saw his face darken and then pity and revulsion leap to his eyes, as if he had been touched by it himself.

"I'm sorry," he said quietly. "Be careful. She is a dangerous woman."

"I know. I think I made a reasonably graceful refusal, but I know she won't forget it. I hope I don't have to treat her again. Perhaps she won't want me to. . . ."

"Don't rely on that, Anastasius. It entertains her to humiliate."

Anna pictured Helena's face. "I think she knows humiliation. She told me Justinian was in love with her. She showed me a beautiful box that she said he gave her." She saw it in her mind as she said it. It was the sort of thing Justinian would have chosen, but surely not for Helena?

Constantine's mouth curled with distaste and perhaps a vestige of pity. "Lies," he said without hesitation. "He disliked her, but he believed that Bessarion could lead the people against the union with Rome, so he hid his feelings."

"She said he quarreled with Bessarion badly, shortly before he was killed. Was that a lie, too?"

Constantine stared at her. "No," he said quietly. "That was the truth. He told me of it himself."

"Why?" she demanded. "Was it about Helena? Did Justinian tell him that Helena had . . . How could he tell him such a thing?"

"He didn't." Constantine shook his head minutely. "It was not to do with Helena."

"Then what?"

"I can't tell you," he replied. "I'm sorry."

The protest welled up inside her. She saw in his face that he knew the answer and that he would not tell her.

"Was it a confession?" she said shakily. "Justinian?" Now the fear gripped inside her like an iron hand closing.

"I cannot tell you," Constantine repeated. "To do so would betray others. Some things I know, some I guess. Would you have me speak that aloud, were it your heart and your secret?"

"No," she said hoarsely. "No, of course I wouldn't. I'm sorry."

"Anastasius . . ." He swallowed hard. His skin was very pale. "Be very careful of Helena, of all of them. There is such a lot that you don't understand, life and death, cruelty, hatred, old debts and dreams, things that people never let go of." He leaned farther toward her. "Two men are dead already, and a third exiled, and that is only a tiny part of it. Serve God in your own way, heal their ills, but leave the rest of it alone."

To argue with him would be pointless and unfair. She had not told him the truth, so how could he understand? They were each trying to reach the other, he failing because he was bound by the sanctity of confession, she because she could not trust him with the truth of why she could not let go of any of it.

"Thank you," she said quietly. "Thank you for listening."

"We shall pray together," he replied. "Come."

She was at the Blachernae Palace, having treated one of the eunuchs for a bad chest infection and been up with him all night until the crisis broke. Then she had been sent for by the emperor over a minor skin irritation. She was still with him when the two papal legates from Rome, Palombara and Vicenze, were granted an audience and were shown in, as was customary, by the Varangian Guard. They were always there, strong men with lean, hard bodies, dressed in full armor. The emperor was never without them, no matter the time of day or night, how formal or trivial the occasion.

Anna stood a little apart, not included, yet neither had she been given leave to go. She recalled her unpleasant journey to Bithynia with Vicenze, during which Cyril Choniates was nearly killed.

All the ritual greetings were exchanged, well-wishes that no one meant. Beside Anna, Nicephoras was watching every inflection while outwardly seeming merely to wait. Only once did he glance at her with a momentary smile. She realized that he would remain here, judging both words and silences, and afterward give Michael his counsel. She was glad of that.

"There is still some dissension among certain factions who do not see the need for Christendom to stand together," Vicenze said with barely concealed impatience. "We must do something decisive to prevent them from causing trouble among the people."

"I'm sure His Majesty is aware of that." Palombara glanced at Vicenze, then away again, both humor and dislike in his eyes.

"He cannot be," Vicenze argued impatiently. "Or he would have addressed it. I seek only to inform, and ask advice." The look of contempt he shot his fellow legate was sharp and cold.

Palombara smiled, and that too was a gesture without warmth. "His Majesty will not tell us everything he knows, Your Grace. He would hardly have led his people back again to their city, and kept them safe, were he ignorant of their nature and their passions, or lacking in either the skill or the courage to govern them."

Anna hid her smile with difficulty. This was becoming interesting. Rome certainly did not speak with a single voice, although it might be only ambition or personal enmity that divided them.

Palombara looked at Michael again. "Time is short, Your Majesty. Is there some way in which we might assist? Are there leaders with whom we might speak, and resolve some of their fears?"

"I have already spoken with the patriarch," Vicenze told him. "He is an excellent man, of great vision and understanding."

For half a second, it was clear in Palombara's face that he had not known that. Then he concealed it and smiled. "I don't think the patriarch is where we need to concentrate our efforts, Your Grace. Actually I believe it is the monks in different abbeys who harbor the greatest reservations about trusting Rome. But perhaps your information is different from mine?"

Two spots of color stained Vicenze's pale cheeks, but he was too furious to trust himself to speak.

Palombara looked at Michael. "Perhaps if we were to discuss the situation, Your Majesty, we might learn of a way in which, in Christian brotherhood, we could find an accord with these holy men, and persuade them of our common cause against the tide of Islam, which I fear is lapping ever closer around us."

This time it was Michael whose face lit with amusement. The conversation continued for a further twenty minutes, and then the two legates withdrew, and shortly afterward Anna went after them, having finally been noticed and given permission to leave.

She was on the way through the last hall before the great doors when she encountered Palombara, apparently alone. He looked at her with interest, and she was unpleasantly aware of a certain curiosity in him because he was clearly unfamiliar with eunuchs. She became self-conscious, aware of her woman's body under the clothes, as if he could see some kind of guilt in her eyes. Perhaps to a man unused to even the concept of a third gender, her masquerade was more apparent. Did she look feminine to him? Or was he simply considering how mutilated she was that her hands were so slender, and her neck, her jaw, lighter than a man's? She must say something to him quickly, engage his intellect away from her physical presence.

"You will find it a difficult task persuading the monks of the truth of your doctrine, Your Grace." Normally she was not conscious of her voice, but now to her it sounded so much that of a woman, without the mellower, more throaty quality of a eunuch. "They have given their lives to Orthodoxy," she added. "Some in most terrible martyrdom."

"Is that what you advise the emperor?" he asked, taking a step closer to her. In spite of his bishop's robes and emblems of office, there was a virility about him that was unpriestly. She wanted to make some uniquely eunuch gesture, to remind both of them that she was not a woman, but she could think of nothing that would not be absurd.

"The last advice I gave him was to drink infusion of camomile," she answered, and was delighted to see Palombara's puzzlement.

"For what purpose?" he asked, knowing she was taking some advantage of him to amuse herself.

"It relaxes the mind and assists digestion," she replied. Then, in case he should think the emperor was ill: "I came to attend one of the eunuchs who had a fever." Now she was aware of her crumpled dalmatica after a long night of nursing and the pallor of her face from weariness. "I have been with him for many hours, but fortunately he is past the crisis. Now I am free to leave, and attend my other patients." She moved forward to pass him.

"The emperor's physician," Palombara observed. "You look young to have attained such responsibility."

"I am young," she responded. "Fortunately the emperor has excellent health."

"So you practice on the palace eunuchs?"

"I make no distinction between one sick person and another." She raised her eyebrows. "I don't care whether they are Roman, Greek, Muslim, or Jew, except as their beliefs affect their treatment. I imagine you are the same. Or have you ceased to minister to ordinary people? That would explain your perception of the monks who do not wish to be driven into union with Rome."

"You are against the union," he observed with faint irony, as if he had known she would be. "Tell me why. Is the issue of whether the Holy Spirit proceeds from the Father only, or the Father and the Son, worth sacrificing your city for—again?"

She did not wish to concede his point. "Let me be equally direct. It is you who will sack us, not we who will come to Rome and burn and pillage it. Why does the issue mean so much to you? Is it enough to justify the murder and rape of a nation for your aggrandizement?"

"You are too harsh," he said softly. "We cannot sail from Rome to Acre without stopping somewhere on the way, for water and provisions. Constantinople is the obvious place."

"And you cannot visit a place without destroying it? Is that what you have in mind for Jerusalem also, if you beat the Saracens? Very holy," she added sarcastically. "All in the name of Christ, of course. Your Christ, not mine—mine was the one the Romans crucified. It seems to be becoming a habit. Was once not enough for you?"

He winced, his gray eyes widening. "I had no idea eunuchs were so savage in argument."

"From the look on your face, you have no idea about them . . . us . . . at all." That was a bad slip. Did he anger her because he was a Roman or because he could not take the gender for granted and made her so aware of her lie and the loss of herself as a woman?

"I am beginning to realize how little I know about Byzantium," he said softly, laughter and curiosity at the back of his eyes. "May I call on you if I need a physician?"

"If you fall ill, you should call one of your own," she responded. "You are more likely to need a priest than someone skilled in herbs, and I cannot minister to a Roman's sins."

"Are not all sins much the same?" he asked, amusement now quite open in his face.

"Exactly the same. But some of us do not see them as sins, and it is the healing I am responsible for, not the shriving—or the judgment."

"Not the judgment?" His eyes widened.

She winced as the barb struck home.

"Are the sins different?" he asked.

"If they are not, then what have Rome and Byzantium been fighting for over the centuries?"

He smiled. "Power. Is that not what we always fight for?"

"And money," she added. "And pride, I suppose."

"Not much is hidden from a good physician." He shook his head a little.

"Or a good priest," she added. "Although the damage you do is harder to attribute. Good day, Your Grace." She moved past him and walked down the steps toward the street.

Thirty-four

∽

ZOE HAD SEEN THE NECKLACE WHEN IT WAS ALMOST FIN-
ished. She had stood in the goldsmith's shop and watched him working the metal, heating it slowly, bending it, and smoothing it into exactly
the shape he wanted. She had seen the stones because he had had them out
in order to make the shapes to hold them: golden topaz, pale topaz almost
like spring sunlight, dark, smoky citrines, and quartz almost bronze. Only
a woman with hair like autumn leaves and fire in her eyes could wear this
without being dominated by it and made to look eclipsed rather than enhanced.

The goldsmith would be flattered that she wore it. It would advertise
his art and earn him more customers. Then everyone would want his
work.

She arrived at his shop at midmorning, gold coins ready in a small
leather pouch. She would not send Sabas for this because she wanted to
make sure the piece was perfect before she passed over her money.

She was irritated to see someone already there, a gaunt-faced middle-
aged man, his graying hair prematurely thin. He was holding coins in his
hand. He closed his fingers over them, smiling, and passed them to the
smith. The smith thanked him and picked up Zoe's necklace. He laid it on
a piece of ivory silk, wrapped it gently, and passed it to the man, who took
it and folded it away until it was concealed by his dalmatica. He thanked
the smith, then turned and walked away toward Zoe, his face alight with
satisfaction.

Zoe's fury overtook her. The man had taken her necklace, and the smith had allowed it.

It was only as the man passed her that she recognized him, even after all these years—Arsenios Vatatzes, Eirene's cousin by marriage, the head of the house whose crest was carved on the back of her crucifix.

It was his family who had robbed Zoe's father in 1204, promising to help in that terrible escape, then betraying them by keeping the relics, the icons, the documents of history that were uniquely Byzantine. They had fled to Egypt and sold them to the Alexandrians to finance a fat, comfortable exile, while Zoe's father, hideously bereaved, a widower with one small daughter, had had to labor with his hands in order to survive.

Now Arsenios was rich and back again in Constantinople. The time was right. She turned away, in case he might recognize her also.

She arrived home with her mind racing. There were a dozen ways of achieving someone's ruin, but it depended upon circumstance, the person's friends and enemies, their family or lovers, their hungers, their strengths, the weaknesses through which they were vulnerable. Arsenios was clever, and it seemed he had wealth, which these days meant power. The Vatatzes had ruled Byzantium in exile from 1221 to 1254. Arsenios's brother Gregory was married to Eirene, who was also of aristocratic descent from the Doukas dynasty. Only a disgrace so clear, so blatant as to be unarguable, would work.

What kind of disgrace? She paced the floor of her room, walked over to the great cross, and stared at it, seeing in her mind's eye the other side with one goal achieved, one of its fourfold emblems meaningless at last. The Vatatzes must be next.

Whom was the necklace for? Someone Arsenios loved, but whom?

It did not take long to find out that he was a widower and had one daughter, Maria, who was soon to make a fortunate marriage into a family with not only wealth, but immense power and ambition. Her beauty and her lineage were her strengths, and therefore Arsenios's strength also. That was where to strike.

The plan took shape in her mind. It would avenge the humiliation she had suffered in Syracuse all those years ago. Arsenios would pay for that, as he would pay for betraying Byzantium.

Anastasius Zarides was the perfect vehicle. But with a peculiar mixture of emotions, she remembered their last encounter. At first she had thought his saving the monk Cyril was just one of those random pieces of good fortune that happen from time to time to anyone. But then she had seen something in the healer's eyes that made her believe he knew she had tried to poison Cyril and had himself worked out exactly how.

She could see him in her mind's eye, and it was almost as if she had caught half an image on some polished surface: herself and yet not herself. The clothes were different, the shape of the body, no lush curves of bosom and hip. Yet the turn of the neck, the refinement of the jaw, just for half a second, the blink of an eye, were the same.

It was a delusion, of course. It was the fire in the mind that was the resemblance, the steel inside.

Of course, Anastasius had serious flaws. He forgave, and that was a weakness that sooner or later would prove fatal. He overlooked faults. Such a defect infuriated Zoe. It was like a chip on the face of an otherwise perfect statue. The mutilation of his manhood was a shame, but he was too young to be of any interest to her, although it was difficult to be accurate about the age of a man who was not a man. A human being without the spirit or the fire to hate was only half-alive. That was a waste. She liked him—apart from that.

She shook herself impatiently. The only thing of importance was that he was the perfect tool for this task and perhaps for others in the future. She realized with surprise just how sorry she would be if it did destroy him.

The sun was making bright patterns on the floor, its warmth soothing her shoulders. What was the cause of this new hate of Anastasius in Helena? Had he bested her too in something, and was she stupid enough to resent it instead of tasting the amusement of it? Zoe's daughter gave in to emotion instead of using it.

The idea that was forming in her mind had far greater possibilities than merely destroying Arsenios. By using Anastasius, she might also learn the answer to several questions that had become more and more insistent lately. Anastasius was always interested in the murder of Bessarion. Zoe had assumed that the law was correct and Antoninus had killed him, and then Justinian had helped him conceal it. She had thought that she knew why, but possibly she had been mistaken. It could be dangerous to be wrong.

Also dangerous was the possibility of Michael learning that she had deliberately ruined Arsenios. If he discovered this, he might deduce that she had also killed Cosmas. He might feel inclined to stop her.

That must be prevented. Michael was clever, inventive, a true Byzantine. Above all, he would save his country, his people, against their will if necessary, but he would live or die to prevent the crusaders from burning Constantinople again.

If Zoe were indispensable to him in any part of foiling Charles of Anjou, then he would protect her from the devil himself, let alone some mere question of the law.

Even as she stood in the sun, the sounds of the street echoing below her, the far light gleaming on the sea, she began to see how she would do it.

It took over two weeks for Scalini, the Sicilian, to visit her, alone and at night, as she had insisted. He was a weasel of a man, but clever and not without a sense of humor, and that quality alone redeemed him in her eyes.

"I have a job for you, Scalini," she told him as soon as he sat in the chair opposite her and she had poured wine. It was long after midnight, and she had only one torch lit.

"Of course." He nodded and reached for the glass. He put it to his long, sharp nose and sniffed. "Ascalon wine, with honey and something else?"

"Wild camomile seeds," she told him.

He smiled. "Where is the job? Sicily, Naples . . . Rome?"

"Wherever the king of the Two Sicilies might be," she replied. "As long as he is not here. By then it would be too late."

He grinned. His teeth were sharp and white, well cared for. "He will not be here yet," he said with relish, licking his lips as if tasting something sweet. "The pope has forgiven the emperor of Byzantium. When he heard this piece of news, His Majesty of the Two Sicilies was so beside himself with rage that he snatched up his own scepter and bit off the top of it!"

Zoe laughed until the tears were wet on her face. Scalini joined in, and they finished the wine. She opened a new bottle, and they finished that as well.

It was coming toward three in the morning when at last she leaned forward, her face suddenly grave. "Scalini, for reasons which are not your concern, I need to have something of great worth to offer the emperor. A year from now may be sufficient, but I need to be certain of it."

He pursed his lips. "The only thing Michael Palaeologus wants is his throne secure and Constantinople safe. He'll trade anything else on earth for the city's security—even the Church."

"And who threatens him?" she whispered.

"Charles of Anjou. The world knows that."

"I want to know everything I can about him. Everything! Do you understand me, Scalini?"

His small brown eyes searched her face, studying inch by inch. "Yes, I understand."

Thirty-five

∞

IT WAS BEGINNING TO DISTURB ZOE THAT SHE DID NOT know for certain who had betrayed Justinian to the authorities. She had assumed it was some clumsiness that had caused Antoninus to be caught, and he had been tortured, which was a common practice.

But on reflection, she doubted that even under torture Antoninus, an unquestionably brave man and a soldier of excellent record, would betray any friend, let alone one who was as close as Justinian had been. Now she needed to know who it had been, and if Anastasius would discover that for her, so much the better.

In the meanwhile, he was treating Maria Vatatzes precisely according to Zoe's plan. The whispers as to the exact nature of Maria's disease were spreading nicely. The tide of anger would in time take back her brother and her father, just as Zoe intended. "If someone is poisoning her, find out who, and give her an antidote," she said to Anastasius. "If anyone knows such a thing, it is you."

"Who would poison her?" Anastasius asked.

Zoe raised her eyebrows. "You ask as if I would know. Her brother Georgios is a friend of Andronicus Palaeologus, as Esaias is, and Antoninus was. They play hard, drink hard, and take their pleasure where they wish. Georgios has a high temper, so I have heard. Perhaps he has enemies? I have wondered if it could have a thread of connection with Bessarion's death."

"After five years?" Anastasius said with disbelief.

Zoe smiled. She was not quite sure how much Anastasius knew, and it was sharp in her memory that this bland-seeming eunuch could bite very hard indeed. "Five years is nothing. There is much yet to learn," she said gently. "Antoninus is dead, but Justinian is still alive. You have asked many questions, but never the only one that I ask and cannot answer. . . ."

"What question is that?" Anastasius's voice had dropped to a whisper. There was no doubt that Zoe had his total attention now.

"Who betrayed Justinian to the authorities?" Zoe answered.

"Antoninus . . . ," Anastasius replied, but the certainty had gone from his voice.

Zoe felt victory sing inside her, at least for this first step. "I assumed it was, but your questions stirred doubt in me. Shortly before Bessarion was killed Justinian quarreled with him, passionately. Justinian went to Eirene about it, but she gave him no help. He went to Demetrios, but he was no help, either. He did not come to me. Why was that?" Zoe could see the thoughts racing behind Anastasius's dark gray eyes. Sometimes for an instant he looked like Justinian, the same expression. Except that Justinian had been such a man!

"Do you think this poisoning of Maria, if that's what it is, could have something to do with Bessarion's murder?" Anastasius asked, doubt still in his voice. "Georgios Vatatzes?"

"It might." Not the truth, but close enough to be believable. "Georgios knew Bessarion, and he knew Antoninus even better."

"Thank you," Anastasius said quietly. "Perhaps that is true."

Anna found Georgios as he was leaving the Blachernae Palace. He was a better-looking man than his father, taller and leaner, without the years of soft living larding his body with fat. He recognized her after only a moment's hesitation.

"Is my sister worse?" he said sharply, stopping in the shadow of the great outer wall with its immense stones fitted so perfectly together and the high windows that let in so much light.

"No," Anna said with rather more certainty than she felt. "But she may be, if I don't find the source of the poison."

He stiffened. "Why do you say it is poison? Or is this just an excuse because you don't know how to treat her?"

"I don't know who is poisoning Maria," she said quietly. "But I think that if you examine everything you know, particularly about other plots, other deaths, you might know."

He looked totally confused. "Whose death?"

"Bessarion Comnenos?" she suggested. "Or Antoninus? Was he not a friend of yours? And Andronicus Palaeologus?"

He froze. "God Almighty! That?" His face was pale.

"Do you know something that could be of danger to someone? Or of use?"

"And they'd poison Maria?" He was aghast.

"Wouldn't they?" she asked. "What was Antoninus like? And Justinian Lascaris?" She almost stumbled over the name.

"They were close friends," he said slowly, remembrance sharpening in his mind as he found the words. "Justinian cared about the Church more than he let on, I think." He frowned. "Antoninus was different. When he was with Justinian, he was thoughtful, loved beautiful things. But when he was with Andronicus and Esaias, he was just like any other soldier, enjoying the moment. I never knew which was the real man."

A shadow crossed his face. "We were going to have a great party the night after Bessarion was killed. Esaias and Andronicus were going to be there. Andronicus planned to have races first—that was Antoninus's idea, like the old days, before the exile. Justinian loved horses, too. He always said we'd know we really had our city back when we opened the Hippodrome again."

"Was Justinian going to be at the party?"

"No. Antoninus said he had to be somewhere else. But what the devil can this have to do with Maria?" Anger darkened his face again. "Just cure her! I'll find out who did it."

It was pointless to argue any further. Anna thanked him and walked away, leaving him staring out across the city toward the western headland and the old Hippodrome.

She turned over everything that he had said. Was the party important? It had been canceled because Antoninus was arrested that day. Had he betrayed Justinian? For what? They had executed him anyway. Or was Zoe right, and it had been someone else? Perhaps Esaias?

What was supposed to have happened at that party? Which was the real Antoninus—the partygoer, drunkard, and lover of horse races whom

Georgios had described and she had heard about from others? Or the man of passion and intelligence whom Justinian would have wanted as a friend?

Anna discovered the nature of the poison afflicting Maria Vatatzes—it was administered through the stems and leaves of the flowers that arrived fresh every few days in Maria's room.

Maria was recovering, but it was too late to save her reputation from the whispers about her virtue. Her marriage to John Kalamanos was canceled. His family would no longer countenance it, and he yielded to their wishes.

Maria was devastated. Even though she was almost in full health again, she threw herself onto her bed and sobbed. There was nothing Anna could do to help. It was unjust, but there was no recourse.

Anna had not been long home after what was her final visit to Maria when Simonis came in to say that there was a gentleman to see her. It was after dark, and Leo was still out on an errand. Anna could see the anxiety in Simonis's face.

Anna smiled. "Show him in, please. I expect he has some matter to discuss which is urgent, if he calls at this hour."

Georgios Vatatzes entered in a towering rage. His face was flushed and he stormed into the room, slamming the door behind him with Simonis barely through it.

Anna squared her shoulders and stood as tall as she could, but she was still several inches shorter than him and half his weight.

"Have you discovered something?" she said as stiffly as she could, but her voice wavered a little, giving her away. She sounded like a woman.

"No, I haven't. In God's name, what does it matter who poisoned her?" His voice was thick with rage. "The Kalamani have withdrawn their offer of marriage, as if our family were unclean. It stains all of us. They won't remember it was some unknown poison, all they'll think of was that the word went around Maria was a whore! You let the filthy gossips say whatever they wanted when you could have told them the truth."

"You could have said it was poison," she countered. "I was not free to."

"Who's going to believe us when you wouldn't back us up?" He was drunk, slurring his words. "The poison worked, didn't it? It didn't kill her, but she might as well be dead." He was standing so close to her that she could smell the acrid sweat on him and the odor of wine.

Her breath was ragged. "You could have told anyone you wished to that she was being poisoned."

"You destroyed her with your sanctimonious silence as surely as if you'd poisoned her yourself," he sneered. "She might as well be dead."

"Because she didn't marry John Kalamanos?" she said. "If he loved her, he would believe what she said and marry her anyway."

Georgios lunged forward and struck Anna across the side of the face, sending her sprawling backward, arms flailing. She caught her left hand on the edge of a small table, and pain shot through her arm. He reached for her, pulling her up by the front of her tunic, and hit her again. She could hardly get her breath for the fear that seemed to paralyze her. She was dizzy and could taste blood. She knew he was going to go on beating her. Any moment her clothes would rip and expose the padding and her breasts. Then it wouldn't matter if he killed her or not, it would all be ended anyway.

The next time he came forward, she managed to roll over sideways, away from him, and reached for the small stool half under the table. His blow landed on her shoulder, numbing her arm. She grasped the stool with her other hand and swung it back toward his face as hard as she could.

She heard him roar with surprise and pain. Then there was a scream that was not hers—and surely was too high-pitched to be his?

There were other people in the room, more shouting and banging, the heavy thud of bone against flesh, and bodies swaying and lashing, weight hitting the floor, finally heavy breathing and no more movement. She was half-blinded and all she could feel was her own pain.

Someone reached for her and she clenched, trying to think how to strike back. She would have only one chance.

But the hands were gentle, lifting her up. A cold, wet cloth touched the throbbing wound in her cheek and jaw. She opened her eyes and saw a man's face, someone she knew, but she could not think from where.

"Nothing is broken," he said with a rueful smile. "I am sorry. We should have been here sooner."

Why could she not remember him? He put the wet cloth to her face again. There was blood on it.

"Who are you?" She wanted to shake her head, but with the slightest movement pain shot through her like a knife blade.

"My name is Sabas," he replied. "But I expect you have never heard it."

"Sabas . . ." It meant nothing.

"Zoe Chrysaphes was afraid for you," he said. "She knew that Georgios Vatatzes had a violent temper, and overbearing family pride."

Her breath caught in her throat, all but choking her. "Had?"

Sabas shrugged. "I am afraid he attacked us also, and in order to subdue him, it was necessary . . ." He left the sentence unfinished.

She sat up a little farther and looked past him. Georgios lay on the floor, blood on his face and his head at an angle that made it clear his neck was broken. Another man stood by him.

"Don't worry," Sabas said hastily. "We'll take him away. Perhaps you should say a burglar attacked you. If anyone asks, you frightened him off."

She laughed abruptly, close to hysteria. "Well, if they look at me, and reckon I made an even worse mess of him, no one will try to rob me again."

Sabas smiled, softening the hard lines of his face. "Bought at a high price, but a good thing." He helped her to stand, guiding her to a chair. "Can your own servants assist you, or would you like us to send for another physician?"

"They can assist me, thank you," she replied. "Would you be kind enough to thank Zoe Chrysaphes for her concern, and your courage? If ever you need any help, it is yours, or your friend's."

He bowed, and then the two of them picked up Georgios and carried him out, leaving Simonis to come in, her face blanched with shock. While she did what she could to clean Anna's cuts and apply ointment to the bruises, Anna's mind raced. She should have known Georgios Vatatzes would take his sister's rejection badly. Or was it more complex than that?

Bessarion's murder again, old fear, old vengeance? And how had Zoe's servants known what to expect and from whom? The answer to that was only too obvious, once Anna faced the facts. Zoe had poisoned Maria, knowing it would ruin the family and intending it to. She had sent Sabas and his fellow servant, not so much to rescue Anna as to make certain that Georgios was killed.

But what had they done to earn Zoe's hatred to such a depth?

Thirty-six

When Anastasius was shown into Zoe's magnificent room, the physician was clearly angry but quietly so, his eyes hard as stones on the shore. He looked appalling; his face was swollen and dark with bruises, and he limped. He dropped herbs on the table as if she had ordered them, but presumably they were to explain to the servants why he was here.

"What are they?" Zoe inquired with interest, as if she had no concern at his appearance, no sudden welling up of fear that he was really hurt.

"The antidote to the poison you used on Maria Vatatzes," Anastasius replied icily. "I brought it so that you know I have it, and other antidotes. And that Arsenios knows I have it."

Zoe raised her eyebrows. "It seems to have taken you rather a long time to find it. I assume you learned nothing about Bessarion's death from Georgios, before he attacked you? Unfortunately you will learn nothing now."

Temper flared in Anastasius's eyes. "It won't take so long if it happens again," he retorted, entirely ignoring the question about Georgios and Bessarion's death. "Because I shall know where to look. Of course, should you be the victim, that would be different. You might find it yourself first, if you are well enough to get out of bed."

Zoe was stunned. Was he threatening her? "How ungrateful of you, Anastasius. After I had the forethought to send Sabas to your rescue." She regarded him up and down carefully. "You look awful. Not that I doubted Sabas, he never lies."

Anastasius's face tightened. "He told the truth. Had he not come, I would be dead. Were I not grateful for that, I would have made it public that you had poisoned Maria. I know that from the flower seller, and she will say nothing, but if harm comes to her, then I will speak. You can't poison everyone. But in case you have a mind to, Arsenios is perfectly aware that it was you who destroyed his daughter, and who caused his son to be killed in disgrace. I have no idea why you hate him, but he knows, and has taken steps to protect himself."

"You're threatening me!" Zoe said in amazement. Perversely, she was pleased.

"That amuses you?" Anastasius said, disgust twisting his mouth. "It shouldn't. People are at their most dangerous when they have nothing left to lose. If you hate Arsenios, you should have left him something worth surviving to save. That was a mistake." He turned and walked out, still limping, but with dignity.

Of course, the question of allowing Arsenios to continue spreading the rumors was settled. Zoe could not. She must deal with him, but the question was how?

Again, poison was the obvious weapon. It was her supreme skill. Of course, Arsenios would never take food or drink from her, even in a public place. She would have to find another way to administer it.

Another hundred candles to the Virgin.

She selected the poison carefully, something to which there was no antidote. It had no color and no odor, and it acted rapidly enough that Arsenios would have no chance to call for help or to attack her before he was incapacitated. It was ideal. This would look like a hemorrhage. No one would ever trace it back to her, either from its nature or because she was known to have purchased it. She had possessed it for years and had never needed it until now.

A further hundred candles to light. The priest smiled at her, knowing her now.

Zoe arrived at Arsenios's home carrying her own most precious and beautiful icon, the dark blue sloe-eyed figure in the frame inset with smoky citrine and river pearls. She wrapped it in silk first, then over that oiled silk, to protect it from the weather should it suddenly rain. The sky was overcast and there was a light wind from the west, but she did not feel the chill in it, even now at dusk. He had agreed to see her only because she was bringing the icon. He sensed she was afraid, at a disadvantage, and his lust for revenge mounted higher. It was what she counted on, but it was a dangerous game.

Sabas was barred from entering and told to wait outside. She was shown into Arsenios's presence. That was what she had expected. She trusted Sabas, but she did not want him to see her kill Arsenios. That might strain his loyalty. He was a good man, but his willing blindness would go only so far.

Arsenios dismissed the servants, telling them the matter was private. He smiled as the door closed, leaving them alone in the room with its walls inlaid with porphyry and its tessellated floor. It seemed he had no more desire to have servants present than she did. Her pulse quickened.

"The icon?" he asked, looking at it as she laid it on the table. "Gorgeous, I trust?"

She allowed herself to flinch, confirming what he already believed. He must not think she was in control, acting.

"From my own collection," she replied huskily. Then she lowered her eyes. "But you know the real from the false." It was time to let him know that she understood his anger and that it was justified. She should seem afraid to anger him further.

"Why do you bring it to me, Zoe Chrysaphes? What are you looking for in return? You never trade except for advantage."

"Trade?" She allowed the tension in her to show in the trembling hand, the uncertain words. "Yes, of course I want something, but not money."

He did not answer her but pulled on a pair of fine, soft leather gloves, so light in weight that he could move his fingers easily in them, and then carefully he unwrapped the icon from its silks.

She watched, listened to the sudden intake of his breath with admiration as the last wrapping fell away and he saw the glowing beauty of the Virgin's face and felt the weight of gold in the frame. She saw the lust for it in his eyes and the delicate movement of his finger as it traced the lines of the frame and moved it so the light caught the gems.

She stood motionless, watching.

He turned and looked at her, studying her face, the rigidity of her body, the power of emotion in her, savoring it. This was what he wanted—her fear.

She started to speak and then stopped.

He smiled slowly and turned back to the icon. "It's exquisite," he said, his voice filled with awe in spite of himself. "But it is rather similar to one I already have."

It did not matter. She had no intention of giving it to him, but she tried to appear crushed and, even more than that, afraid. Again she started to speak and stopped. She looked at him, imagining his cousin Gregory, perhaps the only man she had loved for himself, years ago, and made her eyes plead with him.

Arsenios fingered the front of the icon, picked it up, and examined the back, his heavy-lidded eyes flicking up at her and down at the frame. He saw the small tack she had left projecting, and his smile widened.

Deliberately, she shuddered. She would have gone pale were it within her power.

"Careless," he whispered. "Not up to your usual standard, Zoe." His voice was a hiss, anger flaring in his eyes.

"I'm s-sorry," she stammered, reaching into the folds of her tunic for the dagger in its jeweled sheath, crystals blazing in the light. She pulled it forward enough for him to see it.

He saw it and lunged forward, his fingers grasping her wrist like a vise. She did not need to pretend in order to cry out in pain. She was a tall woman, his height, but she was no match for him in strength. He wrenched the sheath from her easily, bruising the slender bones of her wrist and bending the arm back until it was twisted, bringing tears to her eyes.

He was close to her; she could smell the sweat of anger on him and see the pores of his skin.

"Just a little scratch," he said between his teeth. "An accident with a careless tack, and I would have been dead. Why, Zoe? Because Gregory would not marry you? You fool! Eirene was a Doukas. Do you imagine he would have given that up for you? Why bother? You lay with him whenever he wanted anyway. One doesn't marry a whore."

She did not have to pretend anger, or pain. She let it blaze up in her eyes and tried to snatch back the dagger, but deliberately aiming to the left, as if misjudging.

He laughed, a harsh, ugly sound, and grasped the handle to yank it free. It did not come, and he pulled harder. "You tried to stab me," he said jubilantly. "That's what you came for, to murder me. We struggled, and tragically, in spite of all I could do, you slipped and the knife turned on you—fatally." His lips drew back from his teeth in triumph; he pulled again on the knife hilt, his other hand on the sheath to free it, and felt the tiny needle in his flesh.

It was seconds before he knew what it was; then, as the pain flooded through him, his eyes widened and he stared at her in sudden, terrible understanding.

She stood straight now, shoulders back, head high, but far enough away from him that even if he fell forward, he could not reach her. She smiled, a slow, sweet taste of victory.

"It was nothing to do with Gregory," she told him as he fell forward onto his knees, his face purple, his hands clutching at his stomach. "I had all I wanted from him." That was almost true. "It was your father's theft of the icons when the city was burning. You took our family relics, and you kept them. You betrayed Byzantium, and for that you must pay with your life." She stepped backward as he crawled a few inches toward her. His throat was closing and his eyes bulged in his head. Saliva dribbled from his mouth and there was a terrible hacking, rasping sound in his chest, then he vomited blood in a scarlet tide. He screamed and almost instantly choked as more blood spewed out. His eyes rolled in terror, and he gagged and choked, swallowing, drowning.

She watched a few moments longer until his face turned purple and he lay still. She walked around him and picked up her icon and the knife, rewrapping both carefully in the silk. She walked to the door and opened it silently. There was no one in the hall or the room beyond. She moved soundlessly over the marble and out the great carved front door. Sabas was watching for her and appeared out of the shade. Servants would find Arsenios and suppose he had died of a hemorrhage; perhaps too much wine had ulcerated his stomach.

That night, she celebrated with the best wine in her cellar. But she awoke sometime in the dark, shivering and nauseated, her body running with sweat. She had been dreaming, seeing Arsenios's body on the floor again, vomiting rivers of blood, and the icons on the wall above him, their calm-eyed faces watching his horror. She lay rigid in the bed. What if his servants knew it was poison? Was anyone clever enough to find traces of it? Surely not. She had been careful. He had died dreadfully—quickly, but in agony and horror.

When daylight came, it was not so bad. She could see the realities of her house, her servants moving around. Sabas came in, and at first she dared not meet his eyes, then she could not look away from him. What did he know? To explain herself to a servant would embarrass them both—and yet she wanted to. Desperately she wanted not to be alone.

That night, the dreams were worse. Arsenios took longer to die. There was more blood. She saw his bulging eyes always looking at her, staring, stripping her clothes off literally until she stood in front of him naked, vulnerable, her breasts hanging, her stomach bulging, repulsive. He crawled on the floor after her, refusing to be paralyzed, refusing to choke, to die. He grasped her ankle with his claw of a hand, pain shooting through her again as it had when he had taken her wrist.

He had been going to kill her! He had said so. She had had no choice. She was justified. It was self-defense, to which everyone is entitled. There was no justice in this!

She woke with her body covered in sweat, her clothes sticking to her, ice-cold the minute she threw off the cover and slid out. She knelt on the marble floor, shuddering, her hands folded in prayer, knuckles shining white in the candlelight.

"Blessed Virgin, Holy Mother of God," she whispered hoarsely. "If I have sinned, forgive me. I did it only to prevent him from keeping the icons which belong to the people. Forgive me, please wash me of my sins."

She crept back to bed, still shaking with cold, but she dared not sleep.

The following night she did the same, but spending longer on her knees, recounting to the Blessed Virgin the icons Arsenios had taken and his impiety in keeping them all these years—and that was apart from the less precious, less beautiful ones he had sold, anyone could guess as to whom—the buyer with the most money. As if that mattered!

On the fourth day, she heard the news she had prayed for. Arsenios Vatatzes had been buried. They said he had died of a hemorrhage to the stomach shortly after Zoe had visited him. His servants had found him. She listened carefully, but there was no whisper of blame. She had got away with it!

The conclusion was obvious. Heaven was with her; she was an instrument in the hands of God. The rest was just bad dreams, nothing more. They should be forgotten, like any other nonsense.

Tomorrow she would go out and offer her thanks, with gifts, to the Virgin Mary in the Hagia Sophia, knowing that she had divine approval. Candles were not enough, but she would offer them anyway, hundreds of them, enough to light the whole dome, and also perhaps one of her lesser icons.

Thirty-seven

 G IULIANO DANDOLO ENJOYED BEING BACK IN CONSTAN-
tinople. The vitality of the city excited him; the tolerance and width
of vision was like the wind off a great ocean. It called to him more and
more powerfully each time he saw it.

Now he was here at Contarini's orders to observe for himself, rather
than by rumor, whether Byzantium was finally keeping the rules of the
union with Rome or, as before, paying them lip service while going its
own way.

What he had seen so far should have pleased him for the prospects of a
new crusade passing this way and storming the city and the profit that that
would mean for Venice. But Giuliano could not rejoice in it. He learned
of the strength of the resistance with a sense of foreboding. Not only had
the leaders of opposition to the union been blinded, mutilated, or ban-
ished; many had fled to separatist Byzantine states. The prisons were
crowded, and most embarrassing to Michael, many of his immediate relatives were actively engaged in plotting against him. It seemed he was attacked at the front and beset on all sides.

The Blachernae Palace was beautiful, even if it was poor compared with
the glories of Venice. There were still the marks of fire and pillage all
through it, and it had none of the sheer grace of pale marble and the endless reflections of light that he was used to.

But when Giuliano was face-to-face with Michael, he saw a man of remarkable composure. There was a weariness in the emperor's face, but

nothing of fear. He received Giuliano with courtesy and even a shadow of wit. Against his will, Giuliano felt both a pity and an admiration for him. Whatever Michael lacked, it was not courage.

"And of course there is the East," a eunuch told Giuliano as he was conducted away after his audience was over. The eunuch's name was Nicephoras.

Giuliano dragged his mind back to the issues as they walked side by side along a vaulted corridor paved with mosaics.

"Everything is changing all the time," Nicephoras added, choosing his words carefully. "It appears at the moment as if the greatest threat to us is from the West, the next crusade, but in truth I think we have as much, if not more, to fear from the East. It is simply that the West will be first, if we do not find some accommodation with Rome, however much we hate it. But there is no accommodation to be found with the East." He looked at Giuliano. "There is much balancing to be done, and it is hard to know which way to turn first."

Giuliano wanted to say something intelligent and sympathetic, without betraying Venice or sounding patronizing, but nothing whatever came to him. "I begin to feel as if Venetian politics are relatively simple," he said quietly. "This is like taking out a boat that is leaking in ten different places."

"A good analogy," Nicephoras agreed with appreciation. "But we are good at it. We have had much practice."

Giuliano was still on the steps, leaving the palace, when he came to the bottom at the same time as another eunuch, apparently also leaving. This person was considerably smaller, several inches shorter than Giuliano himself, and more delicate of appearance. When he turned there was a flash of recognition in his dark gray eyes, and Giuliano remembered him from the Hagia Sophia. This was the same man who had seen him clean Enrico Dandolo's tomb and whose face had shown such grief and such compassion.

"Good morning," Giuliano said quickly, then wondered if perhaps he had been precipitate in speaking to him, that it would be taken as overfamiliarity. "Giuliano Dandolo, ambassador from the doge of Venice," he introduced himself.

The eunuch smiled. His face was effeminate, but certainly not without character and again the burning intelligence Giuliano thought he had seen in the Hagia Sophia. "Anastasius Zarides," the eunuch said. "Sometime physician to Emperor Michael Palaeologus."

Giuliano was surprised. He had not placed the man as a physician. But it only reminded him how alien Byzantium was. He hastened to say something else. "I live in the Venetian Quarter." He made a gesture roughly in the direction of the shore. "But I am beginning to think perhaps that restricts me from knowing the city better." He stopped, gazing across the rooftops. The Golden Horn was spread below them, shining in the morning sun, dotted with boats from every corner of the Mediterranean. The air was warm, and Giuliano could imagine he smelled the odors of salt and spice drifting up from the harbor front.

Anastasius followed his gaze. "If I could choose, I would live where I could see the sun rise over the Bosphorus, and that requires some height. Such places are expensive." He laughed with gentle self-mockery. "I would have to save the life of the richest man in Byzantium in order to afford that, and fortunately for him, if less so for me, he is in excellent health."

Giuliano regarded him with amusement. "And if he were ill, would he send for you?" he asked.

Anastasius shrugged. "Not yet, but by the time he is ill, maybe." He was joking, lightly.

"In the meantime, healing merely the emperor, where do you live?" Giuliano kept up the easy tone.

Anastasius pointed down the hill. "Over there, beyond those trees. I still have a good view, although only to the north. But there is an excellent place, my favorite in the city, a hundred yards away, up on that hill, where you can see in almost a full circle. And it is quiet. Very few other people seem to go there. Perhaps I am the only one with time to stand and stare."

Giuliano had a sudden thought that perhaps what he really meant was to stand and dream, but self-consciousness had prevented him from saying so.

"Were you born here?" he asked quickly.

Anastasius looked surprised. "No. My parents were part of the exile. I was born in Thessalonica, and I grew up in Nicea. But this is our ancestral home, the heart of our culture, and I suppose of our faith as well."

Giuliano felt stupid. Of course he was born somewhere else. He had forgotten that almost everyone he spoke to in this city would have been born during the exile and was therefore from somewhere else. Even his own mother had been.

"My mother was born in Nicea," he said aloud, then instantly wondered why. He looked away, keeping his face in profile to Anastasius.

As if sensing something of a retreat, Anastasius changed the subject. "They say that some of Venice is like Constantinople. Is that true?"

"Some of it, yes," he replied. "Especially where there are mosaics. One in particular I like, in a church very similar to one here." Suddenly he remembered how many Byzantine works of art had been stolen in the ruin in 1204 and felt his face grow hot with embarrassment. "And the money exchanges, of course, and the . . ." He stopped. The silk trade had once been purely Byzantine; now the art, the weaving, and even the colors were Venetian. "We've learned much from you," he said a little awkwardly.

Anastasius smiled and gave a slight shrug. "Perhaps I shouldn't have asked. I opened the door to an honest answer."

He was startled. It was a response with more grace than he had expected or perhaps deserved. He smiled back. "We are learning, but there is a vitality here, a complexity of thought we may never acquire."

Anastasius inclined his head in acknowledgment, then excused himself with ease, as if they might meet again with the same interest.

Giuliano walked down the steep street lightly. Anastasius had been born during the exile, and judging from his age, his parents must have been also. It had been over seventy years now. That meant, of course, that Giuliano's own mother had been a child of the exile, even if her heritage was pure Byzantine. And so shortly after the pillage of the city, her hatred for Venice must have been very strong. How on earth had she come to marry a Venetian? More than before, now that he had stood in the wind and the sun and spoken so candidly with another lost, different child of the exile, born away from a spiritual home, he was compelled to find out more about the woman whose child he was.

He began to inquire diligently, and the answers led him to many interesting people and eventually to a woman well into her seventies, who had actually fled the invading armies after the fall of the city. She must have been amazingly beautiful in her youth and in her middle years. Even now she had a depth of passion, a flair and individuality that fascinated him. Her name was Zoe Chrysaphes.

She seemed to be willing to talk about the city, its history, its legends, and its people. The room where she received Giuliano overlooked a vast panorama of the roofs of lesser houses. Standing beside him at the window, she told him of the traders who came from Alexandria and a great river of Egypt that wound like a snake into unknown heart of Africa.

"And from the Holy Land," she went on, extending her arm, jeweled fingers pointing below, down near the sea's edge, "Persians and Saracens, and remnants of the crusader armies of the past, ancient kings of Jerusalem, and Arabs from the desert."

"Have you been there, to the Holy Land?" Giuliano asked impulsively.

She was amused. Her golden eyes flashed at some memory she would not share. "I have never been far from Byzantium. It is my heart and mind, the roots from which I live. In the exile my family went first to Nicea, then east to Trebizund, and Georgia and the shores of the Black Sea. Once, for a while, farther still to Samarkand. Always I looked to come home again."

He was stabbed with the old guilt of being Venetian and his people's part in carrying the crusader army here. It seemed foolish to ask why Zoe had hungered to come home, even though she could hardly know it after so many years and none of her family were left. He must instead ask her the questions that mattered. He might not have the opportunity again, and the hunger ate inside him with a growing need. "You know all the old families," he said a little abruptly. "Did you know of Theodoulos Agallon?"

She stood quite still. "I've heard of him. He has been dead many years now." She smiled. "If you want to know more, I'm sure it can be learned."

He turned away so she would not read the vulnerability in his eyes. "My mother's name was Agallon. I should be interested to know if there was a connection."

"Really?" She sounded interested, not inquisitive. "What was her Christian name?"

"Maddalena." Even saying it was painful, as if it revealed something private that could not be recovered again. He swallowed, his throat tight. His mother was probably dead, and if she wasn't, the last thing he wanted was to meet her. Giuliano turned to look at Zoe, searching for a way to change his mind.

She was staring at him, her brilliant tawny-colored eyes almost at a level with his. "I will inquire," she promised. "Discreetly, of course. An old story, something I heard and can't remember where." She smiled. "It may take me a little while, but it would be interesting. We are linked in love and hate, your city and mine." For a moment her expression was unreadable, as if she contained inside her some other creature, unknowable, driven by pain. Then it was gone again, and she was smiling at him, still beautiful, still full of laughter and a craving for the taste, the smell, and the texture of life. "Come back in a month, and see what I have discovered."

Thirty-eight

ᑎᕈᑎ

ZOE STOOD ALONE AFTER THE VENETIAN HAD GONE. SHE had liked Giuliano. He was handsome. And he cared intensely; she knew that as vividly as she would feel a touch.

She had to hate him. He was a Dandolo. This could be the best of all the vengeances she hungered for. She must remind herself of all that was worst, most rending of the heart and soul. Deliberately, as if taking a knife to her flesh, she lived it again in her mind to remind herself.

At the end of 1203, the besieging crusaders had sent an insolent message to then emperor Alexios III. It was at the instigation of Enrico Dandolo. It was a threat, and the ringleader of a plot against the emperor, his son-in-law, had incited a riot in the Hagia Sophia. They tore down the great statue of Athena that had once graced the Acropolis of Athens in its golden age.

There was more rioting in the city, attempts in the harbor to set fire to the Venetian fleet. The besiegers must fight or die. Dandolo for the Venetians and Boniface of Montferrat and Baldwin of Flanders and other French knights agreed on the division of spoils when the city was sacked.

In March, the Westerners decided to conquer not only Constantinople, but the entire Byzantine Empire. By mid-April, the city was burning and pillage, robbery, and slaughter raged through the streets.

Houses, churches, and monasteries were robbed of their treasures, chalices for the taking of the sacrament were used to swill the wine of drunkards, icons were used as gaming boards, jewels were gouged out and gold and silver melted down. The monuments of antiquity that had been revered down the centuries were looted and broken, imperial tombs, even that of Constantine the Great, were stripped, and the corpse of Justinian the Lawgiver desecrated. Nuns were raped.

In the Hagia Sophia itself, soldiers smashed the altar and stripped the sanctuary of its silver and gold. Horses and mules were brought in to be loaded with the spoil, and their hooves slid in the blood on the marble floors.

A prostitute danced on the throne of the patriarch and sang obscene songs.

The treasure stolen was said to be worth four hundred thousand silver marks, four times as much as the cost of the entire fleet. The doge of Venice, Enrico Dandolo, personally took fifty thousand marks.

That was not all. The four great gilded bronze horses had been stolen and now adorned the Cathedral of St. Mark in Venice. Enrico Dandolo had chosen the bronze horses. He also took the vial containing drops of the blood of Christ, the icon encased in gold that Constantine the Great had carried with him into battle, a part of the head of John the Baptist, and a nail from the Cross.

Last and perhaps worst, there was the Shroud of Christ.

The loss of all these was far more than sacrilege of holy things, it was an alteration of the character of the whole city, as if its heart had been ripped out.

Pilgrims, travelers, the lifeblood of exchange, commerce, the trade of the world, now no longer came here. They went to Venice or Rome. Constantinople grieved in poverty, like a beggar at the gates of Europe. Zoe stood with her hands clenched till her bones ached and there was blood on her palms. If Giuliano died a thousand times over, it would not be enough to pay for that. There would never be mercy, only blood and more blood.

Thirty-nine

OR ZOE CHRYSAPHES TO INQUIRE WAS EXCELLENT, BUT it was not all that Giuliano could do. He also looked in the other quarters of the city for people who knew which families had gone where during the long exile. It had to be done in the time he did not need for his duties to Venice. Toward the end of the month Zoe had set for his return, Giuliano visited the hill from which Anastasius had said he could see in every direction.

It was not difficult to find the exact place, and the view was as spectacular as described. It was also sheltered from the west wind, and there was a balm in the air. Vines below him were in flower and sent up a perfume, delicate and sweet. It was some time before he realized it was the softness of the waning light on the sea that reminded him of home. He looked up, narrowing his eyes, and the small, rippled clouds, like the scales of a fish, were the same also, and mares' tails shredding in gossamer to the northeast, fanning the sun's rays into a skeletal hand.

The following evening he returned, and this time Anastasius was there. The physician turned and smiled but did not speak for several minutes, as if the sea spread before them were eloquent enough.

"It is a perfect place," Giuliano said at last. "But perhaps it would be wrong for any one person to possess it."

Anastasius smiled. "I hadn't thought of that. You are right, it should be here for everyone who can see, and no oaf who can't." Then he shook his head. "That's too harsh. I have been dealing with fools all day, and I am short-tempered. I'm sorry."

Giuliano was oddly pleased to find him fallible. He had been a trifle daunting before, although he realized it only now. He found himself smiling. "Did you know a family named Agallon in Nicea?" He asked the question before considering it.

Anastasius thought for a moment. "I remember my father mentioning a name like that. He treated many people."

"He was a physician also?" he asked.

Anastasius looked out across the water. "Yes. He taught me most of what I know."

He had stopped, but Giuliano sensed that there was more, an intimate memory that was so sweet, it was painful to bring it back now when the reality was gone. "Did you learn willingly?" he asked instead.

"Oh yes!" Suddenly Anastasius's face came alive, eyes bright, lips parted. "I loved it. From as far back as I can remember. He had no interest in me when I was born, but as soon as I could speak, he taught me all kinds of things. I remember helping him in the garden," he went on. "At least I imagined I was helping. I expect I was far more of a nuisance, but he never told me so. We used to tend the herbs together, and I learned them all, what they looked like, smelled like, which part to use, root or leaf or flower, how to harvest them and keep them safe and from spoiling."

Giuliano envisioned it, the small boy and his father teaching him, telling him over and over, never losing patience.

"My father taught me, too," he said quickly, memory sharp. "All the islands of Venice, and the waterways, the harbor, where the shipyards were. He took me to see the builders, how they laid the great keels and attached the ribs, then the timbers, and the caulking, how they seated the masts." It was the same thing, a man teaching his child the things he loved, the skills he lived by. He remembered it so clearly, always his father, never his mother.

"He knew every port from Genova to Alexandria," he went on. "And what was good and bad about each."

"Did he take you?" Anastasius asked. "Did you see all those places?"

"Some of them." He remembered the close quarters of the boats, feeling seasick and shut in, then the strangeness and the excitement of Alexandria, the heat and the Arab faces, and language he did not understand. "It was terrifying, and wonderful," he said ruefully. "I think I was petrified with fear more than half the time, but I would rather have died than said so. Where did your father take you?"

"Nowhere much to begin with," Anastasius replied. "Mostly to see old people with congested chests and bad hearts. I remember the first dead one, though."

Giuliano's eyes opened wide. "Dead one! How old were you?"

"About eight. Can't be squeamish about death if you're going to be a physician. My father was gentle, very kind, but on that visit he made me look at what had killed this patient." He stopped.

"And what was it?" Giuliano tried to picture a child with Anastasius's solemn gray eyes and delicate bones, that tender mouth.

Anastasius smiled. "The man was chasing a dog that had stolen his dinner, and he tripped and fell over it. Broke his neck."

"You're making it up!" Giuliano accused.

"I'm not. It was the beginning of a lesson in anatomy. Father showed me all the muscles of the back and the bones of the spine."

Giuliano was startled. "Are you allowed to do that? It was a human body."

"No." Anastasius grinned. "But I never forgot. I was terrified he'd be caught. I drew a picture of everything, so I'd never have to do it again." There was a sudden sadness in his voice.

"Were you the only child?" Giuliano asked aloud.

Anastasius looked momentarily taken aback. "No. I had a brother . . . have a brother. He is still alive, I believe." He looked disconcerted, annoyed with himself, as if he had not meant to say that. He looked away. "I have not heard from him for some time."

Giuliano had no wish to pry. "Your father must be proud of your skills if you treat the emperor." He meant it as a simple observation, not flattery.

Anastasius relaxed. "He would be." He took a deep breath and let it out slowly. He did not speak for a while, then he turned his back to the sea. "Is Agallon part of your family? Is that why you look for them?"

"Yes." Giuliano had no thought to lie. "My mother was Byzantine." He could see instantly from Anastasius's face that he understood the conflict. "I have made some inquiries. There are people who may be able to tell me more."

Sensing his reluctance, Anastasius said nothing more of it but started to point out some of the landmarks on the dark outline of the opposite shore, beyond which lay Nicea.

Giuliano continued in his quest for hard facts that pointed to the likelihood of a crusade by sea stopping here for provisions and support, rather than going by land, a choice that still allowed for the possibility of passing the city before crossing to Asia and south.

If only Michael could persuade his people to yield to Rome! No crusader would dare attack the sovereign realm of a Catholic emperor! No crusader or pilgrim would gain absolution for that, whatever shrines he visited afterward.

But as Giuliano watched, weighed, and judged, he still felt like a man assessing the chances and profits of war, and he was ill at ease with himself for doing it.

Toward the end of the month, he received a message from Zoe Chrysaphes saying that she had managed to learn some facts about Maddalena Agallon. She was not certain that he would wish to hear them, but if he did, she would be pleased to receive him in two days' time.

Of course he went. Whatever the news was, he was compelled to hear it.

When he arrived at Zoe's house and was admitted by her servants, he was struggling to keep a veneer of composure. She pretended to notice nothing.

"Have you seen more of the city?" she asked conversationally, leading him again toward the magnificent windows. It was early evening, and the light was soft, blurring the harsher lines.

"I have," he answered. "I have taken time to visit many of the places you spoke of. I have seen some views lovely enough to hold me spellbound. But nothing as good as this."

"You flatter me," she said.

"Not you—your city," he corrected with a smile, but his tone allowed that the distinction was minimal.

She turned to look at him. "It is cruel to stretch out the response." She gave a slight shrug. "Some people find spiders beautiful. I don't. The silken thread which traps flies is clever, but distasteful."

He felt his pulse beating so hard, he was surprised she did not see it in his temples. Or perhaps she did.

"Are you certain you wish to hear?" she asked quietly. "You do not have to. I can forget it and tell no one, if you prefer."

His mouth was dry. "I want to hear." In that instant he was not sure if he meant it, but he would be a coward to retreat now.

"The Agallons were an excellent family, with two daughters," she began. "Maddalena, your mother, eloped with a Venetian sea captain, Giovanni Dandolo, your father. It seemed at the time that they were very much in love. But after less than a year, in fact only a matter of months, your mother left him and returned to Nicea, where she married a Byzantine of considerable wealth."

He should not have been surprised; it was what he had expected. Still, to hear it in words so clear in this exquisite room was the end of all denial, all escape into hope.

"I'm sorry," Zoe said quietly. The muted light from the window removed all lines from her face, and she looked as she must have in her youth. "But when Maddalena's new husband discovered that she was already with child, he threw her out. He would not raise another man's son, and a Venetian's at that. He had lost his parents and a brother in the sacking of the city." Her voice cracked, but she faltered for only a moment. "She did not want the responsibility and the burden of a child, so she gave you away. News of it must have reached your father, and he came and found you, and took you with him back to Venice. I wish I could have told you something less cruel, but you would have learned this sooner or later, if you had persisted in searching. Now you can bury it, and not think of it again."

But that was impossible. He was barely aware of thanking her or of struggling through the rest of the evening. He did not know what time it was when he finally excused himself and fumbled his way out into the night.

Forty

THREE MONTHS LATER, GIULIANO ARRIVED BACK IN VENICE to report to the doge. Even more important for him was the need to recapture the old sense of belonging. This was the home where he had been happy, yet he felt a part of him had already left Venice for the last time.

That afternoon, the doge sent for him and he reported to the palace. It still felt faintly alien to find Contarini there and not Tiepolo. That was foolish: Doges died, like kings or popes, and were succeeded by the new. But Giuliano had cared for Tiepolo, and he missed him.

"Tell me the truth of the union," Contarini asked after the formalities had been conducted and all but his secretary had left.

As Giuliano told him the real depth of the dissension that faced Michael Palaeologus, Contarini nodded. "Then a crusade is inevitable." The doge looked relieved. No doubt he was thinking of the wood already negotiated and in part paid for.

"I think so," Giuliano agreed.

"Is Constantinople rebuilding its sea defenses?" Contarini pressed.

"Yes, but slowly," Giuliano replied. "If the new crusade comes through in the next two or three years, they will not be ready."

"Will it be two or three years?" Contarini demanded. "Our bankers here need to know. We cannot commit money, timber, shipyards, or a hope which may be years away. At the beginning of the century, we stopped all other business and threw everything into building for the fourth crusade, and if your great-grandfather had not finally lost his patience with the devious Byzantines and their endless arguments and excuses, then the losses to Venice would have ruined us."

"I know," Giuliano said quietly. The figures were clear enough, but the fires and the sacrilege still shamed him.

He looked up to see Contarini watching him. Were his thoughts so clear in his face?

"What if Michael wins his people over?" Giuliano asked.

Contarini thought for several moments. "The new pope is less predictable than Gregory was," he said ruefully. "He may choose not to believe it. The Latins will see what they want to see."

Giuliano knew that was true. He despised himself for what he was doing, although he had left himself no choice.

Contarini was still guarded, his eyelids heavy, concealing. "Our shipwrights must work. Trade must continue: Whose ships they are is a matter of judgment, careful planning, and foreknowledge."

Giuliano knew exactly what he was going to say next. He waited respectfully.

"If Constantinople is still vulnerable," Contarini went on, "then Charles of Anjou will hasten his plans so he can strike while it remains so. The longer he waits, the harder his battle will be." He paced across the checkered marble floor. "This month he is in Sicily. Go there, Dandolo. Watch, listen, and observe. The pope has said the crusade will take place in 1281 or 1282. We cannot be ready before that. But you say Constantinople is rebuilding, and Michael is clever. Which man will outwit the other, the Frenchman or the Byzantine? Charles has all of Europe on his side, bent on regaining the Holy Land for Christendom, not to mention an overweening ambition. But Michael is fighting for survival. He might not care whether we win Jerusalem or not, if it is at the expense of his people."

"What can I learn in Sicily of his plans?" Giuliano asked reasonably.

"Many a man's weaknesses lie at home, where he does not expect them. The king of the Two Sicilies is arrogant. Come back to me in three months. You will be provided with all you need of money and letters of authority."

Giuliano made no demur, saying nothing of the fact that he had only just arrived back, that he had had no rest and barely time to speak to his friends. He was more than willing to go, because Venice had not healed the ache inside him as he had believed it would.

Forty-one

IULIANO'S SHIP DOCKED IN THE SICILIAN PORT OF PALERMO two weeks later. He stood on the harbor wall in the harsh, eye-searing sun and stared around him. The glittering light off the water was blue to the horizon. The town rose on gentle hills: the buildings pale, soft colors like the bleached earth, with occasional splashes of colored vines or bright clothes strung across the street from window to window in the hot air.

In time he would present himself at the court of Charles of Anjou, but first he wanted to arm himself with some knowledge of the town and its people. He should never forget that he was in what was essentially an occupied city, French on the surface, Sicilian at heart. For that he needed to be among the people.

He set out to look for lodgings, hoping to find a family of ordinary local people who would take him in, so he would have an opportunity to share at least some part of their lives and their less guarded opinions. The first two had no extra room. The third one welcomed him.

The house looked like any other from the outside, simple, badly weath-ered, fishing nets and lobster pots set nearby to dry. On the inside, the poverty was more apparent. The floor of earthen tile was worn uneven by passing feet. The wooden furniture was well used, and the dishes of beau-tiful, heavy ceramic in tones of blue were occasionally chipped. They of-fered him a room and food at a price he thought was too little, and he was uncertain whether to offer more or if it would make his comparative wealth ungraciously obvious.

He ate supper with them, Giuseppe, Maria, and six children of ages from four to twelve. It was noisy and happy. The food appeared plentiful although simple, mostly vegetables from their own rich earth. But he noticed that every scrap was eaten, and no one asked for more, as if they already knew that there was none.

The oldest boy, Francisco, looked at Giuliano with interest.

"Are you a sailor?" he asked politely.

"Yes." Giuliano did not wish to be obviously Venetian, but any lie or evasion would betray him in a way he could not afford.

"Have you been to lots of places?" Francisco went on, his face eager.

Giuliano smiled. "From Genoa right around to Venice, and to Constantinople and all the ports on the way there, and twice as far as Acre, but I didn't go overland to Jerusalem. Once I went to Alexandria."

"In Egypt?" Francisco's eyes were wide, and Giuliano noticed that no one else around the table was paying any attention to food anymore.

"Are you here to see the king?" one of the girls asked.

"He wouldn't be staying with us if he were here to see the king, stupid!" one of the other boys told her.

"Why would anyone want to see that fat bastard?" Giuseppe asked with a savage edge to his voice.

"Hush!" Maria warned him, her eyes wide, conspicuously not looking at Giuliano. "You mustn't say that. And anyway, it's not true. They say Charles is not fat at all. And his father died before he was born, but he's legitimate. It's not the same thing as being a bastard."

Giuliano knew she was not criticizing her husband, she was trying to protect him from indiscretion in front of a stranger.

But Giuseppe was not so easily silenced. "Forgive us," he said. "We take our taxes hard. Charles doesn't tax his own Frenchmen as heavily as he does us." Giuseppe could not keep the edge of bitterness out of his voice that betrayed the hatred close under the surface.

Giuliano had heard it already, even in the few hours he had been here. "I know," he agreed. "It might be unwise to criticize him, but I think it would make you an outcast to praise him. And a liar."

Giuseppe smiled and clapped him on the shoulder. "Wise man," he said cheerfully. "You're welcome in my house."

Giuliano spent four weeks with Giuseppe and his family, listening to their conversations and those of the other fishermen and farmers in the local taverns. He heard the undertones of anger and also a sense of helplessness. He mentioned Byzantium once or twice, and the responses he heard were so open in interest and sympathy, on weighing them afterward, he thought they were innocent of intent.

But the anger was there. It would not take a great deal to ignite it, one act of stupidity that intruded into the fabric of their lives, one desecration of a church, one abuse of a woman or child, and the flame would be lit. If he could see that, then if Michael had spies here, they would see it, too. The question was not if the will was present, but if the coherence of effort could be organized well enough to succeed. If the Sicilians rose up and were crushed, it would be a tragedy Giuliano was not prepared to incite. It would be the ultimate betrayal of hospitality. To eat a man's bread in his own house and then sell him to the enemy was beyond pardon.

Guiliano presented himself at the court of Charles of Anjou, or, as he was known here in Palermo, the king of the Two Sicilies. Giuliano was not surprised by the lavish beauty of the palace, but beneath it all was the comparative austerity of the court. The exorbitant taxes Charles drained from the land were for war, not pleasure. Men dressed simply, and the king himself counted only on the power of his presence to command respect. He was as burning with energy as usual and welcomed Giuliano with an instant recollection of exactly who he was.

"Ah! Returned again, Dandolo," he said enthusiastically. "Come to see how our preparations for the crusade are progressing?"

"Yes, sire," Giuliano answered, investing his expression with far more eagerness than he felt.

"Well, my friend . . ." Charles slapped him on the back. "All goes very well. All Europe is stirring to the call. We are about to unite Christendom. Can you see it, Dandolo? One army under God."

There was only one possible answer. "I can see it in my mind," he replied. "I look for the day when it is more than a vision, an army in the flesh."

"More than the flesh," Charles corrected him, looking at him sideways with sudden acute perception. "We need it in the steel and the wood, the wine, the salt, and the bread. We need it in the will and the courage, and in the gold, do we not?"

"We need all those things," Giuliano agreed. "But we need them supplied willingly, and not at a price we cannot pay. The cause is to win back the Holy Land for Christendom, not to enrich every merchant and shipbuilder in Europe—except justly, of course!"

Charles roared with laughter. "Ever the careful diplomat, eh? What you mean is that Venice will not promise anything until they see which way everyone else jumps. Don't be too cautious, or you'll invest too late. Anyone can tell you are traders, not soldiers." It was said with a smile, but it was an insult nevertheless.

"I am a sailor, sire," he replied. "I am for God, adventure, and profit. No man who will face the sea deserves to be called a coward."

Charles spread his arms wide. "You are right, Dandolo. I take it back. And any man who trusts the sea is a fool. You are more interesting than I thought. Come and dine with me. Come!" He held out his hand, then turned and led the way, certain that Giuliano would follow.

Every time Charles invited him to join in a game of chance, Giuliano accepted. Apart from the fact that one did not easily refuse a king, even if one was not his subject, he needed to be in Charles's company to make any judgment as to his immediate intentions. Everyone knew what they were eventually, he had made no secret of it, but the timing was of intense importance to Venice.

When they played at dice or cards, Charles was highly competitive, but Giuliano learned easily that although he did not like to be beaten, he resented even more bitterly being condescended to. Giuliano needed all his wits to play well and still lose. Once or twice he failed and won. He waited with muscles clenched, ready to defend himself, but after a moment's prickling silence, Charles swore briefly and with considerable inventiveness, then demanded a further game, at which Giuliano made absolutely certain he lost.

The word *Byzantium* awoke a fire in Charles's eyes, as if some legendary treasure had been named. Giuliano saw his hands tighten and the muscles in his thick wrists knot as if to grasp something precious yet infinitely elusive.

It was at sea a few days after that that Charles's more contemplative nature asserted itself. He was less sure of his own skills on the water and took some care not to attempt anything where it was possible he might fail. Giuliano twice saw him move to begin and then change his mind. It was more revealing than he could have known. He was still the younger brother, unwanted, afraid of failure, not confident enough to shrug it away. He needed to be seen to succeed every time.

Yet he had no hesitation in allowing the helmsman to take the boat through heavier seas, close in past jagged rocks of a promontory with the surge roaring past it. It was failure Charles feared, not death.

Giuliano felt a sudden understanding for him, born after his father's death and unloved by his mother. His oldest brother had been king of France and perceived by many as a saint. What was there left for a man of hunger and passion to do except demand attention by achieving the impossible?

They passed the point and were out into calmer deep water, with the mainland falling away to the west and the islands of Alicudi and Filicudi far to the north, Salina, Panara, and beyond that the smoking crown of Stromboli staining the horizon.

Charles swiveled round, ignoring the current now, his face toward the east. "That way lies Byzantium," he said jubilantly. "We'll be there, Dandolo. Like your great-grandfather, I shall leap from my ship to the sand and lead the assault. We too shall storm the walls again and break them down." He lifted both his arms, balancing in the rocking boat, his hands locked into fists. "I shall be crowned in the Hagia Sophia myself!"

Then he turned and smiled at Giuliano, ready at last to talk details about money and ships, numbers of men to be transported with all their armor, horses, engines of war, and other necessary equipment.

Forty-two

⁓

ON THE EARLY EVENING, ANNA STOOD IN THE PLACE HIGH on the hill overlooking the sea where she had stood with Giuliano Dandolo and spoken of the glory of the city spread below them. It was still as beautiful, but it was the shore of Asia beyond that she stared at now. Above it, the sun was making shining towers of the slow clouds sailing like ships around the edges of heaven.

The silence was heavy in the air. Lately she had been so busy with patients that she had had little opportunity to come here, and the solitude was welcome.

Yet she would have liked to be able to speak to Giuliano or even simply meet his eyes and know that he saw the same beauty in it that she did. Words would be unnecessary.

But even as the thoughts came to her, she was conscious of her own foolishness. She could not afford to think of him in such a way. His friendship was something to savor, then to let go, not to cling to as if it could be permanent.

She could stand here and watch the light fade over the water only for a little longer, see the shadows turn gold and then darken and color fill the hollows in purple and amber, blurring the outlines, splashing the windows with fire.

She had not accomplished much in clearing Justinian's name. He was still in a desert monastery, imprisoned and useless, fretting away the hours, let alone the days and the years, while she gathered shreds too small to weave into anything.

She was not even certain that Bessarion's death was a result of his religious fervor. It could have been personal. He had clearly been abrasive, difficult to be at ease with, and Helena had been bored with him. That she could understand too easily.

She had thought that Bessarion himself must be the key to his own death. It had not been difficult to ask about him. The city was still full of memories, and as the stories of torture and imprisonment mounted, his stature as a hero grew. But Anna had found that the humanity of the man eluded her. He had shared the fire of his belief with everyone, but never the hunger of his dreams.

Then why had he been murdered?

It was like looking at a mosaic picture with the center missing. It could have been any of a score of things. Without it she was floundering, wasting more precious time.

Again and again she came back to the Church and its danger of being consumed by Rome. Had Justinian loved it with the passion that would drive him to spend time, energy, and loyalty with people he did not like in order to preserve its identity from corruption?

She shivered in the dying sun, even though the whisper of a breeze rising held no chill at all.

She needed to meet others like Esaias Glabas, who had been an unlikely friend of Justinian's, and Eirene and Demetrios Vatatzes. Eirene sometimes had poor health. Anna must exert all her efforts to become her physician. Zoe could aid her with that.

It took Anna a number of weeks to contrive her first professional call on Eirene. She liked her immediately. Even distressed by illness as Eirene was now, her face was vivid with intelligence and yet startlingly ugly, but Anna realized that that was at least in part because of the strength in her. The consultation was brief. Anna had the impression that it was largely for Eirene to decide whether she wished to trust Anna or not.

However, on the second call Eirene greeted Anna with relief and without prevarication, leading her into a more private room looking onto a small inner court. There were no murals except one simple picture of vines, but the proportions were so perfect that they seemed to form the walls rather than be added to them.

"I am afraid the pain is worse," Eirene said frankly, standing with her arms limp at her sides, as if even in front of a physician she was embarrassed to mention something so personal.

Anna was not surprised. There had been an awkwardness in the way she moved and a stiffness that betrayed locked muscles, and above all fear. Now that she was still, she lifted her left arm and cradled it in her right hand.

"And in the chest also?" Anna asked her.

Eirene smiled. "You are going to tell me that my heart is weak. I shall acknowledge it and save your searching for comforting words." There was a bitterness to her humor, but no self-pity.

"No," Anna replied.

Eirene's eyebrows shot up. "Sin? I'd heard better of you than that. Zoe Chrysaphes said you were no lover of obedient thoughts and the safety of men's beliefs."

"I had not imagined her so sharp of vision," Anna replied. "Or that she looked at me at all, beyond my professional ability."

Eirene smiled widely. In her ugly face, it was like a blaze of sunlight across a bleak landscape. "Zoe looks at everyone, especially those she judges can be of use to her. Don't take it as flattery. It is merely that she weighs every tool to the fraction of an ounce before she considers using it. Now give me a candid answer: What is wrong with me? You looked at me thoroughly enough when you were here before."

Anna was not ready to answer yet. She knew that Eirene's husband was still alive, because his name had been mentioned in her first visit. "Where is your husband?" she asked.

Anger flared up Eirene's face, her eyes burning. "You will answer to me, you impudent creature. My body is my affair, not my husband's."

Anna was stung by surprise and then the instant after by how revealing Eirene's answer had been. What had her husband done to lacerate Eirene so profoundly that the wound bled at a touch?

"Much of your illness comes from anxiety," Anna said, lowering her voice, trying to keep pity out of it. "I know from last time I was here that your son is in Constantinople. I wondered if your husband was traveling, perhaps in dangerous regions. Although I am not sure how many are safe. The sea never changes its shores or its rocks and whirlpools. Pirates come and go."

Eirene blushed. "I apologize. My husband is in Alexandria. I do not know whether he is safe or not. I do not worry about it, because it would be pointless." She turned away and, with an effort, walked upright toward the archway into the court and the high, bright flowers beyond.

So Gregory was still in Egypt, even so many years after most other exiles had returned to Constantinople from every other region.

Anna followed Eirene to the courtyard. It too was sparsely beautiful, clean-lined. The fountain fell into a shaded pool, the water catching the light only at its peak.

She spoke to Eirene of the usual things a physician addresses: food, sleep, the benefits of walking.

"Do you imagine I haven't thought of all that?" Eirene said, disappointment dragging her voice down again.

"I am sure you have," Anna replied. "Have you done them? They will not cure you, but they will allow your body to begin curing itself."

"You are as bad as my priest," Eirene remarked. "Would you like me to say a dozen Paternosters?"

"If you can do it without your mind wandering off to other things," Anna replied perfectly seriously. "I don't think I could."

Eirene looked at her, a beginning of interest in her eyes. "Is that a rather abstruse way of saying that it is sin at the heart of this after all? I do not need to be sheltered from the truth. I am just as strong as Zoe Chrysaphes." A flash of light, almost like a moment's laughter, glanced in her eyes. "Or did you wrap up the truth for her, too, like a child's medicine, hidden in honey?"

"I would not dare," Anna replied. "Unless, of course, I was sure I could do it well enough that she would never know."

This time Eirene laughed outright, a rich sound with layers of meaning, at least some of them malicious. How had Zoe hurt her?

"I have an herbal extract for you . . ." Anna began.

"What is it? A sedative? Something to stop me feeling the pain?" There was contempt in Eirene's face. "Is that your solution to life's griefs, physician? Cover them up? Don't look at what will hurt you?"

Anna should have been insulted, but she was not. "A sedative will relax your muscles so your body does not fight itself and send you into spasm. Relax so you can eat without gulping in air and giving yourself indigestion to cramp your stomach. Relax so your neck does not ache from bearing your head up, and your head pound from the blood trying to pass through flesh that is knotted as if ease were your enemy."

"I suppose you know what you are talking about," Eirene said with a shrug. "You can tell Zoe that my household knows you came on her rec-ommendation. I shall hold her responsible for anything that happens to me. Come back tomorrow."

When she returned, Anna found Eirene much the same. If the pain was less, it could be attributed to the night's rest, partially induced by the seda-tive. She was still tired and in considerably short temper.

Afterward, Anna found Eirene's son, Demetrios, waiting for her. He asked with some concern over his mother's condition. She could easily un-derstand why Helena was attracted to him.

"How is my mother?" he repeated urgently.

"I believe anxiety and fear are eating inside her," Anna answered, not meeting his eyes as she would have were her conscience at ease.

"What has she to be afraid of?" Demetrios was watching her closely, but disguising it in a show of disdain.

"We can fear all manner of things, real and unreal," she replied. "The sack of the city again, if there is another crusade." In the corner of her vi-sion, she saw the impatient gesture of his hand brushing away the idea. "The forced union of the Church with Rome," she went on, and this time he stood perfectly still. "Violence in the city if that should happen," she added, measuring her words as precisely as she could. "Possible attempts to usurp Michael's power over the Church." Her voice was shaking a little now. "By those who are passionately against union."

The silence was so intense, she could hear a servant drop a fork on the tiled floor two rooms away.

"Usurp Michael's power over the Church?" he asked at length. "What on earth do you mean?" He was very pale. "Michael is emperor. Or do you mean usurp the throne?"

Her heart pounding, she met his eyes. "Do I?"

"That's ridiculous! Stay with your medicine," Demetrios snapped. "You know nothing about the world, and still less about the relations of power."

"There is something that disturbs your mother," she lied, her mind racing. "Something keeps her from sleeping and takes the pleasure from her food so she eats it badly and too fast."

"I suppose that's better than saying her illness is caused by sin," he conceded dryly. A sudden, very real sadness crossed his face. "But if you think my mother's a coward, then you are a fool. I never saw her afraid of anything."

Of course you didn't, Anna thought. Eirene's fears were of the heart, not of the mind or the flesh. Like most women, she feared loneliness and rejection, losing the man she loved to someone like Zoe.

Forty-three

༄

A CEILING IN THE PAPAL PALACE IN VITERBO HAD CAVED in, splintering to a thousand shards of wood, plaster, and rubble, killing Pope John XXI. The news reduced Rome to stunned silence, then slowly spread to the rest of Christendom. Once again, the world had no voice for God to lead it.

Palombara heard the news in the Blachernae Palace at an audience with the emperor. Now he stood in one of the great galleries in front of a magnificent statue. It was one of a few that had survived with only the slightest chip in one arm, as if to show that it too was subject to time and chance. It was Greek, from before Christ, preserved here in this seldom used corner, beautiful and almost naked.

Anna was in the same corridor, returning from treating a patient. She saw Bishop Palombara, but he was deep in thought and as unaware of her as if he had been alone. She read in his face in the unguarded moment a vulnerability to beauty, as if it could reach inside him effortlessly past all the barriers he had built up and touch the wounds beyond.

Yet he allowed it. Some part of him hungered for the overwhelming emotion, even if it was so threaded through with pain. Yet its reality eluded him. She knew that when he turned to her, only for an instant she saw it in his eyes.

Then, as if by mutual agreement, he walked away, back toward the main gallery, and she was ashamed of having intruded, even though it had been unintentional.

She heard a noise of swift footsteps and swung around sharply, as if she had been caught somewhere she should not have been. Why should she feel so exposed? Because she had experienced a moment's empathy with the Roman?

This was the immediate razor edge of the Schism, not arguments about the nature of God; it was the poison in the nature of man, where the lines of enormity were drawn in the ground and one was afraid to stretch out the hand across them.

Forty-four

cwɔ

FROM MAY TO NOVEMBER, THERE WAS ANOTHER LONG VOID in struggle between Rome and Byzantium until Pope Nicholas III was elected toward the end of November. He was Italian, passionately so. He dispossessed Charles of Anjou of his position as senator of Rome, so he could vote in no future papal elections, thus considerably reducing his power. He packed the high offices close to him with his own brothers, nephews, and cousins, gaining a stronghold on Rome.

He also required yet another affirmation of the union between Rome and Byzantium. This time it was not Michael and his son who should sign the promises of the new restrictions, it was all the bishops and senior clergy in what remained of the empire.

Anna found Constantine in despair.

"I shouldn't have done it!" he said hoarsely. "But how could I have been wrong?" He seemed almost on the edge of tears, his eyes hot, beseeching escape from a reality he could not bear. He flung out his hands in a gesture of pleading. "Pope John forced the emperor into signing the promise to obey Rome, and a month afterward—just a month—the ceiling of his palace fell in on him. It was an act of God, it had to be."

She did not argue.

"I told the people so," he went on urgently. "Even the cardinals in Rome must have seen it. What more do they need as a sign? Do they not believe it was God who brought down the walls of Jericho on the sinners within?" His voice was rising in a wild plea. "I told them it was the miracle we had waited for. I had promised them that the Blessed Virgin would save us, if only we had faith." He choked, gagging for breath. "I have betrayed them."

She was embarrassed for him. This was the sort of crisis of faith one should have alone and afterward be able to pretend had not happened. "No one said it would be easy," she began. "At least no one who tells the truth. Or that it wouldn't hurt, and we would always win. The crucifixion must have looked like the end of everything."

He breathed out heavily. "We must keep on fighting, to the death, if necessary. We must find new heart somehow. If we haven't the truth, then we have nothing at all." The faintest flicker of a smile touched his eyes, and he moved absently to straighten his robe. "Thank you, Anastasius. Your faith in me has given me strength. This is a setback, it is not a defeat. Tomorrow will see the resurrection, if we have faith." He straightened his shoulders. "I shall begin immediately."

"Your Grace . . ." She reached out as if to touch him, then dropped her hand at the last moment. "Be careful," she warned, thinking of his arrest, perhaps worse. "If you speak out too clearly against the union, you will be thrown out of office," she said urgently. "And then who will minister to the poor and the sick? You will end up in exile, like Cyril Choniates, and what good will that do?"

"I have no intention of being so impractical," he promised her. "I shall walk quietly and keep the faith."

Constantine was on the steps of the Church of the Holy Apostles. A crowd was pressing forward anxiously, looking to Constantine, waiting for him to speak and reassure them, tell them that their ancient comforts were not empty. He was not aware of Anna in the shadow a few yards behind him. His eyes and his mind were on the eager faces in front of him.

"Be patient," he said quietly. In order to hear him, they ceased talking to one another, and gradually the silence spread. "We are entering a difficult time," he went on. "We must be outwardly obedient, or we will cause dissension in the community, perhaps violence. Old ways vie with new ones, but we know the truth of our faith, and we will practice virtue in our homes, even should it become impossible in our streets or churches. We will keep the faith and abide in hope. God will yet rescue us."

The panic ebbed away. Anna could see the faces begin to smile, the jostling cease.

"God bless the bishop!" someone called out. "Constantine! Bishop Constantine!" The cry was taken up and repeated like an incantation.

Constantine smiled. "Go in peace, my brethren. Never lose faith. To the true heart there is no such thing as defeat, only a time of waiting, an exercise of trust, and a keeping of God's Commandments, until the dawn."

Again the cry came, his name, blessings, then again his name, over and over. Anna looked at him and saw the humble bearing of his head, the gesture of declining the praise. But she also saw his body shiver, his fist half-hidden in his robes tighten into a clench, and the sheen of sweat on his skin. When he turned toward her, modestly withdrawing from the adulation, his eyes were shining and his cheeks were flushed. She had seen the same look on Eustathius's face the first time he had made love to her, back in the beginning, when the hunger and the anticipation had burned through both of them, before the bitterness.

Suddenly she was revolted and ashamed, wishing she had not seen it, but it was too late. The look in Constantine's face was printed on her mind.

He did not notice. He was reveling in being adored.

She stood in the shadow and was hot with guilt because she was aware of the ugliness in him, the doubt and then the lust, and she had not the honesty to tell him.

Constantine had given her a link to the vast body of the Church again, a purpose to strive for beyond the daily healing of the sick. To separate from him irrevocably—and it would be irrevocable—would mean standing alone.

Which was the greater betrayal, to face him with the truth or not to face him? She turned and walked away, ahead of him, so she could not see his eyes nor he see hers.

Forty-five

∽

ANNA STOOD IN EIRENE VATATZES'S ELEGANT, QUIET BED-
room and looked down at the woman lying on the bed. Her
clothes were rumpled and marked with blood, and around her neck there
were stains of an ointment. In two places was also the yellow mucus of
suppuration. There was an open ulcer on her cheek and another just under
her jawline on the opposite side. Her hands were covered in red weals,
some already swollen where the pus was gathering into a head.

Anna knew from her son, Demetrios, that his father, Gregory, was due
to return shortly from Alexandria, this time to remain indefinitely. Eirene
was in physical pain, but her distress was greater.

"Is the rest of your body affected as well?" Anna asked gently.

Eirene glared at her. "That doesn't matter." She made a sharp gesture
with her hands. "Cure my face. Do whatever you have to. The cost is
unimportant." She drew in a long breath. "So is the pain." Her voice was
brittle; Anna could hear the edges of the words like shards of glass grating
together.

Anna's mind raced over every possibility she could think of, every treatment, however radical—Christian, Jewish, or Arabic. Were any of them of
use if the source of the illness was the fear in Eirene's mind?

Anna's imagination flew to the wounds she guessed at: the rejection of
clever, ugly, vulnerable Eirene for the sensuous Zoe, who would laugh and
enjoy, then leave, taking whatever she wanted and needing nothing. Was
Gregory a man bored by what he could have and fascinated by what he

could not? How shallow. How cruel. And yet how desperately understandable.

What was the point in healing the skin from outside, only to have it
erupt again a day later?

"Don't stand there like a fool!" Eirene snapped, twisting a little to
look at her. "If you don't know what to do, say so. I'll call someone else.
If you're in poverty, for God's sake take some money, but don't stare at
me as if you expected me to heal myself. What are you going to tell me?
That I should pray? Do you think I haven't prayed all my life, you stupid . . ." Suddenly she turned her face away, tears wet on her blemished
cheeks.

"I am considering what remedies there are, and which would be best,"
Anna said gently. Some form of intoxication would relieve the self-
consciousness that prevented Eirene from allowing her passion or her
anger to show and that had perhaps masked the laughter that could have
made her less easy to read. It might even allow the sensuality that could
have made her entertaining and just beyond Gregory's total reach. It
would be a short-term answer, but what use was a long-term cure if she
perished of misery now?

"I will give you an ointment to take away the heat," she said aloud.

"I don't care what it feels like, you fool!" Eirene shouted at her. "Can
you see nothing, you—"

"And the redness," Anna finished calmly. Eirene needed her to understand, yet if she did, that would be intolerable also, another humiliation.
"And an infusion to heal it from within, so it does not recur," she added.
"For the suppuration you will just have to wait. I will wash them with a
tincture I have prepared, and put on light bandages to keep them from
rubbing."

Eirene looked taken aback, but she would not apologize. Physicians
were like good servants; hardly equals. "Thank you," she said awkwardly.

Anna fetched clean water from one of the servants and dropped in a
small measure of liquid from a little vial. The sharp aroma filled the air,
but it was pleasant, invigorating. She began to wash each individual sore,
working gently and slowly. She intended to be here as long as possible.

Since the last time she had been here, Demetrios's words had raced in
her brain. It still seemed absurd, and she remembered his contempt with
a heat of embarrassment. He had said the idea of usurping Michael was

ridiculous. She knew that to succeed, one would have to overcome the Varangian Guard. Demetrios knew them, even had friends among them. It would not be possible. One would need to have the army with you. Antoninus was a soldier, he would know that. And the navy, and the merchants, which Justinian would know. His ever increasing business had been in such things.

One would need sound economic advice and access to the Treasury. Since then, Anna had learned that the lord of the Treasury was Eirene's cousin Theodorus Doukas, and they were close. Some people had suggested that at least part of his brilliance was actually Eirene's, her foresight, her genius with figures.

And what could the easy, charming Esaias Glabas do in such a plan? Was he cleverer than anyone supposed? And Helena? Was she a part of this plot or merely Bessarion's wife?

"They are not as deep as I had feared," Anna said, dabbing gently at one of the scars, cleaning away the suppuration. "I think it may heal over without leaving a mark. Last time I was here I spoke a little with Demetrios. He was most interesting."

"Really . . . ," Eirene said with skepticism.

"I think so." Anna positioned the bandage, easing it smooth, and bound it lightly. "I'm told he has friends among the Varangian Guard." She bent to her work again.

"Yes," Eirene agreed, wincing as one of the worst sores was washed. "I think they are grateful that a man of Demetrios's rank should befriend them. Some noble families treat them less courteously. Not rudely so much as with indifference." She smiled bleakly. "Like a good servant."

"You mean Bessarion? Or Justinian Lascaris?"

"Justinian less so. Of course to Bessarion they were heathens, for the most part. Certainly those from the far north." She bit her lip, forcing herself not to pull away from the pain.

Anna affected not to notice. "Someone told me Esaias Glabas was talented. Is that true?"

"Good heavens, no!" Eirene said with contempt. "He could tell a story well, and he knew endless jokes, most of them unrepeatable in front of women. He could flatter, and keep his temper even when provoked."

Anna smiled. "You didn't like him." It was more an observation than a question.

"He is not dead," Eirene snapped. "At least not as far as I know. I think Demetrios would have mentioned it."

"They were friends?" Anna did not look up from her work.

"I suppose so. Esaias was really a companion of the emperor's son, Andronicus. They used to go riding together, and to the horse races. And of course drinking, gambling, parties of one sort and another."

"I can't see Bessarion liking that," Anna remarked. "From what people say, he was remarkably serious."

"The word you are looking for is humorless," Eirene said wryly, at last looking at the sore as Anna finished bandaging it. "You are gentle. Thank you."

Eirene was too clever to be fooled. If the wild idea in Anna's mind was right, it would be not only pointless but dangerous to awaken her suspicions. She felt her hands shaking. "I'm sorry," she apologized.

"It's nothing," Eirene said, dismissing the slight brush of Anna's hand over one of the other wounds. "You are quite right. Bessarion did not like Esaias. I think he merely used him."

Anna took a deep, quivering breath. "In his struggle to . . . to save the Church?" She invested her voice with puzzlement, as if she did not understand. "I cannot imagine him working to indulge in such . . . parties."

There was a minute's fleeting pity in Eirene's eyes for the eunuch robbed of manhood, which she took Anna to be, of both its pleasures and its weaknesses. "He didn't," she said gently. "Nor Justinian. Esaias was planning the biggest party with horse races, from the night after Bessarion was killed. It would have been superb. Esaias was a magnificent host; I should add that to his list of qualities."

Anna pretended interest. "Really? Horse racing? That can be exciting to watch. I suppose everyone would have been there, even Bessarion?"

Eirene hesitated.

"Wouldn't they?" Anna's heart was thundering inside her.

Eirene looked away. "No. I believe on that occasion Bessarion was supposed to have an audience with the emperor."

The silence in the room was heavy, almost prickling. Anna started to roll up the unused bandages and put them away. "So the emperor would not have been there?"

"It hardly matters now," Eirene said, a sudden, hard edge to her voice. "Bessarion and Antoninus are dead, and Justinian is in exile." She looked at her bandaged arms. "Thank you."

"I'll come and dress them again tomorrow," Anna told her, standing up. "And bring you more herbs."

Working quietly in the evening, alone in the room where she kept her medicines, Anna crushed leaves, ground roots and stems, sometimes with mortar and pestle, always being careful never to let one herb contaminate another; and all the while, thoughts crowded her mind as she turned over every possible interpretation of what she had learned.

Did she have all the pieces that mattered, if only she could put them in the right order? Bessarion was a religious fanatic devoted to the Orthodox Church. He was a Comnenos, one of the old imperial families. He was passionate to prevent the union with Rome that Michael Palaeologus had already begun, and that was dividing the nation, because he believed it was the only way to avert another invasion.

Justinian had quarreled several times with Bessarion; the last and worst argument was just before the murder. It made a picture she could no longer deny. They had planned to kill Michael so Bessarion could usurp the throne. Justinian would help him. Esaias and Antoninus were to hold Andronicus, perhaps even kill him also. Then Bessarion would withdraw all agreement to the union with Rome—calling on those loyal to the Church to support him, and that support would naturally be led by Constantine.

All the difficulties had been foreseen and planned for. Justinian to deal with the merchants and the harbormasters. Antoninus to hold the leaders of the army; Demetrios himself to have bribed or otherwise won over the Varangian Guard on duty that night and, once the emperor was dead, to give their loyalty to the new emperor, Bessarion.

Who would actually have killed Michael? The Varangian Guard would not let anyone close enough. There could be only one answer to that. Zoe would do it, if she believed it was to save Byzantium.

Anna poured powder into a jar, labeled it, and cleaned her tools, then began again.

Dynasties had changed violently before and no doubt would again. The more she thought of it, the more did Bessarion seem just the nature of fanatic to whom that would be the necessary and noble thing to do.

It was an explanation that answered far too much for her to discount it. She would have to struggle with the rest, but immeasurably more carefully—and never for the second in which it takes to say a word or make an unguarded gesture forget that all the rest of the conspirators were still here, still alive, and perhaps seeking another pretender to the throne, such as Demetrios Vatatzes.

She shivered as the knots of fear wound tighter inside her.

The next patient she treated required several days of her attention, and he was in the Venetian Quarter, down by the shore. He had been quite severely cut when he was attacked in a brawl near the docks. His family were afraid to ask a local Christian doctor, and Anna's reputation had spread.

He was bleeding profusely. She had no choice but to try a method she had seen her father use in extreme cases. He had learned it traveling in his youth, north and eastward beyond the Black Sea. She collected the blood in a clean pot and put it near the fire.

Then she cleaned the wound and packed it with cotton cloth until the bleeding eased. It took some little time, during which she talked to the man gently to ease his fear and gave him a tincture to help the pain.

When the blood in the pot had at last coagulated, she took it and painted it gently on the raw wound, sealing it over. When she was sure there was no more bleeding, she mixed the most healing and strengthening herbs, finely powdered, into a paste softened with butter and used them to prevent the cloth of the bandage from sticking to the wound. She stayed in the house with him, going out only to purchase more herbs and then returning to sit by his bedside.

Hearing the rhythm and patterns of the Venetian tongue around her made it impossible not to think of Giuliano Dandolo. She had no idea why he had left so suddenly, but she was aware of missing him, although in a way his absence was also a relief. It was impossible that they should ever be more than occasional friends, people able to speak of dreams deeper than the surface, joys and sorrows that touched the bone, and laughing at the same moment at small absurdities.

But he awoke something else in her that she could not afford.

Yes, it was a relief that Giuliano Dandolo had gone back to Venice. Like Eirene Vatatzes, she needed a little numbing, a rest from the pain of caring.

Forty-six

NNA RETURNED TO SEE EIRENE AS SOON AS HER VENE-
tian patient was sufficiently recovered. She found the ulcers noticeably improved. Eirene was up and dressed in a simple, almost severe
tunic. Helena called when Anna was there, but she was not received.

"I am in no mood to receive Helena when I look more like the Gor-
gon." Eirene said it wryly, as if it were amusing, but there was pain behind
it, and it showed in her eyes and in the tightness of her shoulders as she
turned away.

Anna forced herself to smile.

"I wonder what Helen looked like, that they were willing to burn a city
and ruin a civilization for her," Eirene went on, pursuing the conversation
as if there were nothing else to remark upon.

"I was taught that their concept of beauty was far deeper than a mere
matter of form," Anna replied. "It needed to be of the mind as well, of the
intellect and imagination, and of the heart. If all you want is a beautiful
face, a statue will do. And you can own it completely. It doesn't even need
feeding." She wondered if Eirene's self-knowledge had created Gregory's
rejection. Was it possible that her belief in her own ugliness had made her
seem so to others? Might they have forgotten it, had she allowed them to?

Anna looked at her. The awkwardness of Eirene's movement was no
more than that of many other women her age. Time and intelligence had
lent a distinction to her features that they would not have had in youth.
Had Eirene not allowed herself to see it?

She both loved and hated Gregory. The look in her eyes, the tension in her hands, gave her away. She believed she could not be loved, not with passion or laughter or tenderness, not with that desperate hunger for her to love in return that made passion a mutual thing.

Later, as Anna stood in the main room receiving payment from Demetrios for the herbs, she was conscious of Helena in a pale tunic trimmed with gold, her hair elaborately dressed. Without intending to, Anna compared her with Zoe, and Helena was still the loser.

"Thank you," Anna said as Demetrios gave her the coins. "I shall return in a day or two. I believe she will continue to recover, and by then it may be time to change the treatment a little." She did not add that she was concerned not to dose Eirene too heavily with the intoxicant she had used, in case she became dependent upon its artificial sense of well-being. She intended to use it only as long as it was necessary to face Gregory's return.

"Don't change it," Demetrios said hastily, his face puckered with concern. "It is working well."

Anna left and walked to her next patient and the one after. It was late and she was tired when she turned aside to climb the steps to her favorite place overlooking the sea.

This place drew her because of its silence. The wind and the gulls were no disturbance to the flight of thought. She was not yet ready to answer Leo's solicitous questions as to her welfare or see in Simonis's eyes the slow dying of hope that they would one day prove Justinian's innocence.

Anna stood on the small, level surface at the top of the path, the wind fluttering the leaves above her. Slowly the color bled away on the horizon and dusk filled the air.

She was annoyed when she heard footsteps on the path below her. Deliberately she turned her back and faced the east and the blurred coast of Nicea, already dark.

She heard her name. It was Giuliano's voice. It took her a moment to compose herself before she greeted him. "Are you back here for the doge again?" she asked.

He smiled. "He thinks so. Actually I am back for the sunset, and the conversation." He was flippant, but there was a rueful honesty there for a second. "Home is never quite the same when you go back." He walked the last few paces and stood beside her.

"Everything is smaller," she agreed lightly. She must not allow her burning emotions to show. She was glad to have her back to the last of the light.

He looked at her, and something of the tension in his face smoothed away. The smile became wider, easier. "The cafés on the waterfront here haven't changed. Neither have the arguments. That's another kind of home."

"We Greeks are always arguing," she told him. "We can't be bothered with subjects about which there is only one valid opinion."

"I noticed," he said wryly. There was still enough light reflected up from the water to see the sheen on his skin, the faint pucker around his eyes. "But the emperor has sworn his loyalty to Rome. Doesn't that end some of your freedom to argue?"

"Not as much as an invasion would," she said dryly. "There'll be another crusade, sooner or later."

"Sooner," he said, a sudden tightness in his voice.

"Have you come to warn us?"

He looked down at his hands resting on the rough wood that formed a kind of railing. "There's no point. You know as much of its coming as anyone does."

"We'll still argue about God, and what He wants of us." She changed the subject. "Someone asked me the other day, and I realized I had never seriously considered it."

He frowned. "I think the Church would say that nothing we could do would be of much value to Him, but He requires obedience, and I suppose praise."

"Do you like to be praised?" she asked.

"Occasionally. But I'm not God." The smile flickered across his face.

"Neither am I," she agreed seriously. "And I like to be praised only if I have done something well, and I know the person speaking is sincere. But once is enough. I would hate it all the time. Just words? Endless 'you are wonderful,' 'you are marvelous' . . ."

"No, of course not." He turned around, his back half to the sea, his face toward her. "That would be ridiculous, and . . . unbelievably shallow."

"And obedience?" she went on. "Do you like it if people do what you tell them to, never because they have thought of it themselves? Not because they care, and want to do it? Without growth, without learning, wouldn't eternity be . . . boring?"

"I never thought of the possibility of heaven being a bore," he said, half laughing now. "But after a hundred thousand years, yes, terrible. In fact, maybe that's hell. . . ."

"No," she said. "Hell is having had heaven and then let it slip from your grasp."

He put his hands up to his face and pushed the heels of his palms hard against the skin. "Oh God, you are being serious."

She felt self-conscious. "Should I not be? I'm sorry. . . ."

"No!" He looked at her. "You should be! Now I know what I missed most when I was away from Byzantium."

For a moment, tears filled her eyes and her vision swam. Then she took one hand in the other and twisted her fingers until the pain reminded her of reality, limits, the things she could have, and those she could not. "Maybe there's more than one hell," she suggested. "Maybe one of them is to repeat the same thing over and over again until you finally realize that you are dead, in every sense that matters. You have ceased to grow."

"I'm tempted to joke that that is pure Byzantine, and probably heretical," Giuliano answered. "But I have an awful feeling that you are right."

Forty-seven

OF COURSE, HELENA HAD TOLD ZOE OF GREGORY VATATZES'S return from Alexandria. She had stood to the middle of the glorious room overlooking the sea and said it quite casually, as if it were of no more meaning than the price of some new luxury in the market: entertaining, but of no matter. How much did Helena know, or worse than that, was there something Zoe did not know?

She stared at the great gold cross. Poor Eirene. She had sought refuge in her intelligence and her anger, instead of using both to win what she wanted.

And Gregory was on his way back at last. He would arrive any day now. Zoe remembered him as vividly as if he had gone only a week ago, not more years than she wanted to count. Would his hair be gray? But he would still be as tall, towering even over her.

Perhaps it was as well they had not married. The edge of danger might have gone; they could have become bored with each other.

Arsenios had been his cousin in the elder branch of the family. He had kept the money and the gorgeous stolen icons, sharing nothing, so his sin had not tainted Gregory. In fact, Gregory had hated Arsenios for it. If he hadn't, Zoe could never have loved him.

But he was still Arsenios's cousin, and he would be concerned by his death, and of course the ruin of his daughter, and the death of his son, which Zoe had so brilliantly contrived. Would he deduce what had happened and how she had brought it about? He had always been as clever as she, or very nearly.

She shivered, although the air from the open window was still warm.
Would he look for revenge? He had had no love for Arsenios, but family
meant something, pride of blood.

She dressed in dark blue one day, crimson and topaz the next, used oils
and unguents, perfumes, had Thomais brush her hair until it gleamed, the
sheen bronze and then gold as she moved, like the warp and weft of silk.

The days went by. Word spread that he was home. Her servants told
her. Helena told her. He would come, he would not be able to resist it.
Zoe could outwait him, she had always been able to do that, whatever it
cost her. She paced the floor, lost her temper with Thomais and threw a
dish at her, catching her on the cheek in a curving gash, seeing the sudden
blood run scarlet on the black skin. She sent for Anastasius to stitch it up,
telling him nothing.

When Gregory finally came, he still caught her by surprise. All the pictures in her mind did not match the shock of seeing him come into the
room. She had been reading, with the lights high so she could see. Too late
to dim them now.

He walked in slowly. His hair was winged with gray but still thick, his
long face sunken below the cheekbones, eyes black as tar. But it was his
voice that always reached deepest into her: the careful diction, as if he
loved the roll of the words; the dark, bass resonance of it.

"It doesn't look very different," he said softly, his eyes gazing around before resting on her. "And you still wear the same colors. I'm glad. Some
things shouldn't change."

She felt a flutter inside her, like a trapped bird. She thought of Arsenios
dying on the floor, spewing blood, his eyes glittering with hate.

"Hello, Gregory," she said casually. She moved a step or two toward
him. "You still look Byzantine, in spite of your years in Egypt. Did you
have a good voyage?"

"Tedious," he replied with a slight smile. "But safe enough."

"You'll find the city changed."

"Oh, yes. Much is rebuilt, but not all. The seawalls are largely repaired,
but you have no games, no chariot races at the Hippodrome," he observed. "And Arsenios is dead."

"I know." She had prepared for this moment. "I feel for your loss. But
Eirene is well, and Demetrios, although I know they missed you." That
was a formality.

He shrugged. "Perhaps," he acknowledged. "Demetrios speaks much of Helena." A slight smile touched his lips. "I thought she would tire of Bessarion. In fact, it took longer that I had expected."

"Bessarion is dead," she replied.

"Really? He was young, at least young to die."

"He was murdered," she told him, keeping her voice perfectly level.

A razor-sharp amusement crossed his face and vanished as quickly. "Indeed? By whom?"

Zoe had not intended to meet Gregory's eyes, but the impulse was irresistible. She saw the fire of intelligence there, and a bottomless understanding. To look away would be a defeat. "A young man called Antoninus, I believe, assisted by a friend, Justinian Lascaris. He disposed of the body."

Gregory looked surprised. "Why? If ever a man were totally ineffectual, it was Bessarion. Surely not over Helena? Bessarion wouldn't have given a damn if she had affairs, as long as she was discreet."

"Of course not over Helena," she said tartly. "Bessarion was leading the battle against union with Rome. He had gained a considerable reputation as a religious hero."

"How interesting." He sounded as if he meant it. "And these other men, Antoninus and Justinian, were for the union?"

"Not at all, especially Justinian," she replied. "They were profoundly against it. That is the part of it which does not make sense."

"This really is interesting," he murmured. "What about Helena? Did she wish to be a hero's wife? Or might a hero's widow suit her better? Bessarion sounds extremely tedious."

"He was. Someone tried to kill him before Antoninus did. Three times. Twice with poison, once with a knife in the street."

"Not Antoninus?"

"Definitely not. He was not incompetent. Far from it. Justinian Lascaris even less so."

"Then perhaps it was Helena after all," he said thoughtfully. "You said 'Lascaris'? A good name."

She did not answer. She could feel her heart pounding and her breath tight in her chest.

Gregory smiled. His teeth were still white, still strong. "That is something you never did, Zoe." He said it softly, as if with approval. "If you were going to kill someone, you would do it yourself. More efficient, and safer. Although even with the greatest care, the utmost secrecy, there is always a way to find out."

"But not to prove it," she said with barely a flutter in her breath.

He moved another step, closing the distance between them. He touched her cheek with his fingers, then kissed her, slowly, intimately, as if he had all the time in the world.

She decided to attack. If in doubt, always attack. She answered him with equal intimacy, her lips, her tongue, her body. And it was he who stepped back.

"You do not need to prove anything," he said. "If what you want is revenge. All you need is to be sure."

"I understand revenge," she answered him, her voice caressing the words. "Not for myself—no one has wronged me deeply enough for that—but for my city, for its rape and the spoiling of its holy relics. I understand it, Gregory."

"I shall never think of Byzantium without thinking of you, Zoe. But there are other loyalties, such as that of blood. One day we will all die, but Byzantium will not be the same after you do. Something will have gone, and I shall regret that!" He looked once more around the room, then quickly turned on his heel and left.

He knew she had killed Arsenios. That was what he had come to tell her. He would let her wait, wondering when he would do it and how. Gregory never rushed his pleasures, either physical or emotional. She remembered that about him. He tasted every bit, slowly.

She stood in her room holding her arms around herself. The rape of Constantinople could not be forgiven until all of it was paid for, not ever put to the back of the mind and allowed to heal.

High among those from whom she must wring the last drop was Giuliano Dandolo, the great-grandson of that monstrous old man who had led the ruinous crusade.

She walked to the window, gazed across at the rising moon spilling silver over the Horn, and began to plan the destruction of Gregory. She regretted it.

She remembered him passionately, with both pleasure and regret. Maybe she would lie with him one last time? She would mourn him, perhaps even more than Eirene would.

Forty-eight

⁓

FOR ZOE, TOWERING OVER SUCH RELATIVELY SMALLER CON-
siderations as how to destroy Gregory was the fact that he was fore-
warned.

Poison was her weapon, either of the mind or of the body. She could
anger, tempt, or provoke people, even mislead them into destroying themselves. Every quality that was power could become a weakness, if carried to
excess. Even the gold byzant, that most exquisite of coins, had two sides.

She stared at herself in the glass. In this dim room, shaded from the
sunlight, she was still beautiful. She had never been indecisive, never a
coward. Would he use those things against her? Of course he would, if he
could find a way.

How? By baiting her to attack him. That is what she would have done.
Use her courage to tempt her to seize the chance, recklessly, and then trap
her. Should she do the same? Bluff? Double bluff? Triple bluff? Abandon
them all and act simply? Nothing Byzantine, nothing Egyptian—just
crude as a Latin and therefore unexpected from her.

What if she just waited and watched, to see what he did? How soon
would he decide to act? After all, it was Gregory who wanted revenge for
Arsenios's death; she could afford time.

Care, always the utmost care.

Even so, three days later, after a trip to the baths and eating fruit afterward, she was dreadfully ill. By the time she got home, she was nauseated
and filled with stabbing pains. Already she was beginning to grow dizzy.

How had he reached her? She had eaten only what she had seen others eat: harmless things, apricots and pistachios from a common dish.

She staggered into her bedroom, Thomais supporting her.

"No!" she gasped as Thomais tried to help her lie down. "I have been poisoned, you fool! I must mix an emetic. Fetch me a bowl, and my herbs. Be quick! Don't stand there like an idiot!" She heard the fear in her own voice as the room swayed and blurred around her, darkening as if the candles were burning down.

Thomais returned with a bowl and a jug of water in the other hand. She set them down and waited, gray-faced, to be told what to do next.

Zoe told her precisely which bottle and which jar to bring. Fingers shaking, she put a tiny spoonful of one in a glass, then two crushed leaves of the other, and drank them. The taste was vile, and she knew that in a few moments the pain would get worse and she would vomit terribly. But it would not last long, and her stomach would be empty. By tomorrow morning, she would begin to recover.

Damn Gregory! Damn him!

It was nearly two weeks before she saw him again. It was at the Blachernae Palace. Everyone who mattered from church or state was there, old blood or new money. A king's ransom of jewels was worn by men and women alike, although admittedly there were few women present. Zoe could not outshine the empress, so she chose to wear no gems at all, simply to use her height and her magnificent hair to accentuate the beautiful bones of her face and thus mark herself as different. Her tunic was of bronze silk, sheened light and dark as she moved, and she wore a rope of gold in her hair like a crown.

Faces turned to stare, and the gasps told her she had succeeded.

She saw Gregory early on—his height made that inevitable—but it was over an hour before he actually spoke to her. They were briefly alone, cut off from the crowd by a row of exquisitely tiled pillars creating a separate room. He offered her a honey cake decorated with almonds.

"No, thank you," she declined, perhaps too quickly.

A slow smile spread across his face. He made no remark, but their eyes met, and she knew exactly what he was thinking, as he knew what she thought.

His smile widened. "You look marvelous, as always, Zoe. You make every other woman in the room appear as if she is trying too hard."

"Perhaps what they wish for can be gained by wealth," she replied, wondering how he would interpret that.

"How tedious," he said, still not moving his eyes from hers. "How very young. What can be bought cloys so quickly, don't you think?"

"What can be bought by one person can also be bought by another," she agreed. "Eventually it becomes vulgar."

"But not revenge," he replied. "The perfect revenge is an art, and that has to be created. It can never be satisfying if it is the work of someone else, do you agree?"

"Oh yes. Creating it is half the flavor. But of course only if it succeeds."

He looked at her, studying her. "Of course it must, but you disappoint me if you think that it must do so immediately. That would be like pouring good wine down your throat, rather than sipping it a little at a time. And my dear, you were never a barbarian to waste your pleasures."

So he had not meant to kill her! Not yet, anyway. He was going to play first, a cut here, a cut there, bleeding away courage a little at a time. It was the insult to his proud name that counted to Gregory, her monstrous temerity in daring to kill one of his blood—in fact, counting Georgios, two. It was war. She smiled up at him.

"I am Byzantine," she replied. "That means that I am both sophisticated and barbaric. Whatever I do, I do it to the ultimate degree. I am surprised you need to be reminded of that." She looked him up and down. "Is your health failing you?"

"Not at all. Nor will it. I am younger than you are."

She laughed. "You always were younger, my dear. All men are. It is something women must learn to accept. But I am glad if you have not forgotten. To forget one's pleasures would be a kind of death, a little one, inch by inch." She smiled at him, eyes bright. "My memory is perfect."

He did not answer, but she saw the muscles tighten in his jaw. Whether he admitted it or not, she still had power to arouse him. It was a great pity he had to die.

He moved a step away, distancing himself a fraction.

She allowed her smile to widen, laughter into her eyes. "Too little, or too much?" she asked softly.

Anger flared up in the stain of blood in his cheeks. He put out his hand

and caught her arm, his fingers hard and tight. She could not have escaped, even had she wanted to. Physical memory of passion was suddenly so sharp that it ran hot through her body.

She looked up at him. If he did not give in to the temptation and make love to her, she would never forgive him. Then killing him would be easy, hardly even regrettable. If he did, and it had all the old passion and strength, then dear God, killing him would be the hardest thing she had ever had to do.

He kept his grip on her arm and strode out, half dragging her along until they were beyond the public rooms in some private quarters with chairs and cushions. For an instant, she was frightened. If she screamed here, not even the Varangian Guard would come. She must not let him see that she was afraid.

But he had seen; he knew it as if he could smell it in the air. He smiled slowly, then allowed himself to laugh, a deep, rich sound of pure pleasure.

She drew in her breath and let it out very slowly. The seconds seemed to be caught, suspended one by one.

Then he let go of her arm and placed his hand on her chest and pushed. She fell backward, surprised and a little ashamed, landing hard on the cushions. She stayed motionless.

"Frightened, Zoe?" he asked.

She still did not know if he was going to make love to her, or kill her, or possibly both. Any word she said might be the wrong one. What was he waiting for?

She let out her breath in a sigh, as if bored.

He tore open her tunic and kissed her, hard, over and over, as he had done in the days when they had loved. Then she knew that at least he would not be able to kill her, not tonight. There were too many old hungers to answer, too much present fire.

For both of them it was easy, as if the years had never happened. They said nothing. Afterward they kissed once, and both knew it would be the last time.

Forty-nine

ᔕ

ZOE KNEW BEYOND ANY DOUBT THAT SHE WOULD HAVE only one chance to kill Gregory. If she lost it, she lost everything. He would not fail.

She was thinking of this on her way home from the baths, her servant Sabas a few feet behind her, when she was bumped unexpectedly hard by a messenger running around a group of women talking in the street. Zoe lost her balance, and in trying to regain it without falling over, she stepped out into the path of the traffic. She was struck by a cart that had just started moving forward. She fell heavily and felt a sharp pain in her lower leg.

There were shouts of alarm and sympathy around her. People rushed forward, Sabas among them, and a tangle of arms thrust out to help her, pushing and shoving to get the cart backward without startling the horse into bolting. Arms pulled her up, tearing her robe, and she was unceremoniously put down on the ground with her back to the wall of the nearest shop while an old woman wagged her head and looked with alarm at the blood staining the fabric.

Then Sabas was there, bending over her. Without asking permission, he tore the hem off Zoe's tunic and used it to bind the wound.

"Look where you're going in future," an old man said waspishly.

Zoe was too shaken to retaliate, but she looked at his face so she would remember it, and one day she would repay his insolence. He saw something in her gaze and hurried away.

Sabas found a carriage and helped her in, and she was carried home, angry and for the moment consumed with pain.

As soon as she arrived, she sent Sabas off again at a run to fetch Anastasius. He was obliged to ask Simonis where Anastasius was and then follow her to another patient who was not seriously ill. Anastasius left almost immediately and accompanied him back.

Zoe was in too much distress to complain about waiting. Blood had soaked through the makeshift bandage, and the wound was throbbing so she could feel it all the way up to the groin. She told Anastasius what had happened and watched while he unbound the bloody edge of her tunic and exposed the wound. It looked horrible, and it turned her stomach and sent a chill of fear through her, but she would not let him see her avert her eyes.

He worked quickly. She noticed that he had beautiful hands, like a woman's—slender, long-fingered—and he moved with both delicacy and strength. She wondered what he would have been like had he been allowed to grow into a man. There was something in the turn of his head, an inflection of the voice, that reminded her of Justinian. It came suddenly as he frowned and bent to look more closely at an herb, then the likeness was gone again.

"I need to stitch the sides together," Anastasius told her. "Otherwise it will take a long time to heal, and it will leave a worse scar. I'm sorry, but it will feel unpleasant."

"Then do it quickly," Zoe ordered him. "I want it healed. And I don't care for blood all over the place."

Anastasius threaded one of his curved needles with silk. "Now please keep perfectly still. I don't wish to cause you any more pain than I have to. Would you like Thomais to hold you steady?"

Zoe looked at Anastasius and met the unflinching gray eyes. It was the first time she had looked at him so intently. He had long eyelashes and his eyes were beautiful, but it was the intelligence in them that excited her, even alarmed her. It was as if his mind touched hers and read it much more intimately than she would have expected.

He had started to stitch, and she had not noticed it. She watched him work quickly, admiring his skill.

"It seems you are busy now, Anastasius," she remarked. "Your reputation has spread. I hear many people speaking of your abilities."

He smiled without taking his eyes from his work. "I am grateful to you for that. I owe my first recommendations to you. I believe it was you who gave my name to Eirene Vatatzes. I have attended her since then."

Zoe froze, her body suddenly rigid.

"I'm sorry," Anastasius apologized. "I am nearly finished."

Zoe swallowed. "Tell me about Eirene. It will take my mind off what you are doing. How is she, now that her husband has returned from Alexandria?"

"Recovering." Anastasius put in the last stitch and, very gently, so as not to pull the flesh, cut the silk with a blade. "It may take her a little while."

"Thank you. Did you meet her husband?"

Anastasius looked up. "Yes. An interesting man. He mentioned that he knew you."

"A long time ago. What did he say?"

Anastasius smiled, as if he knew exactly what was in her mind and in Eirene's. "He said you were the most beautiful woman in Byzantium, not for your face, or even your body, but for the passion in you."

Zoe looked away. She could not face Anastasius's eyes. "Really? No doubt he said it to annoy Eirene. She has a temper, and that amuses him. And what did you say?" she demanded, facing him again, the high color in her cheeks masked as anger.

Anastasius smiled. "My answer was unimportant."

"Oh? What was it?"

"I told him that I was not in a position to appreciate it, but I quite believed him that it was so," Anastasius replied.

She gasped at his nerve, felt the remembered heat scorch up her face again, then burst into laughter, a rich peal of pure delight.

Anastasius poured some fine powder into a small silk sachet and then placed a jar of ointment on the table beside it. "Take a spoonful of this in hot water once a day." He handed her a ceramic spoon, wide but shallow. "Level, do not heap it. Draw a knife over the top to make certain of that. It will keep the infection from getting worse. And put the ointment on if it starts to itch. It probably will do, as it heals. I shall call again in a week to remove some of the stitches, and then take out the rest a week or so after that. But if it gives you cause for anxiety because it is inflamed or it suppurates, send for me immediately. Or if you become feverish."

After Anastasius was gone and Thomais had assisted her to bathe and put on clean clothes, Zoe became aware of the steadily increasing pain in her leg. By nightfall, it was throbbing so powerfully that she could think of little else. She sent for hot water and measured out the powder Anastasius had left and dropped it into the cup. She was about to drink it, and suddenly a hideous thought came to her. What if Gregory was using Anastasius, perhaps the only person outside her own household whom she would trust?

Carefully, in case any of it spilled on her, she threw out the medicine. At first she thought to destroy it with fire and then realized just in time that it might be just as lethal if it was burned and its fumes inhaled. She ended up tipping all the powder into the hot water and pouring it down the drain.

Three days later, she was in even greater pain. In spite of having treated it herself and taken one of her own powders to get rid of fever, the wound was red and angry, and it felt as if it were on fire. Every now and then she was dizzy. She drank glass after glass of water; it tasted even more brackish than usual, and she was always thirsty.

Now she was certain that Gregory was behind the attack and that somehow he had managed to introduce poison into the wound.

"Look for poison!" she told Anastasius when he came. "The wound is infected. Someone is trying to kill me."

Anastasius looked at her, studying her hot, golden eyes, her flushed skin, and then last the raw wound in her leg, which was beginning to suppurate. He touched it gently with one cool finger, then turned to her. "Did you use the medicine I gave you? And don't lie, unless you want to lose your leg."

"No," she said quietly. "I was afraid that whoever poisoned me might have reached you, too."

Anastasius nodded. "I see. Then we had better start again, from the beginning. The infection is serious now. I shall stay here and watch you. I have every interest in your recovery. It would be bad for my reputation if you died, so do as I tell you." He smiled very slightly, a deep, inward humor.

He stayed, nursing her all day and to begin with all night as well. He sat beside her, talking to her through the increasing pain. At first it irritated her. Then gradually she realized that as she answered his questions, she became less aware of how badly she hurt. Obliquely, it was kind of him.

"Demetrios?" she answered his last question, smiling in spite of herself. "Not like his father. Weaker. In love with Helena? Probably not. In love with power, certainly. Thinks he hides it, but he doesn't. Eirene's son, but without her intelligence. Brilliant with money, like her." She laughed, but so deep inside herself that he did not hear it. "Helena thinks he loves her, but then she thinks all sorts of things. Fool."

"Did Justinian love her?" Anastasius asked, sounding only mildly interested, as if he were still trying to take her mind from the pain.

"Loathed her," Zoe answered frankly. Damn it, her leg hurt! She was getting a little dizzy. Was she going to die after all?

He made her drink something more that tasted foul. Had Gregory got to him? She searched his eyes, his face, and could read something in it beyond curiosity, but what?

"Anastasius," Zoe whispered.

"Yes?"

"If I am alive in the morning, I shall tell you why Justinian Lascaris killed Bessarion. Bloody fool! He didn't come to me, and I was the one person who would have believed him. I can see it for myself now. Only mistake he made, but it cost him everything. Idiot!"

Anastasius looked as if she had struck him, his face an odd mixture of ashen pale and red spots on his cheeks, like weals.

The room was beginning to swim around Zoe. She was growing delirious with fever. He forced her to drink something that was even more vile than the last time, but when she awoke at midday she was much improved.

Anastasius was smiling at her. "Better?" he inquired with some satisfaction.

"Much better." She sat up slowly, and he offered her something to drink that was pleasant. "Thank you."

He eased her back down again. He was stronger than she had expected. Or perhaps she was weaker.

"It's morning," Anastasius observed.

"I can see that!" Zoe snapped.

A smile flickered in Anastasius's eyes. "Then you will tell me why Justinian was a fool not to trust you?" he said with an edge to his voice. "Or was I the fool to believe it?"

Memory rushed back. "What was that you just gave me?"

Anastasius smiled. "You haven't answered my question."

"Justinian knew Bessarion was useless," Zoe said quietly. "He would have been a disaster on the throne. But the others wouldn't believe Justinian. They'd put everything into it and the plans had gone too far. The only way to stop it was to kill Bessarion. Antoninus believed Justinian. He helped." She almost laughed when she thought of it, except that it was so futile. "Fool. I would have stopped it. They could have done nothing without me. But Justinian didn't trust me. What was it I just drank?"

Anastasius stared at her as if mesmerized.

"What was it I just drank?" Zoe repeated, her voice more angry and frightened than she had wanted to betray.

"Infusion of camomile," Anastasius answered. "It's good for the digestion. Just camomile leaves in hot water, nothing else. It's bitter because you've been ill. That alters your taste."

She did not want to admire Anastasius, and it was a curious feeling to trust him. Yet at least as far as medicine was concerned, she did. She lay back at last, for the time being content.

After three days, she began to regain strength and the wound was less red and the swelling subsided. After a week, he pronounced it satisfactory and said he would leave and return at the end of another three days.

She thanked him, paid him generously, and also gave him the gift of a small enameled box made of silver and inlaid with aquamarine. He touched it gently, looking first at its beauty, then up at her. His appreciation of it was clear in his face, and she was satisfied. She told him to leave.

Zoe was glad Anastasius had liked it. He had ministered to her not only with skill, but with gentleness. It had given her a serious fright to be so vulnerable. It could not go on like this.

An idea was beginning to take shape in her mind. She would make Gregory's death count. She would contrive a means to have Giuliano Dandolo blamed for it. That way, she could bear to kill Gregory. She could even do it herself.

Fifty

ITH GREGORY, ZOE WOULD HAVE NO SECOND CHANCE.
In a perverse way, this last battle between them was another kind
of bond. She thought of him during the day. She lay awake at night and
remembered how it was to be with him.

Another piece of the plan fell into her hands. It was the street attacks
upon Bessarion and then upon herself that gave her the idea.

The first thing was to plant the seeds in people's minds that there was a
quarrel between Gregory and Giuliano Dandolo. It must be just a superficial word, so slight that the meaning was recalled only afterward and understood then.

The second thing was to go to Bardas, a maker of daggers whom she
knew and had trusted in the past. She put on her heaviest dalmatica and
went out into the windy street and the light rain. Walking quickly, she left
Sabas far behind her as he was used to being, discreet, seeing and hearing
nothing. The pain in her leg was barely there anymore.

"Yes, mistress," the swordsmith said immediately, pleased to see her
again. Only a fool forgot a benefactress or broke his word to a woman who
never forgot or forgave. "What can I make for you this time?"

"I want a good dagger," she replied. "It doesn't have to be the best, but
I want a family crest on the hilt, and I want you to be discreet about it. It
is a gift, and it will be spoiled if anyone else hears of it."

"Your business is no one else's, lady. Whose crest would that be?"

"Dandolo," she answered.

As soon as she had the dagger, which was beautiful—Bardas was even better than his word—she sent a letter to Giuliano Dandolo, who was still lodging in the Venetian Quarter. The message was simple: She had learned more about his dead mother.

Giuliano came, as she had known he would. She looked at him standing in her magnificent room. Although he was ill at ease, trying to hide the eagerness to learn what she had to say burning inside him, he still moved with grace, and grudgingly she admitted to herself he was better than handsome: He had a vitality of mind that she could not ignore. If she had been younger, she would have wanted to lie with him. But he was a Dandolo, and the dream in the eyes, the shape of a cheekbone, the width of his shoulders, or the way he walked could not pardon that.

He made all the usual polite remarks, not rushing into asking for the new information, and she played the game, uncertain whether she enjoyed it or not.

"I have heard more of your mother," she said as soon as the greetings were over and the casual remarks that courtesy required. "She was beautiful, but perhaps you knew that already." She saw the flicker of emotion in his face, the sharp hurt too deep to camouflage. "Perhaps you did not know that Maddalena had a sister, Eudoxia, also beautiful, but regrettably there is considerable scandal about her name." Again she saw the emotion raw in him. A pity she could not be young again. "What I did not know before is that Eudoxia is said by some to have repented deeply in her old age, and to have joined some holy order. I do not know which, but I may be able to learn. It is possible that she is still alive."

"Alive?" His eyes opened wide.

"Please, leave it to me. I have ways which are not open to you, and I can do it discreetly. I will let you know as soon as I have something that is certain."

"Thank you." He smiled at her, a handsome, self-assured man with a charm that came without effort.

"I was three when my mother died," she said to Giuliano, aware that her voice was shaking but unable to control it.

"I'm sorry," he responded with sudden shock, his eyes tender.

She did not wish his sympathy. "She was raped and murdered." Then she wished she had not told him. It was a weakness and a tactical error. He might work out the year, and the circumstances, and then know he could never trust her. "I have something for you," she said hastily, trying to cover it. "I came by it almost by chance, so please feel no obligation." She moved away from him over to the table on which lay the dagger with the Dandolo crest. She unwrapped the blue silk cloth around it and held it out, hilt toward him, crest upward. Bardas had done a perfect job: It looked old and well used, yet every detail of it was clear.

Giuliano stared at it, then looked up at her.

"Take it," she urged. "It should be yours. Anyway, what on earth would I do with a dagger that carried a Venetian crest on it?"

He was not clumsy enough to offer to pay for it. He would give her a gift of appropriate value, a little more than he judged the dagger to be worth.

He weighed it in his hands. "The balance is perfect," he observed. "Where did it come from?"

"I don't know," she answered. "But if I find out, I shall tell you."

"Thank you." He was not effusive, but the depth of his feeling filled his voice, his eyes, even the way he stood and the touch of his hands on the knife.

"Wear it," she said quite casually. "It will become you." She would pray that he did, kneel before the Virgin Mary and beseech her that he did. Unless the dagger was known to be Giuliano's, Zoe's plan would not work.

"I will." He seemed about to add something further, then changed his mind and took his leave.

She watched him go with an odd little pain biting in her side, as if something were slipping out of her hands. Now there was nothing to do but wait, two or three weeks, at least. She had to be sure others had seen Giuliano with the knife and knew it was his.

She waited a month. Time seemed to crawl by like a crippled thing, dragging days behind it. The heat of noon paralyzed, the afternoons were heavy and silent, darkness was a mask that could hide anything, every creak and footstep a possible assassin.

As she had expected, Giuliano sent her a gift: a brooch for her dalmatica. She liked it more than she wished to. It was black onyx and topaz, in a bed of gold. She did not want to wear it, yet she could not resist doing so, her fingers straying to it because it was also beautiful to the touch. Damn him!

Finally she could wait no longer, and she sent for a thief she had used in the past, when necessity dictated. She told him the knife was hers and had been taken in a robbery, then sold to Giuliano Dandolo. She had seen him with it and realized he had no idea of its origin. She had offered to buy it back, and because of the family crest, he had, not surprisingly, refused. She had no recourse but to have it stolen, as it had been stolen from her.

The thief asked no questions and promised to do as she wished, for a price.

Next she wrote a letter to Gregory, disguising her hand to look like that of Dandolo, copying from the letter he had sent her accepting her earlier invitation. She said she had accidentally stumbled on a revealing secret about Zoe Chrysaphes and would be willing to inform Gregory, if Gregory would assist him in a certain diplomatic matter, of no detriment to Byzantium. She signed it with his name, also copied.

Finally she sent a similar letter to Giuliano from Gregory saying he had heard that Giuliano was interested in learning about Maddalena Agallon. He had known and admired her and would be happy to tell Giuliano all he was able to. She signed it "Gregory Vatatzes." She knew his hand well enough to forge it without effort.

Then she sat in the large red chair under the torches and stared at the ceiling, relishing the moment, feeling her heart beat so hard and so high in her chest that she could scarcely breathe.

The night of the assignation between Gregory and Giuliano, Zoe was filled with a torrent of doubts. She stood at the window and looked out at the hazy darkness and the faintly moving gleam of lanterns like crawling fireflies in the streets below. Was she being absurd? Poor Zoe Chrysaphes, once the greatest beauty in exiled Byzantium, the mistress of emperors, soon to be a crazy old woman in the streets, dressed in rags, trying to kill people!

She strode over to the great cross on the wall and stared at it, willing herself to regain the passion of vengeance that would overcome her weakness. The Kantakouzenos were destroyed in Cosmas, and the Vatatzes with Arsenios, the Doukas in Euphrosane; the rest did not matter. Only Dandolo was left, and that would soon be over, too.

She moved to the icon of the Virgin Mary and knelt. "Blessed Mother of God, fill me with strength to complete my mission!" she pleaded.

She looked up at the somber face with its aureole of gold, and it seemed to smile at her. As if some hidden floodgates inside Zoe had opened, the blood throbbed in her veins and her muscles had the vitality of a young woman.

She rose, crossed herself, and hurried out alone in the night, as light and easy in her stride as a deer. It was mild, the wind off the sea smelling of salt. Only when she was half a mile from her home did she realize that the old beggar woman she was dressed to seem would never have walked as she was doing. As she rounded a corner, she bent a little and slowed her pace. She went another mile slowly, painfully.

Gregory had to pass this way to keep his appointment with Giuliano. Here was the place to catch him, in the Venetian Quarter. She had calculated the time he would pass, and before Giuliano could arrive, but only just. It had to be exact. She touched the dagger at her belt, hidden by her cloak, then crossed herself again. Now she must wait.

There was someone coming along the street now. Two young men, arm in arm, drunk, their bodies swaying, making the shadows move. She heard their voices and their laughter and shrank back into the lee of a doorway.

Should she attack Gregory from behind? No, that was a coward's way. He would suspect anyone following him, but not an old woman face-to-face. She bent farther forward, as if age crippled her.

There was laughter down the street, lights going the other way. The wind was saltier here, close to the waterfront.

There was someone else coming, a tall man carrying a lantern. She recognized his step. She hobbled, barely glancing at his face, her voice whining, high-pitched, and servile. "Spare an old woman a few pence? May God bless you. . . ."

He stopped, his hand going toward his side. Money or a weapon? There was no time to wait and see. Zoe drew out the knife from beneath her cloak and clawed upward with it, at the same time kicking him as hard as she could on the shin. He jerked forward with surprise, and she swept the blade hard across his throat, using all her strength, helped by the weight of his body as he lurched off balance from the kick. The lantern crashed and went out, but her eyes were accustomed to the night. There was blood jetting out of his throat, warm and sticky on her hand. She could smell it. He did not even cry out, making only a terrible gurgle as he choked, wrenching around, grabbing at her as his life gushed out of him. He tore at her shoulder, pulling the muscles, hurting as if he had stabbed her, but he was already losing his balance, carrying her down with him. She felt herself falling, and the ground hit her hard with a pain in her elbow that took her breath away.

But his grasp had loosened. She did not want him to go without knowing it was she who had done it.

"Gregory!" she said clearly. "Gregory!"

For a moment, his eyes focused on her and his lips formed something that might have been her name; then the light in him went out, and his tar black eyes were empty.

Slowly, her bones aching, her muscles stiff, she rose and turned to walk away. Her vision was blurred; hot tears streamed down her face. It puzzled her why she felt as if the void were not at her feet but inside her, and she knew with certainty that it would never again be filled.

Fifty-one

ANNA WOKE IN THE NIGHT TO FIND SIMONIS STANDING over her with a candle in her hand.

Simonis's voice was sharp with irritation. "It's a man from the Venetian Quarter, on horseback. Says you're to come right away. There's been an accident and they need help. He wants you to go on his horse. They're mad people. I'll go and tell him to get one of their own." She half turned away.

"Tell him I'll be there in a minute," Anna ordered.

She went with the Venetian, accepting his hand to haul her up into the saddle behind him, clutching her bag.

"You won't need it," he told her. "He's dead. We . . . we need your help to get rid of the body so it won't be found and we won't get the blame for his murder."

She was stunned. "Why on earth would I help you?" she demanded, preparing to slide off and return to her bed.

He urged the animal forward, gathering speed too quickly for her to do such a thing. They clattered down the hill and along the level. If he replied to her question, she did not hear his words. It was a quarter of an hour of clinging to him awkwardly in the hazy darkness, her bag slapping against her legs, before they came to a halt in an alley. A little knot of people had gathered outside the doorway of a small shop. At their feet was sprawled the body of a man. One of the group produced a lantern and held it up. In its wavering light, she could see the fear in his face and the scarlet of blood on the stones.

"We found him in our doorway," the man said quietly. "We didn't do it. He's not one of us, he's a nobleman, and Byzantine. What shall we do?"

Anna took the lantern from him and lowered it to look at the body. She saw straightaway that it was Gregory Vatatzes. His throat had been cut in a terrible, jagged wound, and scarlet with gore on the road beside him was a fine dagger with the Dandolo crest on the hilt. She had seen it before, less than a week ago, in Giuliano's hands. He had cut a ripe peach with it, offering her half. They had laughed together over something trivial. There had been only the one peach. It had been his, and he had shared it with her.

She ran her hands over the body, searching to see if he was armed, if there had been a fight. She was cold with fear that Giuliano could have been injured as well.

She found a weapon, another jeweled knife, this one with a different shape of blade, still in its sheath at his belt and unstained. Gregory had not even drawn it. There was a piece of paper in his pocket: an invitation to meet about three hundred yards from here, signed by Giuliano.

With stiff hands, she tore the paper into tiny pieces and put the Dandolo dagger in her own bag, then turned to the man who had come for her. "Help me move him into the middle of the road. Somebody get a horse with any kind of cart. As many of you as can, climb into it and drive over the body, just once, over his neck, so we can hide the wound. Go on! Quickly!"

Anna bent down, forcing herself to grip Gregory's body. It was heavy. It was hard work to drag it into the middle of the street where the traffic had worn the stones concave over the years. The sweat broke out on her body, yet she was shivering so violently that her teeth chattered. She tried not to think of what she was doing, only what it would cost Giuliano if she failed, and these people who had trusted her and would pay a terrible price to the authorities if it was thought to be murder.

When the task was completed, in swaying, jerking lantern light, the women helped her find the place where Gregory had been killed so that in daylight the blood would not make it obvious he had been moved. They worked hard, with lye and potash and brushes to get rid of every trace, scrubbing, swilling, scraping between the stones.

By the time they were satisfied, the man had returned with the cart, drawn by a swaybacked horse. He did not say where he had got it, and no one asked.

It was a fearful job. The horse was frightened by the smell of blood and death, and it did everything it could to avoid treading on the corpse. It had to be led, talked to softly, encouraged against its will, in order to draw the wheels over Gregory's neck and shoulders.

"It's not good enough," Anna told them, staring at the mangled flesh and hideously exposed bone. She could not leave it looking so obviously like a murder. "Do it once more. No one will believe it an accident if it's clear the cart went over him several times. They might accept that the horse was frightened and backed once. Be careful." The cart began to move, the man dragging at the halter of the reluctant animal, which was sweating, its flanks lathered, its eyes rolling.

"To the left!" she said urgently, waving her arm. "More! . . . That's it. Now forward."

She forced herself to look. The body looked terrible. Anyone seeing it would assume he had been knocked down and then dragged until the wheels finally went over him as the animal panicked. She turned away.

"Thank you," the man said. His voice cracked with emotion. "I'll take you back home."

"You stay here. Clean the cart and the horse's hooves. Do that very carefully or they'll find it if they look. I'll tell the authorities you called me to an accident." She gulped again, her head swimming. "It's easy to explain. Dark night, frightened horse, a man returned from a long exile in Alexandria who didn't know the Venetian Quarter well. Bad accident, but they happen. Don't add to it." She felt her stomach churning. "You found him. You called me because you knew me. You didn't see in the dark how bad it was."

She walked away quickly, and as soon as she was around the corner, she retched. It took her several minutes before she was well enough to stand up and go on. She was less than a mile from the house where Giuliano lodged, and he should have returned by now. The time of his appointment with Gregory was long past. Before she could report Gregory's death to the night watch, she must give Giuliano back the dagger.

She reached the door he used at the side of the house and rapped on it hard. There was no answer. She tried again and waited. She had tried a third time and was about to walk away, but then she heard a brief noise, and the door swung open to show light and the bulk of a man behind it.

"Giuliano?" she said urgently.

He pulled it wider, his face stunned with surprise in the upward glow of the lantern. "Anastasius? What's happened? You look terrible. Come in, man." He pulled the door wide. "Are you hurt? Let me . . ."

She had forgotten how filthy she was, stained with dirt from the street and with Gregory's blood. "I'm not hurt!" she said sharply. "Close the door . . . please."

He was standing in a nightshirt, his hair tousled as if he had already been back in bed. She felt her face burning.

She took the bloody dagger out of her bag and showed it to him, gripping it by the handle, but so that he could see the Dandolo crest. The blade was scarlet with blood—congealing but not yet dry.

Giuliano's face went white. He stared at her in horror.

"I found it in the street a mile from here," she told him. "Beside the body of Gregory Vatatzes. His throat had been torn out."

He started to speak but choked on the words.

She told him briefly how she had been sent for and what she had done. "They'll assume it was an accident. Clean your knife. Soak it until there isn't a smear of blood on it anywhere, even in the crevices of the handle. Did you go to meet him?"

"Yes," Giuliano said hoarsely, having to clear his throat to force out the word. "He wasn't there. That's my knife. Zoe Chrysaphes gave it to me, because it has the Dandolo crest on it. But it was stolen a couple of days ago."

"Zoe?" she said incredulously.

He still did not comprehend. "She's helping me . . . to find my mother's sister, who may still be alive. That's why I went to meet Gregory. He wrote to me, saying he had word of her." He walked over toward a chest by the wall, carrying the lantern with him so he could find the paper. He held it out to her, the light high for her to read it.

It was almost immaterial what it said. It was Zoe's writing. The slant of the letters was different from her usual—bolder, more masculine—but Anna recognized the characteristic capitals. She had seen Zoe's script often enough on letters and instructions, lists of ingredients.

"Zoe Chrysaphes," she said softly, her voice rasped with fury. "You fool!" She was shaking in spite of the effort to control herself. "She's Byzantine to the soul, and you are not only a Venetian, you're a Dandolo! You let her give you a dagger anyone would recognize? Where were your wits?"

He stood frozen to the spot.

She closed her eyes. "Please God, no one will ask you, but if they do, stick to the truth that you were out. Someone may have seen you. I shan't tell you where it happened because you shouldn't know. Don't mention the dagger. I think I'm the only one who really saw it. Just clean the damn thing!" Without giving him more than a glance, Anna opened the door and went out into the corridor and then the street again. Quickly, stumbling and shivering, she hurried to the nearest watch point of the civil authority of the city. Thank heaven it was in the Venetian Quarter still, and the watchmen had no willingness to consider it anything more than the accident it appeared to be.

"And what were you doing there?" the watchman asked her.

"I have several patients in the quarter," she replied.

"At that hour of night?"

"No, sir. I was just a physician they had consulted. They knew that I would come."

"The man was dead, you say. What could you do for him?" The man frowned at her.

"Nothing, I'm afraid. But they were very distressed, especially the women. They needed help . . . treatment."

"I see. Thank you."

She stayed only a little longer, leaving her name and address for them to find her again if necessary. Then, still shaking with horror and fear, still wretched with nausea, the sweat cold on her skin, she began the long walk back up the hill homeward.

Fifty-two

Zoe was too excited to sleep when she returned to her house. She took off her old woman's rags and burned them in the hearth. No one must see them, especially soaked with blood as they were. Fortunately, she had little of it on herself. As if she had merely found herself having a restless night, she sent for Thomais and told her to heat water for her to bathe and to fetch towels. Carefully she chose her most precious, luxurious oils and perfumes and unguents for her skin.

When the water was ready, steam rising, moist on the skin and sweet to the smell, she stepped in slowly, savoring the sensation. The heat, the gentle touch of it, eased out all the tight-knotted aches and fears.

She remembered, with a pleasure made sharper by grief, how Gregory had wanted her, tasted her slowly. It was right that she had killed him physically, violently, face-to-face. That was how they had loved, and hated. Poison was right for men like Arsenios, not for Gregory.

She stood up when the water was cooling and noticed with amusement that Thomais still looked at her with admiration in her eyes.

She dressed in fresh clothes and ordered fruit and a glass of wine. Alone in the silence of the end of night, she stood in front of the window and watched the dawn pale in the east. Today she would go to the Hagia Sophia and offer up her thanks to the Virgin Mary. She would give hundreds of candles, make the whole place a glory of light. Gregory Vatatzes and Giuliano Dandolo destroyed in one superb act. And she was safe.

The dawn broadened. Thomais returned to say that the physician Anastasius had called, requesting to see her immediately.

What on earth could he want at this hour? But since Zoe was up and dressed anyway, it was not an inconvenience.

"Send him in," she ordered. "And bring more fruit, and another glass."

A moment later Anastasius came in, his face ashen except for two high spots of color on his cheeks. His hair was barely combed, and he looked both exhausted and furious.

"Good morning, Anastasius," Zoe said. "May I offer you wine, a little fruit?"

"Gregory Vatatzes is dead," Anastasius said in a hard, thin voice.

"I did not know he was ill," Zoe replied with perfect calm. "From your apparent distress, I assume you attended him?"

"There was nothing to attend," Anastasius replied bitterly. "He was lying in a street in the Venetian Quarter, his throat torn open with the dagger you gave to Giuliano Dandolo."

"Murdered?" Zoe turned the word over on her tongue, as if uncertain of it. "He must have had more enemies than he realized. Dandolo, you said? Really. I believe Gregory spent some time in Venice, before going to Alexandria. Perhaps it was a family feud?"

"I am sure it was," Anastasius agreed. "Dandolo is a dangerous name to carry in Constantinople. With the history it has, I would be surprised if you gave him such a gift." He smiled with scalding irony, his eyes brilliant, the intelligence in them hard and probing. "With the hilt toward him, that is."

A flash of humor lit Zoe's smile for an instant. "You think I should have presented it blade first?"

"I think you did," Anastasius retorted. "Only he did not realize it."

Zoe shrugged. "Then it looks as if he too is a victim of this murder. I'm sorry he is your friend. I would not intentionally have had it so."

"He is not a victim," Anastasius said. "The authorities have concluded that Gregory's death was a tragic accident. He was apparently struck by a horse and cart, in the darkness, of course, and the unfamiliar streets."

"And it tore his throat out?" Zoe said incredulously. "Was it the horse which did that, or the cart?"

Anastasius's face was unreadable. "It looks as if he was in the middle of the street and was knocked down. The wheels of the cart went over Gregory's throat. At least that is what it looked like to me."

"And the Dandolo dagger?" Zoe asked sarcastically. "Was the horse carrying that as well? Or the driver, perhaps?"

"That would have been someone else, who left the scene," Anastasius said. "But since the dagger has disappeared, it doesn't really matter. No one else saw it, and I daresay Giuliano has it back by now, and will take better care of it in future."

Zoe had to control her eyes, her mouth, even the pallor in her face. Anastasius must see nothing.

She stood staring at him, his blazing eyes, the face so strong yet so unmasculine with its soft mouth, passionate and vulnerable. He could not be related to Dandolo. There was no resemblance. Dandolo's mother's family, perhaps? There was no one of his generation except Giuliano himself. Eudoxia had become a nun. Maddalena was dead.

Love? A physically immature eunuch, with a man like Dandolo?

Then like lightning, a wild idea cut across the darkness, dazzling Zoe with its obviousness, and she began to laugh. Perfectly clear now—and yet impossible. But she believed it: Anastasius was not a eunuch at all—he was as much a woman as Zoe herself! Her love for Dandolo was just the same love Zoe would have had for him, had she been the right age and he not a Venetian. Or maybe even if he had been, just not a Dandolo.

Anastasius, or whatever her name was, stood frozen to the floor, staring.

Zoe went on laughing. This person who had been so sad and confusing as half a man was infinitely understandable as a woman.

Finally, Zoe regained control of herself and walked over to the wine and the glasses. She poured a glass to the brim and held it out, offering it.

"No, thank you," Anastasius said coldly.

Zoe shrugged and drank the glass half-empty herself, then filled the other glass. She offered the first glass again.

This time Anastasius took it, drank it to the lees, then put it down and turned on her heel and walked out.

Zoe drank her own glass slowly, savoring it, thinking. She had learned something of delicious and immeasurable value. The power it gave her over Anastasius—no, Anastasia—was limitless. But before she attempted to use it, she would learn all she could about this woman who had chosen to deny herself the greatest natural asset she had. What did she want that she would pay this terrible price for it?

Zoe's mind raced. She had said she was from Nicea, but was that true? Probably. Only a fool created unnecessary lies. The more Zoe thought about it, the more it intrigued her. What passion was immense enough for such a masquerade?

Anastasia was interested in Justinian Lascaris. Was Zarides her true name, or was she too a Lascaris, part of another imperial family? Wife of Justinian? If so, she did not love him, or she would not have so rashly risked her life to save the Venetian. Beyond doubt, she loved the Venetian.

Sister of Justinian! That was what Zoe had glimpsed before. A sister wanting to prove his innocence.

And was Justinian innocent? Zoe had thought not, but could she be wrong? Was there something else she had not guessed at?

The more Zoe could learn about Anastasia the better.

She would also learn more about Giuliano Dandolo's mother and her life and death, so she could twist the knife of pain in his heart. Anything that he could not disprove would do.

Fifty-three

∾

A WEEK AFTER THAT, ANNA RETURNED HOME TO FIND SI-monis waiting for her with a strip of paper in her hand.

"From Zoe Chrysaphes," Simonis said, pursing her lips.

"Thank you." She put down her bag of herbs and oils and opened the paper.

> Anastasius,
>
> Unfortunately I have a slight wound in my leg which needs a surgeon's attention. Please call on me immediately you receive this.
>
> Zoe Chrysaphes

"When did this come?" Anna asked.

"Less than an hour ago. Half an hour, perhaps." Simonis raised her eyebrows. "Are you going?"

"I am," Anna replied. Simonis knew perfectly well that ethically she could not do anything else, nor would she easily survive the damage to her reputation were she to refuse.

What she found upon her arrival at Zoe's was the one thing Anna had never considered. Giuliano was there, leaning casually against the sill of the great window that looked across to the Bosphorus. He straightened up with slight discomfort when Anna came in, and she saw the flush on his cheeks. He acknowledged her courteously, with no shadow in his face from their last conversation or Gregory's murder.

"Ah!" Zoe said with clear pleasure. "Thank you for coming, Anastasius. I have a deep spelk in my leg. I am afraid if it is not removed and treated, it may poison me." She pulled the hem of her gold-colored tunic higher and exposed an angry wound with a spelk of wood sticking out of it and a crust of dried blood around the edges.

"When did it happen?" Anna put her bag on the floor and bent to examine the leg.

"I was walking in the courtyard last night," Zoe replied. "After dark. It did not seem serious enough to call you then, but this morning I realized the spelk was still there."

"Perhaps I should leave you . . ." Giuliano's voice came from behind Anna, the reluctance so sharp that he could not disguise it. "I can return on another occasion." He moved away from the window.

"Not at all," Zoe dismissed the idea. "It is only my ankle. It would be pleasanter for me to have company to take my mind off what Anastasius must do. Please."

Anna looked up and saw Zoe smiling, and inside her own mind she could hear her wild, almost delirious laughter, completely out of control. The sound of it had haunted Anna.

Giuliano relaxed. "Thank you."

Zoe looked at Anna again. "Tell me what you need, and I shall send my maid for it. Hot water, bandages?"

"Yes, please." Anna tried to concentrate her attention on the wound. "And salt."

"You are not one to put salt in anyone's wounds, are you, Anastasius?" Zoe said lightly

"Not so far," Anna replied. "But the thought has occurred to me once or twice. The salt is to clean my knife when I use it, and the ointment for the first layer of bandages. It will be less painful if they do not cling to the flesh, especially if it bleeds."

Thomais brought the water in several dishes, and the salt and a pile of clean linen bandages, then Zoe dismissed her. She rested her leg on a stool, leaving Anna to work on it, ignoring her, and turned to Giuliano.

"I have learned a great deal more about Maddalena Agallon." She said it softly, dropping her voice as if in deep emotion and causing Giuliano to move closer to her and into Anna's range of vision.

"Most of it concerns her life after she left her husband and her infant son." Zoe's face was full of pain, but it was impossible to tell if it was pity for that long ago abandoned child or from the prick of the blade in Anna's hand as she pierced the angry flesh around the spelk of wood.

"Why did she go?" Giuliano forced the words from deep inside him.

Zoe hesitated. "I'm sorry," she said gently to Giuliano, ignoring the wound as if she could not even feel the blade. "It seems she did not want the responsibility of caring for a small boy. She became bored with it. She returned to the life she had had before, but no decent man would have her."

"How did she . . . live?" Giuliano asked, his voice cracking.

Anna looked up and saw Zoe's golden eyes looking back, first at the knife, then at Anna directly. There was triumph burning in her mind, and Anna read it as clearly as words. She bent to the wound again, blade poised.

"Can't you do it?" Zoe asked. "No stomach for it, Anastasius?"

Anna saw her smile, and the knowledge in it bright as a flame, which turned her own stomach cold. Was it conceivable Zoe had guessed she was a woman?

She looked down again and deliberately pushed the point of her knife into the flesh on the other side of the spelk, saw the blood ooze and then flood. She was tempted to push harder, even to slice through an artery and watch it gush, pumping, as Gregory's blood must have, pouring life away.

Zoe turned back to Giuliano. "She turned to the streets, as all women do when there is nothing else," she said, her voice filling the silence of the room. "Especially beautiful women. And she was beautiful."

Anna turned the knife delicately, lifted out the spelk, and dropped it on one of the spare plates.

"As beautiful as Anastasius here would be," Zoe went on. She had not even flinched. "If he were a woman, and not a eunuch."

Anna felt her face flame. She could feel Giuliano's hurt as if the blade had gouged a living organ out of him. She should not be here to witness this awful scene.

She looked up and met Zoe's eyes, bright and hard as agate.

"Have I offended you, Anastasius?" Zoe asked with mild interest. "It is not a bad thing to be beautiful, you know." She turned and looked across at Giuliano, then picked up a paper from the table beside her. "A letter from the Mother Abbess of Santa Teresa. I'm sorry, but you have to know this one day. You have insisted on knowing. Maddalena ended her life a suicide. So many women do, who look to the street for their livelihood."

Every vestige of blood drained from Giuliano's face.

Anna spoke impulsively, out of a passion to protect him. Nothing could undo the wound, nothing could make him imagine she had not heard or seen his pain.

"I suppose some are better at whoring than others," she said, looking Zoe full in the face. "But even the most beautiful fade eventually. The lips crease, the breasts sag, the thighs become lumpy, the skin wrinkles and falls away. Lust becomes empty, and then only love matters."

Giuliano gasped, swinging around to Anna in amazement, even taking a step toward her as if physically to protect her from Zoe's fury.

Zoe's eyes widened. "The little eunuch has teeth, Signor Dandolo. I do believe he likes you. How grotesque."

The blood burned up Giuliano's cheeks and he turned away. "Thank you for taking the trouble to find the information for me," he said, his voice choking. "I will leave you to your . . . treatment." He walked out of the room, and they both heard the footsteps of his leather boots along the marbled corridor.

"You are leaving me to bleed," Zoe remarked, looking down at her ankle and foot, now dripping scarlet onto the floor. "I thought you were a more honorable physician than that, Anastasius."

Anna saw the gloating in Zoe's face. This was vengeance on Giuliano because of his great-grandfather and on Anna for loving a Dandolo. And she did love him; it would be pointless now to deny it to herself.

"It is good for it to bleed," she said, forming the words deliberately, even though her voice shook. "It will carry away the poison the spelk may have left." She picked up the knife again and touched the wound with the point of it, pricking, but no more deeply than she had to. "Then it will be clean, and I shall bind it."

Several moments of silence went by.

"This must be hard for you," Zoe said quietly.

Anna smiled. "But not impossible. I decide who I am, you don't. But you are right: Beauty can be dangerous. It can give people delusions of being loved when in truth they are only consumed, like a peach or a fig. Eirene Vatatzes said that Gregory liked figs."

Zoe's foot dripped blood onto the floor more rapidly, making a little pool of scarlet.

"I think it is ready to be bound up." Anna met Zoe's eyes and smiled. "I have just the ointment here to put on it. It would be very serious if it were to become poisoned now, when the flesh is so . . . vulnerable."

A sudden shadow of fear crossed Zoe's face. She leaned forward. "Be careful," she whispered. "Your love for Dandolo could cost you very dear, even your life. If my foot does not heal, you will regret it."

Anna smiled at her even more widely, her eyes ice cold. "There is nothing wrong with it that removing the spelk did not cure. You were wise enough not to pick a poisonous wood."

The surprise flashed in Zoe's eyes for only an instant. "I would not like to destroy you," she said casually. "Don't oblige me to do so."

Fifty-four

∾

GIULIANO LEFT ZOE'S HOUSE AND WALKED OUT INTO THE broad, open street, barely seeing where he was going. The pain seemed so huge, it threatened to tear through his skin from the inside and overwhelm him. He was filled with shame and the knowledge that this woman he could just remember—a lovely face, tears, warmth, and a sweet smell—not only had not loved him enough to keep him, but had descended to that most despicable of trades.

He had seldom used whores himself; he was handsome and charming and had had no need to. He shivered with a new revulsion at himself when he remembered the times he had.

He barely saw the street around him. Other people were so many blurs of color and movement. He felt sick, cold to the very pit of his belly, and shivering. Thank God at least his father had never known that Maddalena had died by her own hand, beyond the reach of the Church, even in death.

He crossed the busy street, traffic stopping, drivers of carts shouting at him, but their words did not penetrate his mind. He went on down the steep incline toward the Venetian Quarter by the shore.

She had borne him, carried him within her body, and given him life. He hated her for what she had become, yet he had learned love at his father's knee, at his side. Her name had been the last word he spoke. What was Giuliano if he denied her now?

Damn Zoe Chrysaphes—damn her to a hell of pain that would last all life long—as his would.

Anastasius had been extraordinary. He was a true friend, first rescuing him from being blamed for Gregory Vatatzes's murder, which he deserved for stupidity, if nothing else, and then defending him against Zoe. Both times it had been at risk to himself: Giuliano was realizing now just how great a risk. And Anastasius had asked for nothing in return. Still, Giuliano could not bear to be with Anastasius again, after this. He was the one person who had seen and heard, and he would never be able to forget it, even if only in anger at Zoe. Or in pity. It was the pity that hurt the deepest.

After stopping at his lodging, he went along to the busy dockyards, looking for any Venetian ship in the harbor. There were two. The first was a merchantman bound for Caesarea, the second just berthed and due out to Venice again within the week.

"Giuliano Dandolo, on the doge's business," he introduced himself. "I seek passage home, to report to the doge as soon as possible."

"Excellent," the captain said enthusiastically. "A little earlier than I expected, but excellent all the same. Welcome aboard. Boito will be delighted. You may use my cabin. You will not be interrupted."

Giuliano had no idea what the man was speaking about. "Boito?" he said slowly, searching for meaning in it.

"The doge's emissary," the captain replied. "He has letters for you, and no doubt other things too complex or too secret to commit to paper. I was not aware he had even sent word to you yet, but he said it would be today, as soon as possible. Come. I'll take you."

In the cramped but well-furnished cabin that was the captain's domain, Giuliano found himself sitting opposite a narrow-faced, handsome man in his early fifties who produced letters of authority from the doge. He thanked the captain and asked permission to be uninterrupted until he and Giuliano had finished their business.

As soon as the door closed, Boito looked gravely at Giuliano. "I have seen you before. I served Doge Tiepolo. You must have news to have sought me even before I sent you word I was here. Tell me about the Venetian Quarter of the city."

Giuliano had done his job, spoken casually to all the major families in the quarter, and, perhaps more tellingly, listened to the younger men talking in the cafés and bars along the waterfront and in the street where the best food was served from the stalls. They had been born in Byzantine territory. Their loyalties were torn.

"Those who still have family in Venice will probably remain loyal to us," he said carefully.

"And the younger ones?" Boito said impatiently.

"Most of them are Byzantine now. They have never been to Venice. Some of them are married to Byzantines, they have homes and business here. There is always the chance that if loyalty to Venice did not move them, faith in the Church of Rome might."

Boito breathed out very slowly, and his shoulders eased, so slightly that it was visible only in the smallest alteration of the way the creases in his coat changed a fraction. "And you think that faith will not hold them?"

"I doubt it," he answered.

Boito frowned. "I see. And what is the likelihood of Constantinople accepting the union with the Church of Rome? I know some of the monasteries and maybe most of the outlying towns, perhaps all of Nicea, will refuse. There are even members of the imperial family imprisoned for refusing."

Giuliano was Venetian. That was where his loyalties must be. And he had promised Tiepolo. The thought of his Byzantine mother was too bitter even to touch. The friends he had made here were mostly Venetian anyway. Constantinople was Zoe Chrysaphes and people like her. Except Anastasius. But you could not distort the fate of nations or the course of a crusade on the friendship of one person, however passionate, generous, or vulnerable.

Yet Anastasius had not hesitated to risk his life to save Giuliano from prosecution for the murder of Gregory. In fact, he had not even asked Giuliano if he were guilty. And he had been willing to fight Zoe in a way for which she would never forgive him. How does a man honor debts to two opposing forces?

"They need more time," Giuliano answered, dragging his mind back to the moment and this small, wooden-walled cabin, so like all the others he had sailed in. "Give it to them, and they may see the wisdom of it. They need to feel that they are not betraying the faith they understand. You cannot expect a man to deny his God and then be loyal to you."

Boito made a steeple of his long, thin fingers and regarded Giuliano thoughtfully. "There is little time to give them, whether we wish it or not. The doge is certain that Charles of Anjou is already making plans that will considerably further his ambition to rule all the eastern Mediterranean, including those areas of trade and influence which belong rightfully to Venice. I'm sure you don't wish to see that happen."

Giuliano was startled. "But Byzantium won't stop Charles, because it can't. They are subtle and wise, and cruel, but their power is waning. Their strength is exhausted. The sack of 1204 devastated them, and they have not yet recovered."

Boito sat in silence, his hooded eyes distant. Finally he smiled. "Knowledge is what we need, at this point. The doge must know exactly what obstacles lie in the way of the king of the Two Sicilies, and his ambition to be king of Jerusalem also." His expression was enigmatic. He did not say whether it was to remove the obstacles or to strengthen them. Giuliano had a strong impression it might be the latter.

"To be specific," Boito continued, "the doge must know the military situation in Palestine, and what an intelligent man would predict for the future. Say, the next three or four years."

Giuliano turned it over in his mind. It was knowledge of the most intense importance, perhaps to the whole of Christendom and the future of the world. If Charles conquered the Holy Land and united the five ancient patriarchates, it would be the most powerful kingdom in the West.

"I see that you understand," Boito said with an easing of his smile into warmth. "I suggest you go by the safest route possible, and the most inconspicuous. That would be from here down the coast of Palestine to Acre, and then make your way inland. There are always pilgrims. Attach yourself to one of their groups, and you will pass initially unnoticed. When you return, you will report to the doge himself. No one else. Is that clear?"

"Of course."

"The doge needs eyes and ears that he can trust. As you love, and owe, the city of your heritage, Dandolo, the city that has given you hope and honor, give her your service now, for the sake of the future."

"Yes, I will." There was no other possible answer. Apart from anything else, Giuliano had promised Tiepolo.

Fifty-five

∽

ANNA STOOD IN HER HERB ROOM MIXING OINTMENTS AND distilling tinctures. In each of the little wooden drawers of powders, she kept one whole leaf of each type so she would not mistake what it was.

She had watched Giuliano go from Zoe's house almost blind with the pain of what she had told him, and Anna had known also that her own presence there had made it doubly agonizing for him. She did not expect to see him again in the next few weeks or perhaps even months. That hurt her with a persistent ache, like a hunger, but she knew of no way to heal it.

Zoe's extraordinary admissions when she had been feverish made her certain beyond doubt. They had planned to kill Michael Palaeologus, and for Bessarion to usurp the throne and then deny the union and rally the country behind him to save the Orthodox Church from Rome.

But how had they thought to withstand the crusader armies? Or had they not even considered that? Were they so steeped in religious fervor that they believed the Virgin Mary would save them?

Justinian had been levelheaded in Nicea, self-mocking at times; he had far too sharp a sense of wit, and of the ironies of life, to trust a man like Bessarion without knowing exactly what he meant to do and how.

She stood with the leaves in her hand, breathing in their aromatic perfume, trying to steady her racing mind.

How had Justinian discovered the plot? Or had he been part of it from the beginning? Then how had he taken so long to realize it could not work?

She looked at the astrolabe on the table with its beautiful inlays and circles, orbits within orbits. Was the plot like that or far simpler: a desperate agreement by all of them, albeit from different priorities? Bessarion for faith, and perhaps—whether he recognized it or not—for ambition and glory for himself, the old power returned to his family. Helena quite simply for power. She had the honesty, or perhaps the lack of conscience, that she had never pretended faith.

Of Esaias, she still knew little. Others had spoken of him as shallow, but that did not have to be true. Knowledge of the plot made her realize everyone might be utterly different from the character they had presented for the purpose of achieving that one overriding aim.

She had finished putting away the herbs and began pouring the tinctures into vials and labeling them.

Antoninus might have been exactly what he now seemed: a man loyal to the Church even at the cost of his own life; a good friend to Justinian, acknowledging his part in it after torture and only when it was pointless to deny it.

But he had joined with Justinian to kill not Michael, in order to save the Church, but Bessarion, and for what? To save Byzantium, because Bessarion had neither the grasp of reality nor the nerve to do as Michael Palaeologus was doing and make the only peace possible?

Justinian had been devoutly against the union from the beginning. His allegiance to Constantine was witness to that. And Constantine's loyalty to him in return? Was that not one passion that could be trusted?

She stopped working and began to wash her mortar, pestle, and dishes, then put them away.

Justinian was the first, as an outsider, to see Bessarion's weaknesses as well as his dreams and to realize that far from saving Constantinople, he would seal its fate.

She tried to imagine how he must have felt as the evidence forced itself upon him and little by little he understood that Bessarion must not be allowed to take the throne. If Justinian withdrew from the plan, Demetrios would simply take his place. Bessarion must be stopped. He could have gone to him and tried to persuade him, more and more forcefully as Bessarion resisted. The quarrels had become deeper. In momentary desperation he had gone to others, even to Eirene, but not to Zoe. Why had Justinian and she not allied to serve the common cause?

The only one Justinian had trusted was Antoninus, who in the end had gone to his death tortured and alone. Then who had betrayed Justinian to the authorities?

If Bessarion had lived, the plot would have gone ahead. The next evening, they would have attempted to kill the emperor. Zoe had the courage and the skill to do it, whatever Bessarion's failings. But had Zoe honestly believed that Bessarion had the courage and the fire to save both the city from the Latins and the Church from Rome?

And would Bessarion have obeyed her, or was his arrogance such that once on the throne he would have defied all advice, especially from a woman? How had she imagined she could manipulate him? Because she had more political intelligence than he, and more realism? Or more allies? Perhaps knowledge of Michael's network of spies and agents of violence, information, and deceit? Then he could keep his hands clean and still reap the benefits.

Perhaps Zoe would have allowed Bessarion to take the throne and then helped Demetrios Vatatzes to usurp Bessarion. Or was that Eirene's plan?

Justinian had prevented any of it from happening. If he had killed Bessarion, then far from being a conspirator against the emperor, he had saved his life. Had Michael known that? Had Nicephoras?

And a cold and ugly thought: Had Constantine allowed Justinian to be blamed as an act of revenge for his change of allegiance, his understanding of reality?

Fifty-six

ANNA CHOSE HER TIME WITH CARE. FROM HER MANY VIS-
its to the Blachernae, she was familiar with Nicephoras's routine.
She went when she knew he would be alone and undisturbed, unless there
was some crisis. She was uncharacteristically nervous climbing the palace
steps, although she was now well-known, having attended most of the eunuchs at one time or another.

She passed the broken statues, the dark stains of fire, the passages
blocked with rubble because the fabric of the building was dangerous. Perhaps Michael kept it this way so that neither he nor his servants would
ever forget what being faithful to Orthodoxy cost.

She found Nicephoras in his usual room, open onto the courtyard. His
servant went ahead and whispered that Anastasius had come, and a moment later she was shown in. Instantly she saw both the tiredness in his
face and the sudden lift of pleasure at the sight of her.

"We are not falling ill often enough. It seems a long time since you have
been here. What brings you? I have not heard of anyone needing your
help."

"It is I who need yours," Anna replied. "But perhaps I can offer something in return? You look weary."

He gave a little shake of his head. Anna was aware of the loneliness
within him, the hunger to speak of things deeper in the heart than policy
or the realities of diplomacy.

"That vase is new," she observed, looking at a smoothly curved bowl sitting on one of the tables to the side. "Alabaster?"

"Yes," he said quickly, his face brightening. "Do you like it?"

"It's perfect," she replied. "It's as simple as the moon, as . . . as complete in itself, unconcerned with admiration."

"I like that," he said quickly. "You are quite right, many things try too hard. You hear the artist's voice crying through the work for your attention. This has the supreme confidence of knowing exactly what it is. Thank you. I shall like it even more from now on."

"Do I interrupt you reading?" she asked, seeing the manuscript on his desk.

"Ah! Yes, I was. It is about England, and I daresay it would be considered highly seditious here, but it is extraordinarily interesting." His eyes were bright, watching her face carefully.

She was surprised. "England?" To her it meant only a barbarism beyond even the French, and she said as much.

"I thought so, too," he admitted. "But they wrote a Great Charter in 1215, different from our laws of Justinian, because they were created by the barons, the aristocracy, and forced upon the king, whereas ours were codified by the emperor. Nevertheless, some of their provisions are interesting."

She feigned interest, for his sake. "Really?"

His enthusiasm was too keen to be dampened by her lack of it. "My favorite is the dictum that justice delayed is justice denied. Do you not like that?"

"Yes, I do," she said, to please him, then realized how profoundly she meant it. "Very much. It is certainly true. Is that what you were reading?"

"No. Much more recent, actually. Have you heard of Simon de Montfort, the Earl of Leicester?"

"No." She hoped this was not going to be long. "Is he one of the barons who forced this charter?"

"No." He turned the manuscript facedown deliberately. "But you have come about something in particular. I see it in your face. The murder of Bessarion again?"

"You know me too well," she confessed, then felt as if with the words she had betrayed him. He knew nothing at all of her in reality. She could not meet his eyes and was surprised how much that hurt. She had planned in her mind exactly what to say, practicing the details.

"What is it?" he asked.

She plunged in, all her careful rehearsal abandoned. "I believe there was a plot to assassinate the emperor, and for Bessarion to take his place, in order to save the Church from union with Rome. Whoever killed Bessarion prevented that from happening. It was an act of loyalty, not treason. They should not have been punished for it."

His face was filled with a sadness she did not understand.

"Who were the conspirators, apart from Justinian and Antoninus?"

She said nothing. She could not prove it, and in spite of what they had planned to do, it seemed such a betrayal to tell him. He would have to act. They would be arrested, tortured. Horrible pictures filled her imagination: Zoe stripped, humiliated, her body mocked and perhaps touched with fire again. And she could not prove it anyway.

"I did not think you would tell me," Nicephoras said. "I might have been disappointed if you had. Justinian would not either, nor Antoninus." His voice dropped even lower and was rough with pain. "Even under torture."

She stared at him, new terror gripping her like a clenched fist inside her stomach, tightening.

"Is he . . ." She forced the words out between dry lips. She remembered John Lascaris's blind face. Justinian . . . it was almost more than she could bear.

"We did not maim him." Perhaps without meaning to, Nicephoras was taking part of the blame himself. He was the emperor's man. "Justinian could not tell us that they wouldn't try again. Can you?"

She thought about it, struggling, twisting this way and that in her mind, finding no escape. "No," she said at last.

"What is Justinian Lascaris to you that you risk so much to save him?" he asked.

She felt the blood hot in her face. "We are related."

"Closely?" he said in little more than a whisper. "Brother? Husband?"

It was as if time stopped, frozen between one heartbeat and the next. He knew. It was perfectly clear in his face. To deny it would be idiotic.

He waited, his eyes so gentle that it made the tears spill over onto her cheeks for the shame of her deceit. Would he think her disguise mocked him? She kept her eyes down, unable to look at him and hating herself.

"My twin," she whispered.

"Anastasia Lascaris?"

"Anna," she corrected him, as if that tiny piece of honesty mattered. "Zarides now. I'm a widow."

"Whoever the other conspirators are, they are still dangerous," he warned. "I believe you know who they are. One of them betrayed Justinian, I don't know which, and if I did, I would not tell you, for your own sake. They would betray you just as quickly."

"I know—" The words caught in her throat. "Thank you."

"By the way, you should lengthen your stride a little. You still take short steps, like a woman. Otherwise you are pretty good."

She nodded, unable to speak, then turned slowly and walked away, her mind numb, finding it hard to keep her balance. She would have to correct her walk some other time.

Fifty-seven

∾

A WEEK LATER, ANNA HAD JUST SEEN HER LAST PATIENT OF the morning and was standing in the kitchen when Leo brought her a letter from Zoe Chrysaphes.

> Dear Anastasia,
> I have just received news of a most important matter concerning the true faith which we both espouse. I need to inform you of the details as soon as possible. Please regard this as urgent, and call upon me today.
>   Zoe

The blurred writing of her name, using the feminine rather than masculine, was a veiled reminder to Anna of Zoe's power over her. She dared not refuse.

There was no decision to make. "I have to call on Zoe Chrysaphes." She did not want to frighten Leo by telling him that Zoe knew her secret. "It is something to do with the Church. It should be interesting."

But interest was the emotion furthest from her mind when she was shown into Zoe's room. The fear and the loss in their previous encounter seemed to close in on her as if she could never escape it. She felt as though Giuliano must be just out of the line of her sight, and any moment he would move and she would see the pain in his face.

Zoe came forward superbly, head high, back straight. The deep blue-

gray silk of her tunic swirled around her ankles, unbroken by gold ornament, simple as the dusk sky.

"Thank you for coming so quickly," she said. "I have remarkable news,
but before I tell you I must swear you to secrecy. A promise to me is little:
Promise to Mary the Mother of God that you will betray this secret to no
one. I charge you!" Her golden eyes blazed with a sudden flare of passion.

Anna was astonished. "And if I will not do that?"

"We need not consider it," Zoe replied, her smile not wavering. "Because you will. Betrayal of secrets can be a most painful thing. The out-
come can even kill. But you know that. Give me your promise."

Anna felt her face burn. She had walked directly into the trap. "I will
promise Mary the Mother of God," she said with a faint echo of sarcasm.

"Good," Zoe responded immediately. "And most appropriate. Everyone knows that the Venetians stole the Shroud of Christ from the Hagia
Sophia, and also a nail from the true Cross. It is the most holy relic on
earth, and only God knows where it is now. Probably in Venice, or maybe
Rome. They're all thieves." She tried to keep the fury from her voice and
failed. "And the crown of thorns," she added. "But I have word out of
Jerusalem of another relic, nearly as good. It has just come to light, after
more than twelve hundred years."

Anna tried not to care. She should never forget that, above all, Zoe was
a creature of revenge and deception. Only a fool would trust her. Yet she
found herself asking, almost holding her breath for the answer.

Zoe's smile widened. "The portrait of the Mother of God, painted by
St. Luke," she whispered. "Imagine it. He was a physician, like you. And
an artist. He saw her, just as you and I can see each other." Her voice was
husky with excitement. "Perhaps she was older, but all the passion and the
grief would be there in her face." Her eyes were alight with wonder.
"Mary—as an old woman, who had given birth to the Son of God, and
stood at the foot of the Cross at his death, helpless to save Him. Mary,
who knew He was risen, not by faith or belief, or the sermons of priests,
but because she had seen Him."

"Where is this painting?" Anna asked. "Who has it? How do you know
it is genuine? There are more pieces of the true Cross sold to pilgrims than
would furnish a forest."

"Its existence has been confirmed," Zoe said calmly, seeing victory.

"Why do you tell me?" She dreaded the answer.

Zoe's eyes were unblinking. "Because I wish you to go to Jerusalem and purchase it for me, of course. Don't pretend to be stupid, Anastasia. Naturally I will provide the money. When you return with the picture I shall give it to the emperor, and once again Byzantium will have one of the great relics of Christendom. She is our patron saint, our guardian, and our advocate with God. She will protect us from Rome, whether it is the violence of the crusaders or the corruption of popes."

Anna was stunned. Another thought occurred to her. Zoe had said it was to give to the emperor, not the Church. Did Michael know perfectly well that it was Zoe who had been going to kill him, and this was a bargain for her freedom, even her life?

Aloud she asked, "Why me? I know nothing of paintings."

Zoe looked deeply satisfied. "I trust you," she said smoothly. "You will not betray me, because to do so you would have to betray yourself . . . and Justinian. Do not forget how well I know you."

"I can't travel alone to Jerusalem," Anna pointed out, although now her heart was racing at the thought. Jerusalem—so near Sinai. She might see Justinian. Did Zoe think of that, too? "Still less could I return without an armed guard if I am carrying a relic like that," she added.

"I don't expect you to." Zoe gazed out of the window at the fading light of the sky. "I have already made inquiries as to your passage, and arranged it where you will be perfectly safe. Except, of course, from the rigors of a voyage, but that is inescapable." She was smiling. "There is a ship chartered and commanded by a Venetian about to leave Constantinople for Acre, and then its captain, with suitable guard, I imagine, will make his way to Jerusalem. They are willing, for a consideration which I will pay, to allow you to accompany them. The captain will be aware of your purpose, but no one else."

"A Venetian?" Anna was appalled. "They'll let me get the painting, then steal it, probably throw me overboard, and you'll never see the painting again."

"Not this captain," Zoe said with secret amusement. "He is Giuliano Dandolo. I have told him only that it is the picture of a Byzantine Madonna, posed for by a merchant's daughter, perhaps his mother. You would be wise not to tell him differently."

Anna stood rigid. "And if I refuse?" she stammered.

"Then I shall no longer feel bound to be discreet about your . . . identity. To the emperor, the Church, or to Dandolo. Be sure that that is what you want before you provoke it to happen."

"I'll go," she said quietly.

Zoe smiled. "Of course you will." She picked up a package lying on the table at her side and held it out to Anna. "Here is the money, and your instructions, a letter of safe conduct for you, with the emperor's signature. Godspeed, and may the Blessed Virgin protect you." She crossed herself piously.

At the teeming dockside, Anna came to a three-masted Venetian round ship with lateen sails and a high stern. It was broad-beamed, hence the name, and she judged it to be at least fifty paces from end to end. She made inquiries of the sailor at the bottom of the gangway, stating her name and Zoe's, and was permitted to board. She found Giuliano on deck. He was dressed in a leather coat and britches, nothing like the courtly tunic and robes he'd worn in the city. Suddenly he looked Venetian, and alien.

"Captain Dandolo," she said firmly. Whatever the cost, there was nowhere to retreat. "Zoe Chrysaphes told me that you had agreed to take me as passenger on your voyage to Acre, and then afterward to Jerusalem with you. She said she had paid you the price you considered fair." Anna's voice was cold with the tension that knotted inside her.

He turned around slowly, surprise in his face, then a quick flame of recognition suffocated the moment after by memory of the last time they had met.

"Anastasius Zarides." His voice was quiet, not audible twelve feet away where sailors were working on the ropes and rigging. "Yes, Zoe made arrangements for a passenger. She did not say it would be you." His face darkened. "Since when were you her servant?"

"Since she has the power to hurt me," she replied, not flinching from his gaze. "But the commission on which she sends me is good: to bring back a picture which belongs in Constantinople."

"A picture? Did she tell you of whom?"

Anna longed to be able to answer him honestly. Lying was like deliberately staking out a space between them, but the gulf was there already.

"A Byzantine lady of good family," she answered. "But apparently the victim of some tragedy or other."

"Why does Zoe care?"

"Do you think I asked her?" she said with an attempt at light sarcasm.

"I think you might have guessed," he replied. She was not sure if there was gentleness in his voice or sadness.

Now it was her turn to look away, over the choppy waters of the harbor. "I think it is a picture she wants because it will give her power," she answered. "But it could be merely one whose beauty she likes. She has a passion for beauty. I've seen her stare at the sunset till the sight of it should be printed on her soul."

"She has a soul?" he said with sudden bitterness.

"Surely a soul twisted is far worse than no soul at all?" she asked. "It is the loss of what could have been which tortures, the fact that something was within your reach and you let it slip away. I don't think hell is fire and torn flesh and the smell of sulfur choking you. I think it is the taste of heaven remembered—and lost."

"God preserve us, Anastasius!" Giuliano exclaimed. "Where on earth do you come up with things like that?"

He put his hand on her back, swiftly, in a companionable gesture, far from a caress. A moment later he took it away, and it was as if she had lost the warmth of the sun on her.

"You'd better come to Jerusalem with us and get this picture for Zoe," he said cheerfully. "We sail tomorrow morning. But I daresay you know that." He gave a brief laugh, but the smile remained in his eyes. "We've never had a ship's physician before."

Fifty-eight

~

Anna stood at the railing of the ship in the late afternoon sun. It was already low on the horizon, the wind was cold on her face, and the sharp, salt air filled her lungs. They were several days out of Constantinople, having sailed through the Sea of Marmara and into the Mediterranean, and she had begun to find the pitch and slight roll of the deck more natural. She had even grown accustomed to the seaman's britches she had been lent, a tunic and dalmatica being awkward garments in which to climb steps and move easily in narrow spaces. There was no room to hold on to skirts, and they were more immodest than she had previously considered. Giuliano had suggested the change, and after a few hours she had found it agreeable.

Giuliano was busy most of the time. It took all his skill to command men he knew little and to work south at this time of the year, against the current sweeping up from Egypt past Palestine and then westward. Even when they were with the wind, they still had to tack and veer precisely.

She heard his footsteps across the deck behind her. She did not need to turn to know it was he.

"Where are we?" she asked as he stepped beside her.

He pointed. "Rhodes is there, ahead of us. Cyprus over there, farther to the south and east."

"And Jerusalem?" she asked.

"Farther still. Alexandria's that way." He swung around and extended his arm south. "Rome there, to the west. Venice is to the north of that."

This was the first time they had had more than a few moments in which to talk without being overheard by the crew. Zoe and the death of Gregory crowded her mind, but she did not want to say anything that would tear scabs off the wounds and prevent the fragile healing.

She thought of the great rock that was reputed to guard the other end of the Mediterranean from the ocean, which, as far as anyone knew, stretched out to the edge of the world.

"Have you been out through the Gates of Hercules into the Atlantic?" she asked, her imagination fired at the thought.

"Not yet. One day I'd like to." He narrowed his eyes against the sun, smiling. "If you could go anywhere at all, where would you choose?"

She was taken by surprise. Her mind raced. She did not want to talk about old dreams that did not matter anymore. "Venice? Is it very beautiful?" She wanted to hear the urgency and the tenderness in his voice.

He smiled, indulging her. "It's like nowhere else," he answered. "So beautiful you think it must be a city of dreams, an idea floating on the face of the water. Touching it would be like trying to catch moonlight with a net. And yet it is as real as marble and blood, and as brutal as betrayal." There were passion and regret in his eyes. "It has the ephemeral loveliness of music in the night, and yet it stays in the mind as great visions do, coming back again and again, just when you think it has finally left you in peace."

He looked at the darkening horizon. "But I don't think I could forget Byzantium, either, now. It is subtle, wounded, more tolerant than the West, and perhaps wiser." He drew in a deep breath and let it out slowly.

The wind was rising from the north, whitening the wave crests as the current buffeted them. Anna waited for him to speak, happy in the sounds of the water and the creaking of wood.

"I know we want to retake Jerusalem for Christianity," he went on. "But I wonder if we've thought beyond that, to the cost." He gave a hard little laugh. "We sacrifice Byzantium to gain Jerusalem—and lose the world. I don't know. But I've got a decent red wine—"

"Venetian, of course," she interrupted lightly, tearing the thread of tension that was tightening inside herself.

He laughed. "Of course. Come and we'll share it over dinner. Ship's rations, but not bad." He spoke easily, without hesitation.

Banishing thought for anything beyond the moment, she accepted, rising to her feet and having to steady herself to the slight pitch of the deck.

It was a good meal, although she was barely aware of what she ate or of anything beyond the sweetness and the fire of the wine. They spoke easily, of all manner of things, places they had been to, people they had met or known. He described the funny and the absurd with pleasure and, she noticed, without cruelty. The more she listened to him, the more irrevocably she felt bound to the good in him. And the less could she ever tell him the truth. He saw her as a man, but one from whom he need fear no rivalry. She knew that something of his gentleness with her was because he was a whole man, able to taste the physical pleasures of life in a way Anastasius never would, and she was startled by the delicacy he exercised in never overtly mentioning such things.

She left at about two in the morning, when duty called him up to the deck because the weather was worsening. She had drunk more wine than usual, and she felt so close to weeping as she closed the door of her own cabin that the tears actually spilled over her cheeks, hot and painful. Had she been less exhausted, she might have given in and sobbed until she had nothing left inside her. But when would she stop? What end was there, except to treasure friendship, or laughter, trust, tolerance, and the will to share? She would not sacrifice that for some momentary indulgence in self-pity or grief for what she herself had closed the door against.

The following day the weather was bad, a storm driving down from the north forcing them to stand farther out than they would otherwise. Giuliano was fully occupied with navigation and keeping the ship from drifting onto the dangerous troughs where she could lose sails or even a mast.

The next time they spoke it was the morning watch as dawn was rising from the east, where Cyprus lay far beyond view. The sea was calm and there was a slight breeze, smelling sweet and exquisitely clean, the pale light barely tipping the crests of the water, too delicate to be touched with foam. In the silence, they could have been the first humans to see the earth or breathe its air.

For a long time they stood at the rail almost a yard apart, staring across at the radiance spreading over the sky, melting the shadows between one wave and another. She did not need to look at him; she was certain his thoughts were also filled by the enormity of it. It was not frightening to be alone on the ocean's face; in fact, there was a curious comfort in it.

On other occasions snatched in moments here or there, she and Giuliano spoke of memories, experiences good and bad, sometimes matching tall stories. She pulled many from the tales her father had told her that she could identify with well enough. At times when she was embroidering rather a lot, he would realize it and they laughed together. It was a joke with no ill will. She had no need to explain her inventions.

One night when they were on deck, watching the sun sink, squandering fire beyond the black outline of Cyprus, the wind cold in their faces, the conversation turned toward religion and the union with Rome.

"Pride and history apart," he said seriously, "is separation from Rome really worth dying for? Do you think it is?" He was direct, a personal question, not a general one.

She stared at the fading light, changing even as she watched. No two sunsets were ever the same. "I don't know. I'm not sure how much I am prepared to have anyone else tell me what to think. But I also know for certain that I am not prepared to demand anyone else sacrifice their lives, or the lives of those they love, because I'm certain of the differences between the Roman and Byzantine faiths.

"Maybe any Church can only take us so far, provide a framework in which we can climb far enough to see just how much farther there is to go, and that the journey is infinitely worth it. Sooner or later we outgrow it, and it becomes a shackle to the spirit."

"Then how do we do the rest?" There was no banter in his voice. She could hardly see the outline of his head and shoulders against the darkness of the sky, but she felt the warmth of him near her.

"Maybe we have to want it with such a passion of hunger that no one can hold us back from reaching it," she said quietly. "We cannot be led, or commanded. We must labor with our own strength, seeing with the light of the mind, even if it's only a short space ahead. That's enough."

"That's hard." He let out his breath slowly. "I would like to believe it, difficult and lonely as it sounds. Your heaven would be worth looking for, and creating out of my own mistakes, building out of forgiveness, and seeking in every new place."

He leaned back a little and looked up at the sky. "We had better weave some ladders, Anastasius."

Fifty-nine

~

AFTER CALLING AT FAMAGUSTA IN THE EAST OF CYPRUS, they sailed through rough weather, tacking across the wind, coming about hard. The huge lateen sails were heavy, creaking as they fell slack then filled and billowed out again. Every time she marveled at the skill of the men, her hands clenching as she saw the precise judgment and timing and knew how easily a mast could break.

They worked their way steadily south along the coast of Palestine, putting ashore at Tyre, then at Sidon, and finally at Acre, a wide, busy seaport. It spread out from the high, magnificent old crusader walls into trading quarters—Pisan, Genoese, and of course Venetian—quays busy, water dotted with ships.

This was the gateway to the Holy Land and the beginning of the six- to ten-day journey overland to Jerusalem. Anna stayed on the ship while Giuliano went ashore, ostensibly to see to unloading his cargo and obtaining another shipment for the return journey.

She stood on the deck looking at the sun-bleached land, pale docks, and landing piers above glittering bright water. She realized sharply that Giuliano would be judging it all with a military eye, as had generations of men before him from the far, Christian corners of the world, thinking to conquer it—for what? For God? For Christ? Some, perhaps. More probably for glory. It was a land of milk and honey, perhaps, but also of blood.

On the third day, she and Giuliano went ashore. He had sent the ship off down the coast with cargo to return in two months' time, when he and Anastasius would meet them here again. If they were late, then his men would obtain the best cargo they could and wait.

They were dressed in the recognized costume for pilgrims: a gray cowl, scrip, and scarf, a red cross on the shoulder, a broad belt to which was attached a rosary and a water bottle. They each wore a broad-brimmed hat, turned up at the front, and carried over their shoulders a sack and a gourd. Anna also had a small case of medical supplies, a knife, needle and silk, a few herbs, and a pot of unguent. She felt untidy, anonymous, and uncomfortable. She was glad there was no glass in which to see herself.

She looked at Giuliano. At a glance he seemed like anyone else, gray, one of scores of travelers weary, footsore, and a little crazy, a light in the eyes and repetitive songs on the lips. But when he moved he still had the easy gait, the slight swagger of the mariner.

She would have liked to stay in Acre for longer, to walk through the streets of this last stronghold of the Christian kingdom of Jerusalem and see where the men of the past, crusaders, knights, kings, and even queens, had lived; but she knew there was no time.

"We must join with others," she urged. "We need guides."

"Ahead of us." He pointed. "We leave in just over an hour. It'll be hard. And cold this time of year."

They formed a group of about twenty pilgrims, most of them dressed in gray, as Anna and Giuliano were. More than half of them were men, but Anna was surprised how many women there were—at least six. One old woman with a windburned face and gnarled hands clutched the staff she used to support herself. She never stopped muttering the names of all the holy places she had been to, like an incantation. Canterbury, Walsingham, Lourdes, Compostela, and now the greatest of all, Jerusalem. They all had the pallor of a long sea voyage, cramped in ships that gave them barely enough room to lie down and no privacy at all.

A soldier appeared to be the natural leader, and it was he who stepped forward to speak to the dark-skinned Arab who offered to guide them. He was a small, fierce-looking man with hawklike features and broken teeth. Anna did not understand the words, but the meaning was clear. They were haggling over price and conditions. Voices grew louder. The Arab professed astonishment, the soldier insisted. There was a flurry of abuse on both sides. The soldier would not yield his position, and finally there were smiles. Everyone contributed their money.

They set out at midday, walking steadily. Anna did not want to grow close to any of the other pilgrims, since she must always guard her identity. She was in the strange position of being neither man nor woman, but she could not help looking at them with interest and now and then overhearing their conversation. Most of them had come by sea from Venice, which was the meeting place for pilgrims from other parts of Europe.

"Thousands of them," Giuliano told her when they made a brief stop. "The money changers on the Rialto make a fortune. That's mostly what they're complaining about." He indicated a group of the others a few yards away. "And the sea journey. It was rough, and they're terribly cramped."

"It takes a lot of faith to come," she said with respect.

"Or nothing much to leave behind," he added. Then he saw her face. "Sorry, but that's the truth, too. If they survive and get home again, they can wear the palm in their hats for the rest of their lives. It's a badge of honor. They'll be forgiven all sins, and respected by family, neighbors, and friends. And they will have earned it." He saw her puzzlement. "How do I know? I'm a Venetian. I've seen them all my life, coming and going, full of hope, piety, pride." He bit his lip. "We let them all in, sell them real holy relics, and false ones, give them hospitality, guidance, advice, passage to Acre or Jaffa, and fleece them of most of their money."

She pushed her hand through her hair, which was dusty already, and smiled at him. It was an admission he had made, describing the venal side of his city, as well as the clever and the beautiful. He did not say he was ashamed, but she knew it.

Anna was not used to walking all day. Her feet became blistered, and her back and legs ached until she was filled with an all-consuming weariness. She was bitterly aware that Giuliano had so much more strength than she, and she dared not allow him to help her, even when he offered with real concern.

By the first nightfall, they stopped at an inn. She was overwhelmingly relieved just to sit down, and it was only after they had all eaten, around one large wooden board, that she realized she was also glad of the warmth. It was far colder outside than she had expected, and the pilgrim's gray cloak was not as warm as her own woolen dalmatica would have been.

. . .

Over the next days she forced herself to walk on, even when her feet bled. She found herself so weak that she staggered more, often losing her balance and stumbling, but always she rose again. She insisted on privacy for bodily functions, but as a eunuch that was granted her, even if for quite mistaken reasons. No one wished to embarrass her for the organs they rightly assumed she did not have.

They all suffered the same blisters, the cold from the wind and rain, the rough road under their feet, the ache in the bones from nights on hard boards and with too little sleep. The land was hard, built of rock and dust, and the few trees were wind-gnarled. There were long stretches where there was no water at all except what they carried with them. The rain was cold and made mud of the track underfoot, but it was still welcome on the parched skin.

She tried not to look at Giuliano. She knew exactly why the doge had sent someone not only to sail to Acre, but to walk this route, as the crusader army would have to walk it. He would be looking at the fortifications of Jerusalem also, with a soldier's eyes, seeing their strengths and weaknesses, whatever had changed since Western knights and squires were last here. Venice's full profit would depend on the degree of their success.

She did not want to know if that thought was as sour to him as it was to her. He was Venetian. He must see it differently. She thought of the first Roman soldiers, marching in their legions to conquer the troublesome Jews. Could even the boldest of them have imagined one man from Judea would change the world forever? Over a thousand years later, the road was worn smooth with people, summer and winter, who believed that in some way they were following in Christ's footsteps.

Were they, in any way that mattered?

Without having intended to, she looked quickly at Giuliano and found his eyes steady on hers. He smiled, and there was an intense gentleness in him. For a terrible instant, she thought he understood the real nature of her physical weakness; then she realized it was the confusion he read in her that moved him.

Anna smiled back and was surprised how lifted her spirits were, just to know he was there.

Sixty

FIVE DAYS LATER, THEY REACHED THE CREST OF THE SLOPE, legs aching, bodies weary. They had climbed almost three hundred feet since leaving Acre. There before them lay Jerusalem, spread out over the hills, all light and shadow. The sun-facing walls were blistered white, punctured by alleys like dark knife cuts, winding and impenetrable. The rooftops were flat, with here and there the smooth arc of a dome or the sudden, steep sides of a tower.

There were few trees, mostly the silver gray of olives or the dark irregularity of date palms. The huge, crenellated outer walls were unbroken, except for the great gates, now open and crowded by little antlike figures coming and going, tiny spots of color.

Anna stood beside Giuliano and stared in spite of herself, gasping with amazement. She looked at him quickly and saw the same wonder in his eyes.

The Arab signaled impatiently, and they began to move forward toward the Jaffa Gate, where pilgrims entered. As they came closer, the walls became enormous and pockmarked by time and erosion and the violence of siege. The gate itself was vast, like half a castle.

Men crowded outside it, dark-eyed, bearded, robes dusty from the ever creeping sand. They talked, gesticulating with their hands, arguing, haggling over an opinion or a price. A group of children played some game with small stones, throwing them up and catching them on the backs of their thin brown hands, making complicated patterns. A woman was beating a carpet, a cloud of dust rising. It was all so ordinary—daily life and a moment in eternity.

Then reality engulfed them again. There was money to pay, directions to ask, and accommodations to find before nightfall. Anna said good-bye to her traveling companions with real regret. They had shared too many simple, physical hardships for parting to be easy.

The safety of the journey was over; the danger of being too close, of betraying emotion or physical weakness, was past, at least for the time being. A different kind of loneliness was beginning.

They secured rooms at a hostelry. The first night Anna could barely sleep, tired as she was. The night was cold and the darkness full of strange noises and totally different odors from the ones she was accustomed to. The voices she heard were Arabic, Hebrew, and others she could not place. There was a mustiness in the air of closed streets, of animals, and of the dry, bitter smell of unfamiliar herbs. It was not unpleasant, but it left her feeling alien and uneasy.

She read again and again her instructions from Zoe. She must find a Jew by the name of Simcha ben Ehud. He knew where the painting was and would verify it, although Zoe had given instructions for Anna to look at it minutely also. The description was exact. She dared not fail. Not for an instant did she doubt that Zoe would take the first chance she had to use her power to destroy. Once she had the painting, she might well do it anyway. Anna had been naive to imagine she would be able to hand it over and walk away, safe because Zoe had promised. Between now and then, she would have to think of some weapon for her own use. Zoe had no respect for mercy.

After she had the picture, she would have time to think of Justinian and find a way to travel to the monastery in Sinai.

In the morning, she and Giuliano ate breakfast together. They had grown accustomed to dates and a little coarse bread.

"Be careful," he warned as they parted in the street. He was on his way to study first the warren of alleys, the half-hidden waterways of underground rivers and springs. A desert city lives or dies on its water, as does any army besieging it.

"I will," she said quietly. "Zoe gave me the name of the man to ask for, and a story as to why I want the picture. And I know what it is supposed to look like. You be careful, too. Examining fortifications isn't a good thing to be caught doing either."

"I'm not," he said quickly. "I'm a pilgrim, praying in every place Christ walked, just like all the others."

She smiled at him, then turned away quickly and went without looking back. Her feet felt bruised on the uneven pavement; her shoulders bumped one moment against other people, the next against the protruding walls as the alley became narrower. Then suddenly there were steps, and she was climbing down.

She began in the Jewish Quarter, at the address she had been given by Zoe.

"Simcha ben Ehud?" she asked several local shopkeepers. They all shook their heads.

She tried day after day, growing afraid that she was drawing attention to herself. One morning, when she had been in Jerusalem a little over three weeks, Anna was walking up a narrow flight of steps. Legs aching, muscles so weary that she was consumed in the concentration of forcing one foot after the other, she almost collided with a man coming in the opposite direction. She apologized and was about to move on when he caught her by the shoulder. Her first instinct was to fight; then he spoke to her quietly, with his mouth almost to her ear. "You are looking for Simcha ben Ehud?"

"Yes. Do you know where I can find him?" She had a knife at her belt, but she was afraid to reach for it. The man was only an inch or two taller than her, but he was wiry and she knew from the pressure of his hand on her shoulder that he was strong. He had a hawk nose and hooded eyes, almost black, but there was a gentleness in his mouth, even an ease of laughter in the lines cut deep by the passage of emotion.

"You are Simcha ben Ehud?" she asked.

"You have come from Byzantium, from Zoe Chrysaphes?" he returned.

"Yes."

"And your name?"

"Anastasius Zarides."

"Come with me. Follow me, and say nothing. Stay close." He turned and led the way back up the steps and along a narrow lane. Not once did he turn to make sure she was following, but he moved slowly and she knew he was deliberately making sure she did not lose him.

Finally, he turned into a small courtyard with a well and a narrow wooden door at the opposite side. Inside was a room with a stairway to another room above it; this was full of light. In it sat a very old man, white-bearded. His eyes were opaque as milk, and he was clearly blind.

"I have the messenger from Byzantium, Jacob ben Israel," ben Ehud said quietly. "He has come to see the painting. With your permission?"

Ben Israel nodded. "Show him," he agreed. His voice was hoarse, as if he were unused to speaking.

Ben Ehud went to another door, this one no more than three feet high, opened it, and, after a moment's consideration, pulled out a small square of wood wrapped in linen cloth. He took off the cloth and held it up for Anna to see the picture.

She felt a sudden wave of disappointment. It was the head and shoulders of a woman. Her face was worn with age, but her eyes were bright, her expression almost rapturous. She wore a simple robe of the shade of blue traditionally associated with the Madonna.

"You are disappointed," ben Ehud observed. He was waiting, still holding the picture. "Do you think it is worth your journey?"

"No," she replied. "There is nothing special about her face, no understanding. I don't think the artist knew her at all."

"He was a physician, not a painter," ben Ehud pointed out.

"I am a physician, not a painter," Anna argued. "I can still see that that is poor. She was the Mother of Christ. There has to have been something in her greater than this."

He put the picture on the ground and returned to the cupboard. He took out another painting, a fraction smaller, unwrapped it, and turned it toward her.

This one was also of a woman, her face touched by age and grief, but her eyes had seen visions beyond human pain. She had endured the best and the worst and knew herself with an inner peace that the artist had tried to capture, ending with only the grace to understand that he could not catch the infinite with the strokes of a brush.

Ben Ehud was studying her. "You wish for this one?"

"I do."

He wrapped it again carefully and then took another, larger piece of linen and wrapped that around it also. He ignored the first painting as if it were not worth consideration. It had served its purpose.

"I do not know if it is what you hope," he said quietly.

"We will choose to believe that it is," she replied. "That will be as good."

After settling with ben Ehud, she carried the painting back to the hostelry, clutching it inside her robe.

She was not far from the hotel when she was aware of someone behind her. She touched the knife at her belt, but it was little comfort. She had only ever used it for food or a few brief moments of first aid.

She forced herself to walk, rapidly but quelling the panic inside her. She reached the entrance of the hostelry just as Giuliano approached from the opposite direction. He saw the fear in her face, perhaps in the haste of her movement as well.

He grasped her by the arms and pulled her up the steps and then into an archway. Three men, heavily robed in gray, their faces hidden, hurried past them and up into an open square. One had a curved knife still in his hand.

"I've got it!" she gasped as soon as they were in his room and the door latched. "It's beautiful. I think it's real, but it doesn't matter. It's the face of a woman who has seen something of God that the rest of us only hope for."

"And the questions about Sinai?" Giuliano asked. "Was that to do with the painting?"

Anna was startled. She thought she had been discreet, but somehow he had heard.

"That's my own search." She knew as she said it that she was opening a door she would not ever be able to close again. "It has nothing to do with Zoe."

"But she knows about it," he insisted. "That's how she was able to make you come." He was guessing; she could see the puzzlement and the hurt in his face that she had not trusted him.

"Yes," she said without hesitation. She must tell him now; there was no alternative. "There is a relative of mine who has been accused of a crime, and exiled somewhere near here."

"What is he accused of?"

"Collusion in murder," she replied. "But his reasons were noble ones. I think I could prove that if I could speak to him, learn from him the details, not just the pieces I already have."

"Who is he supposed to have killed?"

"Bessarion Comnenos."

His eyes widened, and he breathed out slowly. "You're fishing in deep waters. Are you sure you know what you're doing?"

"I'm not at all sure," she said bitterly. "But I have no choice."

He did not argue. "I'll help you. First we'd better put the picture somewhere where it will be safe."

"Where?"

"I don't know. How big is it?"

She took it out, unwrapped it carefully, and held it up for him to see. She watched his face, seeing the disbelief in his eyes melt away and wonder take its place.

"We must put it on the ship," he said simply. "It's the only place where it'll be safe."

"Do you think those men were after it?" she asked.

"Don't you? And whether they were or not, others will be. If Zoe knew of it, so do they."

"The monastery I want is at Mount Sinai." She forced out the words.

He studied her face, trying to understand. "A relative?" he said softly.

How much dared she tell him? The longer she hesitated, the more anything she said would seem to be false. "My brother," she said in a whisper. "I'm sorry." Now she would have to lie again or tell him that her name before she married was Lascaris. Men did not change their names at marriage, and eunuchs did not marry at all. He would have to think she simply lied about her name, to hide it. This masquerade had once seemed so obvious that she had even become accustomed to thinking of it as easy. Even the freedom to move about the streets she now took for granted.

He was still puzzled. He said nothing, but it was in his eyes.

"Justinian Lascaris," she said, wading in more deeply.

At last, understanding filled his eyes. "Are you related to John Lascaris, whose eyes the emperor put out?"

"Yes." She mustn't elaborate. "Please don't . . ."

He put up his hand to silence her. "You must go to Mount Sinai. I'll take the picture to the ship. I'll look after it, I promise." He smiled with a hard, biting pain of shame. "I'll not steal it for Venice, I give you my word."

"I wasn't afraid you would," she replied.

"We'll go very carefully," he said. "I think we'll be safer outside the city. How long will it take you to get to Mount Sinai?"

"A month, to go there and back," she answered.

He hesitated.

"I'll be back here by the time the ship returns," she promised. "Just keep the picture safe."

"I must see Jaffa, and Caesarea on the coast," he said. "I'll be back in thirty-five days." He looked anxious, on the brink of speaking, and then changed his mind.

There was a sound of footsteps outside in the hostelry corridor and hushed voices arguing.

"We can't stay here," he told her quietly. "You must change your appearance and get out of the city. How are you getting to Sinai? A caravan?"

"Yes. They go every two or three days."

"Then you must get out of the pilgrim gray. That's what they're looking for. I'll go and get you something right now. You could dress as a boy. . . ."

She saw the embarrassment in his face, in case he had insulted her, but there was no time or safety to spare for such things.

She took the initiative. "Better still as a woman," she told him.

He looked startled. "They won't let women into the monastery."

"I know. I'll find another hostelry, on the road outside the walls. Then I'll change back again."

He left and she barred the door behind him. She spent a miserable hour waiting for his return, afraid in case he was attacked. She was too tense to sit or even to stand still. She paced the floor back and forth, only a few steps each way. Five times she heard footsteps outside and thought it was Giuliano, then stood with pounding heart and ears straining as they passed and the silence closed in again.

Once someone knocked, and she was about to undo the bolt when she realized it could be anyone. She froze. She could hear someone breathing heavily just on the other side of the wood.

There was a thump against the door, as if someone had tested it with his weight. She stepped back silently. There was another thump, this one harder. The door shook on its hinges.

There were voices, then quick footsteps. Someone stopped outside the door.

"Anastasius!" It was Giuliano's voice, urgent and sharp with fear.

Relief washed over her like a sudden heat. She tried to loosen the bar and found it jammed by the previous pressure from outside. She jerked her own weight against it, heard it give.

Giuliano stepped in and replaced the bar instantly. He had a bundle of clothes in his arms, some for her and some for himself. "We'll go tonight," he said quietly. "Change into these. I've got merchants' clothes for myself. I'll try to look like an Armenian." He shrugged. "At least I can speak Greek." He began slipping off his gray pilgrim cloak.

Was he coming with her? How far? She picked up the women's clothes and turned her back to put them on. If she made any kind of an issue of modesty now, it would draw his suspicion. If she was quick enough, he might be too occupied with his own clothing to notice anything else.

The dress was wool, dark wine red, roughly shaped, and tied with a girdle. She slipped into it with an ease that tore away the years of pretense as if they had been paper, and once again she was the widow who had returned from Eustathius's house to that of her parents. She bound her hair like a woman's, wrapped the outer robe of darker wool around her, and without thinking adjusted it with the grace she had struggled so hard to abandon.

He looked at her. For an instant his face was blank, then it filled with sharp, painful surprise. He picked up the painting and handed it to her. He turned to the door, opened it carefully with his hand on the hilt of his knife. Having looked to right and left, he nodded at her to follow him.

Outside in the street there were several groups of people standing around, apparently arguing or haggling over the prices of goods.

Giuliano went immediately north, keeping a steady pace she could match without appearing to stride like a man. She kept her eyes down and her steps shorter. In spite of the fear tightening her muscles, she enjoyed the brief freedom of being a woman, as if it were a wild, dangerous escape that would have to end too soon.

Jerusalem was a small city. They walked quickly, keeping to the wider streets where possible.

·They were climbing steadily, the great site of the Temple Mount to their right. She thought Giuliano was making for the Damascus Gate to the northwest and the Nablus Road.

They were accosted once, and Giuliano stopped and turned, smiling, hand on his belt. It was a peddler selling holy relics. He thought Giuliano was reaching for his purse. Anna knew he had a hand on the knife hilt.

"No, thank you," he said briefly. Catching Anna by the arm, he hurried onward.

His grip was warm and harder than it would have been had he touched a woman. She struggled to keep up with him, never daring to draw attention to herself by looking backward.

The Damascus Gate was crowded with merchants, peddlers, camel drivers, and several pilgrims dressed in gray. Suddenly they appeared sinister, and without realizing it, she slowed her step. Giuliano's hand tightened again, pulling her forward.

Did he feel her fear, or the slenderness of her bones, and wonder? They knew so much of each other—of dreams and beliefs—and yet so little. It was all shot through with assumptions and lies. Probably the lies were all hers.

They pushed through the crowds at the gate, and then they were out on the open road. After they had gone swiftly for about two hundred yards and strayed off the path downward, Giuliano stopped. "Are you all right?" he said anxiously.

"Yes," she said. "Do you want to go south now?" She pointed back to the road. "The Jaffa Gate's that way. That's Herod's Gate ahead of us. I could go in there. There's a pilgrim lodging near St. Stephen's. I'll stay there overnight, and go down to the Sion Gate before morning."

"I'll come with you," he said quickly.

"No. Take the painting and go back to Acre and the sea. I'll stay in this until morning, then I'll put on the gray again." She looked at him briefly, then turned away. Beyond his shoulder she saw the scarred hillside with holes in it that seemed at a glance like the eyes and nostrils of a great skull. She shivered.

"What is it?" he asked, swiveling around to follow her line of sight. "There's no one."

"I know. It wasn't that. . . ." Her voice tailed off.

He stood closer to her, his hand on her arm. "Do you know where we are?" he said softly.

"No. . . ." But even as she denied it, she understood. "Yes. Golgotha. The place of the crucifixion."

"Perhaps. I know some people think it's inside the city, and perhaps it doesn't matter. I'd rather it were here, desolate with the earth and the sky. It shouldn't have a pretty church built over it. That is to efface all it means. It had to be terrible, and alone, like this."

"Do you think we'll all come to such a place one day?" she asked. "Or be brought here?"

"Maybe, one day or another," he answered.

She stood still for several moments longer. Then she turned to him. "But I must go to Sinai, and you must go to Acre. I'll see you again in thirty-five days, or as close as I can to that." She found it difficult to keep her voice level, the emotion in control. She wanted to leave before it broke. She glanced down to where he held his sack with the clothes and the picture. "Thank you." She smiled briefly and turned away, climbing back up the steep incline to the road. At the top, she looked at him once and saw he was still on the same spot, still watching her, the skull of Golgotha behind him. She took a deep breath, swallowed, and started walking again.

Sixty-one

∽

GIULIANO WATCHED UNTIL THE SLENDER, LONELY FIGURE of Anastasius disappeared into the distance, then he walked over the rough ground and climbed back up to the road, joining it farther to the south and west. Was that the true Golgotha on which they had stood? The desolation of it seeped into his bones, drowning his mind. *Why hast Thou forsaken me?* The cry of every human soul who looks upon despair.

Was the sad, powerful face on the wooden painting he carried really that of Mary? It didn't matter. The passion was real. Who cared if it was this place or that place? This woman or another?

Why did the sight of Anastasius dressed as a woman trouble Giuliano so much? He not only looked so natural in the clothes, he even changed his walk and the angle of his head. The way he looked at the passing men was feminine, different. His character had changed. He was no longer the friend Giuliano had come to know so well. At least he thought he had. There were days at a time when he forgot that Anastasius was a eunuch. His sexuality, or lack of it, was of no importance. It was his courage, his gentleness, his intelligence, his quick wit and soaring imagination that mattered and made him who he was.

Now suddenly the whole issue was forced into the open. Anastasius truly was a third gender, neither male nor female. He could slip from one to the other as silk changed in the light, almost as if there were nothing innate that defined him.

But it was worse than that. It was something deeper, something within himself, that troubled him. He had found Anastasius dressed as a woman to be beautiful. He knew perfectly well that he was, if not a man, then definitely male, yet momentarily he had responded to him as if he had been female. He had felt protective and then been aware of the sharp stirrings of sexual attraction.

Giuliano was relieved that he had to go to Jaffa and there was no real question of his traveling to Sinai as well.

Yet the moment Anastasius, such a vulnerable figure, was gone, he felt strangely alone. He would soon be surrounded by people, but there was no one to whom he could speak of the burdens inside him, the guilt at having fallen so far short of being the kind of friend Anastasius needed and deserved.

Perhaps worse than that, cutting more deeply into the fabric of himself, he was not the man he himself needed to be. He had realized that perhaps he could not love, passionately or with lifelong honor and completeness, as his mother could not and his father did so unrequitedly. Perhaps the depth of that was not in him. But he had believed that friendship was another kind of love just as profound and just as precious. And he was wrong in that, too.

Had Anastasius the gentleness to forgive that? Out of the great well of his loneliness, the compassion Giuliano had seen in him so often, could he? And should he?

Sixty-two

～

DRESSED AS A PILGRIM ONCE MORE AND HAVING TO FORCE herself to adopt the habits and gestures of a eunuch again, Anna asked the caravan master at the Sion Gate for passage across the Negev Desert to St. Catherine's Monastery in Sinai. She still had a great deal of Zoe's money, more than was necessary to pay for her passage. He haggled a few minutes, but time was short and the money she offered was good, even generous.

Anna was unused to riding a donkey, but since there was no alternative, she accepted the assistance of one of the guides. He was a dark, mild-faced man of whose language she understood only a few words, but his tone of voice was sufficiently explicit that even the camels were obedient to him.

The caravan that left the shelter of Jerusalem numbered as near as she could tell about fifteen camels, twenty donkeys, and about forty pilgrims, plus a number of camel and donkey drivers and two guides. It was apparently a small number compared with what was usual.

It was a journey that began easily as they followed the road south. The first place of any note they passed was desolate, unremarkable, until the man on the donkey beside her crossed himself and began to pray over and over again, as if warding off some evil fate. She was startled by the fear in his voice.

"Are you ill?" she asked in concern.

He made the sign of the cross in the air. "Aceldama," he said hoarsely. "Pray, brother. Pray!"

Aceldama. Of course. The Field of Blood, where Judas slew himself. Surprisingly, it was not fear that took hold of her but a savage and overwhelming pity. Was that really a road from which there was no returning?

When they moved past Aceldama and into the ever-shifting, ever-changing desert, there was nothing left behind but an old grief.

The first night she was stiff and cold, too tired to sleep at first, and very aware of the miserable accommodations: three dirty, leaking sheds where they huddled together, trying to find enough rest to gain strength for the next day.

It was a relief to eat and drink a little and begin the day's journey. At least it was warmer to move, even in the wind, than to lie still.

The scenery changed from black and white to faded colors, bleached by heat and cold, almost devoid of life except for miserable little tamarisk trees thick with thorns. Pale sand gave way to almost black, flat and hard, covered with little flints. Black mountains were dense and jagged in the distance. The wind roared and stung with hard little edges of sand, like myriad insects stinging. They were told quite cheerfully by the guides that at other seasons it was worse.

They were warned not to leave the caravan for any reason whatever. To stray was to invite death. One could become lost in minutes, disoriented, and perish of thirst. The wastes beyond the known path were littered with the white bones of the foolish.

At night, the sky was ink black and burned with stars so low as to seem barely out of reach. Beautiful and alien, they exerted such a profound fascination that Anna found it hard to tear her gaze away from them and remember that she must sleep if she was to survive.

Day followed day. The scenery changed, limitless horizons giving way to lines of hills. Black desert changed to pale or even white with gray lines and shadows across it.

Then at last, on the fifteenth day, almost as if a cloud had cleared, in front of them, two towering summits appeared with a deep-clefted valley between, high and steep.

"The Mountains of Moses," the caravan master announced with pride. "Horeb and Sinai. We will climb. We will be there before nightfall." Anna thought they must already be several thousand feet above Acre and the sea.

At last they reached the outer walls of St. Catherine's. The vast, square fortress towered above them thirty to forty feet high, crammed into the fork between the peaks of Horeb and Sinai. It was built out of smooth, dust-colored rock hewn into giant squares and placed together so one could barely get a knife blade between.

The only way in was to hail the watchtower and request entrance. If it was granted, a small door opened high above and a knotted rope was let down. The guest would place his foot in a loop at the end and, on command, be hauled up.

After only a short hesitation, Anna found herself clinging with desperate hands, numb and dizzy, while she was raised up the outer face of the great wall. The sun burned red and purple on the western horizon. She would have liked to look at the scene until every last vestige of light faded, but already her hands were locked and slipped on the rope. Her legs ached so fiercely, she found it difficult to keep them straight.

She scrambled a little awkwardly through the small door. An elderly monk greeted her civilly enough, but with little interest. Perhaps he was so used to seeing pilgrims that they had all melted into one for him. So many of them would come with impossible dreams, expecting miracles, here where Moses had seen a burning bush from which God had spoken to him.

Sixty-three

～

S HE PRESENTED THE LETTER THAT NICEPHORAS HAD GIVEN
her and asked to see Justinian alone. The letter suggested, without
directly saying so, that she was on the emperor's business, and the monk
did not question it. Nicephoras had been careful to word it ambiguously.

She was conducted into a small, irregular-shaped courtyard, and the
monk leading her stopped. "Take your shoes off," he whispered. "The
place where you stand is holy ground."

Anna bent to obey and suddenly found tears in her eyes. She looked up,
boots in her hand, and saw in the lantern light a huge spread of leaves
where a bush mounded higher than her head and seemed to pour over the
stones. A wild thought came into her head. Was this Moses's bush, which
had once burned with the voice of God? She turned to the monk.

He nodded slowly, smiling.

"You may have a short time until the next call to prayer," he said gently, but the warning was implicit in his voice. She should not forget that
Justinian was a prisoner here and she was being granted a privilege in
speaking alone with him.

She was left to wait in an airless stone cell barely large enough to pace
back and forth more than a few steps. When she heard the door swing on
its heavy hinges, she whirled around.

For the first instant, he looked as he always had: his eyes, his mouth, the
way his hair grew from his brow. Her heart lurched, and she could hardly

breathe. The years vanished, and all that had happened between ceased to be real.

He was staring at her, confused, blinking. There was a first stumbling of hope in his face and then fear.

The monk behind him was waiting.

She must explain quickly, before either of them betrayed themselves. "I am a physician," she said clearly. "My name is Anastasius Zarides. The emperor Michael Palaeologus has given me permission to speak with you, if you will permit me to."

Even though she had pitched her voice with the throaty quality of a eunuch, he recognized it instantly. Joy flared up in his eyes, but he stood perfectly still, his back to the monk still standing behind him. When he answered, his voice trembled a little.

"I will be happy to speak with you . . . as the emperor wishes." He half turned to the monk behind him. "Thank you, Brother Thomas."

Brother Thomas inclined his head and withdrew.

"Anna! What in the name of—" Justinian started.

She cut him off by stepping forward and putting her arms around him. He responded, holding her so tightly that she felt bruised, although the pain was welcome.

"We have only a few minutes." His body was hard, far thinner than last time they had seen each other, so many years ago. He looked older, almost gaunt. The lines in his face were deeper, and there were hollows around his eyes.

"You look like a eunuch," he replied, still holding on to her. "What on earth are you doing? For God's sake, be careful! If the monks find out, they'll . . ."

She pulled away a little and looked up at him. "I'm good at it," she said ruefully. "I didn't dress like this to get in here. Although I would have! I'm like this all the time. . . ."

He was incredulous. "Why? You're beautiful. And you can practice medicine as a woman!"

"It's for a different reason." She also could not bear to tell him that she was unmarriageable, and why. That was a burden he did not need. "I have a good practice," she went on quickly. "Often at the Blachernae Palace, for the eunuchs there, and sometimes for the emperor himself."

"Anna!" he cut across her. "Don't! No practice is worth the risk you're taking."

"I'm not doing it for the practice," she said. "I'm doing it to find out enough to prove why you killed Bessarion Comnenos. It's taken me so long because at first I didn't even know why anyone would, but now I know."

"No, you don't," he contradicted her. His voice dropped, suddenly gentle. "You can't help, Anna. Please don't become involved. You have no idea how dangerous it is. You don't know Zoe Chrysaphes. . . ."

"Yes, I do. I'm her physician." She looked straight into his eyes. "I think she poisoned both Cosmas Kantakouzenos and Arsenios Vatatzes. I'm certain she killed Gregory Vatatzes face-to-face, with a dagger, and tried to have the Venetian ambassador arrested for it."

He stared at her. "Tried to?"

"I prevented it." She felt the heat burn in her face. "You don't need to know now. But yes, I know Zoe. And Helena. And Eirene, and Demetrios," she went on hastily. "And Bishop Constantine, of course."

He smiled at Constantine's name. "How is he? I get so little news here. Is he well?"

"Are you asking me as his physician?" It sounded lighthearted, but she said it because she suddenly realized that he had not seen the darker, weaker side of Constantine, the way he had changed under the desperate pressure of the union, of failure, the burden of leading so much of the resistance almost alone.

His eyebrows shot up. "You're *his* physician, too?"

"Why not?" She bit her lip. "To him I'm a eunuch. Isn't that appropriate?"

He paled. "Anna, you can't get away with this. For God's sake, go home. Have you any idea the risks you're taking? You can't prove anything. I . . . ."

"I can prove why you killed Bessarion," she replied. "And that you had no other choice. You were foiling a plot to usurp Michael, the only way possible. The emperor should thank you, reward you!"

He touched her face so gently she felt little more than the warmth of his hand. "Anna, it was a plot to usurp Michael, in order to save the Church from Rome. It was only when I finally realized that Bessarion had not the fire or the guts to succeed that I changed course. Michael knows that.

"I killed Bessarion," he said in little more than a whisper. "It was the hardest thing I've ever done, and I still have nightmares about it. But if he had usurped the throne, it would have been a disaster for Byzantium. I was a fool for it to take me so long to see that. I didn't want to, and then it was too late. But I'm here because I wouldn't tell Michael the names of the rest of the conspirators. I . . . I couldn't. They were no more guilty than I—perhaps less. They still believed it was the right thing to do for the city—and the faith."

She dropped her head and leaned against him. "I know that. I know who they are, and I couldn't tell him either. But there must be something I can do!"

"There isn't," he said softly. "Leave it be, Anna. Constantine will do what he can. He already saved my life. He'll plead for me with the emperor, if there's a chance."

There was no one else except her to fight for Justinian. And she had more chance of the emperor's ear than Constantine now.

"Who betrayed you to the authorities?" she asked.

"I don't know," he answered. "And it doesn't matter. There's nothing you can do about it, even if you were certain. What do you want, vengeance?"

She looked at him, searching. "I don't want revenge," she admitted. "At least only when I'm not really thinking. Then I'd like to see them pay. . . ."

"Leave it. Please," he begged. "In the end, it isn't worth anything."

"It isn't failure, not if Byzantium survives. And Michael will win that, if anyone can."

"At the cost of the Church?" he asked with disbelief. "Go home, Anna," he whispered. "Please. Be safe. I want to think of you healing people, living to be old and wise, and knowing that you did it well."

The tears blinded her. He had paid so much to give her that chance. And she had made him a promise she knew she could not keep.

"You won't, will you?" he said, touching the tears on her cheek.

"I can't. I don't know that they aren't still planning to kill Michael. Demetrios is a Vatatzes, and a Doukas through Eirene. He could try for the throne. If Michael were dead, and Andronicus, he might have a chance, especially with crusaders at the gates."

He gripped her harder, his hands tight on her shoulders. "I know that!

I think he might have taken over once Bessarion had got rid of Michael for him anyway."

"And you," she added. "You're a Lascaris!"

The key sounded in the lock.

Justinian pushed her away.

She wiped her hand across her cheek to get rid of the tears and forced herself to steady her voice.

"Thank you, Brother Justinian. I shall carry your message back to Constantinople." She made the sign of the cross in the Orthodox fashion, smiled at him once, briefly. Then she followed the monk out into the corridor, feeling her way rather than seeing it.

Sixty-four

⤫

THE JOURNEY BY CARAVAN FROM ST. CATHERINE'S BACK to Jerusalem took fifteen days again. Apparently it always did, whatever one had negotiated.

This time, Anna stared at the stark magnificence of the desert around her with different emotions. It was still beautiful. The shadings ran from black through a hundred shades of umber and gray. In daylight the blue was scorched with the dull ocher of dust on the wind, sometimes raw-edged with cold. Now it was indelible in her heart with the terrible price Justinian had paid for his error, and then to put it right.

She ignored the physical exhaustion, the ache in her body from the hardness of the ground on which she slept.

Had she been in Justinian's place, she might so easily have done exactly the same, if she had had the courage. Bessarion would have been a disaster as emperor, but he was too arrogant to see it, and the others were too far committed to accept such a bitter truth.

Except perhaps Demetrios. Was Justinian right, and he had planned to kill not only Michael and Andronicus, but perhaps Bessarion also? What irony that would have been! The archconspirator to turn against them as soon as the murder of Michael was accomplished, kill Bessarion and claim to restore order, then step into the breach himself, the hero of the hour!

And would he have got rid of Justinian as well? Because as a Lascaris, he was a threat. Then there would be nobody left but himself. Demetrios would console the widow, poor Helena, and in due course marry her and combine the families of Comnenos, Doukas, and Vatatzes in one glorious dynasty.

Were they still plotting? That was something she needed to know, because she realized with some surprise that she was wholeheartedly behind Michael. He was the only hope the city had now.

She arrived back in Jerusalem windburned and exhausted, her bones aching, but she had no time to rest. She must take the next caravan back to Acre and meet Giuliano on the ship. Carefully she counted out what was left of Zoe's money. She smiled. It must have hurt Zoe to change it from gold byzants into Venetian ducats. She could not afford to spend it all yet; she would need to wait in Acre if the ship was late. She would need food and lodging. But she knew that walking for another five days was beyond her physical strength.

She had learned a few tactics since last time and considerably sharper words since her stay in Jerusalem and her journey to Sinai and back. The deal was made, and she rode an awkward and highly ill-tempered mule all the way to Acre. Before they arrived there, the beast had discovered that she too could be stubborn and awkward if she chose. Secretly, she thought that they had gained some mutual respect and was quite sorry to part with it. She spent a few coins on buying it a treat of bread dipped in oil. The animal was most surprised but accepted the gift with something approaching grace.

She had one night to purchase poor lodgings, and she had no breakfast. Then she saw the ship come in, on precisely the day Giuliano had said he would return.

She boarded midmorning, not to betray how eager she was to see him.

He hid his relief in front of the crewmen. However, later, alone on deck as they pulled away in the darkening sky, he spoke to her alone, standing a little apart. His voice was gentle, although he looked not at her, but at the white wake of water behind them.

"Was the journey hard? They say it is."

"I'm not used to riding an ass day after day. A patient little beast, but uncomfortable. The desert's cold this time of year, especially at night. It's beautiful—and terrible."

"And Sinai?" he asked, turning to look at her now. In the stern, his back was to the light as they moved westward. She could not see his face.

"It's over five thousand feet above the sea," she began. "And yet the mountains around almost make it look insignificant, until you get to it, and realize the walls are thirty or forty feet high, and massive. Even if you could get a siege engine up there, nothing could break them. There are buttresses and towers, but no doors near the ground. The only way in is through a small opening near the top. You have to be winched up, standing in a rope stirrup."

"That's true?" he said, his voice hushed with wonder. "I heard it, but I thought it was imagination."

"It's true. Inside it's beautiful, austere, and you can never forget the mountains that seem to be almost hanging over you, blocking out the sky behind, Mount Sinai and Mount Horeb. There is a pathway upward in the cleft between them, steep stairs now. That's where Moses climbed up to meet God. I didn't go. I didn't have time, and I'm not sure if I wanted to. Maybe I would have met God, and I'm not ready." She smiled and looked down. "Or maybe I wouldn't, and I'm not ready to face that, either. But I saw the 'burning bush.' It's still there. It looks like any other bush, but you know it isn't."

"How?" he asked.

"Probably because the monk told me I was standing on holy ground— to take my shoes off."

He laughed, and the tension eased out of his shoulders. Only then did she realize how awkward he had been, without his usual grace. She thought of their parting in Golgotha, of his face when he had seen the painting of Mary—she chose to believe that was who it was. Other moments crowded her mind, and she knew that something had changed. She did not want to understand what it was because it included a hurt she could not reach.

Sixty-five

～

"WELL?" SIMONIS DEMANDED WHEN ANNA WAS HOME AT last, washed and rested and sitting in clean clothes at the table, hot soup and fresh bread in front of her. "What did you learn of Justinian? I can see by your face that he is alive. What else? When will he be home?"

Anna had told Simonis and Leo nothing of Zoe's picture. They had both assumed her entire journey was to gain news of Justinian. Leo had cautioned her against going, saying she would endanger herself for little purpose. Simonis had been furious with him and praised Anna for at last taking the step that she had hoped of her from the beginning.

"I saw him," Anna began. "He is thinner, but he seemed well."

"Drink your soup," Simonis directed. "What did he say?"

Anna felt the knot of disappointment tighten inside her. "He told me what happened," she replied, beginning the soup because its fragrance tempted her and eating would not make what she had to say better or worse. "It was almost what I had believed, from what I learned my-self. . . ."

"You didn't tell us!" Simonis accused, her face darkening again.

Leo touched her arm gently, with a small, restraining gesture.

She shook him off, still staring at Anna. "So how are you going to prove his innocence?" she repeated.

"I'm not," Anna said bluntly. "He killed Bessarion. . . ."

"He couldn't!" Simonis said furiously. "Not Justinian. You, perhaps! You could have—"

"Stop it," Leo said sharply. "You exceed yourself."

Simonis blushed hotly.

Anna too was caught by surprise. "Thank you, Leo," she said to him gravely. "The story is simple, and now that I know from Justinian that it is true, I shall tell you, but if you value your lives, or mine, you will not repeat it." She waited for their word. "This is as Justinian wishes."

Simonis nodded reluctantly, her face still hot and angry.

"Of course," Leo promised.

Briefly she told them, not elaborating any of the details.

Simonis looked crushed. She stared in miserable silence.

"Anna, you must obey Justinian's wishes," Leo said with concern. "You can't let anyone know that you are aware of all this, or they will destroy you."

Simonis was looking at her, too, but she expected action. "You'll go to the emperor and tell him who the other conspirators were," she said as if it were a conclusion they had all agreed. "You'll say you saw Justinian, and he told you who they were. Then the emperor will free him."

"No, I can't," Anna said. "They tortured Justinian to make him tell, and he didn't. You want me to do it now, after the price he has paid. . . ."

Simonis shouted at her, "Men are fools. They keep to people who betray them when there's no sense in it. You must do it for him. That way his hands are clean—"

"Not if she says that it was Justinian who told her," Leo interrupted her.

"It doesn't matter!" Anna said desperately. "He doesn't want it done, by me, or himself, or anyone."

"Of course he does," Simonis contradicted her witheringly. "Why else would he tell you?"

"He didn't need to tell me, I already knew," Anna pointed out. She did not mention her conversation with Nicephoras.

"Oh, so it's your honor now, is it?" Simonis almost choked on her words. "He sits in prison in the desert, beaten and tortured, and you increase your practice here in Constantinople and grow fat, wearing silks, but you don't want to stain some honor you imagine you have. You didn't mind sacrificing his whole future over your mistakes in Nicea, did you? Or have you chosen to forget that? None of this would ever have happened if you'd owned up then. He'd be a doctor and you wouldn't! Where was your precious honor then, you . . . you coward. . . ." Sobbing, gasping for breath, she blundered out of the room and they heard her feet down the passageway.

Anna found the tears were hot in her eyes. "He begged me not to," she whispered. "It's not for me . . . it's for him."

"I will speak to her," Leo said quietly. "Perhaps you should send her back to Nicea. . . ."

"No." She shook her head. "I can't do that."

"You can't excuse what she said," he replied. "It was unforgivable."

"Very little is unforgivable," she said wearily. "And anyway, I can't afford to have a stranger here in her place, not in the house."

"Are you afraid she will betray you?" he asked.

"No, of course not," she denied too quickly. "She would never do that. Justinian wouldn't forgive her."

Anna took the picture to Zoe Chrysaphes the following day. There were no servants present, simply the two of them in the silent room. It was filled with sharp, pale spring sunlight. She handed over the package, quite small, heavily wrapped, just as Giuliano had passed it back to her.

Zoe did not pretend to be interested in Anna. She cut the fastenings with a small, thin-bladed knife, then undid them and stared at the wooden panel. For a long time she did not speak, her face transfixed with crowding emotions: awe, amazement, overwhelming joy. Strangely, there was no open victory in it—rather the opposite: a sense of sudden humility. Finally she looked up at Anna, and her eyes were totally without guile.

"You did well, Anastasia," she said quietly, as one woman might speak to another who was an equal—possibly, for a moment, even her friend. "I could pay you in gold for your skill and your hardship, but that seems crass. There is a jeweled candlestick on the table. It is yours. Take it, and set your taper in it to carry the light."

Anna turned and saw it. It was exquisite: small—not more than a few inches high—but set with rubies and pearls that burned softly even in the harsh morning light. She picked it up and turned to thank Zoe, but Zoe's head was bent and she was totally absorbed in the picture.

Anna left without breaking the silence.

Sixty-six

∽

MICHAEL PALAEOLOGUS, EMPEROR OF BYZANTIUM, STOOD in the pale sunlight in his private chamber. On the chest in front of him was a simple picture, but the face in it was that of the Mother of God. He knew it without question. The artist who had painted it had known, and the passion, the suffering, and the beauty of soul were attempted in the lines. It was not his imagination, not an ideal, he was trying to capture in line and shading what he saw in front of him.

Zoe Chrysaphes had sent the eunuch physician to Jerusalem to bring it back. It was a gift not to the Church, but to Michael personally.

Of course, Michael knew why Zoe had given it to him. She was afraid that he was aware of her part in Bessarion Comnenos's plan to usurp the throne and that one day when Michael would have no need of her, he would take his revenge for that. This was to buy him off. It had succeeded. If it was not the greatest relic in Christendom, it was certainly the most beautiful, the most moving to the soul.

Very slowly he bent to his knees, the tears wet on his cheeks. The Blessed Virgin was back in Byzantium again, in a way she had never been before. How strange that Zoe, of all people, had caused her to be brought.

Sixty-seven

❦

IN CONSTANTINOPLE, THE SUMMER OF 1278 WAS HOT AND still. Palombara was again in the city, surrounded by its vivid mixture of sounds and colors, its racing ideas, its passionate religious debate.

Unfortunately, he had once more been accompanied by Niccolo Vicenze. The Holy Father had told Palombara that Vicenze knew nothing of his real mission, which was supporting the emperor in obeying the act of union with Rome. And naturally to preserve the emperor's life and power, should they be threatened. It was implicit that it was also Palombara's task to be sure he was aware of such threats, whoever posed them.

Of course, what the Holy Father had actually said to Vicenze could be completely different. That must never be forgotten.

The priority now was to deal with Bishop Constantine. He was foremost among those still irrevocably opposed to the union. Arguing with him was pointless. He must be defeated. It was an ugly thought, but too many lives rested on it to be squeamish. The question was one of means.

At Constantine's side, through hunger and disease, had been the physician Anastasius. If anyone knew the bishop's weaknesses, it was he. And what was equally certain in Palombara's mind was that Anastasius would never willingly betray them, least of all to Rome. Deceiving him was not something Palombara looked forward to.

Another thought occurred to him, subtle and dangerous. If he were in Constantine's place, determined at any cost to save the freedom of the Orthodox Church, the one man above all others who stood in his way was

Michael himself. Remove the emperor, put an Orthodox believer in his place, without either his intelligence or his steel, and all this other maneuvering would be unnecessary.

His urgency to see Anastasius doubled. Fragments of conversation came back to his mind, old plots and murders, imperial names like Lascaris and Comnenos, his intimacy with Zoe Chrysaphes, that most Byzantine of women, and his treatment of the emperor.

It was over a week before the opportunity came without forcing it. He had been attempting to cross Anastasius's path by chance, and eventually they met on the hill above the docks. Palombara had just arrived by water taxi, and Anastasius was walking along the cobbles. It was early evening, the sun low and hazy, healing the jagged scars of violence and poverty beneath a patina of gold.

"My favorite time of day," Palombara said quite casually, as if it were a natural thing they should meet again after so long a space of time.

"Is it?" Anastasius said. "You look forward to the night?"

He stood still, and courtesy demanded that Anastasius do the same. "I was speaking of these moments only, not what came before, or will follow."

There was interest in Anastasius's eyes. Palombara knew they were dark gray, but facing the sun as he was, he thought they could have been brown.

Palombara smiled. "There is a tenderness in the shadows," he continued. "A mercy the hard light of morning doesn't allow."

"You like mercy, my lord?" Anastasius said curiously.

"I like beauty," Palombara corrected him. "I like the unreality of the softer light—the permission to dream."

Anastasius smiled, the quick, warm gesture lighting his face. Palombara had the sudden thought that he was beautiful; neither man nor woman, but not a distortion of either.

"I need to dream," he explained quickly. "Reality is harsh, and its fruits will come quickly enough."

"You refer to something specific?" Anastasius glanced to his side at the ruin of a tower; one side of it had crashed to the ground, the rubble still uncleared. "Are you still here trying to persuade us to join Rome in heart, as well as in treaty?"

"Charles of Anjou wants any excuse to take Constantinople again. The emperor knows that."

Anastasius nodded. "He would hardly unite with Rome against a lesser threat."

Palombara winced. "That's harsh. Shouldn't Christendom be united? Islam is rising in the East."

"Do we fight one darkness by embracing another?" Anastasius said softly.

Palombara shivered. He wondered if Anastasius really saw it like that. "What is so different between Rome and Byzantium that you can consider one light and the other darkness?" he asked.

Anastasius was silent for a long time.

"It is all far subtler, a million shades between one and the other," he said at length. "I want a Church that teaches pity and gentleness, patience, hope, forbearance from self-righteousness, but still with room for passion and laughter, and dreams."

"You want a lot," Palombara said gently. "Are you expecting the elders of the Church to produce all this as well?"

"I just need a Church that doesn't stand in our way," Anastasius replied. "I believe God wants us to teach, to befriend, and finally to create—that is the purpose. To become like God, as all children dream of becoming like their fathers."

Palombara studied his face: the hope in it, the hunger, and the ability to be hurt. Anastasius had been right: The thought was beautiful, but it was also turbulent, intensely alive.

Palombara did not believe for an instant that either the Byzantine Church or the Roman would ever accept such an idea. It painted something of an awe and a beauty too limitless for ordinary men to conceive of. One would have to catch some glimpse of the heart of God even to dream so much.

But then perhaps Anastasius had, and Palombara envied him that.

They stood over the darkening seascape, the lights of the dockside behind them. For long minutes, neither of them spoke. Palombara was afraid Anastasius would leave and his opportunity would be lost.

Finally, he spoke. "The emperor is determined to save the city from Charles of Anjou by declaring union with Rome, but he cannot force his subjects to abandon the old faith, not even enough to satisfy appearances from the pope."

Anastasius did not answer. Perhaps he knew it was not a question.

"You ask a great deal about the murder of Bessarion Comnenos several years ago," Palombara pressed on. "Was that a thwarted attempt to usurp the throne, and then fight to keep religious independence?"

Anastasius turned slightly toward him. "Why do you care, Bishop Palombara? It failed. Bessarion is dead. So are those who conspired with him."

"So you know who they were?" he said instantly.

Anastasius drew in a deep, slow breath. "Only two of them. But without those, and without Bessarion himself, what can they do?"

"That question concerns me," Palombara replied. "Any such attempt now would incite a terrible revenge. The mutilation of the monks would seem trivial by comparison. And the only man to win would be Charles of Anjou."

"And the pope," Anastasius added, his eyes catching the light of a cart passing with a lantern held high. "But it would be a bitter victory, Your Grace. And the blood of it would not wash off your hands."

Sixty-eight

"THE HISTORIC ICON OF THE VIRGIN THAT THE EMPEROR Michael had carried into Constantinople when the people returned from exile in 1262," Vicenze said unequivocally. "That is what it will take."

Palombara did not reply. They were standing in the room overlooking the long slope down to the shore. The light danced on the water, and the tall masts of the ships swayed gently as the hulls rolled on the slight morning swell.

"We'll never succeed until we have a symbol of Byzantine surrender to Rome," Vicenze went on. "The icon of the Virgin is it. They believe it saved them from invasion once before."

Palombara had no argument to offer against it. His reluctance was purely practical. "It will be impossible to get it, so the effectiveness of it hardly matters."

"But you agree as to the power it will have." Vicenze stuck to his point.

"In theory, of course." Palombara looked at him more closely. He realized that Vicenze had a plan, one he was sufficiently pleased with that he had no doubt of victory. He was telling Palombara only because he wanted him to know, not to participate.

It meant Palombara must form his own plan, with absolute secrecy, or Vicenze would be there first and take the prize to the pope alone. The secrecy was necessary because it would not be beyond Vicenze's mind deliberately to sabotage Palombara and allow all attention to focus on him, while he executed his own scheme. Palombara could end up in a Byzantine jail, while Vicenze, wringing his hands with hypocritical sorrow, would make his way to the Vatican, icon in hand.

"We must obtain it," Vicenze said with a thin smile. "I will let you know what plan I can contrive. If you can think of anything, then you will naturally inform me."

"Naturally," Palombara agreed. He went out into the air, feeling the faint wind in his face. For several moments he stared over the rooftops toward the sea, then he started to walk. He just wanted the comfort of movement, the cobbles under his feet and the ever changing sights.

Michael could not be bought with money or coerced with office. The only thing he cared about was saving his city from Charles of Anjou and the duplicity of Rome. No, that was not true. He would save it from anyone, Christian or Muslim. It had always been Byzantium's art through the centuries to form alliances, to deal in trade, to turn its enemies against one another. Could he be persuaded to ally with Rome against the hot wind of Islam that was already scorching the southern borders?

What could bring such an alliance into being? An atrocity in Constantinople itself. Something that would enrage Christendom and draw the two opposing Churches into each other's arms, at least long enough to send the icon to Rome as proof of Byzantium's good faith.

An outrage, but not murder. Burn a shrine and see that the Muslims were blamed, and there would be rage among the people. Then they would accept any price Michael was able to pay, even tribute to Rome.

Palombara knew how to do it. He had papal money, even some that Vicenze knew nothing about. And he had contact with people who understood how to arrange precise and limited violence, at a price. He would be very, very careful indeed. No one would know, most particularly not Niccolo Vicenze.

The burning of the sacred shrine to Saint Veronica was spectacular. Palombara stood in the street at dusk, anonymous in the gathering crowd, and felt the searing heat as the flames consumed the fragile buildings and scorched the walls of the surrounding houses and shops.

Near him an old woman howled, tearing at her hair, her voice rising in pitch until it was close to a scream. The roar of the fire grew louder, the crackle of wood explosive, sending sparks and burning cinders high into the air.

The heat drove Palombara backward and he reached out to pull the old woman to greater safety, but she snatched her arm away from him.

Gradually the flames subsided, starved of something to consume. But the rage that followed it was as white hot as the heart of the fire had been. Palombara did not need to fan the flames.

He asked for an audience with the emperor and was granted it. When he entered the emperor's presence, Michael looked tired and worried, and his temper was extremely short.

"What is it, my lord bishop?" Michael said tersely. He was robed in a red dalmatica crusted with jewels. The Varangian Guard remained at the doors, very much in evidence.

Palombara did not waste time. "I came to offer the sympathy of the Holy Father in Rome upon your loss, Majesty."

"Rubbish!" Michael snapped. "You have come to gloat, and to see what profit you can make out of it."

Palombara smiled. "Profit for all of us, Majesty. If Islam rises in the south to even more power than it has now, and continues to press the borders of Christendom, it will take more than a crusade to keep them from attacking us, and then inevitably, a full invasion. And I am not speaking of centuries in the future, Majesty, perhaps not even decades."

Michael's face was pale under his black beard, but his expression did not change. He had led his people in exile; he knew war well and carried the scars of it on his body. He was prepared to pay the last, desperate price of compromising his religious faith to preserve his people. Michael Palaeologus, emperor of Byzantium and Equal of the Apostles, knew the taste of failure, defeat, and the art and cost of survival.

Palombara was touched with an amazement of pity for this very human man in his gorgeous robes and his still ruined palace. "Majesty," he said humbly, "may I suggest a more final recognition of Byzantium's union with Rome, one upon which no enemy, either through malice or stupidity, can cast doubt?"

Michael looked at him with cold suspicion. "What have you in mind, Bishop Palombara?"

Palombara found himself hesitating before he could force the words to his mouth. "Send to Rome the icon of the Holy Virgin that you carried above you as you entered into Constantinople after the exile," he answered finally. "Let it come to Rome, as a symbol of the union of the two great Christian Churches of the world, willing to stand side by side against the tide of Islam rising around us. Then Rome will forever be mindful of you, and that you are the bastion of Christ against the infidel. And if we let you fall, then the enemies of God will be at our own gates."

Michael was silent, but there was no anger, no will to fight the impossible or make a show of injured dignity. Michael was a realist. He was neatly caught. The irony of it was not lost on him, but he who had thought himself so clever was utterly out of his depth.

"Look after her well," Michael answered at last. "She will not forgive you if you defile her. That is what you should fear, Palombara: not me, not Byzantium, nor even the connivings of Rome or the floods of Islam. Fear God, and the Holy Virgin."

A week later, the ancient icon that had saved Byzantium centuries ago was delivered to the beautiful house where Palombara and Vicenze lodged. They stood in one of the large reception rooms and watched as it was unpacked in silence.

Vicenze was overwhelmed by Palombara's success. He stood in the sunlight streaming in through the windows, and his pale face was bleak.

Looking at him, Palombara saw a rage and envy that was real.

Then, as Michael's man worked on the packing, Palombara saw a new expression enter Vicenze's face, a vision beyond his own failure to gain the icon.

The last wrapping fell away, and each man silently leaned closer to gaze on the somber, beautiful face and, as close to it as they were, the marks of time and weather visible in the minute cracks in the paint, the pinhole marks in the gold leaf. The banner itself was rubbed smooth by many hands, and the oil from human skin over the generations had polished the surfaces of the wood where it was held.

Vicenze opened his mouth to say something, then changed his mind.

Palombara did not even look at him. The chill dreamlessness of Vicenze's face would infuriate him.

It was simple enough to hire a ship. Palombara made the agreement with one of the many captains in the port of Constantinople. Vicenze oversaw the carter who was actually carrying the icon, which was even more carefully packed in an outer wooden crate. It was discreetly marked so they could identify it easily, but no one else could guess the contents.

They took little with them, not wanting to give notice to servants or the ever present watchers and listeners that they might not be returning for some time. In fact, it was possible they might be elevated to the cardinal's purple and not return at all. Palombara regretted leaving behind some of the exquisite artifacts he had purchased while here, but it was necessary in order to create the illusion that he was merely visiting the dockside and would return before dusk.

However, as he arrived on the quay, he saw with disbelief their ship pull away. The water churned around the hull as it gathered speed, oars dipping rhythmically until they should be beyond the harbor shelter and find the soft wind to fill the sails. Vicenze stood on the ship near the rail. The sun in his pale hair was like a halo, and his wide, flat mouth was smiling.

Palombara broke into a sweat of blind fury. He had never experienced defeat so total and so consuming that no other emotion was possible.

"My lord bishop," a voice said, sounding concerned, "are you ill, sir?"

Astonished, Palombara looked at the speaker. It was the captain of the ship, to whom he had not yet paid the money, believing that that fact alone would hold him loyal. "They've taken your ship," he said harshly, flinging out his arm to point into the bay where the hull of it was already growing smaller in the distance.

"No, sir," the captain said incredulously. "My ship is over there, waiting for you and your cargo."

"I just saw Bishop Vicenze on board." He gestured out to sea again. "There!"

The captain shaded his eyes and followed Palombara's gaze. "That's not my ship, sir. That is Captain Dandolo's."

Palombara blinked. "Dandolo? He took the package onto his own ship?"

"He had a big package, sir. Several feet high, and wide, about the size you described to me."

"Bishop Vicenze brought it?"

"No, sir. Captain Dandolo brought it himself, sir. Will you still be wanting to sail to Rome, sir?"

"Yes, by God in heaven, I will!"

Sixty-nine

∾

ONSTANTINE STRODE THROUGH THE HARD, BRIGHT SUN
to visit Theodosia Skleros, the only daughter of Nicholas Skleros,
one of the wealthiest men to have returned to Constantinople after the
exile. None of the family wavered in their devotion to the Orthodox
Church and consequently in their loathing of Rome and all its abuse of
power.

Theodosia was married to a man who in Constantine's opinion was
worthy of neither her high intelligence nor, more important, her great
spiritual beauty. Still, since he was apparently her choice, Constantine
treated him with all the courtesy he would grant to any man with such an
exceptional wife.

He found Theodosia at prayer. He knew she would be alone at this
hour, and no caller would be more welcome than he.

She greeted him with a smile of pleasure and perhaps surprise also. Usually he sent a message before he came.

"Bishop Constantine," she said warmly, coming into the spare, elegant
room with its classical murals of urns and flowers. She was not a lovely
woman, although she walked with grace, and her voice had a richness to
it, a care and clarity of diction that made listening to her a joy.

"Theodosia . . ." He smiled, already the weight of his anger easing.
"You are most gracious to receive me when I took no care to ask if it was
convenient."

"It is always convenient, my lord," she replied, and she invested it with such sincerity that he could not doubt it. Standing here in the shadow away from the harsh sunlight, she reminded him of Maria, the only girl he had ever loved. It was not that their faces were alike; Maria had been beautiful. At least that was how he remembered her, but they had been little more than children. His elder brothers were young men, handsome and bawdy, feeling their new strength and exercising it, not always with kindness.

It was just after Constantine was castrated. His body ached now at the remembrance of it: not of the physical pain, but of the emotional shame. Not that the pain was negligible, but the wound had healed in time. He wished that had been true for Niphon too, but it had not. He had been the youngest brother, confused by what had happened to him, not understanding. His wound had become infected. Constantine had never been able to forget his white face as he lay on the bed, the sweat-soaked sheets damp around him. Constantine had sat with him, holding his limp hand, talking to him all the time so he would know he was never alone. He was still a child, soft-skinned, slender-shouldered, and so frightened. He had looked so small when he was dead, as if it had never been possible he would grow up.

They had all grieved for him, but Constantine the most. Maria was the only one who had understood how deeply it had cut into all that he was.

She had been the most beautiful girl in the town. All the young men had wanted to court her. But it seemed she had chosen brash, charming Paulus, Constantine's eldest brother.

Then suddenly, without anyone knowing the reason, she had turned away from him and wanted instead to be with Constantine. Theirs had been a pure friendship, asking nothing but understanding, the joy of sharing both beauty and pain, the exhilaration of ideas, and sometimes, on wonderful occasions, laughter.

She had wished to become a nun; she had confided that to him, softly, with a shy smile. But her family forced her to marry into a wealthy family with whom they had ties, and Constantine had never seen Maria again, nor had he ever learned what had happened to her.

She remained for him the ideal not only of womanhood, but of love itself. Now as Theodosia smiled at him in her quiet, grave way and offered him honey cakes and wine, he saw in her dark eyes something of Maria

again, an echo of the same trust in him. A peace settled inside him so
sweet, he began to find again the courage to fight harder, with new power,
more belief.

It gave him the confidence to try a more dangerous path, one that repelled him, and yet in Theodosia's piety and unquestioning devotion to
the faith, he understood the necessity of using every weapon within his
reach.

It was strange to visit Zoe's house afterward. Constantine had no delusions
that she welcomed him out of anything but an intense curiosity to know
what he could want with her.

He had forgotten how striking she was. Although she was in her late
seventies, still she walked with her head high and the same grace in her
steps, the suppleness of body he remembered.

He greeted her cautiously, accepting hospitality in order to make it
clear that he intended the visit to have meaning.

"You must be aware of the danger we are in, perhaps even more than I
am," he began. "The emperor sees it as so imminent that he has taken the
icon of the Virgin which he carried in triumph and sent it to Rome. He
told me that was to preserve it, should the city be burned again. But he has
not told the people this. Presumably he is afraid of panic."

"All times require care, my lord bishop," she answered, although there
was no belief or acceptance in her face. "We have many enemies."

"We were preserved, in spite of the earthly strength of our enemies," he
replied, "because we believed. God cannot save us if we will not trust
Him. We have an advocate in the Blessed Virgin. I know that you know
this, which is why I came to you, even though we are not friends, and I do
not trust you in most things, I admit that. But in your love of Byzantium,
and of the Holy Church we both believe in, I trust you with my life."

She smiled, as if some faint amusement overrode all that she heard in
him, but her eyes were hot and still, and there was a color in her cheeks
that owed nothing to art. Now was the time to tell her his purpose.

"I trust you because we have a common cause," he said again. "And
therefore common enemies in the powerful families who, for one reason
or another, support the union."

"What have you in mind, Your Grace—precisely?"

"Information, of course," he replied. "You have weapons you cannot use, but I can. Now is the time, before it becomes too late."

"Is it not already too late?" she said coolly. "We have had at least this much common purpose for years."

"Because you will not part with the kind of information I want while it is still of more value to you," he replied. "You cannot use it with impunity. I can."

"Possibly. I can think of nothing I know which will enlarge the Kingdom of God." There was a flicker of amusement in her eyes. "But perhaps you have more in mind than reduction of the realm of the devil?"

He felt a chill. "My enemy's enemy is my friend," he quoted.

"And which particular enemy are you referring to?" she asked.

"I have but one cause," he replied. "The preservation of the Orthodox Church."

"For which we need also to preserve the city," she pointed out. "What is your plan, Bishop?"

He looked at her unflinchingly. "To persuade the great families who support the union to change their allegiance from expediency to trust in God. If they will not do so willingly, then I shall, in the interest of their souls, remind them of some of the sins of which I can absolve them, before God, if not before the public—and of course of what awaits those without forgiveness."

"A little late," she said.

"Would you have given me such weapons earlier, when Charles of Anjou was not preparing to sail?"

"I am not sure if I will now. Perhaps I would prefer to use them myself."

"You have power to wound, just as I have, Zoe Chrysaphes," he said with a slight smile. "But I have power to heal, and you do not." He named three families.

She hesitated, studying his face, then something seemed to amuse her, and she told him what he needed to know.

Seventy

PALOMBARA ARRIVED IN ROME ONLY DAYS AFTER VICENZE. The voyage had been good enough for time and seamanship, but the taste of defeat had robbed him of any pleasure at all. He had landed at Ostia, and even the briefest inquiry had told him Vicenze had beaten him by at least twenty-four hours.

The pope and the cardinals were already assembled in the anteroom to the pope's chambers in the Vatican Palace when Palombara strode in, still travel stained, his clothes shabby with dust and sweat. At any other time he could have been barred entrance in his disheveled state, but the buzz of excitement was in the air, as in a summer lightning storm when the wind was dry, prickling on the skin like the touch of a hundred flies. People started to speak and then stopped. Eyes darted everywhere, seeing him and smiling. Did he imagine the mockery, or was it only too real?

The huge crate stood with its wood neatly opened; only the cloth covering protected the icon of the Blessed Virgin that Michael Palaeologus had carried in triumph when his people had returned home.

Vicenze stood a little to one side of it, his face burning with victory, his pale eyes glittering. Only once did he look at Palombara, then away again, as though he were insignificant, a man who had ceased to matter.

A workman stepped forward at his signal. There was no other sound in the room, no rustle of heavy robes, no shifting of feet. Even the pope seemed to be holding his breath.

The workman reached up and pulled off the protecting cloth.

The pope and the cardinals craned forward. There was utter silence.

Palombara looked, blinked, and stared. God Almighty! What met his gaze was not the exquisite features of the Virgin, but a riotous profusion of naked flesh, in exuberant, joyful detail and painted with great skill. The central figure was a smiling parody of the Virgin, but so overtly feminine that one could not look at it without a quickening of the pulse, a remembrance of the hot blood of passion. One lush breast was exposed, and her slender hand rested intimately on the groin of the man nearest to her.

One of the less abstemious cardinals exploded with laughter and instantly tried to suffocate it in a fit of coughing.

The pope's face was scarlet, although there could have been more than one reason for that.

Other cardinals choked. Someone snorted in disgust. Another laughed quite openly.

Vicenze was white to the lips, his eyes as hectic as if he were consumed with fever on the edge of delirium.

Palombara tried for a full minute to look as if he were not laughing, and failed. It was exquisite. He too owed someone a debt he would never be able to pay.

Palombara had no choice but to go when Nicholas sent for him.

The Holy Father's expression was unreadable. "Explain yourself, Enrico," he said very quietly. His voice trembled, and Palombara had no idea if the emotion all but choking him was fury or laughter.

There was nothing to offer but the truth.

"Yes, Holy Father," he said piously. "I persuaded the emperor to send the icon to Rome. It arrived at the house we had taken for our stay in the city. It was unpacked in front of us, and it was quite definitely a very somber, very beautiful picture of the Virgin Mary. It was repacked in front of us, ready to ship."

"This tells me nothing," Nicholas said dryly. "Who obtained it? You?"

"Yes, Holy Father."

"And what did Vicenze do about it? Don't tell me this is his revenge for your superiority? He could never have done this to himself. The laughter will follow him to the grave, as well you know." He leaned forward. "This looks a great deal more like your wit, Enrico. For which I shall pardon you . . ." The faintest twitch pulled the corner of his mouth, and with difficulty he controlled it. "If you return the icon of the Virgin to me forthwith. Discreetly, of course."

Nicholas might not have a towering faith with a light to lead Christendom, but he unquestionably had a sharp sense of humor, and to Palombara that was a grace sufficient to redeem him from almost any other failure.

"Is it still in Constantinople?" Nicholas asked.

"I don't know, Holy Father, but I doubt it," Palombara replied. "I think Michael was honest."

"Do you? Then I am inclined to accept that," Nicholas said thoughtfully. "You are a cynical man. You manipulate others, so you expect them to do the same to you." He raised his eyebrows. "Don't look so crushed! So where is the icon, whoever has it? I do not require to know, if such knowledge would be embarrassing."

"My guess would be Venice," Palombara replied. "The captain who brought Vicenze and the icon to Rome was a Venetian—Giuliano Dandolo."

"Ah! Yes, I have heard of him. A descendant of the great doge," Nicholas said quietly. "How very interesting." He smiled. "When you return to Constantinople you will take a letter for me, in which I shall thank the emperor Michael for his gift of good faith and assure him that the union is regarded with the utmost gravity and honor by Rome." He looked at Palombara steadily. "You will return to Byzantium, taking Vicenze with you."

Palombara was horrified at the thought.

Nicholas saw his distress and chose to ignore it. "I do not want him here in Rome. I quite see that you do not want him, either, but I am pope, Enrico, and you are not—at least not yet. Take Vicenze. You still have work to do there. Charles of Anjou will sail, and then it will be too late to stop him. Perhaps you can find some Byzantine friend who will curb his excesses for you. Godspeed."

Palombara had no choice but to leave the reclaiming of the icon to Nicholas. If Dandolo had any sense, he would yield it easily enough. God knows, Venice had relics to spare. And to steal from the pope, and thus from the heart of the Church, was a dangerous thing to do.

Possibly Dandolo might present it to the Holy Father himself, with any claim he could think of as to how it had come into his possession. Nicholas might be inclined to forgive him for it and pretend to believe any tale of its adventures.

Seventy-one

∞

DURING THE VOYAGE BACK TO CONSTANTINOPLE, PALOM-
bara and Vicenze had barely spoken to each other, and then only in
a bitterly civil manner, as was necessary in front of the sailors. It deceived
no one.

Now Palombara went to the one person who had the power and the
means to destroy a papal legate. He needed to convince her of the need.

Zoe welcomed him with interest, her curiosity sharpened. However, he
was not blind to the hatred in her eyes, the hunger to hurt him because he
was the one who had persuaded Michael to give the icon of the Virgin to
Rome.

Instead of telling her that he too believed in the need for Byzantium to
survive, with its values and its civilization, he told her of the shipping of
the icon. He described his own fury as he saw Vicenze in the stern of the
ship, waving at him. He touched briefly on his seemingly endless voyage
in pursuit, but only for dramatic effect. Then in detail, drawing it out, he
told her of the unveiling, the moment of incredulity, and then in much
freer detail than he would have to any other woman, he described the picture, and the cardinal's horror, the pope's laughter, and Vicenze's incan-
descent rage.

She laughed until the tears ran down her cheeks. In that moment, he
could have reached across and touched her and she would not have pulled
away. As thin as spider's silk and as strong, it was a bond neither of them
would ever forget, an unbreakable intimacy.

"I don't know where it is," he said softly. "I would guess in Venice. I imagine Dandolo took it from Vicenze. He is the only one who had the chance to. But I will see that the pope receives it, and perhaps even sends it back."

"And what are you going to do, Enrico Palombara? You must deal with Vicenze."

"Oh, I know!" he assured her, smiling bitterly. "This pope would protect me today, but tomorrow could be different." He shrugged. "Over the last few years, popes have come and gone faster than the weather has changed. Their promises are worth nothing, because their successors are not bound by them."

She did not answer him, but there was a sudden light in her eyes, a different understanding. It took only an instant for him to know that she had let slip the dream of defying the union and seen the reality, and its flaws. It was his first step toward convincing her. He must tread lightly. The smallest attempt at deception and he would lose her.

She searched his face, curiously, quite frankly. "You are trying to tell me that union with Rome may not be as bad as I had supposed, because little note can be kept of actual practice. A pope's word is worth little, so ours need be worth no more. As long as we are discreet and do not force anyone's attention to us, we may quietly do as we have always done."

He smiled his acknowledgment.

Although she understood perfectly, she was enjoying playing with him. "And what is it you would like of me, Palombara?"

"I find it inconvenient always having to watch over my shoulder," he replied.

"So you wish Vicenze . . . got rid of? You think I can do that? And that I would?"

"I am quite sure you could," he replied. "But I don't want him killed. I would be suspected, whatever the circumstances. And of rather more practical importance than that, he would only be replaced, and by someone I don't know, and therefore would find harder to predict."

She nodded. "You have been in Byzantium long enough to learn a little wisdom."

He smiled and inclined his head. "I need Vicenze's attention diverted, something that will give him no time to concentrate on destroying me."

She considered carefully. "You cannot afford to leave alive someone who will kill you if they can. Sooner or later they will find the opportunity. You cannot stay awake all the time. One day you will forget, be at a disadvantage, too tired to think. Seize the time, Palombara, or he will."

He realized with a wave of certainty that she was speaking from her own experience, and the instant after he knew exactly where and when. The grief was for Gregory Vatatzes, but she had had no choice, for her own survival. Was Arsenios Vatatzes's death her doing also? One of her vengeances?

"The important thing is that only you and I know this." He chose his words carefully, edged with double meaning. "While I appreciate your help, I cannot afford to be in your debt."

"You won't be," she promised. "You have given me knowledge of papal plans which enables me to . . . revise my situation on the union with Rome. That is important to me."

He rose to his feet and she did also, standing close enough to him that he could smell the perfume of her hair and her skin. If the balance between them had been just a little different, he would have touched her, and maybe more than that. As it was, their understanding was deep, even intimate. She would curb Vicenze for him, and it would amuse her to do so. If he ever presented a danger to her, with intense regret, she would kill him. They both knew that, too. The difference between them was that apart from his admiration for her, his involvement was ultimately sealed in his mind, his urgent, busy intellect; there was no wave strong enough to knock him off his feet, bury him, pummel him, and carry him far, far out of his depth. Whereas she cared passionately.

He envied her that.

Seventy-two

CONSTANTINE PACED THE FLOOR OF HIS BEAUTIFUL ROOM with the icons, grasping at the air with his hands.

"Please help her, Anastasius. She is so wounded by the betrayal, she is ill with grief. I think she does not care if she lives or not. I have done all I can, but I am no use. Theodosia is a good woman, perhaps the best I know. How can a man abandon a wife of years for some . . . some harlot with a pretty face, just because she may give him a child?"

"Yes, of course I'll go to her," Anna replied. "But I have no cure for grief. All I can do is wait with her . . . try to persuade her to eat, help her to sleep. But the pain will still be there when she wakens."

Constantine breathed out a great sigh. "Thank you." He smiled suddenly. "I knew you would."

Anna found Theodosia Skleros suffering in spirit as deeply as Constantine had said. She was a dark-haired woman of great dignity, if not beauty. She was sitting in a chair, staring out of the window with unfocused eyes.

Anna carried over another chair and sat near her, for a long time saying nothing.

Finally Theodosia turned to her, as if her presence required some response. "I don't know who you are," she said politely. "Or why you have come. I did not send for you, and I seek no counseling. There is no purpose you can serve here, except the easing of your own sense of duty. Please feel released from obligation and leave. There is probably someone you can serve elsewhere."

"I am a physician," Anna explained. "Anastasius Zarides. I came because Bishop Constantine is deeply concerned for you. He told me you are the finest woman he knows."

"There is no comfort in being 'fine' alone," Theodosia said bitterly.

"There is not much comfort in doing anything alone," Anna replied. "I hadn't imagined you did it for comfort. From what Bishop Constantine said, I had thought it was simply who you were."

Theodosia turned slowly and looked at her, very slight surprise in her face, but no light, no hope. "Is that supposed to cure me?" she said with mockery. "I have no interest in being a saint."

"Perhaps you would like to be dead, but you haven't the anger yet to commit that sin, because it would be irrevocable. Or perhaps you are just afraid of the physical pain of dying?"

"Please stop insulting me and go away," Theodosia said clearly. "I have no need of you." She looked back out of the window.

"Would you want him back, if he came?" Anna asked her.

"No!" Then Theodosia drew in her breath sharply and turned to face Anna again. "I'm not grieving for him, I am mourning what I believed he was. Perhaps you can't understand that. . . ."

"Do you imagine you are the only person to taste the dregs of disillusion?"

"Did you not understand me when I told you to go away?"

"Yes. The words are simple enough. You keep twisting your hands. Your eyes are sunken and your color is bad. Do you have a headache?"

"I ache everywhere," Theodosia replied.

"You are not drinking enough. Your skin will begin to hurt soon, I expect, then your stomach, although I imagine that pains you already. And you will become constipated."

Theodosia winced. "That is too personal, and it is not your business."

"I am a physician. Are you trying to punish someone by deliberately afflicting your body? Do you imagine your husband cares?"

"My God, you are cruel! You're heartless!" Theodosia accused.

"Your body doesn't care about just or unjust, only practical," Anna pointed out. "I cannot stop your heart aching, any more than I could stop my own, but I can heal your body, if you don't leave it too long."

"Oh, give me the herbs, then go away and leave me in peace," Theodosia said impatiently.

But Anna stayed until Theodosia was asleep. And she returned every day for the next week, then every second or third day. The grief did not go, but the urgency of it abated. They spoke together of many things, seldom personal, more of art and philosophy, of tastes in food, of works of literature and thought.

"Thank you," Constantine said to Anna a little more than a month later. "Your gentleness of spirit has bound the wound. Perhaps in time God may heal it. I am truly grateful."

Anna had seen Theodosia at her deepest distress, at her most vulnerable and humiliated. Anna understood very well why she did not wish their association to continue. It was forever taking the plaster off the wound to look at it again. It was wiser to leave it alone to mend unseen.

She acknowledged Constantine's thanks and changed the subject.

Seventy-three

༄

ANNA PICKED DELICATELY AT THE HERB LEAVES IN HER small garden. It was time to harvest many of them. The wild poppy heads were nearly ready to gather. She watered and tended the hellebore, aconite, digitalis, pennyroyal, and the mandrake she was carefully encouraging. If it grew successfully, she would take some of it to Avram Shachar. It would be a small gift in return for all his kindness.

Here in the shelter of the house on one side, and the outer wall on the other, the sun was warm on her shoulders, a memory of summer as the year faded fast. If the union did not become real enough to hold off Charles of Anjou and his crusaders, next summer might be the last before they attacked.

Would she be one of those who tried to escape, or would she stay, as perhaps a physician should? She would be needed here.

And afterward, what then? Life in an occupied city, under an enforced crusader rule. There would be no Orthodox Church then. But if she was honest, it was becoming more and more difficult for her to ally wholeheartedly with the Orthodox faith. She was beginning to accept that the way to God was a solitary one, born of a passion and a hunger of the spirit that no hierarchy, no ritual however beautiful, could give you, nor in the end prevent you from achieving.

She missed Giuliano. She could still remember, as if it had been moments ago, the look in his face when he had seen her in a dress. It was almost as if part of him had known and been repelled so intensely that it had churned his stomach, filled his mind with an inner betrayal he could not bear.

Afterward on the voyage back, he had made a massive effort of will to forget it, but nothing could erase the knowledge from his mind or hers. In a way, they had gone back almost to the beginning again, strangers feeling their way delicately.

Now she would do for him the only thing she could: release him from his own sense of being tainted by his mother's betrayal, unloved and possibly unable to love, as if her blood in him were a poison in his soul.

If she was able to discover more, perhaps it would not be as bad as Zoe had said.

Where would Zoe have looked for Maddalena Agallon? Was there still an Agallon family in Constantinople, or had they remained in the cities of their exile?

Anna collected what she had harvested and took it inside. She washed her hands, separated the leaves and roots, labeled them, and put them away, all except the lemon thyme and the mandrake root big enough to harvest. She wrapped them separately to take.

She would begin her quest by asking Shachar. Months passed as she awaited his answers.

She came in answer to his summons. The heavy skies of early winter were closing in, and his message told her to come warmly clothed and prepared for a long ride.

"I have made inquiries about the Agallons. We are going to a monastery," Shachar informed her. "It is several miles outside the city. We may not be back until morning."

She felt a quickening in her pulse, fear, and surprise.

He smiled, leading the way through to the back courtyard of his house where she had never been before. Two mules were ready, and obviously he intended to leave without delay.

They were a mile beyond the outskirts of the city, and it was dark, almost moonless, when he spoke to her quietly. "I have found Maddalena's sister, Eudoxia. I have little idea what she will tell you, but she is old and ill, a nun in a monastery. You are calling as a physician to see her and possibly treat her. You may ask what you wish, but you will have to accept whatever she says, and under whatever conditions she imposes. Your treatment is not conditional. If she chooses to tell you nothing, then still you will do your best for her."

"I?" she said quickly. "What about you?"

"I am a Jew," he reminded her. "I will be your manservant. I know the way and you do not. I will wait outside. You are both a Christian and a eunuch, the ideal person to treat a nun."

They rode together in silent companionship for another two hours until the black mass of the monastery loomed out of the shadows on the hillside. It was a huge building with small, high windows, like a fortress or a prison. Shachar was admitted only as far as the shelter of the kitchen.

Anna was conducted along narrow stone corridors to a cell where an old woman lay on the bed. Her face was ravaged by age and grief, but it still held the remnants of great beauty.

Anna did not need to ask who she was. The likeness to Giuliano jarred her as if she had been physically struck.

She tried to swallow the tightness in her throat and thanked the nun who had escorted her, then stepped into the room. There was a plain wooden crucifix above the bed, and near the door was a dark, severe, and beautiful icon of Mary. "Sister Eudoxia?" she said quietly.

The woman opened her eyes curiously and then sat up a little farther on the bed. "The physician. They are kind to have sent for you, but you are wasting your time, young man. There is no cure for age, except God's cure, and I think I shall gain that quite soon."

"Do you have pain?" Anna asked, sitting down.

"Only such as mortality and regret bring to all of us," Eudoxia replied.

Anna reached for her pulse and felt it, thin but regular enough. She did not have a fever. "It is not a trouble. Do you sleep well?"

"Well enough."

"Are you sure? Is there nothing I can do for you? No discomfort I can ease?"

"Perhaps I could sleep better. Sometimes I dream. I would like to do that less," the old woman replied with a slight smile. "Can you help that?"

"A draft could ease you. What about pain?"

"I am stiff, but that is time catching up with me."

"Sister Eudoxia . . ." Now that the moment had come, what Anna had to say seemed intrusive, and she was ashamed.

The old woman looked at her curiously, waiting. Then she frowned. "What troubles you, physician? Are you looking for a way to tell me I am going to die? I have made peace with it."

"There is something I would like very much to know, and only you can tell me," Anna began. "I recently sailed to Acre, on a Venetian ship. The captain was Giuliano Dandolo. . . ." She saw the shock in Eudoxia's face, the sudden leap of pain.

"Giuliano?" Eudoxia said, no more than a breath between her lips.

"Can you tell me about his mother?" Anna asked. "The truth. I will tell him only if you give me permission to. He suffers bitterly, believing that she left him willingly, not loving or wanting him."

Eudoxia put a frail, blue-veined hand up to her cheek, fingers still slender. "Maddalena ran away with Giovanni Dandolo," she said quietly. "They were married in Sicily. Our father followed her, found her, and took her away by force. He brought her back to Nicea. He married her to the man he had chosen for her in the first place."

"But her marriage to Dandolo . . . " Anna protested.

"Father had it annulled. He did not know that Maddalena was already with child."

Eudoxia was pale; tears welled in her eyes. Anna leaned over with a soft muslin and wiped them gently. "Giuliano?" she asked.

"Her husband accepted the situation to begin with. He took Maddalena to live some distance away. However, when the baby was born, and was a boy, he became jealous. He was brutal, not only to Maddalena, but he threatened the child also. At first it was only in little ways, and Maddalena thought he would get over it." Her voice was strained with old grief, sharp again as when it was new. "But Maddalena's husband knew she still loved the boy's father, and every time he looked at the child, it was a reminder, another twist to the knife of his jealousy. His violence increased. Giuliano began to have accidents. Twice the servants rescued him only just in time from being seriously injured, perhaps killed."

Anna could imagine it only too vividly: the fear, the shame, the constant anxiety.

"To protect the boy, Maddalena took him and fled," Eudoxia continued. "She came to me. I was married then, and happy enough. My husband bored me." She flinched at the admission. "He was wealthy, and gave me a good life, but he could not give me children. In fact, he could not . . ." She left the sentence unfinished.

Anna smiled and touched the thin hand on top of the nun's gown. "Did you help Maddalena?"

"I did as she asked, which was that I should rear the child as my own. My husband agreed. I think at first he was quite happy to do it. I took Giuliano, and gave Maddalena what support I could." She blinked, but not fast enough to hold the tears. "I loved the boy. . . ."

"Go on," Anna whispered.

"All was well, until Giuliano was five. My husband became possessive, and even more . . . dogmatic, more boring. I . . ." She let out her breath in a sigh. "I was beautiful when I was younger, like Maddalena. We were so alike people sometimes mistook one of us for the other. . . ."

Anna waited.

"I was lonely, both in mind and in body," Eudoxia went on. "I took a lover—in fact, more than one. I behaved badly. My husband accused me of being a common whore, and said that he had witnesses to prove it." She gave a deep, shuddering sigh. "Maddalena took the blame. She insisted it was she, and not I, who had been with the man. She did it for Giuliano's sake—I know that—not mine. I could care for the boy, she couldn't."

Anna found she could barely swallow the pain choking her throat.

"Maddalena was found guilty, and suffered the penalty for being a whore. She died not long afterward, beaten and destitute. I think by then she wanted to die. She never stopped loving Giovanni Dandolo, and there was nothing else left for her."

Eudoxia's voice was choked with tears. "My husband knew it was I who had been in the tavern that night, and he knew why Maddalena had lied for me. He forced me to grant him a divorce, and to take the nun's veil. But he refused to take Giuliano. He would put him on the street, or sell him to some dealer in children, for God knows what use." She shivered. "I took him myself. I ran away from Nicea and begged and stole and prostituted my way to Venice with him. There I gave him to his father. A Dandolo, he wasn't difficult to find. I thought of staying in Venice, even of dying there. But I hadn't the courage. There was something in me which needed a better atonement than that. I came back and took the veil, as I had promised my husband I would. I have been here nearly forty years. Perhaps I have made my peace."

Anna nodded, the tears wet on her own face.

"A human mistake, a loneliness and a hunger so easy to understand. Of course you have made your peace. Now may I bring Giuliano so you can tell him?"

"Please—please do!" Eudoxia cried. "I . . . I did not even know if he was still alive. Tell me, is he a good man, a happy man?"

"He is very good," Anna replied. "And this will give him a greater gift of happiness than anything else possible."

"Thank you." Eudoxia sighed. "Don't bother with the draft for sleep. I shan't need it."

Seventy-four

G IULIANO HAD GIVEN THE ICON TO THE POPE. HE WOULD have liked to give it back to Michael, but with reluctance he understood why that could not be. If he did, it would only necessitate Michael packing it up and sending it again. It could be lost at sea, especially at this time of year.

So when the pope's envoy had approached him in Venice, he had produced the icon immediately and presented it to the man to take with him to Rome, a gift from the Venetian Republic, which had rescued it from pirates. No one believed that, but it did not matter. They split a good bottle of Venetian wine, laughed hard, and the envoy left with the icon, well guarded by a number of soldiers.

Giuliano left for Constantinople and arrived six weeks later, sailing up the Sea of Marmara against a heavy wind and glad to dock at last in the Golden Horn. The familiar outline of the great lighthouse, the warm red of the Hagia Sophia, were strangely pleasing to his mind, yet even as he thought of it, he was also aware that it was an illusion of safety.

As soon as he stepped ashore, the harbormaster gave him a letter with his name on it and the word *urgent* on the outside. It had already been there two days.

Dear Giuliano,

Through the good offices of my friend Avram Shachar, I have found a close relative of your mother. However, there is little time. She is old and very fragile. I have visited her, and I fear she has not long left.

She told me the truth of your parents, and I could repeat it to you myself, but it would be far better that you should hear it from her. It would also bring her great peace.

I promise you it is a story you will want to hear.

Anastasius

Giuliano thanked the harbormaster and returned to his ship. He handed over command to his lieutenant, and without even changing his sea clothes, he went straight to Anastasius's house.

Anastasius stood at his doorway, talking to Leo. He turned and saw Giuliano, and his face lit with pleasure.

Giuliano strode forward and clasped his hand, forgetting for a moment how slender it was. He eased his grasp. "Thank you more than I can say."

Anastasius took a step backward, but he was still smiling. He regarded Giuliano's disheveled clothes, the leather worn with use and still stained here and there by salt water. "We should go tonight. It will be a hard ride," he said apologetically. "But we shouldn't wait."

Giuliano dismissed the inconvenience instantly but was glad to rest an hour or two.

Leo went to hire horses for the journey, and Anastasius himself prepared and served them a brief meal.

"Is Simonis ill?" Giuliano asked.

Anastasius smiled bleakly. "She has chosen to live elsewhere. She comes in during the day, now and then."

He did not add any more, and Giuliano sensed that the subject was painful.

They set out at dusk, at first riding side by side. He was excited, longing to hear the story, afraid of what it would be, how it might damage the fragile defense he had built against the truth.

Rather than endure his own thoughts, he told her about the icon and how he had stolen it from Vicenze, replacing it with the other picture, and what he had heard of its unveiling in front of the pope and all the cardinals. They both laughed so hard that for several minutes they were breathless.

Then the road narrowed and they were obliged to go single file, and further conversation was impossible.

When at last they arrived at the monastery, they were tired and cold, but they did little more than take a hot drink and wash off the dirt of travel before Anastasius asked to see Eudoxia.

They found her pale, breathing shallowly, and close to death, but her joy at seeing Giuliano, knowing immediately who he was, transfigured her.

"So like your mother," she whispered, touching his face with her fragile hand, cold when he clasped it in his. She told him the story, as she had told it to Anastasius. Giuliano was not ashamed to weep for his mother, for his own misjudgment of her, or for Eudoxia.

He stayed with her for most of the night, tiptoeing away to his own rough bed only toward dawn.

He rose late the following day and attended a service with the nuns. He could never thank his aunt enough. He sat with her again, helped her eat a little and drink, all the time telling her about his life, his travels at sea, and especially his journey to Jerusalem.

He found it hard to leave, but her strength was slipping away and he knew it was right to let her rest. There was a peace in her smile, a calmness in her, that had not been there upon their arrival.

And most profoundly, he marveled at the truth. His mother had loved him. All that had been broken inside him was healing. How could he ever thank Anastasius for that?

He and Anastasius set out, riding single file again, down the new pathway, and he was glad of the chance to be alone with his thoughts. In one day, what had been a feeling of abandonment and shame had become the deepest love imaginable. His mother had sacrificed every happiness she had so that he would survive and be loved.

Now his Byzantine heritage was rich with passionate, lifelong, and selfless love. Surely no child had been loved more? He was glad that in the darkness of the long ride, Anastasius could not see the tears on his face and that with the frequent need to pass single file on the rough road, there was little chance to speak.

Seventy-five

∾

ANNA SAT WITH EIRENE VATATZES IN HER RICH, UNFEM-
inine bedroom with its somber colors and rigid patterns on the
walls. It was at once beautiful and lonely. Now it smelled stale, of perspi-
ration and decay. She did all she could for Eirene to lessen the pain, and
simply by being there, by a touch, a word, to still some of her fear. She did
not lie to her; it would have been pointless. She knew Eirene would not recover this time. Each day her strength lessened and her times of complete
lucidity became briefer.

Anna dearly wished that she could ask Eirene some of the unanswered
questions about the plot to usurp Michael.

Eirene tossed in the bed, turning over, dragging the sheet with her. She
moaned in pain. Anna leaned over and straightened it where it was crumpled, then dipped a small cloth in a bowl of cool water and herbs and
wrung it out, freeing the perfume of it into the air. She placed the cloth
gently on Eirene's brow, and for a few moments she was quiet.

Maybe only Demetrios's intentions now were important. But Eirene
was Anna's patient, and she could not tax her with it. For nearly an hour
she lay motionless on the bed, as if she were sinking into the last peace of
death. Then she gasped and started turning again and again, tangling the
covers.

"Zoe!" she said suddenly. Her eyes were closed, but there was such an
expression of ferocity in her face that it was hard to believe she was not

conscious. "Soon you'll be all alone," she whispered. "We'll be dead. What will you do then? Nobody to love, nobody to hate."

Anna stiffened. She knew what Eirene was thinking—Zoe and Gregory. The jealousy still corroded her inside; nothing could take that away. Anna put out her hand and laid it gently on Eirene's wrist.

"He had to die," Eirene began again, shaking her head abruptly from side to side. "Deserved it."

Anna was startled. Was Eirene's unforgiveness for her husband really so deep that she had wanted Gregory dead, his throat torn out and his body left bleeding on the stones of some street he did not know?

"No, he didn't deserve it," Anna said aloud, not knowing if Eirene still remembered what she had said or even if she could hear anything at all outside her own head.

Eirene's voice came back so strongly, it startled her. "Yes, he did. He kept the icons his father stole when they were leaving the burning city. He should have given them back. I could have killed him myself, if I'd dared. I should have."

Anna looked at her and saw her eyes were open and clear, the anger burning hot in them. "You knew that Gregory had the icons from the sack of 1204?" Anna asked.

"Not Gregory, you fool!" Eirene said witheringly, now fully conscious. "His cousin Arsenios. That's why Zoe killed him." She closed her eyes again, as if too weary to be bothered with anyone so stupid. "Gregory knew that," she added as if it were an afterthought. "Revenge. Always revenge." She sighed and seemed to drift into sleep again.

Anna pieced it together. Zoe had killed Arsenios in revenge for his keeping the icons, and Gregory knew it. He would have felt compelled to retaliate for his cousin's death, and knowing that, Zoe had struck first.

But Zoe's revenge had not been only Arsenios's death, it was his daughter's humiliation and his son's death as well. And unwittingly, Anna had contributed to that in her medical treatment of the daughter. She was cold now at the thought. No wonder Eirene hated Zoe. How could she not?

She looked down now at her lying on the bed. Eirene's face was not so much at peace as totally empty of passion or even intelligence. Had Gregory ever loved her? Did he care about her ugliness, or had she cared about it so much that in the end she had forced him to care also?

For another two days, Eirene seemed to remain much the same. She was often asleep, but apparently easier in her mind, the pain less acute. Then quite suddenly she became worse. She woke in the night barely able to move, her body drenched in sweat. Anna treated her with herbs and drugs as much as she dared. But sometime after midnight of the third day, Anna was standing close to the bed looking at Eirene, and she saw that even in the warm glow of the candlelight her face was haggard and there was a gray pallor to her skin.

Eirene opened her sunken, clouded eyes and stared at Anna.

Anna ached with pity for her, but Eirene was beyond physical help. "Would you like me to send for Demetrios?"

"Given up at last?" Eirene's lips were dry and her throat tight. "Give me some more of that herb that tastes like gall." She blinked and stared at Anna. She must know she had not long, and the breaking of her body consumed her.

Anna ached to help her, but if she gave Eirene another dose of the poppy, it might kill her. She decided to do it anyway.

Anna nodded and turned aside to reach for the small bottle. She would put it with a lot of water—in fact, mostly water. The illusion of opium might help as much as the reality. After Eirene took three or four sips, Anna laid her back as gently as she could, straightened the covers, then went to the door and called the servant.

"Fetch Demetrios," she told him. "I think she has not long left."

The servant went away, footsteps rapid on the tiled floor. He returned ten minutes later to say that Demetrios had gone out earlier and not yet returned. Apparently, he had not expected to be needed so soon.

"If he returns, tell him his mother is dying," Anna answered, then turned away and went back into the room.

The candle guttered. She lit another.

Suddenly Eirene opened her eyes again, and her voice was quite clear. "I'm going to die before morning, aren't I."

"I think so," Anna replied honestly.

"Fetch Demetrios. I have something I need to give him."

"I already sent for him. He's not in the house, and the servant cannot tell me where he is."

Eirene was silent for a few moments. "Then I suppose you'll have to do," she said at last. "Gregory thought Zoe loved him, but she betrayed him with Michael," she said. "You didn't know that, did you?" There was satisfaction in her. "Michael is Helena's father. Imagine that! That would have given Bessarion a double right to the throne, don't you see?"

A chill thought struck Anna. This could alter more than she could imagine. It explained Helena's part in the usurpation totally. "How do you know that Helena is really Michael's child?" she asked.

"I have letters," Eirene said, biting her lip as the pain washed over her again. "From him to Zoe."

Anna was skeptical. "How did you get them?"

Eirene smiled, although it was more a baring of the teeth. "Gregory took them."

"Does Zoe know you have these letters?"

"She knows Gregory did. She didn't know I took them from him. He never dared challenge me for them back."

Anna's mind was in turmoil, racing from one new meaning to another. "Helena doesn't know?" she asked yet again.

"It is better she doesn't," Eirene repeated wearily. "She would become impossible to manage."

"Why should I believe all this?"

"Because it is true," Eirene replied. "I bequeathed some of the letters to Helena. My cousin will give them to her in time But the rest are there in my safe box. The key is under my pillow. Give them to Demetrios." She smiled slightly. "Once Helena knows, then she'll have the power. That's why Zoe has never told her." She took a long, shuddering breath. "But now I don't care. It'll be hell for Zoe . . . every day." A faint smile parted her lips, as if to taste something sweet.

She closed her eyes, and gradually all expression emptied out of her face. She slept for perhaps half an hour.

There was a noise in the corridor outside, and the door swung open. Demetrios came in, dalmatica swirling, wet from the rain, his eyes dark and angry.

"Mother?" he said quietly. "Mother?"

Eirene opened her eyes, taking several moments to focus. "Demetrios?"

"I'm here."

"Good. Get Anastasius to give you . . . the letters. Don't lose them! Don't throw . . ." She took a long, deep breath and let it out with a sigh, a little gasp in her throat. Then silence.

Demetrios waited for several more minutes and then stood up. "She's gone. What letters was she talking about? Where are they?"

Anna took the key from under the pillow and went to the box behind the icon on the wall, as Eirene had told her. The letters were in a neatly tied bundle.

"Thank you," he said, taking them from her hand. "You can go. I would rather be alone with her."

There was nothing for Anna to do but obey.

Seventy-six

∾

ZOE HEARD OF EIRENE'S DEATH WITHOUT SURPRISE; SHE had been ill for some time. It was not exactly grief Zoe felt, for they had been both friends and enemies. What troubled her was that they had also been co-conspirators against Michael, when Zoe had believed that Bessarion could have usurped the throne and led a resistance against the union with Rome and that such a thing would have saved both Constantinople and the Church.

Now she knew that that could never have succeeded. Justinian had realized it and done what Zoe should have done herself. His action had had the advantage that it was he who had paid the price for it, not she.

The thought that gnawed at the back of her mind as she paced the floor in her marvelous room was that Anastasius, inquisitive and unpredictable, was the one who had treated Eirene in her last days. Sometimes when people are ill, frightened, and realizing that death cannot be held at bay any longer, they tell secrets they never would have were they going to face the results.

And then there was Helena. She had changed since Eirene's death. She had always been arrogant, but there was a self-confidence in her now that was disturbing, as if nothing frightened her anymore.

Did she think that now Eirene was dead, Demetrios would marry her? That made no sense. He would have to observe a decent period of mourning.

But as Zoe thought back on Helena's mood, her behavior, there was certainly no new warmth toward Demetrios; if anything, rather the opposite. She seemed consumed in herself. It was something far more powerful than security or status; something, perhaps, like a glimpse of the throne!

Could there be another attempt at usurpation, one that this time might succeed? The situation was vastly changed, and this time Zoe would have no part in it. But could she betray it to Michael? She could not. Her part in the last plot had been too close. If Helena attempted and failed, Zoe would be ruined.

Michael was their only hope. His overthrow would bring chaos to the empire, and to her personally, a whole new balance of relationships. Worst of all, Helena would exercise her long-hoped-for revenge.

In the end, survival was all. Byzantium must not be raped again. Whatever was paid to prevent that, it was not too much.

Seventy-seven

∽

THE MAN WHO BROUGHT THE MESSAGE FROM THE POPE was obviously tired and profoundly unhappy. Courtesy required that Palombara offer him refreshment, but as soon as the servant had gone to prepare it, he pleaded to know the news.

"God knows we tried to create a union, but we have failed," the man said miserably. "The king of the Two Sicilies is gathering more ships and more allies with every passing week, and we can no longer pretend that the Orthodox Church is one with us in spirit and intent. It is only too obvious that their acceptance of our hand of friendship is a farce, a convenience to protect their physical safety, no more."

Palombara's mind was heavy with the terrible inevitability of it. Yet he had hoped that somehow the passion for survival would overcome.

"If you wish to return to Rome, my lord, the Holy Father gives you leave to do so." The messenger's voice dropped. "The Holy Father has recognized that he no longer has any control over the actions of the king. There will be another crusade, perhaps as soon as 1281, and it will be an army such as we have not seen before." He met Palombara's eyes. "But if you wish to remain in Constantinople, at least for the time being, there may be some Christian work to do here." He made the sign of the cross, naturally in the Roman way.

After the man had gone, Palombara remained alone in the great room, watching the afternoon sun sink over the ferries and water taxies and the distant business of the harbor. Rome saw Constantinople's tolerance of ideas as a moral laxity, its patience with even the most ridiculous or abstruse idea, rather than suppression of it, to be a weakness. They did not see that blind obedience eventually ended in the suffocation of thought.

Palombara did not want to return to Rome and work at some timeserving job shuffling papers, delivering messages, playing at the politics of office. He faced the window, and the light came in on his face. He closed his eyes and felt its warmth on his eyelids.

The darkness was closing in, but he was not yet ready to give up. If Charles of Anjou landed here, Palombara might save something from the wreckage. Definitely he could not simply walk away.

He found the words quite clear in his mind. "Please, dear Lord, do not let all this be destroyed. Please do not let us do that to them—or to ourselves."

He stood silent for a moment.

"Amen," he added.

Seventy-eight

GIULIANO DANDOLO RETURNED TO VENICE WITH A SHIP filled with gold from all over Europe. In England, Spain, France, and the Holy Roman Empire, men were preparing for a great crusade. Some of the ships were built already. The shipyards worked night and day. Charles of Anjou had paid his share of the contract; he would receive what he had ordered.

Nevertheless, Giuliano was not happy as he stood on the balcony and stared at the splendor of the dying sun over the Adriatic.

The doge had told him that Venice had abrogated the treaty it had made with Byzantium. It had lasted just two years. Giuliano had had nothing to do with it, neither its creation nor its destruction, yet he felt racked with shame for the betrayal of it.

He stared at the light on the water, watching it change. The translucency of it, the moving shadows, were so subtle that one nameless tone vanished into another. It was like the Bosphorus.

What would happen to Constantinople when the crusaders landed?

The whole issue of fighting over faith was absurd. How far from the teachings of Christ were all these quarrels as to who had power or rights over what. He remembered the conversations he had had with Anastasius at sea and in that desolate site that might, or might not, have been Golgotha.

The thought of Anastasius cut to the heart of his pain. How would the crusaders treat him? How could he protect himself? The thought of it was

too terrible to allow into Giuliano's mind. It was the whole city that mattered, and all the lands around it, but in the end, as perhaps with everyone, it all came down to those you knew, the faces, the voices, the people
you broke bread with and who trusted you.

The shadows were stronger. The light was fading rapidly.

Seventy-nine

༶

ANNA HAD BEEN CALLED YET AGAIN TO THE HOUSE OF Joanna Strabomytes, even though the servants did not know if there was money left to pay her. It did not matter. Payment was not part of Anna's decision to come. She was here not to prolong her suffering, only to ease the pain of her letting go.

Joanna was wasted by disease so that she looked far more than her forty-odd years, and now she had little time left. The draft Anna had given her had afforded an hour or so of peace, and she was no longer troubled by needless pain of body or the torment of mind that twisted inside her. She had said little about it. It had wounded her so deeply, it had robbed her of words, other than the same question over and over—couldn't her husband have waited?

Leonicus had left Joanna as she was dying, because he was in love with Theodosia, whose own husband had so cruelly abandoned her. Leonicus would not wait until he was free; he wished his own happiness now, this week, this month. Or perhaps Theodosia wanted it, and he had not had the courage or the honor to deny her.

For once, the hot, still room was silent as Anna stood at the end of the bed making certain Joanna was really asleep before she turned and walked away. She went out briefly into the courtyard, where in spite of the summer heat she could at least escape from the odor of herbs and the bodily functions of the dying.

Theodosia had been a religious woman all her life. Anna pictured her at prayer, kneeling before Constantine in devout gratitude for the sacrament of repentance and absolution. Theodosia knew the bitterness, the shock, of being rejected. How could she, of all people, do this to another woman? What sweetness was there in taking any man at such a price?

Would Anna have wanted even Giuliano this way?

Theodosia had been in good health when her husband had gone, and it had hurt her almost beyond bearing, bringing her to the edge of suicide. Anna remembered it still with pity. Joanna was ill and dying. Could Theodosia really mean to do this? Was Joanna suffering some kind of delusion, a despair that was part of her illness? Perhaps it was Anna's judgment that was hasty, partial in knowledge and therefore completely unfair?

During one of Joanna's better spells, Anna gave careful instructions to the servants. Then, after returning to her own home to collect more herbs, she went to Theodosia's house and requested to see her.

"I am sorry, but the lady Theodosia is unable to receive you," the servant said some moments later.

Anna insisted upon the urgency and importance of her errand. The servant took the request again. The second time, it was Leonicus who came to the entrance himself. There was a sadness in his eyes as well as a certain anger when he faced Anna.

"I am sorry, but Theodosia does not wish to speak with you," he said. "She has no need of your services, and there is really nothing further to add. Thank you for coming, but please do not do so again." He turned and walked away, leaving the servant to close the door in Anna's face.

Anna returned to complete her care for Leonicus's wife and ease her pain of mind and body as well as she could. She mixed herbs for her, sat with her when she could not sleep, spoke to her of anything and everything she could think of that was funny, kind, or offered any beauty. And then she held her hand as her consciousness slipped away, and then finally her life.

By September, much of the overt anger at Rome's demands upon the Church was swept away by the more urgent anxieties of news about the gathering armies to the west.

Anna was in the Blachernae Palace, having attended various eunuchs who were indisposed with minor illnesses, when she was sent for to go to

Nicephoras's rooms. She found him unusually grim, his face dark with anxiety.

"I have just received news from Bishop Palombara," Nicephoras said. "The pope is dead."

"Again? I mean . . . another pope?" She could scarcely believe it. "So we have no leader in Rome to argue with, even if we wanted to?"

"It's far worse than that," he said quickly, no longer even attempting to mask his fear. "Pope Nicholas exacted from Charles of Anjou an oath not to attack Byzantium. Nicholas's death frees him from that. Apparently oaths do not carry from one pope to another." Bitter humor flashed in his eyes for an instant, then was gone.

Anna was stunned. "What does the emperor say?" She heard her voice wavering.

"I am about to tell him." Nicephoras drew in his breath deeply, then let it out in a sigh. "He will find it very hard. I would like you to come with me . . . in case he is . . . ill."

She answered only with a nod, and as he turned to lead the way to the emperor's rooms, she followed him with a heavy sense of foreboding.

Michael was sitting at a table writing when she entered behind Nicephoras. The strong sunlight slanted across the chair, the papers spread across the tabletop, and the assorted pens. It was a cruel light, and it laid bare his weariness. The heavy gray was not only in his hair, but in his beard; but more than that, there were shadows around his eyes, and his skin had a thin, papery texture. Even the iron will that had carried him to military victory was fading. Perhaps harder than that of arms was the victory of the mind over the fractiousness of his people, the ceaseless threats to his power, his life, his family, the quarrels over every conceivable issue arising from union with Rome. And every year there was at least one ugly suggestion that this person or that had more right to the throne than he. He was never safe from the threat of a usurper.

"Yes?" he asked, looking up at Nicephoras. Reading bad news in the man's face, he tensed, a tightening of expression that was barely perceptible to Anna.

Briefly, Nicephoras told the emperor that Pope Nicholas III was dead. There was no need to add that there was now nothing to prevent Charles of Anjou from sacking Constantinople as he wanted to and in time conquering what was left of the Byzantine Empire.

Michael sat perfectly still, absorbing the shock. Anna saw the exhaustion in him, the fight not to crumple under the blow. He had preserved his people in the city for eighteen long, difficult years, and now she was seeing clearly at what cost it had been to himself.

Was it surprising if he felt beaten, even by fate, now that yet another pope was dead? Anna felt it, too, a gathering of dread. She was afraid of a future without him.

Constantine was ill again and sent for Anna. She took the herbs she thought she would need and followed his servant along the busy street and finally up the steps into Constantine's increasingly handsome house. Every time she went there, there was some new ornament or embellishment, always the gift of a grateful petitioner that the bishop explained he could not refuse.

She found him lying in his bed, his face pale. From the position of his heavy body, he was apparently in some discomfort. She considered it was probably caused largely by anxiety, a stomach too clenched with emotion to digest his food.

"I must be well in two weeks' time," he told her with some concern, his eyes narrowed, his lips tight.

"I will do all I can," she promised. "You would greatly improve your health if you were to rest more."

"Rest!" His body flinched as if she had hurt him. "Every hour is precious. Do you not know the peril we are in?"

"I know, but your health still demands that you rest. What is happening in two weeks' time?"

He smiled. "I am going to perform the marriage ceremony for Leonicus Strabomytes and Theodosia. It will be in the Hagia Sophia—a truly splendid occasion. An example to the people of the blessing and mercy of God. It will uplift everyone and fire a new piety in them."

Anna assumed she must have misunderstood. "Theodosia Skleros?"

He looked at her steadily. "Does your largeness of heart not extend to her, Anastasius? I have given Theodosia a special icon of the Blessed Virgin Mary as a token of her absolution."

Anna was amazed. "Theodosia and Leonicus committed real sin, and they did it knowingly, and with choice. They deliberately took what was not theirs, and they kept it. They haven't repented a jot!" She said so to him harshly, her words tearing out of her all the loneliness and her own weight of guilt that she had carried through the years, knowing the fault was still in her. "It is a mockery of those who are truly sorry, and have paid long and bitterly."

"I asked no payment of her, except humility and obedience to the Church," he retorted. "You have sins also, Anastasius. It ill becomes you to judge when you yourself have neither confessed nor repented. I don't know what your sins are, but they are heavy and deep. I know that, because I see it in your eyes. I know you ache to confess and find absolution, but your pride holds you prisoner, and you cling to it rather than to the Church."

She said nothing, almost breathless with the accuracy of his blow, deep as the bone, shocking her with pain.

He sat up, his hand on her wrist, his face close to hers. "You are in sin, Anastasius. Come to me and confess, in humility, and I will give you pardon."

She was frozen inside, as if he had in some profound way assaulted her. She could only remove his fingers from her arm and straighten the bottles on the table, then turn and leave, walking in a daze of misery and wild, twisting confusion. Never in her life had she felt more absolutely alone.

Eighty

୦୪୦

IT WAS AUTUMN OF 1280, A MONTH AFTER THE WEDDING, before Anna saw Theodosia again. They passed in the street without speaking, and Anna felt strangely snubbed, while being quite aware that it was foolish of her. They had not been friends; they had shared an experience of deep pain in Theodosia's life, and it was easy to understand why she would avoid someone who had seen her at her most vulnerable.

She stood in the street, the wind harsh in her face. Perhaps Constantine was right. Did Anna fail to forgive Theodosia because she could not forgive herself, for Eustathius and the child she had not wanted because it would have been his? It was she who was wrong, not Theodosia. She should go to her and apologize. It would be galling, bitter to swallow, but nothing less would make it right.

She started to walk again, urgently, even up the steepening incline, needing to have the apology made before her resolve weakened.

Theodosia received her reluctantly. She stood looking toward the window. Anna barely noticed that the room was more ornate than before, the floor newly tiled in marble, larger torch brackets gilded at the top.

"Thank you for coming," Theodosia said politely. "But I believe I told you last time you called that I have no need of your services." She turned and looked momentarily at Anna, and there was a curious emptiness in her eyes.

"I came to apologize to you," Anna said. "I presumed to think that you could not have been absolved for taking Joanna's husband from her when she was dying. That was arrogant of me to the point of absurdity. It is none of my business, and I have no right even to think it."

Theodosia shrugged slightly. "Yes, it is arrogant, but I accept your apology. I have the Church's absolution, and that is really all that counts." She half turned away.

Anna contradicted her. "Your face, your eyes, say that it doesn't count at all, because you don't believe it."

"It isn't a matter of belief, it's fact. Bishop Constantine said so," Theodosia replied tartly. "And, as you say, it is not your concern."

"The Church's absolution, or God's?" Anna refused to be dismissed.

Theodosia blinked. "I am not sure that I believe in God, or resurrection and eternity in your Christian sense. Of course I can't imagine time ending, no one can. It will go on, what else could it do? A kind of endless desert stretching without purpose into the darkness."

"You don't believe in heaven," countered Anna, "but surely what you have described is hell? Or one kind of hell, if not the deepest."

Theodosia's voice was tinged with sarcasm. "Is there deeper than that?"

"The deepest would be to have held heaven in your hands and let it slip away, to have known what it was and then lost it," Anna replied.

"And would the God you believe in do that to anyone?" Theodosia challenged. "It's bestial."

"God doesn't do it," Anna answered her without hesitation.

Theodosia's voice was harsh with pain. "Are you saying I did that to myself?"

Anna opened her mouth to deny it, then realized it was dishonest. "I have no idea," she said. "Did you have heaven, or only something that was good, and at least a belief in joy in some reachable future?"

Theodosia stared at her, anger, confusion, and grief in her face.

Anna felt a moment of pity so fierce, it took her breath away. "There is a way back," she said impulsively, then instantly knew it was a mistake.

"Back to what?" Theodosia asked, surprise in her voice, as if she had taken a step only to find the ground beneath her was no longer there.

Now it was Anna who turned away, walking alone to the door and outside into the street. She moved along the cobbles slowly, up steps and down them.

Punishment was for society's sense of order, necessary for survival. Theodosia executed her own punishment, and it was far more terrible than God would have given her, because it was destructive. God's punishment should be for the healing of the sinner, freeing him from the sin, to move on without it. By denying Theodosia's sin, Constantine had injured her in lying, and she had injured herself, because she knew better.

Anna turned the corner, and the wind was cold in her face.

She could not let the matter rest. She went to Constantine and found him busy ministering to supplicants of one sort or another.

"What can I do for you, Anastasius?" he asked guardedly. They were in his ocher-colored room facing onto the courtyard.

There was no purpose in trying to be tactful. "I have just visited Theodosia. She has lost the strength and comfort of her faith."

"Nonsense," Constantine said sharply. "She attends Mass every Sunday."

"I did not say she has fallen from the Church," Anna replied patiently. "I said she is without that inner light of hope, the trust that keeps us going even when we cannot see the way at all, but still feel the love of God . . . in the dark."

She saw a flash of amazement in Constantine's eyes, as if he had caught a glimpse of something he had barely guessed at before.

Anna went on with a surge of belief within herself. "She does not believe in a God who overlooks her offense without healing it, as if neither she nor it mattered. If she were to offer some deep penitence, a sacrifice of something important to her, she might be able to believe again."

Constantine looked at her with a strange mixture of wonder and hostility. "What had you in mind?" he said coldly.

"Perhaps to part from Leonicus for a while—say, two years? It was being with him when Joanna was dying that was wrong. She could devote her time to caring for the sick, as Joanna was. Then she would come back from it whole, able to take up and treasure what she had paid for, albeit with pain. Then she could accept forgiveness, because she was honest."

Constantine raised his eyebrows. "Are you saying that she has not accepted God's absolution?" he said incredulously.

"The Church's, not God's. Please . . . at least offer Theodosia the chance to earn back her faith," Anna pleaded. "What are any of us without it? The shadows are closing in everywhere, armies on the outside, and selfishness, fear, and doubt within. If we haven't even a pinpoint of faith that God is absolutely good, a pure love of the heart and soul, what hope is there for any of us?"

Constantine blinked and stared at her. "I'll see her," he conceded. "But she won't agree."

Eighty-one

~

CONSTANTINE HAD BEEN CERTAIN AT THE TIME HE GAVE absolution to Theodosia that he was the instrument of her salvation and that she would be eternally grateful to him for that.

Now he felt the deep, gnawing pain inside him that Anastasius was right. He recalled Theodosia's desperate humiliation after her husband left her. She had been grateful for Constantine's support, his assurance, his constant promise to her of God's guidance and blessing.

Lately when they met she was courteous, but her eyes were blank.

She received him, and he felt his belly tighten with apprehension.

"Bishop Constantine," she said courteously, coming forward to greet him. "How are you?" She looked magnificent in an emerald green embroidered tunic and a dalmatica crusted with gold, gold ornaments in her dark hair. Somehow the hues, rich as they were, leached the color out of her skin.

"Well enough," he replied. "Considering that we live in such threatening times."

"We do," she agreed, turning her eyes away as if regarding some danger beyond the gorgeous painted walls of the room. "May I offer you refreshment? Perhaps some almonds, or dates?"

"Thank you." Having food would make his task easier. It would be too discourteous to ask him to leave while he was eating. "I have not had time to speak with you in the last month or two. You look disturbed. Is there anything with which I can help you?"

"I am well, I assure you," she said.

He had given much thought as to how he could broach the subject of penitence with any delicacy at all. "You have not been to confession lately, Theodosia. You are a fine woman, you have been as long as I have known you, but we all fall short at times, even if it is no more than a lack of complete trust in God, and His Church. That is a sin, you know . . . one it is hard not to commit. We all have doubts, anxieties, fear of the unknown."

"What is it you expect me to confess?" she asked, and he heard the bitterness in her voice. Anastasius was right. Constantine looked around the room. "Where is the icon?" he asked. Theodosia would know which one he meant; there was only one icon that had passed between them, his gift to mark her absolution and return to the Church.

"In my private apartments," she replied.

"Does it help your faith to look at her and remember her sublime trust in God's will?" he asked. " 'Be it unto me according to thy word,' " he quoted Mary's answer when Gabriel had told her she would be the Mother of Christ.

The silence was harsh between them. "Confession and penitence can heal all mortal sin," he said gently. "That is the Atonement of Christ."

She faced him. "Believe what you wish to, Bishop, if it comforts you. I no longer have that certainty. Perhaps one day I may regain it, but there is nothing you can do for me."

He was annoyed. She had no right to speak to him in such a way, as if the sacrament of the Church were ineffectual.

"If you accepted a penance," he said firmly, "such as parting from Leonicus for a space, and devoting yourself to caring for the sick, then—"

"I do not need a penance, Bishop," she cut off his words. "You have already absolved me from any error I may have committed. If my faith is less than it should be, that is my loss. Now please leave, before Leonicus returns. I do not wish him to think that I have been confiding in you."

"Do you need human love so much that you would forfeit divine love to keep even the semblance of it?" he asked with a terrible pity.

"I can love a human being, Bishop," Theodosia said fiercely. "I cannot love a principle men adhere to when it suits them. What you preach is a set of myths and ordinances, rules that move with your own convenience. Leonicus is a human man, not perfect, maybe, as you say, not even loyal, but real. He speaks to me, answers me, smiles to see me, even needs me at times."

He bowed to the inevitable. "You will change your mind one day, Theodosia. The Church will be here, and willing to forgive."

"Please leave," she said softly. "You don't love God any more than I do. You love your office, your robes, your authority, your safety from having to think for yourself or from facing the fact that you are alone, and you mean nothing—just like the rest of us."

Constantine stared at her, shuddering in her despair as if it were cold water lapping around his feet, ice cold as it crept up to his knees, his thighs, the mutilation where his organs should have been. Was it true of him also, that it was the Church he loved, not God? The order, the authority, the illusion of power, and not the passionate, exquisite, everlasting love of God?

He refused to think of it, thrusting it out of his mind. He turned on his heel and strode out.

"I offered it to her," he told Anastasius later. "But she would not accept any penance at all. But I had to try." He looked at Anastasius, searching for the respect that should have been in his eyes, the acknowledgment of patience and honor. He saw only contempt, as if he were making excuses. It appalled him how much that hurt.

"Your arrogance is blasphemous!" Constantine cried out in sudden, overwhelming outrage. "You have no humility. You are quick to suggest penance for Theodosia, but your own sins go unconfessed. Come back to me when you can do so on your knees!"

White-faced, Anastasius walked away, leaving the bishop glaring at his back, still wanting to say more but lost for words hard enough, sharp enough, to wound the heart.

The pain of Anna's disillusion was deep. She had once seen so much that was good in Constantine, perhaps because she needed to. Now the ordinances of the Church were closed to her because she had not the belief to trust them. How could she? In offering such an empty forgiveness to

Theodosia, Constantine had poured away the possibility of Anna's absolution also.

She could lean only on her own understanding of God, seeking that
flame in the night, the warmth that wrapped around the heart when she
was alone on her knees.

Perhaps that was as it had to be. When there was no one beside you,
you looked upward. It is the darkness that tests the light. She must accept
being alone, not looking for the support or the forgiveness of others, but
working in her mind and her soul until she found it for herself.

Eighty-two

OE PACED THE FLOOR OF HER GREAT ROOM, EACH TIME she turned gazing at the great cross, only the back of which carried a name still burned on her heart—Dandolo, the greatest of them all. She must create a way to be revenged on him and his heirs, on Giuliano, before the crusaders came again and it was too late. The year of 1280 was waning fast, and the invasion would be soon now, perhaps even next year.

By the window, she stopped and stared out at the darkening winter sky. Helena had been particularly arrogant lately. Several times Zoe had caught a look in her eyes that seemed to be laughter, close to mockery, as some people see in another's defeat. Zoe was growing more and more certain that Helena knew Michael was her father and that she was planning to use it for her gain.

Perhaps it would be a good idea to send Sabas to watch her rather more carefully. Helena had appeared cooler toward Demetrios. The signs were tiny, a little less voluptuousness in her dress, a momentary distraction of mind now and then that clearly had nothing to do with him, an inattention to his words. Was there someone else? There was no better pretender to the throne.

She was still pondering this when one of the servants came in. He stood in front of her with his eyes on the beautiful tessellated floor, not daring to raise them.

"What?" she demanded. What news could paralyze the idiot like this?

"We have just heard that Doge Contarini abdicated a few weeks ago," he replied. "There is a new doge in Venice."

"Of course there is, fool!" she snapped. "Who is it?"

"Giovanni Dandolo—" His voice cracked with nervous tension.

She made a suppressed noise of fury and told him to get out. He obeyed with indecent haste.

So there was another Dandolo in the Ducal Palace in Venice. Beyond her reach—but Giuliano was not. What relationship was there between him and this new doge? It did not matter; old Enrico was common to both of them, and that was all that counted.

Giuliano might now be returned to Venice, to a higher calling. She must exact her revenge quickly, before that too slipped out of her grasp.

She was still considering this when an old friend called. He came in white-faced, his body tense, hands curling and uncurling even as he spoke.

He stammered over his words. "You may wish to go, although I can't imagine it, not now. It is too near the end. Charles of Anjou's armies are besieging Berat."

Berat was the great Byzantine fortress in Albania, just 450 miles away and holding the key to the land route from the west.

"When it falls," he went on, "Constantinople will lie open and unde-fended before him. The emperor has no army capable of withstanding an assault from the land, or from the sea when the Venetian fleet arrives. Per-haps that will not even be needed? They can take what they want of food and stores and sail on to Acre."

She was cold inside, as if his framing it in words had made it real.

"Zoe?" he prompted.

But she did not answer him. There was nothing to say. She received it in silence, as the darkness of the night comes without sound.

He crossed himself and left.

Her nightmares of childhood returned. She woke sweating alone in the darkness. Even in the winter night her body was seared by a heat that still lay in her dreams, but how much longer would that be true? When would the acrid smell of smoke, the crushing and the screaming, be real? Pictures danced before her of her mother, clothes torn, thighs scarlet with blood, her face distorted with terror, trying to crawl back to protect her child.

When she rose in the morning, people around her were packing up, ready to leave if the news got worse, gathering in little huddles in street corners, stopping every stranger to ask if there was any further word.

Zoe put together jewels and artifacts, things of great beauty, a winged horse in bronze, necklaces of gold, dishes, ewers, gem-encrusted reliquaries, alabaster and cloisonné jars, and sold them.

With the money she bought great vats full of pitch and had them piled up on the roofs of her house. She would burn the city down herself and destroy the Latins in their own flames before she would let Constantinople be taken again. This time she would die in the fires; never would she run away. Let them all leave, if they were coward enough. She would do it alone, if necessary. She would never surrender, and she would never run away again.

Eighty-three

∞

PALOMBARA FINALLY RETURNED TO ROME IN FEBRUARY OF 1281. There was a faint buzz of excitement in the street as he walked toward St. Peter's and the Vatican on his first morning back. In spite of the cold wind and the beginning of rain, there was an energy in the air.

He came to the open square and crossed it to the steps up to the Vatican. A group of young priests were standing on the bottom step. One of them laughed. Another chided him gently, in French. They noticed Palombara and spoke to him courteously in heavily accented Italian.

"Good morning, Your Grace."

Palombara stopped. "Good morning," he replied. "I have been at sea for several weeks, from Constantinople. Do we have a new Holy Father yet?"

One of the young men opened his eyes wide. "Oh yes, Your Grace. We have order again, and we will have peace." The young man crossed himself. "Thanks to the good offices of His Majesty of the Two Sicilies."

Palombara froze. "What? I mean, what offices could he exert?"

The young men glanced at each other. "The Holy Father restored him as senator of Rome," he said.

"After his election," Palombara pointed out.

"Of course. But His Majesty's troops surrounded the Papal Palace at Viterbo until the cardinals should reach a decision." He smiled broadly. "It clarified their minds wonderfully."

"And quickly," one of the others added with a little laugh.

Palombara found his heart beating high in his chest, almost choking him. "And who is our Holy Father?" He was assuredly French.

"Simon de Brie," the first young man answered. "He has taken the name of Martin the Fourth."

"Thank you." Palombara said the words with difficulty. The French faction had won. It was the worst news he could hear. He turned to go on up the steps.

"The Holy Father is not here," one of the priests called out after him. "He lives in Orvieto, or else in Perugia."

"Rome is governed by His Majesty of the Two Sicilies," the first young man added helpfully. "Charles of Anjou."

In the following days, Palombara came to appreciate just how profound was the victory of Charles of Anjou. He had assumed that the healing of the rift between Rome and Byzantium was a firm accomplishment, but the last shreds of that loosened and fell apart as he overheard the speculation around him of how finally they would end the wavering and deceit of Michael Palaeologus and force a true obedience, a victory for Christendom that had meaning.

At last Palombara was sent for when Martin IV was making one of his rare visits to Rome.

The rituals were the same as before, the professions of loyalty, the pretense at trust, mutual respect, and of course faith in their ultimate victory.

Palombara looked at Simon de Brie, now Martin IV, his trim white beard and pale eyes, and he felt the coldness enlarging inside him. He did not like the man, and he certainly did not trust him. De Brie had spent most of his career as diplomatic adviser to the king of France. Old loyalties did not die so easily.

Looking into the hard, broad-boned face of the new Holy Father, Palombara was absolutely certain that, likewise, Martin neither liked nor trusted him.

"I have read your reports on Constantinople, and the obduracy of the emperor Michael Palaeologus." Martin spoke in Latin, but with a considerable French accent. "Our patience is exhausted."

Palombara wondered whether the new pope spoke in the plural as if his office entitled him to think of himself in the royal form or if he actively meant himself and his counselors and advisers. He had a growing fear that it was Charles of Anjou.

"I wish you to return to Byzantium," Martin continued, not looking at Palombara, as if his feelings were irrelevant. "They know you, and more important, you know them. This situation must be resolved. It has dragged on far too long."

Palombara wondered why he did not send a Frenchman, and as soon as the idea had formed in his mind, he knew the answer. There was no glory in failure. He looked up and met the cool, faintly amused stare of the Holy Father.

Martin raised his hand in blessing.

Eighty-four

ᘒ

IN MARCH, GIULIANO WAS IN THE PRIVATE QUARTERS OF the new doge, overlooking the canal, seeing the light on the ever shifting water, the sound of it through the open windows like the breathing of the sea stirring in its sleep.

They had been eating a light supper and reminiscing about Giuliano's father, who had been the doge's cousin. There were exaggerated tales of fishing, wine drinking, brawls, and loves.

They were laughing when there was a sharp rap on the door, and a moment later a stiff gentleman in an embroidered doublet came into the room and bowed from the neck.

"There is extraordinary news from Berat, Your Serene Highness," the gentleman said. "There is a soldier here with a firsthand account of it, if you will receive him."

"Yes. Send him in. Then give him a good meal and wine."

The man bowed and left. A moment later he conducted in a soldier, obviously newly landed, still wearing his worn and bloodstained clothes.

"Well, tell me!" the doge ordered.

"The fortress at Berat has been relieved and Charles of Anjou's army completely routed," the man exclaimed. "Your Serene Highness."

The doge was startled. "Routed? Are you sure?"

"Yes, sir," the sailor replied. "Apparently Hugues de Sully himself, their great hero, undefeated before, was captured." His face was flushed with his delight, not only for the news he carried, but clearly also that he should be the one to tell the doge.

"Really?" The doge glanced at Giuliano. "Do you know this de Sully?"

"No, sir," Giuliano admitted.

"A Burgundian. A huge man, enormous, a symbol of their invincibility." The doge held his hands out far apart to suggest his size. "With hair like a roof on fire. Never seemed to get tired, so I am told. In the last two years he has been ordering boatloads of soldiers, horses, arms, money, siege engines. He has taken them to the Balkans to march first on Thessalonica, then on to Constantinople." The doge turned back to the soldier. "Tell me more." There was the beginning of a slender thread of skepticism in his voice. "De Sully had an army of above eight thousand men when he marched from Durazzo to take Berat. What happened to it?"

"Yes, Highness," the soldier agreed, his eyes still brilliant with triumph. "But the Byzantines dared not lose Berat, it holds the gateway through Macedonia, and thus all the way to Constantinople itself. Lose Berat and the empire is Anjou's for the taking. Michael Palaeologus is no fool—well, not militarily, anyway."

"But he has no army of size, skill, or experience to relieve the city when it is surrounded by a force such as de Sully's, or led by such a man," the doge said. "My information was that they were starving and obliged to smuggle food in by putting it on rafts and floating it down the river by night. What happened?"

The soldier grinned. "I wasn't there, but I heard it from several who were. De Sully was always arrogant, but he let it pickle his wits. He thought no one would touch him. He rode out to inspect the defenses with only a very small guard. The Byzantines ambushed him and took him prisoner, letting his whole army see what they had done." His eyes danced with delight. "It was as if the Byzantines had gouged out the hearts of the lot of them. The entire Angevin army turned tail and fled."

He laughed. "They did not stop running until they reached the Adriatic Sea. Hugues de Sully and the rest of the prisoners were transported back to Constantinople to be paraded through the streets, for the immense good cheer of the crowd."

Giuliano looked from one to the other of them, seeing the undisguised pleasure in the doge's face.

"Thank you," the doge said sincerely. "You did excellently to bring such news, and so rapidly. Venice is grateful. My chamberlain will give you a purse of gold so you may celebrate appropriately. Then go wash, eat, and drink to our prosperity."

The soldier thanked him profoundly and left, still grinning.

"This is excellent," the doge said as soon as he was certain they were alone. "After this, any crusade will have no choice but to go by sea, which means in Venetian ships." He laughed. "I have an excellent red wine. Let us drink a toast to the future."

But Giuliano woke the following morning with an ache inside himself so deep, it consumed all the elation at victory he had felt the night before. With pale, sharp daylight came reality. Charles of Anjou coveted Constantinople, his soul starved for it. Giuliano had seen it in his eyes, in his clenched fist, as if he could grasp it and hold his fingers around it forever. He wanted to take it by violence and crush it unconditionally.

Giuliano knew Charles's brutal rule. He had seen it in Sicily, where he taxed his own people into penury. What would he do to a conquered nation, as Byzantium would become? He would crush it, burn it, murder its people.

Such thoughts of Byzantium were disloyal to all that had bred and nurtured Giuliano, and to the promise he had made to Tiepolo on his deathbed, but he could not deny himself.

Perhaps the decision had been there for a long time, and he had needed only to be here in Venice, to see the vast shipyards busy night and day, to make him face the reality of it. He could no longer belong to a place, with the ease of friendship it gave and its torture of conscience. He must choose a morality, a people and belief that he loved and that had held truths bigger than comfort or acceptance.

He might never again serve this doge or any other. The knowledge came with a wrenching loneliness and a sudden high, bright freedom. He must do what he could to prevent the invasion. Charles of Anjou had friends in Rome, but somewhere he must have enemies. Sicily was the place to seek them.

He returned to Sicily, finding lodging again with Giuseppe and Maria, where he had stayed before.

"Ah, Giuliano!" Maria said with joy lighting her face as she came out to greet him in the front room with its shabby chairs and well-trodden floor. She flung her arms around him, holding him tightly, then blushed as she realized that she was making a spectacle of herself.

"Have you come to stay for a while?" she asked him. "You must eat with us. Tell us everything. Are you married yet? What is her name? What is she like? Why did you not bring her?"

"No." Giuliano was used to her questions and shrugged them off without offense. "I'm here because no one can cook like you, or make me laugh as hard."

She dismissed this with a wave of her hand, but she colored with pleasure.

"I've been to all sorts of places," he said, following her into the busy, chaotic kitchen where loaves of bread and vegetables were piled up, olives in pottery jars, lemons, onions rich gold and wine-colored, and bright fruit.

"Sit," she ordered him. "There, out of my way. Now tell me about all these places. Where is it you've been that's better than here?"

"Jerusalem," he said, grinning at her.

Her hands stopped midair and she turned to look at him gravely. "You wouldn't lie to me, would you, Giuliano? That would be very wicked."

"Certainly not!" he said with much indignation. "Do you want me to tell you about it?"

"If you don't tell me, I won't feed you. And every word had better be true."

He told her many things, and the warmth of her friendship eased out the aches from his body and at least some from his heart.

And after Maria had gone to tidy up and the children were in bed, he stood outside with Giuseppe staring across the harbor. They walked together down to the wall to watch the sea lapping against the stones.

"How is it, really?" Giuliano asked. "People complain, but they always do. Is it worse?"

Giuseppe shrugged. "People are angry, and they are afraid. The king is planning another crusade, and as always we are going to pay for his ships and his horses and his armor." They were going to pay Venice, of course, but he did not say that. It lay an unspoken wound between them.

"The king has friends," Giuliano said grimly. "The pope is his man. And of course his nephew is king of France. Hasn't he any enemies?"

Giuseppe stared at him in the fading light. "Peter of Aragon, so they say."

"Real enemy, or just a petty difference?"

"Real enough, the way I hear it. And John of Procida, for whatever that's worth."

Giuliano could not remember hearing the names before. Peter of Aragon explained itself. But John of Procida he did not know. He repeated the name as a question.

"Portugal," Giuseppe replied, with real anxiety sharpening his voice in the darkness. "What are you going to do? Be careful, my friend. The king has ears everywhere."

Giuliano smiled and said nothing. It was safer for Giuseppe that he did not know.

A man named Scalini made inquiries and obtained Giuliano passage to the coast of Aragon. It was hard labor being an ordinary seaman; however, that was the only vacancy open to him. Perhaps it was wiser than being conspicuous by seeking command. He also chose to use his mother's name of Agallon. He was surprised how much pleasure it gave him, even though at times he forgot and was slow to answer.

In Aragon, Giuliano heard more and more anxiety about the growing influence of France through an overtly French pope and a projected crusade led by a prince of France. He began to join in the conversations.

"Bad for trade," he said, shaking his head judiciously.

"You think so?" the man asked.

"Look at Sicily!" he exclaimed. "Taxed until they can barely afford to eat. Everywhere Frenchmen in the major offices, all the castles, the best lands. Frenchmen in the churches, and marrying the girls. You think they'll give us a chance to trade on equal terms when they hold the Mediterranean from Egypt to Venice, Sicily, and all the French coast? You're dreaming!"

"Venice won't allow that!" another man interrupted. "Never."

"I don't see them doing anything to stop it." Giuliano felt another stab of disloyalty, but what he said was true. "They're selling them the ships. They'll profit, as always. They have a treaty with the French pope. No doubt they're getting something from that."

The fear was growing, and Giuliano worked to foster it. It would reach the ears of the soldiers and the princes and add to their anger, which was already set against the king of the Two Sicilies.

By October, he had planted all the seeds of trouble he could in Aragon and was in Portugal when he heard that Pope Martin IV had excommunicated Michael of Byzantium from the fellowship of the Christian Church. Charles of Anjou was now the most powerful sovereign in Europe. Perhaps most important of all, the pope was under his influence and in his debt.

Who would dare to ride against a Catholic king who so clearly had the unconditional favor of the pope? Would they then find themselves excommunicated also? Did this now threaten anyone who raised his hand, or his voice, against the crusade and Charles of Anjou?

Giuliano felt that the darkness was closing in on all liberty and honor, and on the people he cared about profoundly.

Eighty-five

ᑎᗯᑎ

ON MARTIN'S ORDERS, PALOMBARA WAS IN CONSTANTINO-
ple again late in 1281. But in spite of the euphoria of the citizenry
after the relief of Berat, a sense of anxiety crowded within him that
matched the darkness of the fading year.

Martin IV had excommunicated the emperor Michael. The words
echoed in Palombara's head like the closing of an iron door. It was a
stepping-stone to invasion. Martin was sending Palombara with a death
sentence for the city, and they both knew it.

And once again he was accompanied by Niccolo Vicenze.

"They were practically dancing in the streets," Vicenze said to him over
dinner one evening, referring to the Byzantines rejoicing over Berat in the
spring. "Didn't the fools realize it only meant that he would come by sea
instead of by land?" He smirked as he said it, but Palombara saw the flare
of temper beneath it in his pale face, as if he were savoring the vision of revenge when the great fleet of Charles of Anjou would sweep across the sea
and break the city walls to enter with fear and death, as before.

Palombara had begun by disliking Vicenze, but as he looked at him
across the table now, he realized he actually hated him. "I think the point
is that they have proved to themselves that they can win, albeit with the
aid of a miracle," he replied coldly.

"And are they relying on another miracle?" Vicenze asked with a sarcastic pitch to his voice.

Palombara put an equal surprise in his reply. "Really, I have no idea. If you wish to know, you should ask one of their bishops. Perhaps Constantine could enlighten you."

"I don't care!" Vicenze snapped icily.

Later, alone, Palombara walked up the steep incline to a place where he could see over the narrow stretch of water to Asia. He was on the edge of the Christian world, and beyond it was a yet unknown force.

Yet it was the West that had destroyed Byzantium in the past and was poised to do so again.

What could he do? His mind ranged over a dozen options, all of them useless. The answer was not what he wished, yet he cared enough to be honest with himself and admit that it was the only one. He turned away from the cold wind and the sea and started to climb up the steep street toward the magnificent house of Zoe Chrysaphes.

She greeted him with amusement.

"You did not come merely to inform me that you are in Constantinople again," she observed. "Or to commiserate with us over the excommunication of the emperor." There was self-mockery in her face and a certain bitterness.

He smiled back at her. "I did consider asking your help in converting him to the Roman faith."

She started to laugh, then stopped herself, and it was only just before it turned to weeping.

"Of course," he continued, "that would achieve nothing. The pope is a Frenchman, bought and paid for by His Majesty of Naples. That is a debt you could pay for forever without having purchased anything."

She was surprised by his candor. "So what is it you want, Palombara?" she asked without disguising her curiosity, and with a certain warmth.

"Should we expect God to achieve by miracle what we could do for ourselves, with labor and a degree of intelligence?" he asked.

"How very Roman of you," she said with mockery, but she was far too interested to disguise it. "What miracles did you have in mind?"

"Saving Constantinople from defeat and occupation by Charles of Anjou," he replied.

"Really? Why?" She stood perfectly still; only the flames of the fire in the great hearth gave an illusion of movement in the room.

"Because if Byzantium falls, then the rest of Christendom will not be far behind it," he replied. That was not the whole truth. Part of Palombara's motivation was anger at the hollowness of the papacy, the departure from the passion and the honor that it should have had. And part of it was, to his surprise, that he had come to admire the subtlety and the intricate, devious beauty of Byzantine culture. If it was ruined, the world would lose.

She nodded slowly. "Why are you telling me? It is the pope who needs to know. He is shortsighted, and worldly. Why do you suppose we in the Orthodox Church hate the idea of owing him allegiance?"

"I came to suggest a different course of action."

Her eyes widened. "Different from what?"

"From pouring Greek fire over the walls onto the heads of the invaders," he replied with a smile. "Not that I have anything against that. I would just like to strike a little sooner."

He had her complete attention.

"At his support in Europe, before he sets sail," he continued. "Particularly in Spain, Portugal, possibly parts of France. To foment trouble, insurrection, to appeal to self-interest, trade, to make very clear indeed some of the disadvantages if Charles of Anjou succeeds."

"Trouble costs money," she pointed out, but the flame was back in her eyes. "Michael's Treasury is fully engaged in armaments for defense."

Palombara knew that Michael's Treasury was all but empty, but he did not say so. "What about the great merchant houses of Constantinople?" he asked instead. "Could they not be persuaded to contribute—handsomely?"

Very slowly, she smiled. "You know, my lord bishop, I think they could. I am sure there are . . . ways to convince them."

He kept his eyes on hers. "If I can be of assistance, please tell me."

"Oh, I will. May I offer you wine? Almonds?"

He accepted, as if to eat and drink together sealed a bargain.

Eighty-six

ᵒᵛᵒ

THE WINTER SEEMED TO ZOE UNNATURALLY DARK, BUT after Palombara's visit the cold no longer touched her bones. She knew what she was going to do, it merely required a little thought as to exactly how.

She knew from Scalini and other men like him that the forces of the new crusade were gathering in the West. He had brought her word of siege engines, catapults, horse armor and trappings ready for the foot soldiers and the mounted knights that would mass in Sicily. They would storm Constantinople, then ride in triumph into Jerusalem, with Charles of Anjou at their head. Anyone in their path would be trampled. A road stained with blood had never troubled crusaders.

Also of great concern to Zoe was the change in Helena. It dated since soon after Eirene's death—so soon, in fact, that it was hard to believe they were unconnected. The conclusion was unpleasantly clear. Somehow Helena had found out who her father was.

Zoe stood warming herself by the fire. The thought of Helena kept returning to her mind, so sharp that it was as if someone had left a window open, letting in a knife cut of ice-laden air from outside.

Helena would not stand on the walls with her mother and pour fire on the invaders, then die in her own funeral pyre. She was a survivor, not a martyr. She would find a way to escape and start again somewhere else. And she would certainly escape with money.

Michael would never yield. He would die before he accommodated

Charles. Not that Charles would leave him alive anyway. He would destroy all royal claimants, and if Helena did not know that, then she was a fool. Her birth would be her death sentence. Charles would leave his puppet emperor without a rival of any sort.

The answer came to Zoe with the scorching heat of the Greek fire she planned to use. If Charles wanted to hold Byzantium with a hand of peace, to free his armies to go on to Jerusalem, what better than to marry his puppet emperor to a legitimate heir of the Palaeologi? Murder Michael and Andronicus, and who was left? Helena!

Zoe's mind raced, horrified. It was betrayal beyond imagining.

She sat with her arms around herself, shivering in spite of the fire. Before it came anywhere near that, she must raise the money Palombara had suggested, buy all the trouble, anger, and rebellion she could. And she knew now exactly where that money was coming from.

Her power had always lain in knowledge of other people's secrets and the proof that could ruin them. The man to help her now was Philotheos Makrembolites. She had heard only last week that he was on his deathbed. Perfect! In pain, frightened, and with nothing to lose.

Zoe went to her herb room and prepared various mixtures for the relief of different kinds of pain. She also collected sleeping powders, sweet-smelling oils, and restoratives that would give a short-lived clarity to the mind, even if after that there was only the slipping away into the last silence.

She bathed and dressed, perfuming herself but wearing rich, sober colors, as befitted one going to visit the dying. She did not worry that Philotheos would not receive her. He had a withered arm from the fires of 1204 and a bitter heart. He would want to relive old wrongs and would not be unwilling to help her exact a vengeance that was beyond his own reach. Secrets were worth nothing in the grave.

He received her in his dim, overhot room with as much curiosity as she had hoped. He hoisted himself onto his elbows, wincing with pain and screwing up his face into a snarl, drawing his lips back from stained teeth. "Come to gloat at my death, Zoe Chrysaphes?" he said, his breath wheezing out of his lungs with a sound like tearing cloth. "Make the most of it. Your turn will come, and you'll likely see the city put to blood and fire again before that happens."

She put down the leather satchel in which she had brought the herbs and ointments. They knew each other far too well for pretenses. She would not have come except for good reasons of her own.

"What's in there?" he asked, eyeing it suspiciously.

"Relief from pain," she answered. "Temporarily, of course. It will all be finished when God wishes it."

"You are little younger than I am, for all your paint and perfume. You smell like an alchemist's parlor," he responded.

She wrinkled her nose. "You don't. Rather more like a charnel house. Do you wish a little ease or not?"

"What's the price?" His eyes were yellowing, as if his kidneys were failing him. "Have you spent all your money? No more charms to get men to give it to you?"

"Keep your money. You can bury it with you, for all I care," she replied. "Better that than let it fall into crusader hands. They'll probably dig you up anyway, just to see if there's anything worth taking."

"I'd rather they ravaged my corpse than my living body," he retorted, looking her up and down. His gaze lingered on her breasts and then her belly. "Perhaps you'd better kill yourself before they come."

"Not before I've finished what I mean to do." She would not be distracted by his spite.

Interest flared up in his face. "What's that?"

"Revenge, of course. What else is there left?"

"Nothing," he answered. "Who is there to pay anything now? The Kantakouzenos are all gone, and the Vatatzes, the Doukas, Bessarion Comnenos. Who's left?"

"Of course they're gone," she said impatiently. "But there are new traitors who would sell us again. Let us begin with the Skleros, then perhaps the Akropolites, and the Sphrantzes."

He breathed out with a harsh rattle in his throat, and a little more of the color drained from his face.

She was seized by a fear that he would die before he could tell her what she needed to know. There was a jug of water on the table. She rose, took a small glass, and measured a portion of liquid into it from one of the vials she had brought, then added a little water. She returned to the bed and held it for him.

He drank the potion and choked. It exhausted him for several minutes, but when he finally opened his eyes again, there was a touch of color in his cheeks and his breathing was easier.

"So what is it you want, Zoe Chrysaphes?" he asked. "Charles of Anjou will burn all of us. The only difference is that I shall not feel it, and you will."

"Probably. But you know many secrets about the old families of Constantinople."

"You want to damage them?" He was surprised. "Why?"

"Of course I don't, you fool!" she snapped. "I want them to crush the rebellions and back Michael. You want my herbs. You may roast in the flames of hell tomorrow, like a pig on a spit, but tonight you can be a lot easier, if you tell me what I want to know."

"All the shabby and fraudulent secrets of the dissenters to union?" he said, turning the idea over in his mind. "I could tell you those. There are plenty of them." His smile was cruel and sharp with pleasure.

She remained with Philotheos three long days and nights, portioning out the medicine, keeping him alive using all the skills she had. Little by little, laced with viciousness, he told her the secrets that she could use to bleed the Skleros dry of money, and the Sphrantzes and the Akropolites. It would be worth thousands of gold byzants. Used with skill and care, as she would, it might just foment enough doubt and rebellion in the West to weaken even the strength of Charles of Anjou.

The day after Philotheos died, Zoe was at the Blachernae Palace and told some of her plan to Michael as they walked together along one of the great galleries. The light streaming in through the long, high windows showed cruelly the chipped marble of pillars, the broken hands of a porphyry statue.

The emperor looked at her wearily, and the defeat in his face frightened her. "It's too late, Zoe. We must think of defense. I tried everything I know, and I couldn't carry the people with me. Even now, they don't see the destruction awaiting them."

"Not from Charles of Anjou, maybe." She leaned closer to him, ignoring all the rules of etiquette. "But they will understand shame in the eyes of their peers, the men they see every week, the men they talk to in business and government. The men they will do business with, even in a new exile. They will pay to avoid that."

He looked at her more closely, his eyes narrowing. "What shame, Zoe?" She smiled. "Old secrets."

"If you know them, why didn't you use them before?" he asked.

"I've only just learned them," she replied. "Philotheos Makrembolites is dead. Did you know that?"

"Even so, it is too late. This pope is France's creature. Spain and Portugal will ally with him. They can't afford not to. All the gold in Byzantium won't change that."

"He's pope for as long as he lives," she replied softly. "What does he need the King of the Two Sicilies for now? Are you saying he will honor all his debts?"

"He'll pay them only if there is something he still wants," Michael agreed.

"Think of your own people," she urged. "Think of their suffering in the long years of exile, and of those who never came back. We have been here a thousand years, we have built great palaces and churches. We have created beauty to the eye, the ear, and the heart. We have imported spices, colored silks like the sun and the moon, jewels from the corners of the earth, bronze and gold, jars, urns, bowls, statues of men and beasts."

She spread her hands. "We have measured the skies and traced the paths of the stars. Our medicine has cured what no one else could even name." She spoke with intense intimacy. "But more than any of these, our dreams have lit fire in the minds of half the world. Our lives have brought justice to rich and poor, our literature has furnished the minds of generations of people, and made the world sweeter than it would ever have been without us. Don't let the barbarians kill us again! We will not rise a second time."

"You don't know when you are beaten, do you, Zoe?" he said with a soft, sweet smile.

"Yes, I do," she answered. "I was beaten the first time, seventy years ago. I saw the fires of hell consume everyone I loved. This time, if it happens, I will go with it." She took a breath. "But in the name of the Holy Virgin, I will not die without a fight. If we fail, Michael, history will not forgive us."

"I know," he admitted quietly. "Tell me, Zoe, Cosmas Kantakouzenos is dead, and Arsenios Vatatzes, and Georgios, and Gregory, and now Eirene. Why is Giuliano Dandolo still alive?"

She should have known he would have understood all along and allowed her to take her revenge only if it suited him.

He was waiting. "He is still useful to me," she replied. "He is courting enemies of Charles of Anjou, awakening trouble in Sicily. I will have Scalini kill him when we don't need him. I would have liked something more elegant, but we no longer have time," she added.

He nodded, his eyes sad. "A pity. I liked him."

"So did I," she agreed. "What has that to do with it? He is a Dandolo."

"I know," he said softly. "It's still a pity."

Eighty-seven

～

ZOE STOOD AT THE OPEN WINDOW AND STARED AT THE FAR light on the sea. The wind stinging her face was sharp off the water; it still carried the smell of ice from the east, but also present in the breeze was the promise of spring. Zoe's plans were maturing nicely. She had the money, albeit under bitter protest. Yesterday the Skleros had yielded. And she had exacted an extra price, just as a surety, that they should cease their opposition to the union with Rome. Constantinople needed every shred of power or influence it had with the West. Survival depended on it.

And Zoe's efforts would thwart Helena, which compared with the survival of Byzantium was trivial, but there was still a dark sweetness to it.

Thomais was at the door. She looked frightened. "Bishop Constantine is here to see you, my lady. He is very angry."

Zoe had expected Constantine to be angry. "Let him wait a few minutes, then send him in."

Thomais looked cornered. "Are you well?" she asked. "Shall I bring you an infusion of camomile? I can tell the bishop to come another day."

Zoe smiled at the thought. It was almost worth doing simply for the satisfaction of it. She was still considering her answer when she saw the large figure of Constantine, magnificently robed, in the passage behind Thomais; obviously he was intending to come in, with or without permission.

Thomais turned to face him.

"Get out of my way, woman." His face was white and his eyes blazing.

Now that he was closer, Zoe could see the gleaming silk of his dalmatica, in spite of the inclement weather. It flowed around him, fluttering wide with his movement, making him appear even larger.

His arrogance was intolerable to Zoe. She had a wild idea to wait until Thomais had retreated and closed the door, then take off her tunic and stand naked before the bishop. It would appall him so terribly, he would never exercise such high-handedness again. And it would be funny.

Thomais was waiting for her to give the order.

"Send Sabas to wait outside the door," Zoe told her. "I doubt His Grace will continue with such ill manners, but if he does, I would like you and Sabas to be within call."

Thomais obeyed. Constantine came in and shut the door, almost catching the end of his tunic between it and the jamb.

"You seem to have lost control of yourself," Zoe observed coolly. "I would offer you wine, but you appear to have had more than sufficient already. What is it you wish?"

"You have betrayed the Orthodox Church," he replied through clenched teeth, the muscles of his smooth, beardless jaw bulging.

Theodosia Skleros would have told him. No doubt she had asked absolution again for the sins of her brothers.

Constantine's eyes glittered with a fanatic anger, and there was sweat beading his skin. "You have foresworn all that you professed to believe and broken the covenants of your baptism." His voice trembled. "You have abandoned the faith, blasphemed God and the Holy Virgin, and you are excommunicated from the fellowship of Christ. You are no longer one of us." He flung out his arm, fingers pointing at her almost as if he would jab her. "You are denied the body and blood of Christ. Your sins are upon your own head, and in the Day of Judgment He will not atone for you. The Holy Virgin will not intercede for you before God, her prayers will not speak your name, nor will she hear your words at the hour of your death. Among the company of saints, you no longer exist."

She stared at him. It could not be true. He was standing in the light, alone, the rest of the room blurring around him so she could not see it. There was a strange, fuzzy sound in her ears. She tried to speak, to tell him he was wrong, but she could not find any words, and the pain in her head was unbearable.

She put up her hands to block it out, and then suddenly she was on the floor. Darkness and light splintered into each other in total and incomprehensible silence. Then nothing at all.

Constantine had expected her to be terrified. Zoe had committed the ultimate sin. But he had not thought that she would be so affected that she would be struck speechless and fall to the ground unable to move.

He looked where she lay, her eyes half-open but apparently sightless. Was she dead? He moved closer and stared. He could see her chest rise and fall with her breathing. No, he had not killed her. Better than that, she was sightless and dumb, but still alive to know it.

Victory soared up inside him, as if he were suddenly without weight. He turned on his heel and walked to the door. He pulled it open and saw the servants standing in a huddle. He drew in his breath and let it out slowly. "Be warned," he said, measuring each word. "The Holy Church of Christ will not be mocked. Your mistress made light of her oaths and betrayed her promises. I have delivered God's message to her, and He has struck her down." He gestured behind him to where Zoe lay. "Call a physician if you wish, but he cannot undo the work of God, and he would be a fool to try."

Eighty-eight

∽

ANNA HAD BEEN SENT FOR AND ACCOMPANIED THE WHITE-faced messenger to Zoe's home. Sabas was waiting for her and took her immediately to where Zoe was lying on her bed, Thomais at her side, her face impassive.

"Bishop Constantine excommunicated her from the Church," Sabas informed Anna. "God has stricken her, but still she lives. Please help her."

Anna moved forward and looked down at Zoe. Her tunic was crumpled and she lay awkwardly, as if placed there by someone who dared not touch her with any more intimacy. Her eyes were almost closed, but she was breathing quite regularly. Without thinking, Anna smoothed Zoe's dress over her stomach and thighs, then she felt her pulse. It was weak but quite regular.

"Is it not the bishop's doing?" Thomais asked.

Anna hesitated. Constantine would not have poisoned her or struck her. He might have frightened her into an apoplectic fit if he had invoked the deep terror inside her of the punishment of God, the abandonment of all light and hope.

She touched Zoe's hand, gently. It was warm. She was not dead or even dying. "We must not let her get cold. And put a little ointment on her lips to stop them drying. I will fetch herbs and come back."

Thomais stared at her, her face filled with doubt, perhaps fear.

"God may have struck her," Anna said gently. "If He takes her life, that is His judgment. It's not mine."

She did all she could for Zoe, waiting and watching to see if her condition changed. On the fifth night, she was sitting in the corner of Zoe's room next to a painted and inlaid screen, half asleep. The room was almost dark. One small candle burned on the table about seven feet from Zoe, just enough to see her outline, not enough to shine on her face.

She still had not opened her eyes or stirred more than to move one hand a few inches. Anna did not know if she ever would again. Thinking of the destruction Zoe had caused, Anna should have been glad. It confused her that she felt instead a sense of loss and a troubling pity.

She was almost asleep when she was suddenly, terrifyingly aware that there was someone else in the room. He was moving soundlessly, no more than a shadow passing across the floor. He couldn't be a servant or he would have spoken.

She froze, her breath caught in her throat. She watched as he crept toward the bed, a small man, dressed not in a tunic but a shirt and britches. He had a pointed beard, and as he came closer to Zoe the candlelight touched his face and she saw that he had sharp features, thin and clever. His hands were empty.

Her mind raced. She knew from the awkward way the man's jacket lay over his hip that he had a knife at his belt, and Zoe was defenseless. If Anna called out, there was no one near enough to hear or come in time to help. Anna herself would be dead before then.

She must move silently or the intruder would hear her and strike, probably Zoe first and then her. She had nothing near her, no heavy bowl, no candlestick. But there was the tapestry. If she threw that over him, it might confuse him for long enough to reach for the candlestick on the table.

"Zoe," he said quietly. "Zoe!"

Could he not see she was not asleep but senseless? No, thank God the candle was small and far enough from her that her face was in the shadow.

"Zoe!" he said more urgently. "It is going well. Sicily is like a tinderbox. One spark, one wrong word or move, and it will burn like a forest fire. Dandolo has worked well, but he has just about served our purposes. Give me the word, and I'll kill him myself. One quick thrust and it will be over. I'll use the Dandolo dagger you gave him." He gave a low, soft laugh. "Then he'll know the message of death comes from you."

Anna broke out in a sweat. Whatever happened, she must not move or make the slightest sound. If he knew she was here, he would kill her, too.

Her nose itched. Her mouth was dry. Still the intruder sat silently by Zoe's side.

Then she heard a footstep outside the door, a brief knock, and the door opened. The intruder moved toward the tapestry like a shadow.

Anna turned as the door swung open and Thomais entered. Only then did Anna see, in the widening light, that one of the windows was not fastened.

Anna stirred, as if just waking up. "I'll come and get a little wine," she said sleepily to Thomais. "Can you find me some cakes? I'm hungry."

Anna walked over to the door, not even glancing at the shadow beyond Zoe's bed where the intruder had melted into the corner. He would not hurt Zoe, and if Anna was out of the room for a few minutes, he would leave as he must have come, through the window into the night.

She must see that from now on all the windows and doors were more carefully barred.

Two days later Zoe opened her eyes, puzzled, frightened, unable to speak. She tried, but the words were garbled, animal sounds. Thomais tried offering her a pen and a piece of paper. She gripped the pen awkwardly, made a few scratches on the white surface, and gave up.

Helena was informed that her mother was awake but unable to speak. She came, stared at Zoe with a strange pleasure, then turned and left. It was after she had gone that Zoe spoke her first comprehensible word. "Anna . . . " she said clearly.

It was a slow task. By evening, Zoe had managed a few more simple words and names, requests, movement that was a little more coordinated. Anna looked at the terror in her eyes and in spite of herself felt a sharp pity for her. She wished Zoe could have died simply, at the first blow of the apoplexy, rather than inch by inch like this.

And Anna also knew that if she recovered, the intruder would be back, and Zoe would give the order for Giuliano to be murdered. If she could not stop Zoe, perhaps she could find the intruder and stop him. There was only one man she could trust and who had the power to help— Nicephoras.

It was late and raining hard when she reached the Blachernae Palace, and it took her several minutes of argument to persuade the guard to allow her in and then to disturb Nicephoras to receive her.

He looked troubled; his face was grave, still heavy with sleep, his beardless cheeks soft. "What is it?" he asked anxiously. "Is Zoe dead?"

"No, she's not dead," Anna replied. "In fact, she may recover completely. Her progress is very rapid, and she has a will of iron."

Briefly, Anna told Nicephoras of the intruder, his assumption that Zoe could hear him, and his promise to kill Giuliano as soon as she gave the word. "He is trying to provoke a rising in Sicily, against Charles of Anjou . . . I think," she added. "But Giuliano Dandolo is an ally, not an enemy. If we destroy those who serve us, or allow them to be destroyed, we will not find many wanting to help us next time we need them. And there will always be a next time."

Nicephoras smiled. "From your description, it has to have been Scalini. I will not allow Dandolo to be killed—at least not at Zoe's behest. What else happens to him in Sicily is outside my control. I think Scalini has now served his purpose. And he is Zoe's creature, not ours."

"Is he?" she asked quickly.

"Oh, yes." His expression was bleak. "But I know where to find him. He will not leave Constantinople, I promise you."

"Thank you," she said with profound gratitude. "Thank you."

Zoe continued to recover. In another few days she could form sentences, although many words still eluded her. She began to eat and to drink all the herbs Anna mixed for her. Surprisingly, she was a good patient, obeying every instruction, and she progressed accordingly.

Two weeks after her initial attack, the four Skleros brothers publicly declared total allegiance to the emperor Michael in his efforts to save the empire and privately changed from giving a large donation to the Church to giving a significant part of their fortune to Zoe, to further whatever civil unrest she could effect in the dominions of Charles of Anjou.

Eighty-nine

CONSTANTINE STOOD ALONE IN THE COURTYARD STARING at the fountain, and in his mind everything shrank into a tiny, crystal-clear picture, sharp-edged as a polar wind and just as simple. He could see the whole pattern as clearly as a great mosaic, every piece in its place. His whole life, every experience good and bad, had been leading up to this time when his understanding was like a shaft of light and at last undeniable. Even betrayed, he had not abandoned the cause. From that surely he must conclude that God would never abandon him?

His task now was the one above all others. Zoe Chrysaphes must be stopped. He had struck her down once, with the power of God in his hand, and Anastasius the vain, the shallow, and fickle as water, had healed her.

He must go to Zoe late in the evening, when he was certain to find her alone. His resolve was absolute. He could not leave the destiny of God's people on earth in the slippery hands of Zoe Chrysaphes.

It was a dark night, cloud-covered and windy, with pieces of debris blown rattling along the street. He would not have chosen to be out, but this must be done. And perhaps such a night was created for decisions that could never be reversed.

He was admitted warily by her servants and shown into the entrance room with its old mosaic floors and arched doorways leading to her private apartments; but he had to insist, even imply the threat of excommunication to them, in order to see her alone. After his last visit, Zoe's servants mistrusted him.

Finally, only Anastasius stood in his way.

"I will see her alone," Constantine said firmly. "That is her right. Would you deny her the final sacrament of extreme unction? Can you face God yourself, if you do such a thing?"

Anastasius reluctantly stepped away, and Constantine went in, closing the door behind him.

The great room was as magnificent as always. The torches were burning in their ornate stands, yellow flames giving it a warm, peaceful feeling, like a fine painting framed and dusted with gold. The great crucifix was hanging in its usual place. It was beautiful, but Constantine did not like it. There was something almost barbaric about it. It made him uncomfortable, like a sort of indecency.

Zoe sat in a huge chair with her back to one of the tapestries, all wines and scarlets and purples, with threads of bronze. She was wearing red again, a brazen color. It lit her face, which was not as gaunt as it should be after her illness, and showed off those golden eyes.

"I know what you have done, Zoe Chrysaphes," he said quietly. "And what you plan to do."

"Really?" She seemed barely interested.

He leaned closer. "There are plans in heaven that earth knows nothing of," he said harshly. "That is the meaning of faith. Trust God that He will provide for us whatever is necessary."

Her fine eyebrows rose. "Do you believe that, Bishop Constantine?"

"I more than believe it," he said with ringing certainty. "I know it."

"You mean I cannot change you?" she persisted.

"Not at all." He smiled.

"You have such faith!" Her voice was slow, almost a caress.

"I have," he declared.

"Then why are you here?"

He felt the heat in his skin. Zoe had nearly tricked him.

"To save your soul, woman!" he retorted.

"You told me I had already lost it," she reminded him. "Are you going to forgive me after all?"

"I can do," he told her. "If you repent, and come back as an obedient daughter of the Church. Recant all that you have said in support of union with Rome, forgive your enemies, return the money to the Church you have taken, and submit yourself to discipline. Continue the rest of your days in prayer to the Holy Virgin, and you may at the last be washed clean."

"All that before Charles of Anjou burns us to the ground again?" she said with mocking incredulity.

"God can do anything!" he said forcefully. "If you repent, and obey."

"I don't believe you," she said softly. "We must help ourselves."

"You blaspheme!" His voice rose in amazement and fury. "God will strike you dead!" He lifted his hand and pointed at her, jabbing his finger in the air as if it were a weapon.

She sat staring at him, smiling slightly lopsidedly, the right side of her face a little stiff. "Then my physician will heal me . . . again," she replied. "You have the power to destroy, and he to make whole. Think of that, Bishop! Which of you does that make the greater?"

He lunged forward and seized a cushion from the nearest chair. He flung himself on top of her, pressing the soft, stifling fabric over her face. She struggled, arms and legs thrashing, but he was more than twice her weight and he held her down, crushing her lungs, suffocating her. It was only a few hideous moments before she stopped moving, and his rage went cold, his body covered in icy sweat. He stood up slowly and looked at Zoe where she lay sprawled on the floor, hair tangled, tunic up around her thighs. He should remember her like this: broken, without dignity, at once both exciting and disgusting in her suggestion of sensuality.

Feeling a revulsion he could barely control, he touched her hair with his hand to straighten it around her face. It was soft, so soft that he could barely feel it. The backs of his fingers brushed against her cheek. Her skin was still warm.

He shuddered convulsively. This was obscene! He wanted to strike her, tear down one of the huge tapestries and cover her with it.

But of course he must not do that. He was a bishop, tending a penitent sinner on her deathbed.

He pulled her tunic down as far as it would go. It was not far enough. It still looked as if she had had it lifted, as if . . . He refused to follow that thought. His mutilation burned in his soul. He lifted her thighs; she was heavy and warm. Then he pulled her tunic straight.

He stood up, his whole body trembling.

He waited several more minutes, then walked to the door and opened it. He stopped abruptly or he would have bumped into Anastasius standing just beyond it.

He looked Anastasius straight in the eye. "She repented of all her errors and saved her soul. It is a time for great rejoicing. Zoe Chrysaphes died a loyal daughter of the true Church." He took a deep, steadying breath. "She will be buried in the Hagia Sophia. I shall offer the funeral Mass myself." He forced himself to smile. It was like the rictus of the dead on his face.

Anastasius stared in total disbelief, his eyes wide and, unbelievably, filled with grief.

Constantine crossed himself and walked past him, his huge hands clenched, his heart pounding with victory.

Ninety

∽

ANNA WALKED INTO THE ROOM AND STARED DOWN AT the body of Zoe. She saw the blue face, the bitten lip, and the blood on it. She bent down beside her, pushing back a stray lock of hair off her brow. Gently she lifted one eyelid. She saw the tiny pinpricks of red and knew what had happened. She stood up slowly and faced Thomais.

"Lay her out," she said. "Make her look beautiful." Her voice strangled in her throat. It was not only Zoe who was dead, it was Constantine also, and in an infinitely more terrible way.

Anna went outside into the rising wind and the first spots of rain. She walked alone to Helena's house to give her the news. She did not want to do it, so it was best done quickly. Now the weight of what Constantine had said lay increasingly heavily on her. He would claim that Zoe had taken back all her support for union with Rome and died in the bosom of the Church. He would make pomp and display of it.

Helena took a long time to appear. The servants had admitted Anna only with great reluctance, but she had told them why she had come, and not one of them wished to tell Helena of Zoe's death themselves. Anna waited, grateful for the wine and bread she was offered. She was cold through to the bone now, and her eyes stung with tiredness and with sorrow.

Helena came across the room, and Anna rose to her feet.

"What on earth have you to say that cannot wait until morning?" Helena said irritably.

"I am very sorry indeed to tell you that your mother is dead," Anna replied.

Helena's dark eyes widened in momentary disbelief. "Dead?"

"Yes."

"Really? At last." Helena straightened her back and held her head a little higher. A slight smile touched the corner of her mouth, and one might have thought it was superb courage and dignity in the face of loss. Anna had the ugly thought that in fact it was an attempt to contain her victory.

She felt the tears for Zoe welling behind her own eyelids. Something of Byzantium was gone. It was more than an age that was past, it was a passion, a fury, a love of life, and its leaving took something irreplaceable from the world.

Ninety-one

PALOMBARA LANDED IN CONSTANTINOPLE WEIGHED DOWN by the bitter news he carried. The fleet of Charles of Anjou had sailed for Sicily, and from there it would leave for Constantinople. They could count the time until invasion in weeks.

Back again at the house he shared with Vicenze, Palombara found him busy in his study, writing a pile of dispatches. Vicenze, secretive as always, turned them upside down the moment he saw him in the doorway.

"Good voyage?" Vicenze asked politely.

"Good enough," Palombara replied. He held out the letters the pope had sent Vicenze, still sealed.

Vicenze took them. "Thank you." He looked at Palombara. "I don't suppose you've heard yet, but Zoe Chrysaphes is dead. Had an apoplexy or something. Bishop Constantine said a requiem Mass for her in the Hagia Sophia, the hypocrite. Said she died reconciled to the Orthodox Church. Damn liar!" He smiled.

Palombara was stunned. It had seemed as if nothing could destroy Zoe. He stood still in the middle of the floor and was overwhelmed with loss, as if Byzantium itself had begun to die.

Vicenze was still staring at him, still smiling. Palombara had an almost overwhelming desire to strike him so hard that it would break his teeth.

"Perhaps it's just as well," he said as calmly as he could. "Charles of Anjou has set sail for Messina. At least she will be spared knowing that."

He went to see Helena Comnena to offer his condolences. She had moved into Zoe's house, and she received him in the room that had once been her mother's. The view was the one Palombara remembered, but the colors were already different. The new tapestries were pale, intricately detailed. There were blues and greens, no warmth of the earth tones.

Helena's perfectly balanced face, with its winged eyebrows, almost like her mother's, was lovely. But he had no sense of the steel within. There seemed to be in her a hunger without joy.

"I am grieved to hear of your mother's death," he said formally. "Please accept my condolences."

"Personally?" she asked. "Or do you speak for Rome?"

He smiled. "Personally."

"Really?" She regarded him with dry, rather sour amusement. "I had not realized that you were fond of her. I rather assumed the opposite."

He met her dark eyes. "I admired your mother. I enjoyed her intelligence and her infinite capacity to care about everything."

"Admired her . . ." Helena repeated the words curiously, as if she found them inappropriate. "But surely she was nothing that Rome approves of? She had no humility, she was never obedient to anything but her own desires, and she was certainly very far from chaste!"

He was angry with her for not defending her mother. "She was more alive than anyone else I know."

"You sound like the eunuch physician Anastasius," she observed sourly. "He mourns her, which is stupid. She would have destroyed him without a thought, if it had been worth her trouble." There was contempt in her voice and a sharp edge that Palombara recognized with surprise as resentment.

"You are mistaken," he said icily. "Zoe admired Anastasius greatly. Quite apart from his medical skill, she liked his wit and his courage, his imagination, and the fact that he was not afraid of her, or of life."

Helena laughed. "How quaint you are, Your Grace. And how terribly innocent. You know nothing."

He forced himself to smile. "If you have your mother's papers, I daresay you are aware of a great deal that others are not. Some of it will be very dangerous. But you must already know that?"

"Oh yes, very dangerous indeed," she said in little more than a whisper. "But you are foolish to pretend that you know of what you speak, Your Grace." Her smile was bright and hard. "You don't."

What was it that obviously pleased her so much? She was looking at him and gloating. Why?

"It seems not," he agreed, lowering his eyes as if he were crestfallen.

Helena laughed, a shrill, cruel sound. "I see my mother did not share it with you," she observed. "But she discovered that your precious eunuch, whom you admire so much, is actually the most superb liar! His entire life and everything about him is a lie."

Palombara stiffened, anger swirling up inside him.

Helena looked at him with derision. "Or to be accurate, I should say 'her whole life.' " She went on, "Anna Zarides is as much a woman as I am. Or at least legally she is. There must be something repulsively wrong with her that she would masquerade as a man all these years, don't you think? Wouldn't you say it was a sin? What do you think I should do, Bishop Palombara? Should I assist in her deceit? Is that morally right?"

He was so stunned he could hardly find his voice. Yet as Helena said the words, he believed them. He looked at her face, shining with malice, and he hated her.

Then he smiled. Her envy was so highly visible. Zoe was gone, and now Helena could not taste her victory completely. Without Zoe to see, there was no flavor in it. But she could at least destroy Anastasius, the daughter Zoe had preferred.

Palombara met Helena's eyes and saw the fury in them. "My condolences," he repeated, then excused himself and walked away.

Outside in the street, the sense of triumph wore off within moments, replaced by fear. If Anastasius was actually a woman and Helena knew it, then she was in the most intense danger. If Helena chose to expose her, he did not know what punishment Anastasius would face, but it would be savage.

Zoe had known and had not betrayed Anastasius's secret. That too was a mystery. She must, in her own way, have had a great respect, even a kind of affection, for her.

He walked along the busy street with the crowd jostling around him. News of the fleet having left for Messina had reached Constantinople with the ship on which Palombara arrived. Fear spread like fire on the wind, sharp and dangerous, edged with panic, quick to violence as the threat became suddenly no longer a nightmare, but a reality.

He walked more rapidly, facing into the wind. The more he considered what Helena had said, the more it frightened him. Should he find Anna Zarides and warn her? But what use would that be? There was nothing she could do, except perhaps flee, like so many others. But would she do that? It led him to the question of why she had ever begun such a desperate course in the first place.

Dressed as a woman, she would be beautiful. Why did Anna Zarides not use that? What could have compelled her to such an act, and over the space of years? Who or what did she care about to this cost?

To find out, he began with a man he knew quite well who had been a patient of Anastasius's for some time. From him, Palombara learned of people she had treated without charge in her work with Bishop Constantine.

The picture emerged of a woman dedicated to medicine, absorbed in its practice but also fascinated by its details, its art, its curiosities, and the endless learning it inspired. Yet she was not without fault. She made errors of judgment, and she had a temper. Palombara became increasingly aware of a sense of guilt within her, although he had no idea what caused it. The more he learned, the more he was fascinated by her, the more intense became his need to protect her.

Over and over again, Anna Zarides appeared to have asked about the murder of Bessarion Comnenos.

Had she had some relationship with him? But she had not been to Constantinople before, and he had never left it since the return now nearly twenty years ago. It must be someone else. The obvious candidate was Justinian Lascaris, the man exiled for Bessarion's murder.

Justinian Lascaris was in exile near Jerusalem; this much he also learned. Her husband? Then she was a Lascaris as well, at least by marriage, a member of one of the imperial families with a passionate vengeance to wreak against the Palaeologi.

It was imperative Palombara see Anna Zarides where Vicenze would not know of it. His curiosity was cruel, endless, and still fueled by his need for revenge over the substitution of the nude painting for the icon of the Virgin.

So Palombara made his inquiries obliquely, as if they were of interest rather than importance, and it was three days before he finally presented himself at her house.

He noticed that she looked tired. There were fine lines around her eyes and a pallor to her skin. She had to be even more aware than he of the fear in the city and how short a time they had left before the end.

"How can I help you, Bishop Palombara?" she asked, looking at his eyes, his face, then at the way he stood. She could have seen no signs of illness in him, because there were none.

"I was grieved to hear of the death of Zoe Chrysaphes," he replied. He saw the answering emotion in her, a sharper sadness than he would have expected, and he liked her for it. "I went to convey my sympathies to Helena Comnena."

"That was gracious of you," she responded. "How does that reflect on your health?"

"It doesn't." He did not alter his steady gaze. "She told me that in her mother's papers she discovered something . . . startling. It is a piece of information which I fear Helena will use to her advantage, unless she can be prevented."

Anna clearly had no idea what he was referring to. He hated what he had to do, but her ignorance compelled him to act.

"Is Justinian Lascaris your husband or your brother?" he asked bluntly.

She stood completely motionless, the remnants of color draining from her skin. At first there was nothing in her eyes, as if she were too stunned to react at all; then the fear came, violent, all but consuming her. She breathed slowly, her chest heaving.

"My brother," she said at last. "My twin brother."

"I came to warn you, not to threaten you," he said gently. "You might prefer to leave the city."

The ghost of a smile crossed her face. "But there will certainly be work enough for a physician when the city falls." Her voice was thick with emotion, as if she found the words hard to say at all.

"Helena hates you," he said urgently. "She's changed since Zoe's death. It's almost as if it has freed her. I'm sure she's planning something. If she has access to Zoe's papers, then she may have taken up funding the rebellion against Charles in the West." Had he said too much?

Anna smiled. "I'm sure she has something planned," she agreed bitterly.

"Then go!" he argued. "While you can."

"I'm Byzantine, and I should run while you, a Roman priest, will stay?" she asked.

He did not answer. Perhaps in the end there was nothing else to say.

Ninety-two

CONSTANTINE WAS DESPERATE. IT WAS THREE WEEKS SINCE he had killed Zoe Chrysaphes and then a few days later conducted the funeral service for her in the Hagia Sophia. He had offered the Mass and given a eulogy almost fit for a saint.

Now in the solitude of his courtyard, the euphoria had passed and he was dogged by nightmares. He fasted, he prayed, but still they haunted him. Of course it was the work of God that he had destroyed Zoe. He had only ever allied with her in her plot to overthrow Michael so that Bessarion, a true son of the Church, could defy the union with Rome and save the faith.

And then Justinian Lascaris had killed Bessarion, so it had never come to fruition. Should he have agreed with Michael to help Justinian escape death? Perhaps Justinian had been right, and Bessarion would never have had the passion or the skill to defend them, or on the other hand, maybe Justinian had intended to take the throne himself?

Constantine had not pleaded for Justinian's life. Far from it. He was afraid that if Justinian had lived, he might have betrayed them all. But Michael wanted to save him and had used Constantine's name to do it, saying he had yielded to his pleas for mercy.

Now Zoe still plagued his dreams: She lay on her back, a lush, full-breasted woman, thighs apart in a mockery of his own emptiness. It was a humiliation, an obscenity, yet he could not look away.

Everything was sliding out of control. The emperor had betrayed the entire nation by selling out to Rome, and worse than that, he had done it so publicly that there was hardly a man, woman, or even child in Constantinople who did not know of it.

Now was the time for a miracle. Another month, two months, and it would be too late.

Yet Constantine was startled when his servant informed him that Bishop Vicenze was here and wished to speak with him. He disliked the man intensely, not only for his calling to undermine the Church in Byzantium and the fact that he came from Rome, but personally as well. Vicenze lacked any kind of humility. Still, Constantine had prayed for a miracle, and he must not stand in the way of its occurrence, if in some way Vicenze was part of it.

Constantine set aside the text he was reading and stood up. "Have him come in," he instructed.

Today Vicenze was dressed very plainly, almost as if he wished to pass unnoticed, whereas usually he was self-important.

They exchanged formal greetings: Constantine guardedly, Vicenze with uncharacteristic ease, as if keen to reach his purpose for having come.

Constantine offered him wine, fruit, and nuts. Vicenze accepted his hospitality, making light conversation of irrelevances until the servant had left. Then he turned straight to Constantine, his eyes brilliant with urgency.

"The situation in the city is very serious," he said, his voice sharp. "Fear is mounting every day, and we are on the brink of civil unrest, which could be disastrous for the well-being of the poor and the most vulnerable."

"I know," Constantine agreed, taking a handful of almonds from the exquisite porphyry bowl. "They are terrified of the army that Charles of Anjou will bring. They grew up on tales of crusader murders and destruction." He could not resist saying that, reminding Vicenze that because he was Roman he was partisan in the atrocity.

Vicenze bit his lip. "They need something to restore their faith in God, and in the Blessed Virgin," he said firmly. "Faith is greater than all the fear in the world. Brave men, giants in the cause of Christ, have faced crucifixion, lions, the fires of torture, and not flinched. They have gone to martyrdom because their faith was perfect. We are not asking that of the people, only belief, so God can work the miracle that will save not only their souls, but their bodies as well, maybe even their homes, their city. Has not the Blessed Virgin done it before, when the people trusted in her?"

In spite of his loathing for the man, Constantine was drawn into his vision. He spoke the truth, pure and lovely as the first light of dawn in a blemishless sky. "Yes . . . yes, she has, in the face of the impossible," he agreed.

"The invaders are coming by sea," Vicenze countered. "Has not God power over the wind and the waves? Could Christ not walk upon the water, and calm the storm—or cause one?"

Constantine felt his breath tighten. "But it would be a miracle. We have not the passion of faith to bring such a thing to pass."

"Then we must gain it!" Vicenze said, his eyes gleaming. "The faith of the people could save them, and surely there is nothing else left that will?"

"But what can we do?" Constantine said in a whisper. "They are too frightened to believe anymore."

"All they need is to see the hand of God in something, and they will believe again," Vicenze replied. "You must perform a smaller miracle for them, not only to the saving of their bodies, and your city and all it has been in the world, but to the saving of their souls. They are your charge, your holy responsibility."

"I thought you wanted their loyalty to Rome?" Constantine said.

Vicenze gave what passed for a smile. "Dead they are lost to all of us. And perhaps it has not occurred to you, but I do not want the souls of the crusaders stained with Christian blood either."

Constantine believed him. "What can we do?" he asked.

Vicenze took a deep breath and let it out softly. "There is a fine man, a good man, one who has helped his fellows, given of his means to the poor, and is deeply loved by all who know him. He is a Venetian living here, by the name of Andrea Mocenigo. He is aware of the situation—that we stand on the brink of destruction—and he will help."

Constantine was lost. "How? What can he do?"

"Everyone knows Mocenigo is ill," Vicenze said. "He is prepared to take a poison which will make him collapse. I will carry an antidote to it, and when you come to bless him, in the name of God and the Holy Virgin, I will give it to him, discreetly, and he will recover. People will see a miracle, dramatic and unmistakable. Word will spread, and faith will leap up again as a fire. Hope will be restored." He did not add that Constantine would be seen as a hero, even a saint.

A sharp whisper of doubt stabbed Constantine's mind. "Then why do you not do it yourself? Then the people would give Rome the credit."

Vicenze's mouth turned down at the corners. "The people mistrust me," he said simply. "It must be someone they have seen in the service of God all their lives. I know of no one else with that reputation in Constantinople. "

All this was true, Constantine knew. This was what he had worked and waited for all his life.

"Who knows?" Vicenze went on. "Maybe God will grant you a real miracle. Is this not the purpose for which you have lived?"

It was. Whatever Vicenze did, whatever that loathsome Palombara said to him, Constantine would be unshakable, without doubt or fear, his mind as clear as a burning light. He would not fail.

But he still would use his mind, his experience, and his own safeguards. He would say nothing of them to Vicenze, who for all his unwitting usefulness was still the enemy.

"I do not want a theological debate about it!" Constantine said furiously to Anastasius when asking for his help and receiving in return a passionate argument against the whole idea. "I want you there as a physician to attend Mocenigo, in case Vicenze is not to be trusted."

"Of course he is not to be trusted," Anastasius said bitterly. "What on earth can I do?"

"Carry another dose of the antidote," Constantine retorted. "You cannot refuse to do that. If you do, you are turning your back on Mocenigo, and on the people."

Anastasius sighed. He was caught, and they both knew it. If he spoke out against the plot or betrayed its nature to the people, it would shatter the belief they were clinging to, perhaps even provoke the final panic that could crush them all.

Ninety-three

⌒⌀⌒

ANNA ENTERED THE HOUSE OF MOCENIGO WITH ONLY A faint thought in the back of her mind that this was where Giuliano had lived for so long. All her conscious thought was for Mocenigo's distress. She could feel the anxiety and the fear as soon as she entered. There was that peculiar, tense hush that comes with awareness of profound suffering that is expected to end in the death of someone who is deeply loved.

Mocenigo's wife, Teresa, met her at the door of his room. Her face was pale and hollow-eyed from lack of sleep, and her hair was pinned back simply to keep it out of the way, with no thought for beauty.

"I am glad you have come," she said simply. "The last medicine seems to have made him worse. We rely entirely upon Bishop Constantine. God is our last refuge. Perhaps He should have been the first?"

Anna realized that Mocenigo himself might be party to the miracle, but his wife was not. It was too late to matter now. Anna followed her into Mocenigo's room.

It was stifling. The sun beat on the roofs and the windows were closed. The air smelled of body fluids, of pain and disease.

Mocenigo himself was lying on top of the bed. His face was scarlet and bloated, sheened with sweat, and there were blisters around his mouth. The small vial of liquid in the pocket of Anna's robe did not seem much remedy for this terrible distress.

Mocenigo opened his eyes and looked at her. He smiled, even through the pain that all but consumed him. "I think it will take a miracle to bring me back from this," he said, dry humor lighting his face for an instant, then vanishing. "But even for a day or two, it would be worth it, if it strengthens the people's faith. Byzantium has been good to me. I would like to repay . . . a little."

She said nothing. The deceit of it saddened her, and she hated Constantine for forcing her to be part of it. Yet perhaps Mocenigo was right, and the people would be richer for it. It was his last gift to those he loved.

There was a faint noise from outside, as if the crowd were growing larger. Word had spread that Mocenigo was dying and that Constantine would shortly come to see him. Was it grief or hope that brought them? Or both?

There was a roar and then a cheer. Anna knew that Constantine had arrived. A moment later, one of his servants came to the sickroom door and requested that Mocenigo be brought out where his well-wishers could see him.

Anna stepped forward to refuse him. "You can't—"

But she was overridden. Constantine's servant was giving orders, and other people were coming in, solemn-faced, preparing to put him on a litter and lift him out. No one was listening to Anna. She was merely a physician, where Constantine spoke for God.

She followed outside. Mocenigo was in such distress that he said nothing, too weak to protest. His wife, ashen-faced, simply obeyed Constantine's servant.

There were now more than two hundred people in the street, and soon it would be three hundred and then four.

Constantine stood on the top step, holding up his hands for silence. "I have not come to give this good man the last rites or prepare him for death," he said clearly.

"You'd better prepare us all!" a voice shouted. "We're just as done for as he is!"

There was a roar of agreement, and several people waved their arms.

Constantine raised his hands higher. "The threat is real, and terrible," he cried loudly. "But if the Holy Mother of God is with us, what can it matter if all men are against us, or the legions of darkness either?"

The noise subsided. Several people crossed themselves.

"I come to seek the will of God," Constantine went on. "And if He grants me, to beseech the Holy Virgin to allow this man to be healed of his affliction, as a sign that we too will be healed of ours, and saved from the abominations of the invaders."

There was a moment's incredulity. People turned to one another, puzzled, daring to hope. Then the cheer went up even more loudly than before, a little hysterical, hundreds willing themselves to believe, they knew the strength of faith to make such a miracle possible, and all the wild hope that went with it.

Constantine smiled, lowered his hands, and turned to Mocenigo. The sick man was now lying on the pallet in front of him, breathing shallowly, but seeming to be at ease.

The crowd fell into an almost paralyzed silence. No one even shuffled a foot.

Constantine lowered his hands and placed them on Mocenigo's head.

Anna searched with increasing panic for sight of Vicenze in the crowd; then she saw him, close by but not to the fore, as if he were here only to witness. Better it were so.

Constantine's voice rose clear and charged with emotion. He called on the Holy Virgin Mary to heal Andrea Mocenigo, as a blessing to him for his faith and as a sign to the people that she still watched over them and would keep and preserve them in the face of all adversity.

Vicenze stepped forward, and as Constantine raised Mocenigo up, Vicenze passed him water and together they ministered to him. Vicenze stepped back.

Everyone waited. The air seemed dense with the burden of hope and fear.

Then Mocenigo gave a terrible cry and clutched at his throat, his body twisting in agony. He tore at himself, screaming.

Anna ran forward, pushing everyone out of her way, even though she already knew it was too late. The antidote Vicenze had given Mocenigo was poison. Perhaps hers would be poison to him as well. She dared not use it in what would surely be a useless attempt now.

Mocenigo was choking. She got to him just as he writhed and fell off the litter, vomiting blood. There was nothing she could do but support him so he did not choke and drown. Even so, it was only moments before he gave a last, agonizing convulsion and his heart stopped.

The nearest man in the crowd howled with terror and rage, then charged forward, knocking Constantine off his feet. Others followed, shouting and lashing out. They hauled Constantine half up, dragging him along, all the time cursing him and beating his head and face and body with fists, kicking him and hurling anything they could grasp. It seemed as if they would tear him apart.

Anna was appalled by the savagery of it, and even as he was thrashed and hauled and half carried away, she could see Constantine's terror. Then there was another face in the crowd she knew, Palombara. Their eyes met for an instant, and she understood that he had foreseen it: Vicenze's plan, the poison, the violence.

She laid Mocenigo down. There was nothing anyone could do for him now, except cover his face so his last agony was given some privacy. Then she lunged forward, striking at those in her way, shouting at them to leave Constantine alone.

She screamed until her throat ached. "Don't kill him! It won't . . . For the love of God, stop it!" A blow landed on her back and shoulders, sending her forward, crashing into the man ahead of her, then another blow drove her to her knees. All around were faces distorted with hate and terror. The noise was indescribable. This must be what hell was like—blind, insane rage.

Anna clambered to her feet, was almost knocked over again, and started to move in the direction she thought they had dragged Constantine.

She shouted, pleading with them, but nobody was listening. Someone howled in terror: It was a man's voice, shrill and unrecognizable. It was hideous with the indignity of its nakedness. Was it Constantine, reduced to the least he could become? She lunged forward again, striking and shouting and kicking to make her way.

Palombara saw her for an instant, then lost her again. He knew what she was doing. He understood the horror and the pity in her. That brief second when he met her eyes, it was as clear to him as if he had felt it himself, the passion for life, the courage that could not deny, whatever the cost. She was vulnerable. She could be so desperately hurt, even killed, and he could not bear that. He would not live with that light gone.

He fought his way toward her, his priest's calling forgotten, his robes torn, his fists bleeding. He ignored the blows that landed on him. He knew they hated him. To them he was Roman, a symbol of all that had accomplished their ruin time and time again. Still, he must reach Anna and get her out of this; what happened after that was in the hands of God.

Another blow knocked him almost senseless. The pain was stunning, taking his breath away. It seemed like minutes before he could get his balance back, but it must have been only seconds. He lashed out, shouting at the huge man in front of him.

Palombara hit him. It felt good to put all his weight behind it, all the fury and frustration he had ever known. For an instant, that man was every cardinal who had lied and connived, every pope who had failed his promises, who had equivocated, stuffed the Vatican with his sycophants, been a coward where he should have been brave, arrogant where he should have been humble.

The man went down, teeth broken on Palombara's fist, his mouth gushing blood. Hell, but it hurt! Palombara's hand stabbed with pain right up to his shoulder, and it was only then that he noticed the broken shard of tooth, like bone, embedded in his knuckles.

Where was Anna? He plowed forward, beating and flailing, knocked sideways again and again by blows himself. There was a gash in his shoulder bleeding badly, and it hurt to breathe.

Then she was there in front of him, dust and blood on her clothes, a bruise on her cheekbone. There was too much noise for him to speak to her; he simply grasped her arm and dragged her after him in the direction he thought would lead to escape. He kept her in the shelter of his own body, taking the blows meant for both of them. One to his chest hurt so intensely that he stopped, for seconds unable to draw any breath into his lungs. He was aware of her holding him. Without realizing it, he had sunk to his knees. The crowd was parting a little. He could see clear space ahead.

"Go!" he said hoarsely. "Get away from here."

Still she held him. "I'm not leaving you. Just breathe slowly, don't gasp."

"I can't." His chest was tighter. There was blood in his throat. It was getting harder to concentrate, to stay conscious. "Go!"

She bent down to him, holding him closer, as if she would give him her strength. She was going to wait with him! He did not want her to. He wanted her to survive. Her passion, with its cost, had shown him that hell was worse and heaven far, far more exquisite than he had dreamed—and both were real.

"For God's sake, get out of here!" he rasped, his mouth filling with blood. "I don't want to die for nothing. Don't . . . don't do that to me!

Give me something . . ." He could still feel her arms around him, then just as the darkness had closed over him, he felt her let him go, and suddenly it was light. He knew he was smiling. He meant to.

Anna staggered to her feet. In a few moments, there was a break in the crowd and she saw someone holding out a hand to her. She took it and was pulled beyond the fury into a calm, dusty space. Then a door was opened and she was inside a house. She thanked the man. He looked exhausted and frightened, possibly no older than his twenties.

"Are you all right?" she asked him.

He was shaking, embarrassed by his own weakness. "Yes," he assured her. "More or less. I think they killed the bishop."

She knew Palombara was dead, but this young man was speaking of Constantine. To him, Palombara was a Roman and of no importance.

The young man was wrong; Constantine was badly beaten, but he was definitely alive and still conscious, although in great pain. His servant, arms bloody, face swollen with bruises, came to Anna and asked her help. They had carried him into a nearby house, and the owner had given up his own room so Constantine could have the best bed, the greatest comfort possible.

She went with the servant; there was no alternative she could live with.

The owner of the house and his wife were waiting, white-faced, horrified at the violence, the tragedy, and above all at what appeared to be a total collapse of sanity.

"Save him," the wife pleaded as Anna came in. Her eyes beseeched Anna for some hope.

"I will do all I can," Anna said, then followed the servant up the narrow stairs.

Constantine was lying on the bed, his torn and bloody dalmatica removed. His tunic was crumpled and filthy with dirt from the street, but someone had done his best to straighten it and make him as comfortable as possible. There was a ewer of water on the table and several bottles of wine and jars of perfumed unguent. One look at Constantine's face told her that they would do little good. His ribs were broken, his collarbones, and one hip. He was certainly bleeding inside where no one could reach it.

She sat on the chair beside him. To touch him would only cause greater pain.

"God has left me," he said. His eyes were empty of all passion, looking inward on an abyss from which there was no return.

Christ had promised that in the resurrection every human being would be made whole again; not a hair of the head would be lost. That must mean that everything would be restored as it should have been, without accident, withering, or mutilation. Should she tell him that? Would it be of any comfort now, when it was his soul that had been squandered? That was the inner self that remained into eternity.

She remembered Constantine working so hard, until his face was gray with exhaustion and he could barely keep his balance, yet none of the poor, the frightened, or the sick were turned away. What uncontrollable hunger had blurred his vision so badly that he had ended in twisting it all until nothing was honest anymore?

"God doesn't leave people," she said aloud. "We leave Him." Her voice was shaking.

His eyes focused on her. "I served the Church all my life . . ." he protested.

"I know," she agreed. "But that's not the same thing. You created a God in your own image, one of laws and rituals, of office and observances, because that requires only outward acts. It's simple to understand. You don't have to feel, or give of your heart. You missed the grace and the passion, the courage beyond anything we can imagine, the hope even in absolute darkness, the gentleness, the laughter, and the love that has no shadow. The journey is longer and steeper than any of us can understand. But then heaven is higher, so it has to be steep, and far."

He said nothing, his eyes bottomless, like pits dug out of his soul.

She reached for the towel, wrung out the water, and washed his face. She hated him, yet at this moment she would have taken his pain if she could.

"A Church can help," she went on, in order to fill the silence, so he knew she was still there. "People can always help. We need people. There's nothing if we don't care. But the real climb is made not because this person or that person told you what to do, or lifted you on the way, it is made because you hunger for it so much, no one can stop you. You have to want it so that you will pay what it costs."

"Didn't I save souls?" he pleaded.

How could she refuse him? Love forgave. In all her anger and pain, she must remember she walked beside, not above. She too needed grace. If it was for a different sin, it was no less necessary.

"You have helped, but Christ redeemed them, and they saved themselves by being the best they could, and trusting in God to mend what was left."

"Theodosia?" he asked. "I gave her absolution. She needed it. Wasn't I right?"

"No," she said softly. "You forgave her without demanding penance because you wanted to please her. You lied to her, and it destroyed her faith. Perhaps it was fragile anyway, but she couldn't trust a God who would permit what she did to Joanna. You would have known that, if you'd thought about it honestly."

"No, that's not true." But there was no conviction in his voice.

"Yes, it is. You defaced your own truth."

He stared at her, and very slowly something of what she had said became real to him, and the abyss widened.

She saw it and was seized with pity, and then remorse. But it was too late to take it back. "She walked there willingly." She touched the cloth to his face again, very gently. "We all do." She met his eyes. Whatever she would see there, she had no right to look away now.

She took his hand in hers. "We all make mistakes. You are right, I have made some for which I have not yet repented, and I need to. But we are here to help, not to judge. Only God can teach you how to do that, not even the best of men, not when the pain is beyond bearing. Be gentle. Reach out. What gain is in it for you doesn't matter."

His face was ashen, his lips dry, as if he were already dead. He said the words so softly she had to strain to hear: "I am become Judas . . ."

She bathed his face and hands, his neck. She wet his lips and touched his skin with the perfumed unguent. It may have eased the pain for a while. Certainly he seemed calmer for it.

After a few moments longer, she stood up and went out of the room to ask for water to wash some of the dust and blood off herself. Every part of her body hurt. She had not realized it until now, but her left arm was soaked with her own blood, and her ribs were so badly bruised that it hurt to move. One side of her face was painful and swelling up so that her eye was half-closed, and now that she moved, she limped badly.

It was half an hour later when Anna returned to the upper bedroom to sit with Constantine again, in case there was something she could do for him. Perhaps as much as anything, it was so as not to leave him alone.

She stopped abruptly just beyond the door. The candle was still burning, although the flame was wavering. The bed was empty. Even the sheet was gone. Then she realized that the window was open and it was the slight draft of air from it that was moving the candle flame. She walked over to close the window and saw the torn end of linen tied around the central bar. She leaned out slowly and stared downward.

Constantine's body hung about four feet below her, the sheet tight around his neck, his head lolling sideways. It was not possible that he could still be alive. His last words came back to her, and the Field of Blood beyond Jerusalem. She should have known.

Dizzy and sick, she staggered back into the room and sat down hard on the bed. She remained motionless for some time. Was she guilty of this? Should she have done more to prevent Constantine from ever being involved in trying to create a miracle?

Vicenze had designed it to fail. They should have known that from the start. Palombara knew it. And at the thought of Palombara she leaned forward, buried her face in the blanket, and wept. It was a kind of ease after all the horror and the fear to let the tears come and simply to grieve.

She had lost too much. Constantine was gone in a way that left only pain and a bitter grief. Palombara was different, yet she felt an ache of loss for him, too, because she would miss him.

Later, Anna went back to see Teresa Mocenigo and gave her whatever comfort she could. When it was daylight, she went with her to face the remnant of the crowd still left. Quietly and with the dignity of grief, Teresa asked them to honor Mocenigo's life by behaving now with the honor that was the best in them. They must deal with Vicenze according to the law. Guilty as he was, to murder him would be to stain their own souls.

Finally, Anna returned to her home to tend to her own wounds of heart and her bleeding, aching body. She wept for her own painful emptiness, for Giuliano, for the loneliness that was at the back of everything.

Ninety-four

IN MARCH OF 1282, THE VAST FLEET OF CHARLES OF ANJOU anchored in the Bay of Messina in the north of Sicily. Giuliano stood on the hillside above the harbor and stared at its size and power, and his heart sank. The force under Charles was enormous, and more ships were expected from Venice. Maybe Pietro Contarini would be with them. He had spoken of it the last time they had met, before that final parting. And it was final. They would not meet as friends again, Pietro had made that clear. His loyalty was always to Venice first. Giuliano could no longer promise that.

He watched now as the fleet commanders walked along the quay and then up the broad streets to be welcomed by the royal vicar and governor of the island, Herbert of Orleans. He lived in the great fortress castle of Mategriffon, known as "The Terror of the Greeks." That was the thought uppermost in Giuliano's mind as he thought of the crusader forces pillaging the countryside for food and beasts, in the name of Christ's war to recover the land of the Savior's birth and set it again under Christian rule.

Giuliano set out to walk back over the rough terrain of the central mountains, the cone of Etna always on the skyline. He wanted to be back in Palermo before the French forces reached it. If they were to make a stand, he would do it with the people he cared for most, with Giuseppe and his friends.

Not only did his legs ache—his blistered feet remind him with each step—but he was sick at heart at the senseless violence of it, the hatred that drove ignorant men to plunder and destroy. The loss would be immeasurable, not only in life but in beauty and glories that took the breath away, such as the Palatine Chapel with its great soaring Saracen arches and exquisite Byzantine mosaics. Centuries of profound and exquisite thought would be wiped out by men who could barely write their own names.

Perhaps worst of all was the lie that this was done in the service of Christ, the blind belief that sins would be forgiven, that this sea of human blood could wash anything clean.

How had the message of Christ ever come to be twisted into this atrocity?

Giuliano reached Palermo tired and dirty and went quickly through the familiar streets in the clear early morning sun. There was little sound but the music of the fountains, the occasional hurrying footsteps, then the breathless hush of waiting.

Maria was already up and busy in the kitchen. When she heard him at the door she whirled around, carving knife in her hand. Then she saw him and her face flooded with relief. She dropped the knife and ran to him, throwing her arms around his body and hugging him to her so hard that he was afraid she would hurt her own soft flesh in doing it.

Gently he disengaged himself and stepped back.

She looked him up and down. "Food, then clean clothes. You're filthy!" She turned away and began to get out the bread, oil, cheese, and wine, frantic to do anything useful. He saw over her shoulder how little there was in the cupboards.

"When are they coming?" she asked finally when she set a generous plate of food—too generous—on the table in front of him.

"Share it with me?" he asked.

"I've already eaten," she answered.

He knew it was a lie. She never ate before her family did. "Then eat some more," he insisted. "It will make me feel at home, not like a stranger. It may be the last meal we can eat like this, together." He smiled, tears prickling his eyes for all that would be lost.

She obeyed, taking bread and a little well-watered red wine. "They'll be here today?" she asked. "Aren't we going to fight, Giuliano?"

"Probably tomorrow," he answered. "And I don't know if we're going to fight or not. The whole island is angry, but it's just under the surface, and I can't read it well enough."

"It's Easter Monday tomorrow," she said very quietly. "The day our Lord rose from the dead. Can we fight on Easter Day?"

"You fight on any day, to save the people you love," he replied.

"Maybe they won't fight?" she said hopefully.

"Maybe." But he had seen them and knew otherwise.

Easter Monday was beautiful. The justiciar, John of Saint Remy, celebrated the feast in the palace of the Norman knights as if he and his men were unaware of the tension and hatred churning around them in the people they oppressed. But then, they had refused to learn the Sicilian customs or even their language.

Giuliano stood in the streets and gazed at the Sicilians pouring into the open, filling the alleys and squares with music, dancing. The women's skirts and bright scarves were like flowers in the wind. Was all this energy the joy at the risen Lord, the belief in life everlasting, or just the breaking of unbearable tension as they waited for horsemen to arrive and take from them the last vestige of what they possessed, not only food but dignity and hope?

Half a dozen young men passed him, arms around girls with swaying skirts, laughing. One of the girls held out a hand to him, smiling.

He hesitated. It was churlish not to join them, and it set him apart when he hungered with something close to despair to belong, at least emotionally. He was part of their battle, and he would be part of their victory or loss.

He stood up and ran the few paces after them, taking the girl's hand. They reached an open square where music was playing and began to dance. He danced with them until he was exhausted and out of breath.

A young man offered him wine, and he took it. It was rough and a little sharp to the taste, but he drank it with pleasure, passing the bottle back with a smile. The girls began to sing, and everyone else took up the chorus. Giuliano did not know the words, but it did not matter, he caught the tunes quickly. No one else seemed to care. The wine passed from hand to hand, and he drank probably more than he should have.

The jokes were funny and silly, but everyone laughed too easily and too loud. Now and again he caught someone's eye, a young man with curly hair, a girl with a blue scarf, and saw for an instant the grief they also knew was coming.

Then someone started a song or told another joke, and they all laughed, arms around one another, holding too tight.

He thanked them when he left to go.

He was tired and hope was fading, raw on the edge of despair, when he set out with Giuseppe, Maria, and their children to attend the Vespers service at the Church of the Holy Spirit, half a mile or so to the southeast beyond the old city wall. It was an austere building, and its spare beauty exactly suited his mood.

The square was crowded with people, as if half the countryside had chosen to come here for this most holy celebration. They milled around, excitement charging the air as if there were a storm to come, in spite of the calm spring evening.

Giuliano looked up at the columns and tower.

A dozen yards away a man began to sing, and quickly others joined in. It was beautiful, totally appropriate as they waited for the Vespers bell to ring and the service to begin, yet to Giuliano it seemed jarringly normal, when nothing else was.

Abruptly the singing stopped.

Giuliano swung around and saw horsemen in the street to the north that opened into the square, then to the east as well, leading from the city walls. There must have been a score of them or more, a foraging party come to take what they could. They looked happy and a little drunk.

The pounding of his heart almost choked him.

Gradually the singing stopped as the Frenchmen came forward, apparently intending to join in. They began singing loudly in French.

The man beside Giuliano swore. In the crowd people moved closer to one another, men reaching a hand to clasp a child or a wife. There was a low rumble of anger.

The Frenchmen were laughing, calling out to the pretty women as one or another caught their eye.

Giuliano felt his muscles ache and his nails bite into the palms of his hands.

One of the Frenchmen called out to a small boy and beckoned him over. The child hesitated, backing a little behind his mother's skirts. She moved a little farther in front of the boy. One Frenchman shouted something, another laughed.

Giuliano heard a cry and saw an officer. He held a young woman by the waist and drew her away from the crowd into the mouth of a quiet alley. Suddenly his hands were all over her body and she was struggling to avoid him, turning her head this way and that as he tried to kiss her.

Giuliano pushed his way forward past an old woman and several children, but he was too late. The young woman's husband had already pulled his dagger. The French officer lay sprawled on the stones, his chest scarlet and blood pooling on the stones beneath him.

Someone gasped and stifled a scream.

All around the square, Giuliano saw Frenchmen draw their swords to avenge their comrade. Within seconds the Sicilians had their knives drawn also, and the fighting escalated. There were curses, shouting, the sun bright on steel, and blood on the stones.

Above them all, the bells of the Church of the Holy Spirit began ringing the call to Vespers, and those were echoed by the bells of every other church in the city.

Giuliano was surrounded. Where were Giuseppe and Maria? He saw Tino, one of their children, looking dazed, his face white. He lunged forward and seized the boy's hand. "Stay by me," he ordered. "Where's your mother?"

Tino stared at him, too terrified to speak.

Ten feet away, a French soldier swung his sword and a Sicilian fell to the stones, blood gushing from his arm. A woman screamed. A Sicilian lunged at the man, arm out holding a dagger. The Frenchman fell and Giuliano dived forward to take his sword, then whirled around and snatched the child's arm.

"Come!" Giuliano shouted, dragging him along. He wanted to find Giuseppe and Maria and the other children, but he could not afford to let go of this one.

All around the square and in the streets leading off it men were fighting, and some women, seeming just as good with the knives. The French were badly outnumbered, and already there were men on the ground, some struggling to rise, others lying still. Generations of oppression and abuse, of poverty, fear, and humiliation, were finding a passion of vengeance at last, and the savagery was unstoppable.

They kept to shadows and narrow ways. It was a risk, in case they should find the way blocked, but the fighting in the square was worse. A few yards to the left, they could hear the shouts of "Death to the French!" and the call on the men of Palermo to unite and take back their freedom and their dignity at last.

Giuliano started to run as fast as he could with the boy. After covering the complete length of the alley, they burst into the quiet courtyard of a Dominican convent. The scene that met their eyes was hideous. A dozen Sicilians held ten friars at knifepoint.

"Say '*ciceri*,' " one of the Sicilians ordered. It was the test of nationality. No Frenchman could pronounce the word.

The first friar obeyed and was let go, staggering, tripping over his torn habit, almost numb with fear.

The second was given the same order.

He stumbled and failed.

There was a cry of "French!" and Giuliano grasped Tino and swung him around just as the Sicilians slit the friar's throat and he fell forward, gushing blood.

Tino howled in fear. Giuliano picked him up and slung him over his shoulder, then barged back out the way he had come. He stood in the alley trying to draw the air into his lungs, still clinging to the boy's small body.

He had wanted the Sicilians to rebel, to cast off the yoke of oppression, but he had never imagined this terrible violence. Had Giuliano known the hatred was so close to the surface, would he still have tried to waken it?

Yes. He would, because the only alternative was worse—endless subjection until the life and the heart were crushed out of them. The same slow death awaited Byzantium.

He carried Tino the rest of the way. Men crazed with sudden power, gore-stained scarlet, saw the child and let him pass, and Giuliano was ashamed of his own safety for that reason. But he did not stop, even when he heard men pleading for their lives, women screaming, fighting. He felt Tino's fingers gripping him, and he kept moving.

When at last he reached Giuseppe and Maria's house, Giuliano was exhausted and shivering. Fear that they would not be there turned his stomach to water.

He was still yards from it when the door opened and Maria came out. She saw him and choked back a cry as he put Tino in her arms.

Giuseppe was in the doorway, tears running down his cheeks, the candlelight yellow behind him, a knife in his hand, preparing to defend his remaining children if Giuliano had been an enemy. His face split in a smile and he ran forward, dropping the knife and clasping Giuliano so tightly that he all but cracked his ribs.

Maria urged them inside, and obediently they followed her. Giuseppe barred the door after them.

"Go back to Gianni," Giuseppe said to Maria. As she left, he looked at Giuliano. "He's hurt," he said simply. "She can't leave him." The explanation was unnecessary, but Giuseppe could not take his eyes from Tino for more than a few moments, and he kept touching the boy's head, as if to assure himself that he was real and alive.

A little after first light, one of the other fishermen came, a man called Angelo. The children were asleep, and Maria was upstairs with them.

"We're going to meet in the town center," Angelo said gravely to Giuliano and Giuseppe. His face was burned and there was a cut on his brow, blood congealed, and his left arm was in a makeshift sling. He was filthy and he moved stiffly, as if his limbs hurt. "We must decide what to do now. There are hundreds dead, maybe thousands. The corpses of people block the alleys, and the stones are red with blood."

"There'll be war," Giuliano warned.

Angelo nodded. "We must prepare for it. They have called for men from every district and trade so we can choose someone to represent us and ask the pope to recognize us as a commune, and ask for his protection."

"From Charles of Anjou?" Giuliano said incredulously. "What the hell do you think the pope is going to do? He's French, for God's sake!"

"He's Christian," Giuseppe replied. "He can give us his protection."

"Are you waiting on that?" Giuliano was appalled.

Giuseppe gave him a bleak smile, a flash of the old humor in his eyes.

Angelo nodded. "Runners have already gone out to all the towns and villages, closest ones first, to tell them what has happened and to call on them to rise up with us. The whole island will turn against the Angevins. We are going to march on Vicari and give them all the choice of leaving with safe conduct to sail back to Provence."

"Or what?" Giuseppe asked.

"Or death," Angelo replied.

"I imagine they will choose Provence," Giuliano said dryly.

"And you, my friend . . ." Giuseppe turned to Giuliano, his face puckered with anxiety, his eyes gentle. "What do you choose? These were Frenchmen tonight, but by next week, or next month, they may be Venetians. The fleet lies at Messina. You are not Sicilian. This is not your quarrel. Any hospitality we gave you you have more than repaid. Go now, before you act against your own people."

Still exhausted, aching, his clothes sticking to him with other men's blood, Giuliano realized how alone he was. "I don't have people of my own," he said slowly. "I have friends, I have debts, and people I love. That isn't the same thing."

"I don't know what debts you have," Giuseppe answered. "None to me. But you are my friend, which is why I give you leave to go, if honor pulls you. I am going to Corleone with Angelo to tell them to rise also, and then after that on to other towns, and if I survive it, to Messina."

"To the fleet?"

"Yes. Maria and the children will be safe here now. Angelo and his family will protect them."

"Then I'm coming with you." Already in his mind he knew what he was going to do. It surprised him. He barely had time to be afraid or realize the enormity of it, but now that it came to the moment, there was no choice after all.

Giuseppe grinned and held out his hand. Giuliano clasped it.

Ninety-five

∽

GIULIANO WENT WITH GIUSEPPE AND THE OTHER MEN, leaving Palermo and traveling hastily, often by night. By the middle of April, the whole island of Sicily was in revolt; only one French overlord was spared, because of the humanity he had shown in his rule. Every other garrison was taken and the occupants put to the sword.

By the end of the month, Giuliano stood beside Giuseppe on the hillside overlooking the harbor of Messina. Below him lay the massed fleet of Charles of Anjou, ships of every size and rig he could name, at least two hundred of them crowded together so they darkened the sea and there was barely room for others to swing at anchor without touching one another.

How many catapults did they carry? How many siege towers to storm the city walls? How much Greek fire to ruin and burn?

"They look deserted," Giuseppe said quietly, squinting into the sun.

"They probably are, all but a watch," Giuliano replied. Two days earlier, Messina also had risen against the French, who had retreated to the great granite castle of Mategriffon but had not had the strength to hold it. "But they are still a threat to Byzantium. The Venetian fleet is coming with more men, more ships, more armor. The siege engines are still there, and the horses can always be stolen again."

Giuseppe stared at him. "What do you want? To sink them?"

Giuliano knew that he would be breaking the oath he had made to Tiepolo that he would never betray the interests of Venice. But the world was not the same as it had been when Tiepolo was alive. Venice was not the same; Rome certainly wasn't.

"Burn them," he said softly. "Pitch. Small boats, ones we can tow behind a rowing boat. It must be when the wind is right, and the current—"

"And you would do that? You . . . a Venetian," Giuseppe said softly.

"Half Venetian," Giuliano corrected him. "My mother was Byzantine. But that has nothing to do with it . . . or not everything, anyway. It's wrong. To conquer Byzantium is wrong. There's nothing Christian in it. It doesn't matter who they are, or what are their beliefs. The point is that it should not ever be who we are."

Giuseppe stared at him. "You are a strange man, Giuliano. But I'm with you." He held out his hand, offering it.

Giuliano took it and gripped it hard, holding on to it.

They gathered allies among the Sicilians who had lost relatives, friends, and brothers to the French. They found the boats they needed and the pitch. It was not as much as Giuliano would have liked, but they could not risk waiting any longer.

He stood alone on the quayside, watching the sun set in the west, sulfurous, underlighting the clouds that would make it darker and obscure the moon. He could never watch the sky now without a memory of Anastasius stirring in his mind. Their quiet conversations haunted him when he least expected it.

And it was Anastasius who had given him more than peace with his mother. He had healed that deepest wound.

What part had that in the terrible thing Giuliano was planning to do? While others were helping him, it was his moral decision. There were so many ships, some with men still aboard. He wanted to destroy them all, so they would never carry war to Byzantium. Did it matter that they would also not recapture Jerusalem? Would the crusading knights make anything better than it already was in that troubled city, anything safer or kinder than now?

It was too late to change the decision, even if he wanted to. His mind was afraid of failure, afraid of the horror he was about to unleash, but he was not in doubt.

Stefano, the strongest rower and most familiar with the Bay of Messina, set out first, rowing one boat and towing the other with the pitch and oil in it.

Giuseppe set out next when they judged Stefano to be halfway across, although they could not see him, hidden by the forest of ships at anchor. He would look as if he were some kind of supply boat. With a second unmanned boat behind him, he would not be mistaken for a fisherman.

"Good luck," Giuliano said quietly, crouching low on the shore and pushing the stern away as Giuseppe bent at the oar.

Giuseppe saluted him silently, and within moments he was twenty feet away, oars dipping without sound, rhythmically, the waves slapping against the sides. He had to work to keep from being carried inshore by the current.

Giuliano waited until he could only just see him, then he waded in, climbed into his own boat, and grasped the oars. He was used to the open sea and to giving orders rather than bending his own back, but urgency drove him now, the emotion high in his chest, almost in his throat, as he felt the wind and the water begin to fight against him.

He had not rowed in a long time, and his shoulders ached. He would have blisters on his hands before the night was out. He must be upward of the easternmost warship before he lit the pitch and cast off. Stefano would be first. When he saw the fire start, Giuseppe, in the second boat, would light his, then finally Giuliano. They would all have to row out to sea, against the current and the wind, to be sure of not getting caught in the flames themselves.

He looked over his shoulder, straining in the darkness to see the spark as soon as it showed. Like the others, he had tinder, torches, and oil to make sure the fire took hold before he cast off the burning boat. If he cut it loose too soon and the flames died, it would all have been for nothing.

He reached the point as closely as he could judge, but had to keep his hands on the oars to avoid drifting into the fleet. Slowly he turned so the fireboat was behind him and he was looking westward across the bay. Where were the others?

The water was slapping hard against the hull of the boat. He had to lean on the oars to keep his distance from the nearest warship. The current was running fast, and the wind rising. His back ached, and the muscles of his shoulders cracked.

He strained his eyes to see. Then suddenly there it was, a wick of light, growing, a yellow flame, bigger and bigger. Then another, closer to him, tiny at first but swelling, billowing in the darkness.

He slipped the oars and grasped for the tinder, taking a moment to find it in the darkness at the bottom of the boat. Then he had it. He fumbled for the torch, found the first one, then the second, and a third for safety. The tinder refused to ignite. He was drifting toward the warship, the sea taking him faster and faster. His fingers were clumsy. He must steady himself. He had one chance!

Then the tinder caught and the spark lit the torch. It flared up. He touched it to the second. They burned hard and hot. He hurled the first one into the boat of oil and pitch. The flame took a moment, then roared up. He lit the third torch from the second and threw them both also. The flames were high and hot already. He must cut the rope or it would take him with it. Away to the west, the flames were mounting as the fireboats caught the seaward vessels.

The rope was thick and wet. It seemed to take forever to saw through it. Why hadn't he brought a sharper blade? Patience! At last it was cut through and fell into the sea. He sat back on the thwart and grasped the oars, throwing his weight into pulling, one stroke and then two, three. He was too close to the warships. He could hear men shouting, panic in their voices. To the west, the flames were hard and bright. The first ship was ablaze, fire up to its masts, leaping high.

He pulled as hard as he could, digging the oars deep. He must pull evenly. Tear a muscle now and he would burn with them. He must get away, then back to shore. Were Giuseppe and Stefano all right? Had they the strength to make shore? He should have told Giuseppe, out in the middle of the bay, to make for the farther shore, not try to beat against the wind back to the east.

No, that was stupid; he wouldn't have to be told!

The light was growing stronger as the ship in the middle of the bay burned more strongly. The canvas of the furled sails was on fire. Then the Greek fire in the hold exploded, white hot, like the heart of a furnace. Pieces of flaming debris were sent high into the air. Giuliano leaned on the oars and caught his breath for a moment as a streamer of flame shot into the sky and landed on another ship, catching immediately on the dry wood. Other pieces fell into the sea. He stared at the beauty and horror as one ship after another burned until the whole bay was an inferno like the floor of some visionary hell.

Another ship with Greek fire exploded, sending debris soaring into the air. The roar of it was deafening, and the heat seared Giuliano's skin even as far away as he was.

A blazing plank of wood splashed into the water only a few feet from him. Galvanized into action, he grasped the oars and threw his body against the weight of them, sending the boat hurtling forward.

Fifteen minutes later, he reached the eastern shore a hundred feet from where he had set out and stood to watch as one of the warships listed and dropped lower in the water.

By morning, there would be little left of Charles's fleet. The fact that Giuliano, a Venetian, had lit the fire that destroyed it was perhaps some small measure of redemption for Venice from its ravage of Byzantium seventy years ago.

He turned slowly and made his way toward the town. He could see his way quite clearly in the light of the flames. They roared up into the sky, casting a glare over the drifting wreckage, the water of the bay now showing brazen between the jagged black skeletons of the ruined ships. It lit the fronts of the houses red and yellow, and as Giuliano came closer to the buildings, he could see their windows, brilliant panes of flat gold in the darker stones.

People were crowding out to watch in amazement and horror at the sight. Some clung to each other as each new explosion filled the air with sound and fury. Others stood paralyzed, unbelieving.

Giuliano increased his pace, striding out. Giuseppe and Stefano would go back into the hills, up toward Etna, where the servants of Charles's men would never find them, but he needed to go to Byzantium. He must carry the news.

The massive buttresses of Mategriffon towered above him, men on the battlements staring into the inferno on the sea, their faces lit like effigies of copper. Giuliano looked up and for a moment saw Charles himself, his features twisted with rage and the dawning understanding of what had happened to the precious dreams of his lifetime.

For an instant he looked down, perhaps saw something familiar in Giuliano's stride or the dark outline of his figure as he passed a wall, pale in the reflected light. Charles stiffened with recognition.

Giuliano lifted his arm in a salute. In spite of his weariness and the ache in his body, he quickened his pace. He must be gone before archers could be summoned or soldiers called to hunt him down.

Ninety-six

ZOE WAS DEAD, AND AFTER THE DEATHS OF CONSTANTINE
and Palombara, Anna felt a new constriction and grief even tighter
inside her. The fear in the city increased as people waited for more immediate news of the invasion. Rumors spread like brushfire, leaping from
street to street, growing more distorted with each new telling.

People hoarded food, weapons; those near the walls stored pitch to light
and pour on the enemy when they came. Every day more people left, a
constant bleeding away of those who had the means to travel and somewhere to go. As always, the poor, the old, and the sick remained.

Fishermen still went out, but they stayed close to the shore and were in
by nightfall, boats moored or pulled up the beach, guards on watch
against theft.

Anna still treated the sick and found among them more injuries due to
the clumsiness of fear and carelessness because muscles were clenched, attention divided, people sleepless with the constant watching and listening
for news of disaster.

She could give some relief for the physical distress, but the reality of
what lay ahead she could not treat. It was only by being constantly concerned with the small duties she could perform that she could ignore the
greater truths.

There were few she cared for personally now. Nicephoras would stay as
long as the emperor did. For them to run away was unthinkable. She
spoke also to Leo.

"When the crusader fleet arrives, it will be too late," she said quietly to Leo one evening after a supper of fish and vegetables. "We have done all we could for Justinian. I can look after myself. I will feel better if I know you are safe."

Leo put down his fork and looked at her with eyes filled with reproof. "Is that what you expect of me?" he asked.

She looked down at her plate. "I care about you, Leo. I want you to be safe. I shall feel a terrible guilt if you suffer because I have brought you here."

"I came willingly," he told her.

She looked up, meeting his eyes. "All right, then I shall feel a bitter grief if something happens to you!"

"And Simonis?" he asked quietly. She still came two or three times a week, but she chose times when Anna was out. It was almost as if she watched the street and waited for the opportunity.

In his face, Anna saw compassion and anxiety and felt ashamed that she had not thought of his loneliness before now. He and Simonis had lived and worked in the same house all their adult lives. They had differed over many things, and he deplored what she had said to Anna over Justinian. He had always thought her favoring of Justinian was wrong but owned that his of Anna was just as much at fault. Leo must miss Simonis, even the familiarity of their quarrels. More than that, he was now afraid for her.

"I'm sorry," Anna said quietly. "If there is an invasion . . . when . . . she should be with us. Please ask her if she will come back . . ." She stopped.

"What is it?" he asked.

"Unless she is safer where she is," Anna finished the thought.

Leo shook his head. "Safety is being with your own people. When you are old, it is better to die with your family than escape and live with strangers."

Without warning, tears filled Anna's eyes. "Ask her . . . please."

Simonis came back three days later, nervous, defiant, determined that Anna should speak first. Anna was startled by how much thinner she was, the bruised look in her face. It had been months, but she seemed weary, as if her joints were stiff.

Anna had planned what to say to Simonis, but now that she saw a lonely old woman who had lost everyone she loved, the prepared words vanished.

"I know it is a great deal to ask you to stay," Anna said quietly, "and I will understand if you don't wish to, when—"

"I'm staying," Simonis cut across her, her black eyes fierce. "I do not desert because a battle is coming."

"It's not a battle," Anna pointed out. "It's death."

Simonis shrugged. "Well, I wasn't going to live forever anyway." Her voice trembled a little, and that was the end of the conversation.

Anna took a brief respite from attending the sick to go again to the Hagia Sophia, not so much for the Mass as to look at the unique beauty of it while it was still there.

As she walked through its outer aisles and saw the gold of the mosaics, the exquisite, brooding, sloe-eyed Madonnas and somber figures of Christ and his Apostles, she thought of Zoe and was touched by grief far deeper than she would have expected. Byzantium was less without her. Life was grayer.

"Can't make up your mind whether to be on the floor of the men or the women, Anastasius?"

She swung around and saw Helena standing a few feet away. She was magnificently dressed in a dark red tunic and a dalmatica of such a rich blue as to be almost purple, or as close as anyone dared come who was not of the imperial house. The gold borders on it and the reflection of the red made one look a second time to be certain.

Anna wanted to answer with some cutting reply, but all such thought was crowded out of her mind by the sight of a man behind Helena. Anna knew his face, although she had not seen him in at least two years. It was Esaias, the only other man, apart from Demetrios, who had survived the assassination plot unscathed.

Why was he here in the Hagia Sophia with Helena, and she dressed almost in purple? Helena Comnena, Zoe's daughter to the emperor. She had not married Demetrios. If all she wanted of him was his imperial name, there was no point now. In a matter of weeks, the throne would be in the hands of Charles of Anjou, to give to whomever he wished—some puppet who would rule it at his behest.

Nicephoras had assumed it would be Charles's son-in-law, but perhaps it would not! Could he have something different in mind, something to curb an ambitious daughter, reward a more trustworthy lieutenant, and at the same time buy from a troublesome people a degree of peace with a turncoat Palaeologus queen? What an exquisite betrayal!

She must not let Helena see the thought in her eyes. She must say something quickly, not a polite reply, which Helena would know was masking another truth.

"I was thinking of your mother," Anna said, smiling slightly. "Watching Giuliano Dandolo clean the tomb of his great-grandfather. That was the one vengeance she didn't achieve."

Helena's expression froze. "That was all a waste of time," she said coldly. "An old woman living in the past. I live for the future, but then I have one. She hadn't. What about you, *Anastasia*—is that your name?"

"No."

Helena shrugged. "Well, no matter—whatever it is, you have no place here anymore. I don't know what delusion ever brought you in the first place."

Anna would have been stung had not her thoughts been racing as to what Esaias was doing with Helena. She remembered his part in the original plot. It was he who had courted the young Andronicus, with the intent of murdering him also.

If she was planning an alliance of some sort with Charles of Anjou, then was Esaias the one who carried word back and forth? Helena would never be fool enough to commit anything damning to paper. Nor would she travel herself. And she would not have trusted any of Zoe's men.

Helena was waiting for a response.

"It's over now anyway," Anna said quietly. She knew Justinian was guilty of Bessarion's death, in an act of loyalty to Byzantium, and in a few weeks, even days, it would no longer matter anymore.

Helena lifted her head a little higher and walked away. In dark, glowing reds, Esaias followed after her.

Anna walked slowly into one of the small side chapels and bent her head in thought close to prayer.

She lifted her eyes to the somber face of the Madonna above her, surrounded in a million tiny bricks of gold: If she could tell Michael something he did not know, something he believed still mattered, she might persuade him to pardon Justinian. A letter from the emperor could still be law with the monks of Sinai.

How much proof would it take for Michael to believe? In this darkening time, might he be more willing than before to perform one last act of clemency? Perhaps she might yet succeed.

She closed her eyes. *Mary, Mother of God, forgive me for giving up too soon. Please. Perhaps you can't save the city. We should have saved ourselves. But help me free Justinian . . . please?*

She looked up at the strong, beautiful face. "I don't know whether we deserve your help, maybe we don't, but we need it." Then she swiveled around and walked quickly and silently after Helena, so she could follow Esaias when the Mass was over. She needed to know everything about him that she could.

She told Leo and Simonis because she needed their help.

"What do you want me to do?" he asked, puzzled.

They were sitting over an early supper.

"I need to know if he's traveled," she replied. "I can't prove where to, but I can gain some idea if I can find out which ships he sailed on—"

"I'll find out when," Simonis interrupted.

They both turned to her in surprise.

"Servants know," she said impatiently. "For heaven's sake, isn't it obvious enough? Food, supplies, packing clothes, maybe closing off part of the house! He might have brought treasures for himself, for his house, new clothes. They will know where he went, one of them will have gone with him. And they will certainly know for how long."

Leo looked at Anna. "And when we know, what are you going to do?" he asked grimly, his face shadowed, eyes filled with sadness.

"Tell the emperor," she replied.

"And he will execute Helena," Simonis said with satisfaction.

"More likely have her murdered in private," Leo said before turning to Anna. "But not before she has told the emperor everything she knows about you, including that you are a woman and have fooled him all these years. That you have treated him personally—*very personally.* You will not walk away without paying for that, perhaps with your life. Will you buy Justinian's freedom at the cost of your own?" he asked, his voice no more than a whisper. "I am not sure if I am willing to help you do that."

Simonis blinked, hesitated, looking first at Anna, then at Leo. "Neither am I," she said at last.

"Don't you want to stop Helena, if that is what she plans to do?" Anna asked. Receiving no response, she tried again. "We may be killed when the city is taken anyway. Please, find this for me."

"You should live!" Simonis said angrily, the tears running down her face. "You're a physician. Think of all the trouble your father took to teach you."

"Find out, or I'll have to," Anna said. "And you would be better at it than I would."

"Are you ordering me to?" Simonis responded.

"Would that make any difference? Because if it would, then yes, I am."

Simonis said nothing, but Anna knew she would do it, and do it with courage and dedication. "Thank you," she said with a smile.

Simonis stood up and stalked out of the room.

It was a few days later that enough information was pieced together for Anna to be certain that Esaias had traveled to Palermo and to Naples on Helena's behalf, and that Helena at least believed that she had a promise from the king of the Two Sicilies for her to rule Byzantium, as consort of the puppet emperor he would place on the throne. Her Comnenos and Palaeologus heritage would legitimize the succession in the eyes of the people. She would be empress—a feat Zoe could never have achieved.

Anna went to the Blachernae Palace to speak to Nicephoras. She would do it straightaway, before she lost her nerve, before she allowed Leo or Simonis to dissuade her.

She climbed the steps and went in through the huge entrance, acknowledged by the Varangian Guard, who knew her well. How many more times would she do this? Could it even be the last, this evening, as the dusk settled purple over Asia and the last light flickered on the waters of the Bosphorus?

She asked to see Nicephoras, telling his servant that it was urgent.

He was used to her calls and did not question her. Ten minutes later, she was alone with Nicephoras in his room. It looked exactly as it had the first time she was here. Only Nicephoras himself was changed. He looked tired and much older. There were hollows around his eyes and blue veins in his hands.

"Have you come to say good-bye?" he asked, making no attempt to smile. "You have no need to stay, you know. I will remain with the emperor. The injuries we are about to receive cannot be healed, except by God. I would like to think you are safe. That would be a gift you could give me."

"Perhaps this will be good-bye." She found this meeting harder than she had been prepared for. Her voice wavered, and she mastered it only with difficulty. "But that is not what I came for. I came because I have news of Helena Comnena which you should know."

He gave a slight shrug. "Does it matter now?"

"Yes. I have proof that she has been in communication with Charles of Anjou, to make an agreement with him."

Nicephoras was startled. "What could she possibly offer him?"

"A kind of legitimacy. A Palaeologa wife for whatever puppet he puts on the throne of Byzantium."

"None of Michael's daughters would betray him by doing such a thing," Nicephorus replied instantly.

"Not a legitimate daughter—illegitimate."

His eyes widened with incredulity, then dawning horror. "Are you sure?" he breathed.

"Yes. Eirene Vatatzes told me. Gregory knew, from Zoe. Whether it is true or not hardly matters, although I believe it. The thing is that Helena believes it, and Charles of Anjou may choose to."

"How was Helena in communication with Charles? Letters? Do you have them?"

"She wouldn't be so foolish. Words, a signet ring, a locket, things whose meaning is clear only when you know it already. All these, through Esaias Glabas. He was part of the original plot to murder the emperor, which my brother, Justinian, foiled. He is the only one left, apart from Demetrios Vatatzes, for whom Helena has no further use."

"And you have come to tell the emperor?"

Her hands were clenched so tight, her muscles ached and her breathing was ragged. "I want something in return, because Helena will denounce me to the emperor, and he will not forgive me for having deceived him."

Nicephoras bit his lip, and his face was bleak. "That is true. What do you want, Anna? Freedom for your brother?"

"Yes. A letter of pardon would still achieve that. Please."

Nicephoras smiled. "I think that would be possible, but you must not lie to him, about anything. It is too late for that now. You must tell him that you are a woman, and that you deceived him in order to learn the truth and prove Justinian's innocence."

She felt herself go cold. She could not get enough air into her lungs. "I can't. It would mean I had deceived you also. He can't forgive you for that, because you should have told him, and had me imprisoned . . . at the very least."

"I should have," he agreed. "But I don't think he will have us executed now. These are the last days, and I have served him since my childhood. As much as it is possible, we are friends. I do not think he can afford to cast aside a friend in these last few months before the midnight of our empire."

"Then . . . then we had best do it," she said, her voice cracking.

He looked at her steadily for several seconds; then, when she did not avert her eyes, he reached for a small gold-and-enamel bell and rang it.

A member of the Varangian Guard appeared almost immediately. Nicephoras gave him an order to bring Helena Comnena to the emperor, straightaway, on pain of death.

Startled, pale-faced, the man withdrew to obey.

"Anna," he said, "we have much to say before Helena comes."

He led her along the familiar corridors with the ruined statues. She found herself trembling, ridiculously close to weeping as she thought how all this would soon be smashed again, trodden through by people who did not love it, did not even imagine the beauty of mind and heart it had once been.

Too soon, Anna was in the formal room where the emperor received his subjects. Nicephoras went in ahead of her, then returned to conduct her in.

She followed, bowing low, not meeting the emperor's eyes until commanded to do so. When he spoke, she looked up. What she saw chilled her. Michael Palaeologus was not yet sixty, but he was an old man. He had the hollow-eyed look of one whose days were numbered.

"What is it, Anastasius?" he asked, searching her face slowly. "Have you come to tell me anything I do not already know?"

"I'm not certain, Majesty." She was trembling and her words stuck in her throat, all but stopping her from breathing.

Nicephoras plunged in for her. "Majesty, Anastasius has word of an act of betrayal you may choose to allow, or choose to prevent. Perhaps it will come to nothing in the end, anyway."

"What betrayal, Anastasius? Do you imagine it matters now?"

"Yes, Majesty." Her voice was trembling, her body was cold. "Helena Comnena has been in communication with Charles of Anjou."

"Really? Telling him what? How to invade our city? How to break its walls so the crusaders of the pope can put us to fire and the sword again, in the name of Christ?"

"No, Majesty. So that when he has taken us, and killed those loyal to you, the empire, and the Church, he can crown a new emperor in your place, with a wife who can claim two royal names, and an inheritance sufficient to give him some hold on the people's obedience."

Michael leaned forward a little in his chair, his face pale, the lamplight catching the white in his hair and beard. "What are you saying, Anastasius? Be careful whom you accuse. We are not fallen yet. It may be only a few days, even hours, but I still hold life and death in Byzantium."

Her body shook. "I know, Majesty. Helena is the widow of Bessarion Comnenos, and . . . and also she is your illegitimate daughter by Zoe Chrysaphes. She did not know this until Eirene Vatatzes died. Her mother never told her."

He sat immobile for so long, she was afraid he had had some kind of seizure. "How do you know this, Anastasius?" Michael asked at length.

"Eirene told me," she said in a whisper. "I cared for her at her death. She wanted Helena to know, so she would take her own vengeance on Zoe, because Gregory loved her and not Eirene."

"That I can believe," Michael said. "And why do you tell me now, on the eve of ruin?"

"I did not know of Helena's plan until I saw her in the Hagia Sophia, wearing blue that was almost purple, then I sought for the proof." She swallowed. "Now I have it. May it please Your Majesty, I would like a last act of mercy from you, while you can give it, because you have the power of death, and also of life. Please give me a letter of pardon for my brother,

Justinian Lascaris, who is imprisoned at St. Catherine's in Sinai, for his part in the murder of Bessarion Comnenos."

"He is in prison for his part in the plot to usurp the throne," Michael corrected her.

"The plot failed because he could not dissuade them, so he killed Bessarion," she argued. She had little to lose now.

He spread his hands slightly. "So Justinian was your brother. Why do you call yourself Zarides? Is Lascaris too dangerous a name for you? Or are you ashamed of it?"

Looking at Michael's eyes, she knew he would not forgive her. "It is not Justinian's fault," she whispered. "He knew nothing of it."

"Of what?"

Michael was waiting. In a few days they might all be dead, and it would be too late. She thought of Giuliano, whom she would never see again. Perhaps that was just as well. He would not forgive her either.

"I am a good physician, Majesty, but I am not a eunuch," Anna said huskily.

The emperor did not understand.

"I am a woman. Zarides was my husband's name, so it is mine. I was born Anna Lascaris, and gave it up only reluctantly." She could feel the hot tears stinging her eyes and her throat so tight that it ached almost too much to breathe.

There was such silence in the room that when one of the Varangian Guard at the far end shifted the position of his feet on the floor, the rustle of it was audible.

Michael sat back, staring at Anna. Then suddenly he burst into laughter, a rich, jubilant sound of sheer, hilarious delight.

Anna could not believe it.

Then the Varangian Guard at the end of the room, obedient as always, laughed as well.

Nicephoras joined in, a note of relief near hysteria.

The tears spilled over Anna's eyes and she laughed as well, although it was closer to sobbing. She did it only because she had to. If the emperor laughed, then everyone must, too.

Then just as suddenly Michael was sober again, the sound cut off instantly. He stared at Nicephoras. "You knew this, Nicephoras?"

Nicephoras flushed deeply. "Not in the beginning, Majesty. By the time

I did, I also knew that she would not hurt you. Indeed, I trusted her more than any other physician, both for her skill, which is great, and for her loyalty, which I knew I could rely on."

"I imagine you could," said Michael. "You are highly fortunate that I have the humor of despair, or I might not find this so amusing."

"Thank you, Majesty."

"Why tell me, Nicephoras? If you had said nothing, I would not have known. Why risk my anger?"

"Helena Comnena knows, Majesty. And in revenge for Anna Lascaris telling you of her plan, she will understandably in time betray Anna's secret to you."

"I see." He leaned back in his seat again. "Of course she will."

Michael turned to look at Anna, a look of fascination in his black eyes. "You would make a handsome woman. I can imagine Helena hates you. Zoe liked you, you know. Did she know you are a woman?"

"Yes, Majesty."

"That explains much that I found curious. How Byzantine—" His voice choked suddenly in emotion, and the words died in his throat.

Anna looked away. To watch him now was intrusive. She stood still, because she had not been excused, but she kept her eyes downcast.

There was a disturbance outside, and the door opened. Two of the Varangian Guard appeared, with Helena between them. As in the Hagia Sophia, she was dressed in blue that bordered on purple.

"Come!" Michael ordered.

The Varangian Guard marched her forward, half dragging her, her feet stumbling. They stopped in front of the emperor, still holding Helena by both wrists. Her face was flushed, her hair half pulled undone from its elaborate coil, as if she had struggled hard. For once, in her fury, she had an echo of Zoe's magnificence.

One of the guards opened his fist and let fall in Michael's lap a ring, a locket, and a small box.

The calm leached out of Helena's face.

"Your pact with Charles of Anjou," Michael said quietly.

Her face twisted in a sneer. "You believe that . . . liar?" She jerked her head toward Anna, stopping short only as the bindings caught her wrist. "That physician of yours is a woman, Majesty! Did you know that? A woman, as much as I am, poking and prying at your body, without shame. You take her word over mine?"

Michael looked Anna up and down. "Are you sure he is a woman?" he asked curiously.

Helena gave a bark of laughter. "Of course I'm sure. Rip off her tunic, and you'll see!"

"How long have you known?" he asked.

"Years!"

"And you did not think to tell me before today? Why is that, Helena Palaeologa?"

Too late she realized her mistake. Her eyes were wild, like those of an animal scenting blood and death.

Michael continued, "She is Anna Lascaris. Of imperial blood, like yours—or mine. She told me herself. But she is an excellent physician, and that is what I required of her. That—and loyalty."

Helena drew in her breath as if to speak, then understood that it would change nothing, and she let it out again soundlessly.

Michael made a small, quick gesture with his hand, and the Varangian Guard tightened their grip on Helena and turned, pulling her away. She sagged a little, as if the strength had left her legs and she had difficulty holding herself up.

"I never trusted Zoe," Michael said, his voice soft with regret. "But I liked her. She was a magnificent woman, all fire and passion, and within her own dreadful code, a kind of honor." He turned to Anna. "You will have your letter. You had best hurry, while my word is good. When the city falls, it may mean nothing." He smiled bleakly. "But Helena has friends. You would be advised to leave here as a woman. It would be best for you that as far as they know, both you and Helena came into the palace—and neither of you left."

It was a moment before Anna's voice would come, and even then it was husky, a little tremulous. "Yes, Majesty. Thank you."

Nicephoras reached out his hand and took her elbow, guiding her backward, out of Michael's presence.

As soon as they were alone, in a corridor beyond the great hall, she turned to him. "Will they imprison Helena? What happens when the city . . . falls?"

"The Varangian Guard will break her neck," he told her. "With Charles's fleet on the horizon, no one will care. Come. I will find women's clothes for you, and while you are changing, I will write the letter and the emperor will sign it. Then you must go." He smiled. "I will miss you."

She touched his hand. "I will miss you, too. There is no one else with whom I can talk as we have." Then she looked away, in case he found the loneliness in her too much an echo of his own.

Nicephoras went with her down to the quayside. The summer night was brilliant with stars, but it was too late for the water taxis. Instead there was one of the emperor's barges waiting to take her across the Golden Horn to Galata. This was the last time she would set foot in Constantinople. She was glad it was too dark for him to see the grief in her face, the love of all that was over and on the brink of destruction.

"You cannot come back," he warned. "I will send messages to your servants. It is better if they stay here for a few days, at the very least. Helena's friends and allies will be watching. Esaias and whoever else, Demetrios, perhaps, and others. Helena was like her mother in one thing: Come victory or despair, triumph or ruin, she never forgot a vengeance. You do, sometimes easily, and Zoe thought that was a weakness in you. It kept you from being truly like her."

She was surprised. "Like her?"

"She saw in you her own passion for life, but weakened by the power to forgive. But I think in the end she realized it was really your strength. It made you whole, where she was not."

A tide of guilt swept over Anna that she was not worthy of this praise. Certainly she had forgiven many things, small and unimportant. But she had kept the greatest ones, where the injury had wounded her where no healing was possible. She had never forgiven her husband, Eustathius. She had hidden the revulsion she had felt, the guilt because she could not love him, could not bear to carry his child, or for the hunger that had burned inside her, unanswered. She had never let go of blaming him for her own act of provoking that terrible searing, debasing fight. She remembered the shame even more than the pain and the blood.

Was she blaming him because he had allowed all his frustration, his fury of helplessness, confusion, and defeat, to explode in violence? Or was it her own guilt because she had half wanted him to descend so far?

Yes, he had been brutal, but that was a burden on his soul that she could not reach or help now. The time when perhaps she could have was past, and she had wasted it. That was something else for which she needed forgiveness.

She tried to think of what had been good in him. It was difficult, until she thought first of what had been wounded also, and then the pity came, scouring deep with the awareness that she should have been gentler. If she had helped him, instead of lashing out from her own hurt, he might have found the best in himself.

She remembered his skill with animals, how he spoke softly to his horses, sat up all night with them when they were wounded or ill, his total joy at the birth of a foal, and how he had praised the mare, stroked her, loved her. She found the tears wet on her own face with regret that she had let that slip away from him, selfish with her own need.

She let go of her anger and in the darkness bowed her head.

I'm sorry. She said the words in her mind, humbly and passionately. *Please God, forgive me. Help me to be whole in spirit, to give others the mercy I so desperately need myself.*

Slowly she felt the burden dissolve, and absolution enfolded her like an embrace, easing out all the old pain and washing it away. The ache disappeared, and a sweet warmth filled the emptiness inside.

They reached the edge of the water. The barge was ready, knocking gently against the steps as the ripples carried it. It was time to go.

There was nothing more to say. She was dressed as a woman again; the only other time in nearly ten years had been in Jerusalem with Giuliano. This was difficult. She put her hand up and touched Nicephoras's face, then kissed his cheek. Then, as his arm tightened around her for a moment, she slipped away and went down the steps into the boat.

It was dawn when she arrived at Avram Shachar's house, by now long familiar to her. It was far too early to expect anyone to be up, but she dared not wait in the streets. A woman alone was more vulnerable than a eunuch would have been. Even with a fuller tunic and her figure unbound so the outline of her breasts and hips was clear, she had to keep reminding herself that now she looked utterly different. Beneath the minimal veil of decency, her bright chestnut hair was visible.

The heat was oppressive and would be worse when the sun rose. The streets were parched and dusty with summer drought.

She knocked on Shachar's door and waited. After several minutes had gone by, she knocked again, and almost immediately he appeared, blinking a little, obviously woken from sleep.

"Yes?" He looked her up and down, puzzled but gentle as always. "Is someone in your house ill? You'd better come in." He stepped back and pulled the door wide for her.

She followed him through to the room where he kept his herbs, treading softly to avoid disturbing the rest of the household.

He lit the candles and turned to look at her again, his face anxious, as if he knew he should know her and was embarrassed that he did not, searching his memory.

"Anna Zarides," she said quietly.

His eyes widened in amazement when he realized who she was. "What has happened? Tell me. What can I do?"

"I have the emperor's pardon for my brother," she replied. "I have to leave Constantinople, but I need to go to Sinai anyway, before the city falls, so I can have Justinian freed while the emperor's word still counts. Can you help me? I don't know how I'm going to do it. I need to get a message back to Leo and Simonis, and have them come with what money I can raise. I dare not return to the city myself."

He nodded slowly, beginning to smile.

"And I must see that they are taken care of. Leo might come with me, but Simonis should go back to Nicea."

"Of course," he said softly. "Of course. I will see to it. First you must eat, then rest."

Ninety-seven

ᴄᴡᴏ

GIULIANO HAD LEFT SICILY IN HASTE, KNOWING THAT Charles would search for him and execute him if he was found. He had taken the first ship leaving and made his way east, stopping at Athens and Abydos only to change ships and go on again as fast as possible. Now at sunrise he was in the harbor of Constantinople at last. He went ashore immediately after he had washed, shaved, and made himself as tidy as possible. He had nothing but the clothes in which he had set fire to the fleet in the Bay of Messina. And what he had bought in haste in Athens.

He walked up the dockside into the narrow streets and made the climb up to the Blachernae Palace. With a stab of grief, he was aware of the pall of fear that hung over the city. No one could fail to notice the empty shops and houses, the unnatural silence, the sense of abandonment. It was as if they were already dying.

When he reached the palace, he was stopped by the Varangian Guard. They would be at their posts until they were mown down or hacked to pieces, but never with their backs to the foe.

"Giuliano Dandolo," he said, pulling himself to attention. "Newly landed within the hour, from Messina. I bring good news to His Majesty. Please take me to Nicephoras."

The first guard, a huge man with pale hair and sea blue eyes, looked amazed. "Good news?"

"Excellent news. Do you expect me to tell you before I tell the emperor?"

They found Nicephoras in his rooms alone. Bread and fruit lay on a small table. He was standing in the center of the floor. He looked older than when Giuliano had last seen him, and touched by a loneliness so sharp that even with good news bursting inside him, Giuliano could not be unaware of it.

"May I offer you food? Drink?" Nicephoras asked.

Giuliano knew he must look exhausted, even unkempt, but he could not take the smile from his face. He had such a gift to give.

"The crusader fleet is sunk," he said, as if it were a reply. "Burned in Messina harbor. Charles of Anjou will never sail in it to Byzantium, or Jerusalem, or anywhere. It lies at the bottom of the sea."

Nicephoras stared at him, his face slowly filling with wonder. "Are you . . . sure?" he whispered.

"Perfectly." His voice was vibrant, cracking with excitement. "I saw it myself. I was one of those who set the torches. I shall never forget it as long as I live. When the Greek fire in the holds exploded, the sea was like the floor of hell."

Nicephoras put out his hand and grasped Giuliano's with a strength that almost crushed it, a power Giuliano would never have believed him to possess. There were tears in his eyes.

"We must tell the emperor."

This time there was no waiting for Michael to receive them, no formal admission to the throne room. They strode in past the Varangian Guard as if it were any other room in the world.

Michael was hastily dressed, but wide awake. His eyes burned black, intensely alive in spite of his haggard face and the hollows where the bones of his head seemed to strain the parchment-thin skin.

"Majesty," Giuliano said quietly.

"Speak!"

Giuliano looked up and met Michael's gaze as if they had been equals. "Charles of Anjou will never threaten Byzantium again, Majesty. His fleet lies burned at the bottom of the Bay of Messina. He is a finished man. Even Sicily will breathe free from his oppression."

Michael stared. "You have seen this yourself?"

"Captain Dandolo set the torches, Majesty," Nicephoras offered.

"You are Venetian," Michael said incredulously.

"Half, Majesty. My mother was Byzantine." He said it with pride.

Michael nodded slowly, the tension and pain easing out of his body, the smile spreading over this face, his eyes bright. He waved at Nicephoras, still looking at Giuliano. "Give this man everything he wants. Give him food, wine, rest, clean clothes." He took the gold-and-emerald ring from his finger and held it out.

Giuliano looked at its burning beauty.

"Take it," Michael told him. "Now we will hear the city rejoice. Nicephoras! Have the good news spread. Let there be dancing in the streets, wine and feasting, music, laughter. Put on our best clothes." He stopped and looked again at Giuliano. "Zoe Chrysaphes is dead. It's a pity. How she would have laughed at the irony of this. Byzantium thanks you, Giuliano Dandolo. Now go and eat, drink, take your ease. You will be paid in gold."

Giuliano bowed and withdrew, dizzy with triumph.

But once in the corridor, he could think only of telling the people he cared for in the city, starting with Anastasius. He must tell him first; all the others could hear afterward. The news would be everywhere, but he must tell Anastasius himself, see his joy, his relief.

"Thank you, but I must tell my friends the news," he said to Nicephoras beside him. "I want to do that myself. I must be there when they hear."

Nicephoras nodded. "Of course. You will find Anastasius in Galata, in the house of Avram Shachar."

"Not here? Not in his own house?" A chill touched Giuliano. "Why? Is something wrong?" Suddenly the news was hollow. He realized how intensely he had been looking forward to telling Anastasius.

"You will find him much . . . changed," Nicephoras replied. "But quite well."

"Changed? How?"

"Shachar lives in the Street of the Apothecaries. It will all explain itself. Go. Before they leave for the south. Leo and Simonis went from here yesterday already. You have little time." He smiled. "Byzantium owes you much, and we will not forget."

Giuliano clasped his hand again, the emperor's ring digging into his flesh, then he turned and left.

.   .   .

As soon as Michael Palaeologus, Equal of the Apostles, was alone, he went to his own rooms and closed the doors. He was tired. The long battle had exhausted him, and there was a weakness inside him that he knew would not heal.

He bent in front of the locked cabinet and took the key from around his neck. He slipped it in the lock and opened it.

She was there, as always, her calm face in its sublime beauty, the Mother of God that St. Luke had painted and Zoe Chrysaphes had given him. He knelt in front of her, the tears sliding easily down his face.

"Thank you," he said simply. "In spite of our weakness and our doubts, you have saved us from our enemies. And a greater miracle than that, you have saved us from ourselves."

He crossed himself in the old Greek way, but he remained on his knees.

Giuliano found the Street of the Apothecaries, but it seemed to take an age, and all the way down the hill from the palace, into the docks, and on the quayside waiting for the water taxi, his mind was racing. What had Nicephoras meant? What sort of change? He did not want Anastasius different from the passion and the courage, the wit, and the gentleness that he remembered. He wanted the same warm, clever, and vulnerable person he had known and cared for so profoundly.

He strode up the Street of the Apothecaries in the hot summer sun, past the empty shops and markets, the deserted houses. The news would be here any moment, spreading like fire. He wanted to be the first to tell Anastasius.

"Where is the shop of Avram Shachar?" he called out to a man slowly opening his door and peering out.

The man pointed.

Giuliano thanked him and increased his pace.

He found the right door and banged on it, too hard, and realized with embarrassment that he was being rude.

"I'm sorry," he said as soon as it was opened. "I'm looking for Anastasius Zarides. Is he here?"

Shachar nodded, but he did not step aside or invite him in.

"I'm Giuliano Dandolo, a friend of Anastasius. I have great good news. Charles of Anjou is fallen. His fleet is sunk—burned, and at the bottom of the sea. I want to be the one to tell him. . . ." He realized he was gabbling and took a breath to steady himself. "Please."

Shachar nodded slowly, his eyes searching Giuliano's face. "That is true?"

"Yes. I swear. I have already told the emperor. But I want to tell Anastasius myself—and you."

Shachar's face split into a broad smile. "Thank you. You had better come in." He pulled the door wide and pointed to a room at the farther end of the corridor. "The herb room is there. Anastasius will be working with them. No one will disturb you." He seemed about to add something more, then changed his mind.

"Thank you." Giuliano brushed past him and went down to the door. Then apprehension swept over him. What changes had Nicephoras meant? What had happened? Was Anastasius ill? Injured?

He knocked hard on the door.

It opened and a woman stood just inside. She was taller than average, with a slender throat, high cheekbones, and bright chestnut hair. There was something beautiful in her that tugged at him as if he had known her for as long as he could remember, yet he had never seen her before.

The color swept up her skin in a burning tide.

"Giuliano . . ." Her voice was husky, as if she found it difficult to speak.

He did not know what to say. He knew now. He felt a rage of embarrassment burst open inside him for all the things he had said, the emotions, the stories shared about which he could recall not the words, but the intense feeling of companionship, almost intimacy, as if nothing need be hidden.

Then he remembered the awakening of physical hunger in himself and the shame and confusion that had all but crippled him. He had struggled with such pain to stifle that.

It seared through him with shock. What had she felt?

He averted his eyes and saw the herbs and ointments packed away, as if to travel.

"Is Shachar leaving?" he asked impulsively. "Are you?"

She smiled, blinking rapidly as if to dispel tears. "The crusaders will come any day now. When they do, it will not be good for Jews to be here—or Muslims."

"Is that why . . ." He looked at her woman's tunic. It embarrassed him,

and pleased him, to see how feminine her body was beneath it, as rich as
Zoe's.

"No . . . ," she said quickly. "Helena was going to ally with the invaders, to rule with them. She's Michael's illegitimate daughter. I found
proof of her plans and I told the emperor. She told him I was a woman."

He caught the pain in her voice, then looked up and saw it harsh and
sad in her face. He could only imagine how it hurt.

"Anas—" He stopped. He did not know her name.

"Anna Lascaris," she whispered.

He reached out his hand, not to touch her, just in a gesture. He thought
of all his own disillusion, the dreams and the friendships failed, the long
loneliness of it.

"It's over now," she said quietly. "The emperor allowed me to go, but I
cannot stay in the city. Simonis will go home to Nicea. If that falls, too—"

"It won't!" he cut across her urgently. "None if it will. Byzantium is safe,
at least from Charles of Anjou. His whole fleet is at the bottom of Messina
harbor. I saw it myself. The crusade will never happen." The joy and relief
welled up inside him. He wanted to take her in his arms and hug her so
hard that he lifted her off her feet, whirled her around. He ached to do it
with an almost physical pain. But it would not end there.

"You don't have to leave . . . ," he said.

She met his gaze, studying him. "Yes, I do. Helena had friends, allies.
They will know I was responsible for her betrayal to Michael. They killed
her in the palace. Broke her neck. They won't forgive me for that."

He tried to imagine it, the passion and violence.

"And I have Michael's letter of pardon for my brother," she went on. "I
must take it . . ."

"To Jerusalem?"

"And then Sinai."

If she was not here, what use was Byzantium without her?

"Are you going back to Venice?" Her voice caught on the words.

"No." He shook his head fractionally. "I was one of those who set the
fleet on fire." Why the sudden modesty in front of her? Because boasting
was shallow and in the end without meaning. What he wanted above anything and everything else was to go with her to Jerusalem, not only the
Jerusalem of the world, but the destination of the heart.

"Shachar doesn't have to leave Byzantium," he said softly. "He'll be safe here. I'll go with you—if I may?"

The color swept up her face again, but this time she did not look away. "I'm . . . I'm not a eunuch anymore. . . ."

"I know."

"Do you?" It was a question. He saw the fear in her eyes. Something hurt her almost more than she could bear. Her body was stiff, as if pain filled her and ran out of control.

What did she believe he meant? "As your husband," he said quickly.

She wanted to look away, but this was the moment when the last deceit must go, whatever it cost. "I cannot have children," she whispered. "It's my own fault. I've regretted it with all my time and my strength, but it changes nothing. I hated my husband, and I provoked him until he beat me—" She stopped, the grief inside choking her. She wanted passion, the giving and the taking, with a fierceness that consumed her, but the lie could destroy everything.

"I can live without children," he said quietly, touching her cheek with his fingers. "But I cannot be fully alive without you. I should be alone, always alone, and that is to be shut out of heaven. Marry me, and we shall travel to Jerusalem. We'll find that pathway of the spirit that goes always upward, or make it. There will be people to defend, and to heal."

She reached up and closed her hand over his, putting it to his lips. "I will," she promised. "I will."

Book List

∾

Byzantine Dress: Representations of Secular Dress in Eighth to Twelfth-Century Painting (The New Middle Ages) by Jennifer L. Ball

Byzantine Monuments of Istanbul by John Freely and Ahmet S. Cakmak

Byzantium and Venice: A Study in Diplomatic and Cultural Relations by Donald M. Nicol

Byzantium: The Surprising Life of a Medieval Empire by Judith Herrin

The Christian East and the Rise of the Papacy: The Church 1071–1453 A.D. (Church History Vol.4) by Aristeides Papadakis and John Meyendorff

Chronicle of the Popes: The Reign-by-Reign Record of the Papacy over 2000 Years by P. G. Maxwell-Stuart

Constantinople: Istanbul's Historical Heritage by Stephane Yerasimos

Constantinople: Capital of Byzantium by Jonathan Harris

The Crusades: A Short History by Jonathan Riley-Smith

Emperor Michael Palaeologus and the West: 1258–1282: A Study in Byzantine-Latin Relations by Deno John Geanakoplos

Every Day Life in Byzantium by Tamara Talbot Rice

Flavours of Byzantium by Andrew Dalby

Fourth Crusade and the Sack of Constantinople by Jonathan Phillips

Geography, Technology, and War: Studies in the Maritime History of the Mediterranean, 649–1571 (Past and Present Publications) by John H. Pryor

God's War: A New History of the Crusades by Christopher Tyerman

Hagia Sophia: Architecture, Structure, and Liturgy of Justinian's Great Church by R. J. Mainstone

The Hagia Sophia by Kariye Museum

The Icon by Kurt Weitzmann

The Last Centuries of Byzantium 1261–1453 (Second Edition) by Donald M. Nicol

Liturgy of Justinian's Great Church by R. J. Mainstone

Lives of the Popes: Illustrated Biographies of Every Pope from St. Peter to the Present by Michael J. Walsh, consultant editor

Medicine in the Crusades: Warfare, Wounds and the Medieval Surgeon by Piers D. Mitchell

Medieval and Renaissance Venice by Kittell and Madden

Naples: An Early Guide by Enrico Bacco

The Oxford History of Byzantium by Cyril Mango

Pilgrimage: The Great Adventure of the Middle Ages by John Ure

Short History of the Papacy in the Middle Ages by Walter Ullmann

The Sicilian Vespers: A History of the Mediterranean World in the Later Thirteenth Century (Canto) by Steven Runciman

Venice (Wonders of Man Series) by John Hagy Davis

Women, Men and Eunuchs: Gender in Byzantium by Liz James

ABOUT THE AUTHOR

ANNE PERRY is the bestselling author of two acclaimed series set in Victorian England: the William Monk novels, including *Execution Dock* and *Dark Assassin,* and the Charlotte and Thomas Pitt novels, including *Buckingham Palace Gardens* and *Long Spoon Lane.* She is also the author of the World War I novels *No Graves As Yet, Shoulder the Sky, Angels in the Gloom, At Some Disputed Barricade,* and *We Shall Not Sleep,* as well as seven holiday novels, most recently *A Christmas Promise.* Anne Perry lives in Scotland. Visit her website at www.anneperry.net.